MW00427740

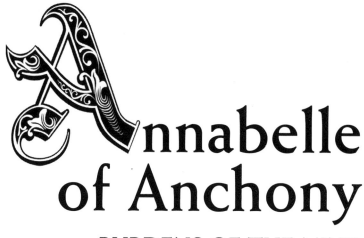

Annabelle of Anchony

BURDENS OF THE MIND

Book One

Ruth Apollonia

Available from:
Marian Helpers Center
Stockbridge, MA 01263

Prayerline: 1-800-804-3823
Orderline: 1-800-462-7426
Websites: TheDivineMercy.org
marian.org

ISBN: 978-1-59614-504-7

Marian Press Edition Publication date: July, 2019

Imprimi Potest:
Very Rev. Kazimierz Chwalek, MIC
Provincial Superior
The Blessed Virgin Mary, Mother of Mercy Province
April 30, 2019

Nihil Obstat:
Dr. Robert A. Stackpole, STD
Censor Deputatus
April 30, 2019

Dedication

To my parents, Grant and Rose Ann, whose unselfish love, encouragement, and guidance throughout my life have allowed me to spread my wings and fly into unknown areas. To my brothers, John, Paul, and Jeff, whose brotherly love, with its many unique manifestations, has been a source of both pleasure and "torture" throughout my life, and has influenced me more than I know.

To my heavenly mother, Mary, and her Immaculate Heart, whose intercession I credit for the success of this story. As in all things you wish, may these pages lead their readers closer to your Son.

Acknowledgments

Some may know — most may not — that the *Annabelle of Anchony* series was originally published through a vanity press that was closed in 2017, making the three formerly published novels no longer available. So I first want to thank Marian Press for taking a chance on my series and "resurrecting" it from the out-of-print world.

I want to specifically thank Mary Clark, Daniel Seseske, and Chris Sparks for their input and ideas, given so that *Annabelle* can not only live, but thrive better than ever!

I want to acknowledge those who helped me with the original developing, editing, or marketing when this book was first released in 2012: Paul Anderson; Sheridan Irick; Elena Rodriguez; Rev. Dylan Schrader, PhD; and Patti Sexton.

I would be amiss if I did not thank the *Annabelle of Anchony* fans out there for their support and encouragement throughout the years: Thank you!

Contents

CAVES

The small child, in her ripped and tattered dress, crouched in the cold, damp cave, just out of sight of the five masked men searching for her. She was frightened, and she was alone.

"Annabelle! Annabelle!" the men called in hopes of locating the little 5-year-old girl.

She dropped her head onto her bent knees while pulling her dress closer around her legs; she dared not answer. Teardrops formed in her eyes with a slight whimpering from her voice; she moved further into the cave thinking about her mamá and papá, sisters and brothers. Leaning up against the cold rock, she closed her eyes, tasting the salt from her tears. The fading slit of light from the cave opening vanished completely as the sun faded into the night.

"Annabelle." A kind, gentle voice whispered as the little girl was gently shaken awake. "Don't be afraid. I'll hide you from those men." In the glow from his torch, the man's appearance was initially alarming, with his long, raggedy hair and unkempt beard, but the little girl looked past the hair and into his eyes; they were kind like those of her papá.

He knows my name. She trusted him.

"Follow me. I'll lead you far from those men searching for you." The man placed a fur shawl over her tiny shoulders. The odor of the leather was a new experience for the little girl. The stranger guided her deep into the cave, up and down, left and right, until the little girl was sure those men could never find her — and she could never find her way out. After being carried for what seemed like hours to the young Annabelle, she emerged into a towering, open cavern.

"I'm sorry, my sweet child, but we must remain here until those men have left." His words echoed in the vastness.

"It's so dark," the small child whispered as she stared up into blackness.

"I know, but you have nothing to fear in the dark. It's only the men searching for you that should give you fright." He gathered some stashed wood to start a fire.

Annabelle looked around the dark cavern as far as she could see with the dim light from the torch. She found the side of the cave and slid down it until she was seated. A few moments later a fire erupted. Annabelle saw the majesty of the cavern, and it took her breath away.

"Wonderful, isn't it? It makes you want to praise the Great Creator."

An awe-stricken Annabelle was mesmerized by the flickering light dancing along the naturally painted cavern walls.

"How did He do it?" the small child asked with a furrowed brow.

The man chuckled. "Only God knows. Our minds are so narrow that we'll never be able to fathom the ways of God."

The little girl's eyebrows raised as she continued to stare at the walls.

The man continued: "What we are able to understand about God's ways is like the size of this little rock" — he pointed to a small rock the size of the tip of his thumb — "and God's knowledge is like the size of this cavern. How tall do you think this cave is?"

She shook her head as she looked to where he pointed. "I don't know."

"Truly right."

Annabelle listened intently as the man spoke of God. *He knows my name; he knows God. Is he an angel?* The little girl grinned, certain she had figured out his secret.

The man took a double glance when he saw her ear-to-ear smile. He could tell her mind was turning. "What brings such a look?"

She did not hesitate: "You're an angel!"

The man chuckled and grinned as he shook his head.

"You know my name," the small girl insisted, to prove her point.

"I heard the men calling, and I figured it had to be you, since I have seen no other little girls around this area in a while." He then added, "Peter. Peter is my name."

Annabelle scanned the area again. "You live here?"

"No, not here. Not in *this* cave." She stared at a wall full of sticks but did not question their presence. The man saw her spy his pile. "God told me to be prepared for a visitor."

Annabelle's face lit up as she exclaimed, "God speaks to you?!"

The man shook his head and grinned, touched by such innocence. "God speaks to all of us."

Annabelle heard a rustling above her. She turned her head toward it. "What's that?"

"Fear not, child. They are only bats."

"Bats?"

"We are overrunning their space, but as long as you stay quiet and don't disturb them, they'll not bother you."

Annabelle moved closer to Peter, the stranger, her angel. "They bite?"

"Little one, I will not let them harm you."

Annabelle did not understand how Peter could tell her they would not cause her harm. *An angel could keep such a word.* Her thoughts were interrupted by the rumbling of her stomach.

"You're hungry? I am as well." Peter pulled a small sack from around his waist holding a tiny portion of the forest's fresh supply of berries.

"We thank You, Father, for the berries You have provided for us to eat, the fire to keep us warm, and this cave to keep us hidden. We thank You for Your Passion, Death, and Resurrection. May Your will be done in our lives. In the name of the Father, and of the Son, and of the Holy Spirit. Amen."

Annabelle stared at Peter and then commented with a smile, "You pray like Papá."

"Do I now?"

Annabelle nodded her head with a distant look in her eyes and then started to cry.

Peter wrapped his giant arm around her little frame. "There now, there now. I'm sure your papá would want you to have courage … to trust in God."

As her upper body shook with her sobs, she hugged Peter as hard as she could, wanting to be hugging her papá and mamá. Peter picked up the small child, placed her in his lap, and soothingly rocked her back and forth as he sang a little tune that he had sung to his children: "Where the angels sing and you see the spring. Follow the cave in and you will find the hidden haven."

Annabelle whispered into Peter's ear between her sobs, "Papá sings me that." Peter squeezed the young girl tighter. She fell asleep, safe in Peter's arms.

She awoke to the flickering fire. Whether it was night or day, she could not tell in the deep cavern. Forgetting for a moment where she was, she quickly remembered when she saw Peter restlessly fidgeting in his sleep. As he was bombarded with unpleasant dreams, the light of the flames danced upon his perspiring skin. Annabelle could tell he was not at peace. She approached him slowly and cautiously extended her hand toward him, but he awoke before she made contact. His startle frightened her so that she lost her balance, and fell backwards onto her bottom as Peter, in a half-awake, half-asleep state, called: "Clare!"

Annabelle's body shook as her tattered dress was further dirtied on the cave floor. With an open mouth, she gasped for air as her heart pounded quickly in her chest.

"Oh ..." Peter awoke completely. "It's you ... Annabelle."

Tears started to form in Annabelle's eyes.

Peter reached out his arm. "It's all right, it's all right."

She continued to stare at him, unsure what to think.

He moved closer to her. "Why did you awake?"

Annabelle pushed herself into a squatting position. "You made noises ..." With great concern in her emerald eyes, she asked, "You all right?"

A tear almost dripped down Peter's cheek. "I am now. Thank you." He pulled her closer and hugged her. "Are you tired? How about you go back to sleep then?" He picked her up and took her back to her bed of moss. He sat by her even after she had fallen asleep — silently watching her breathe in and out — thinking of the little girl he lost.

"Annabelle, Annabelle ... arise, my little one. The men are gone."

"Gone? I can go home now?" the wee little one asked with great hope.

The man's countenance turned somber as he shook his head, replying, "I don't know ... if they left a boat ... yes." But Peter knew they had not left a boat.

Annabelle followed the man, her angel, who had given her food, warmth, and protection — for what seemed, to the young child, like months — as she crouched about the cavern. Nearing the mouth of the cave, Annabelle squinted as they approached the sunlight. She felt the damp chill from the cave subside.

"Living in a cave for a week makes you thankful for the sun, doesn't it?" Peter looked at the small girl, though she did not reply.

As Annabelle stood at the opening of the cave, she beheld a beautiful sight: a deep blue sea with roaring waves that crashed along the rock wall.

Peter looked at the 20-foot width of beach to the right of the cave, the only sand on the whole island. "There are no boats," he observed.

"No boats," the little girl echoed.

"I'm sorry, child, but you can't go home today."

Annabelle thought about what the man said and started to cry.

"I know you miss your family," he said, trying to comfort her.

Annabelle was missing her family, but what made her cry was the thought of being alone on the strange island. She shyly asked, "Can I stay with you?"

Peter saw the concern in the little girl's emerald eyes and was overtaken by her absurd fear. A hearty laugh escaped his lips as he replied, "My child, I would not let you be alone." He wrapped his large arm around her tiny frame and moved her closer for an embrace.

Annabelle hugged him and whispered, "My angel."

Peter smiled. After a moment of embrace, he responded, "It is safe now to go to my dwelling. Follow me."

They made their way through the thick forest. After 30 minutes of walking, Peter picked up the little girl, who had succumbed to the rough terrain and weakness. Hours later they came upon a wall of vines and sticks carefully placed in front of the mouth of a cave.

"You live here?" The 5-year-old was filled with wonder as the man removed the wall to reveal the hidden entrance.

"I do," he answered.

She pointed to the door leaning up against the side of the rock wall. "What's that?"

He was hesitant to give her an answer, but he would not lie: "That is to keep out the bears."

"Bears? What's that?"

He patted her on the head. "An animal you don't want to meet. Do not fret, though. I have not seen any bears on this side of the island in quite some time; it was just to keep it safe."

Annabelle swallowed hard and looked around. "Your neighbors?"

The man's grin faded as he said, "I was the only one on this island … until you came."

The little girl gasped. "No mamá?"

He knelt down to her level. "My mamá has been gone for a while."

She traced the path a teardrop would fall down his cheek. "Are you sad?"

Peter was profoundly moved by her innocence. He had seen such cruelty in the world, such pain and horror. Her simple action made his heart churn within his chest. He was forced to turn from her emerald eyes. "I chose to come to this island, to live here alone. Call me a recluse, a hermit, if you like."

She hugged him. "Peter …" He moved so he could see her face. "You're not alone now."

He hugged her harder as a tear escaped his eye.

The little girl awoke to the sound of sizzling meat and the sight of fresh berries.

"Here's the morning meal," Peter offered.

"What's that?" the girl asked as she scrunched up her nose at the squirrel meat.

"Tree animal." The little girl's eyes bulged as she vehemently shook her head. "Have you ever had it? Then why do you act as if you hate it? When you live in the forest, you must eat what the forest yields."

The girl never stopped shaking her head.

"Berries it is for you then." He placed the large leaf full of berries on the flat rock he used for a table and sat down. He bowed his head and prayed. "Dear Lord, I thank You for this day and for the little friend You have brought into my life. I only hope I can serve her as You wish me to do. Thank You for the food You have placed into our hands and for all the graces and gifts You give. I lift up to You Sara, Clare, and my sons. And above all, Lord, may Your will be done. Amen." He finished with the Sign of the Cross. Annabelle followed suit.

"Who is Sara and Clare?" the small girl asked, before placing a large blackberry in her mouth.

"Are," Peter corrected and then answered, "My wife and daughter."

Her emerald eyes came alive in excitement. "Angels have kids!"

Peter shook his head. "I am not an angel, child. I am man, as you are. One who tries to always do God's will, as hard as it may be." Peter seemed to go off to another time and place. "But I was not always as I am now."

After the simple breakfast was over, Peter brought Annabelle to the corner of the cave where a trunk sat closed and dusty. "When I came here, I brought this chest along. I know now why I was to bring it."

The little girl's eyes sparkled in wonder when he opened up the old oak trunk. Inside was a lady's dress, a green tabard, a chess set, and some other mementos. Annabelle was impressed with it all. She fingered the meticulous embroidery upon the fine dress.

Peter studied her movements. "My wife crafted that." He looked across the cave as he thought about his wife. "She was fine with a needle."

"Mamá is too." Her sad eyes looked up at him.

He stepped close to her and petted the back of her head.

"Did she make many plain linens into something fine?"

Annabelle slowly nodded her head as she smiled and explained, "She let me sit on her lap when she was working. That was" — the little girl lowered her head — "until Crisa. Then Mamá would never hold me. She was always holding Crisa."

"That might be your memory of it, but that doesn't mean that's how it was. Although your mother didn't hold you as much, that doesn't mean her love for you waned. You should be thankful that you have a younger sister. You are blessed, and your parents are blessed. A baby is a gift from God." His eyes began to water.

The little girl looked around the large cave. She bit her lip and looked at a satchel sitting on a ledge in the middle of the cave wall. "What's that?" Her little finger followed her gaze.

"That ..." Peter knelt down beside her. "That is to be respected."

"A bag?" she asked with great confusion.

"What's *in* the bag," he answered back.

She turned her little face toward him. "What's in it?"

He stood up. "That, my little one, is not for you to know." He patted her on the head as she stared at the leather satchel, tilting her head in wonder. Peter shook his head. "You are not to look in it. Do you understand?"

She turned toward him. "Because it's so special?"

Peter smiled. "That's right."

Rivers and Berries

"You have to get in the river. You have dirt all over."

She looked down at her dirty legs and arms but insistently shook her head.

"You want to be dirty the rest of your life?" Peter asked as he rinsed off his face and gruff beard, chest high in the river, donned in his leather attire.

"No!" she yelled at him from the bank as she flared her nostrils and put her little fists on her hips.

"What is it then?"

"Mamá won't let us."

"She won't let you get wet?" Peter asked as he rinsed down his hair.

Annabelle folded her arms in silent protest.

"I don't believe that," Peter stated as he approached.

Annabelle turned her back on him, insisting she would not be going into the river.

"You're taking a bath." Peter's voice was right behind her. She felt his grip and tried to get away. Her little legs kicked in the air as he carried her into the river.

"No!" He squatted down into the river, soaking her completely, and quickly emerged. Annabelle was crying and gripping on to him for all her life. "No! No!"

"Annabelle … Annabelle …" Peter realized how frightened the young girl was. He looked into her eyes. "I won't let go." He walked her over closer to the bank and set her down where she could touch. She still gripped him with all her strength. "Child." He sat down beside her, his head out of the water. "Do you not know how to swim?"

"We aren't supposed to. We aren't supposed to." The little girl insisted as salty tears ran down her cheeks. "The twins. The twins!"

"Twins?"

"Waterfall!" the little girl shouted as the tears streamed down her face.

Peter looked over at the 25-foot waterfall to the north. It was noisy but not ominous. He then recalled the terrain of Anchony. There were two rivers that converged into one in the south-central section. Both the Angler River and the Barstow River were riddled with fearsome waterfalls.

Peter could tell he would get nowhere with the girl today. He picked her up and carried her out of the river.

In the light of the early morning, Annabelle was skipping outside the cave as Peter worked with a deer hide. She saw a couple of colorful butterflies fluttering peacefully around; she followed them, in awe of their bright colors. Looking back, she could no longer see Peter, but she could hear the powerful waterfall. She followed the sound and stood next to the foaming liquid. She studied the river and shook her head. Turning away, she spotted a berry bush. They looked like the berries Peter had given her. She decided to pick them for Peter, but her eyes enticed her, and she could not wait until she found Peter to eat these berries. She helped herself to all that she had picked and then skipped her way back to the cave. She soon began to feel ill.

"Is something wrong, Annabelle?" Peter asked.

The little girl held her stomach as she grimaced out in front of the cave. "Don't feel good."

"Your stomach is hurting? Did you eat something in the forest?" Peter's eyes wandered to the path from where she had returned.

Annabelle's memory was fogged by the nausea and cramps. Recalling the berries that had enticed her, she nodded her perspiring head.

"What did you eat?" An alarmed Peter stood up. "Was it a berry or a leaf?"

"Berry," a weak Annabelle whispered.

"What color?"

"Red."

"Where?"

"By the river."

"How much? How much, Annabelle?"

"I don't know … hand size … ohhhh …" She fell to her knees in agony.

Peter did not waste a moment. He picked up the small child and took her to the spring. Picking a leaf, he smashed it up and told her to eat it.

"I don't want to. I'm not hungry … stomach hurts." She tried to move his hand from her mouth.

"You have to eat it. I'm not giving you a choice." He shoved the small pieces into her mouth and sealed her lips with his fingers and commanded, "Chew it and swallow." Annabelle struggled but she could not get away. She was forced to swallow. "Good. Now drink." Peter filled his cupped hand with spring water and presented it to the little girl. She did as commanded.

She felt worse, far worse. Her stomach churned and rolled and roared. Her countenance turned pouty as her eyes squinted, her jaw tightened, and her eyebrows protracted. "Woooorse," was all she could mutter. Peter nodded his head. She turned on to her belly and expelled the contents of her stomach.

"Good," he said.

She then vomited again. Peter patted her on the back. She was quivering and perspiring, and extremely weak. She crawled away from the former contents of her stomach and laid her cheek on the soft grass. "Sometimes in life, Annabelle, things get worse before they get better."

Annabelle stared at the man who had forced her to eat a bitter leaf that caused her to vomit. "I got sick."

Peter nodded his head. "I fear you had to. If you did not purge yourself of those berries, your body would feel worse ills. I only hope that your body was freed of it with enough haste."

A few minutes later, Annabelle's intestines were grumbling and cramping. "I still hurt," an exasperated Annabelle informed Peter.

"Your hardship is not yet over."

Annabelle made a terrible grimace.

"I wish I could help you, but I can't ... I will pray for you and for your unease." Peter sat down and stroked the young girl's back. "Think of all the people you could be helping with your pains right now."

Annabelle was in too much discomfort to question him. But he answered her unspoken questions anyway: "Unite what you suffer with Christ. Offer it up for all the souls in Purgatory. That way it is not wasted. You do not suffer for no reason — you suffer to help others. It will help you feel better."

"What ..." Annabelle doubled over as she felt another cramp. "... what do I have to do?"

"Offer it up for all the souls in Purgatory."

"Offer up?"

"Give it to God," Peter restated.

"I'll feel better?" She doubled over again in agony.

"It will make you feel better, but not in the way you would like right now."

I give it to God for the souls my angel is talking about. Another severe cramp hit her. "Ohhhhh." Each cramp weakened her dwindling strength. She still felt a little nauseous and wished she could vomit to alleviate her misery.

The little girl continued in this fashion for about an hour and a half until her bowels let loose. She would feel instantly better, but then her intestines would start to cramp even more. The severe diarrhea lasted until there was nothing left in her digestive track to dismiss. Meanwhile Peter, her angel, sat by praying for her — but not in words she could understand.

As night fell, she collapsed in weakness and fatigue. She had not stopped perspiring or quivering. Peter picked her up and took her back to the warm dwelling, placing a wet leaf on her head.

Annabelle opened her eyes sometime in the night. Peter was at her side.

"Drink," he said, offering her a deerskin water pouch. The leather smell was repugnant. She pushed it away.

"You must drink." Peter placed it to her lips. The liquid felt cool, but she could not get herself to swallow. She closed her eyes and moved her head away from the spout, eventually drifting off into sleep as the echoing laughter of her brothers and sister resounded in her thoughts.

"Let's play hide and seek," William stated.

"Annie's it!" Thomas declared.

"Don't want to," Annabelle responded. But her brothers and older sister, Isabella, had disappeared. She found herself walking through a field of tall grass.

"Where'd you go? Don't leave me alone. I don't see you."

More laughter. She turned around and found Isabella behind her. Isabella pushed her and she fell backwards — down, down, down into a dark cave, where the only light was from the hole from which she had descended. She looked up and spied William, Thomas, and Isabella laughing.

"Help! Help! Will, Thom, Isa! Papá, Mamá! Isa, help me!" Her sister's countenance turned serious, and then she disappeared.

Her mother was there holding Cristine, singing to Cristine, dancing with Cristine.

"Mamá, help!" But her mother was too busy to notice her.

Her father appeared. "Umm ... we do have a problem. Now, what is the best way to go about this?"

Michael, her father's confidant, responded, "Well, we should get a rope ... 20 feet. Do you think that's long enough?"

"Maybe 45."

"Actually, I agree — 80 feet."

"Then what will we do?"

"We can lower it down and then she can climb up," her father said.

"Do you think she can do it herself?"

"Of course she can. She wouldn't be my daughter if she couldn't."

"All right, then what will we do?"

"Then we will ... Oh look, one of the horses got out ..." They turned away.

"Help me!" a desperate Annabelle cried. "It's dark!" She looked around. She was no longer in the cave but on a beach all alone with the stars above her, the sea before her, and the trees behind her. The chilly wind bit at her as her breath bellowed out in front of her. There was an owl with his big eyes staring at her, watching her every move.

"For who ... who ... whom are you looking?" the owl addressed her.

"I ... I'm alone."

"So be it." The owl took off into the night sky, vanishing above the sea as the woods were engulfed in fire. The fire crept up around her, surrounding her, suffocating her. She lay down in the sand, too petrified to move, as the flames reached closer and closer.

Annabelle opened her eyes with a gasp and a pounding headache. She was in the cave dwelling. There — the warm fire, and there — Peter, her angel.

She watched the shadows cast by the fire dance along the cave walls. *They're fighting. Who will win?* Slowly, her eyes closed again.

She found herself in a pretty gown at an elegant ball laughing with Isabella. The door opened and all the music stopped. A tall man entered. His face could not be seen. He approached. Annabelle looked around. She was no longer in pretty clothing but in rags. Isabella had disappeared; everyone had disappeared. The man came closer and closer. Annabelle did not shout or try to get away. She was complacent as the unknown man took her away.

Annabelle was in the forest eating the red berries. Her stomach began to shake and a plethora of snakes burst forth from her stomach. The snakes slithered into a big frying pan and were cooking for breakfast.

She heard the sizzling of meat and awoke to see Peter cooking next to the fire. Her stomach grumbled, but she did not wish to eat. She closed her eyes again.

"Annabelle, you must eat."

"No."

"You must. I shall make you something you can handle. Sleep, my child, I shall return soon." She heard his footsteps move farther away. She tried to go back to sleep, but she could not; she was alone in the cave with the fighting figures on the wall. She sat up against the rock; using what energy she had, she gathered her knees to herself and cried. *Alone, alone. I'm all alone.* She was alone, all alone. Her sobs wet the air, and her crying killed the silence.

Peter ran in. "My little Annabelle, what's wrong?" Annabelle held out her arms, she only wanted comfort. Peter went to her, and she crawled into his lap and wailed. He rocked her back and forth soothingly. "Why are you crying?"

"Don't leave me alone. I was alone when I was taken." She was unaware of where the words had come from, but once spoken, she recognized them as truth.

"Do you know who took you?"

Annabelle thought about the question for a while and then shook her head as fresh tears rolled down her cheeks. "Their faces were hidden." She tried to shake away the memory of the homemade disguises, constructed not only to cause fear because of the anonymity of the wearer, but fear at the sight of them, as well.

"It's all right, it's all right, shhh …" Peter tried to calm her. "Tell me about your family, your parents, your brothers and sisters." Peter distracted her from her present state. "How many do you have?"

"Four." The little girl wiped her left eye with the back of her hand.

"What are their names?"

"Will — he's the biggest; Thom and Isa; and then there's Crisa."

"Two brothers and two sisters, huh?"

Annabelle nodded her head.

"I'm certain they miss you."

"Not Crisa; she has Mamá … and Mamá has Crisa."

"No, your mamá probably grieves for you the most. For she is the one who sacrificed her body to give you life, carried you until you were big enough to live in the world, and is always there for you when you're hurt with a hug and love. A mother's love never fades …" Peter shook his head as he added, "She will never stop missing you."

The little girl thought about her mother and about Cristine, whom she called Crisa. She was suddenly ashamed of her selfish actions — all the fits and taking Cristine's toys. She lowered her head.

Peter continued, "You will always be in their hearts. As, I'm certain, they'll be in yours. Now, are you better?"

"I was alone but not now."

"Yes, my little one, I will always be with you, as long as

God allows me. There will come a day, though, when I, too, will no longer be with you. But fear not, for God is always with you. If you are afraid, run to Him. He will calm your fears. If you feel alone, flee to Him for He is always there. Don't ever be afraid to go to God." The small child silently listened to his words with her ear pressed close to his chest, listening to the rhythm of his existence.

A day later, when Annabelle was feeling much better and was no longer having erratic dreams, Peter asked, "Annabelle, did you learn anything from your sickness?"

"Being sick doesn't feel good, but it can help others."

"Yes. Anything else?"

She stared at him.

"Do not eat anything unless you know it's safe," Peter said.

"What's safe?" the little girl asked.

"You don't know, Annabelle, but I do, and I will teach you."

And so began her education in the ways of the forest: which leaves to eat and berries to pick; which trees, flowers, and roots had healing properties; where to gather water and eggs; how to avoid dangerous animals. Most importantly, Peter taught Annabelle how to be thankful for nature and all that God had placed before her to use.

"Look here, Annabelle." Peter squatted next to the river, pointing to a frog.

The little girl came to him with her hand full of freshly picked wildflowers. She gasped and dropped her flowers to investigate the reptile. It jumped into the river. She fell backwards in surprise but was quickly on her feet again. "What is it?" she asked as she searched for the frog in the shallow water.

"It's a frog." He watched her closely, hoping she would follow it into the river.

She gasped again. "I see it!" She pointed, and the frog hopped farther into the shallow river. She looked back at Peter.

"Where'd it go?" he asked as he scratched his head, pretending he did not know.

"Ummm." The little girl bit her lip and took a few steps into the shallow water. The frog hopped in front of her, splashing water upon her dress. She emulated its hop into the river. It hopped again. She looked cautiously for it and took a few more steps into the river. Noticing she was knee high in the cool water, she quickly looked back at the shoreline. Peter was standing behind her.

"See — you're fine. And I will teach you how to swim, so you will have nothing to fear."

"But Mamá —"

"Your mamá was fearful for a reason, but I will teach you so you need not fear. You must trust me. The danger on this island is not to know how to swim."

The little girl bit her lip, thinking of all the advantages of being able to swim. "Could I swim with the frogs?" the sweet girl timidly asked.

Peter laughed. "If that's what you would like to do."

She thought about it for a moment and then slowly nodded her head.

"Good." He waved her over to the bank where he began instructing her in swim techniques.

The young girl soaked up the lessons, and she no longer had any fear of the water. She would bravely jump into the river and chase after reptiles and fish. Peter never had to order her into the river again; his trouble became keeping her dry.

The Island

"Peter, where are we?" the little girl asked as Peter fingered some tracks in the mud.

"I call this place the Forbidden Island. It is off the northeast coast of Anchony."

"Why you call it that?" She picked a petal off the flower she was holding.

"Do you remember the 20-foot strip of sand between the rock wall and the forest?" he asked.

Annabelle nodded her head.

"Well, that is the only shore on the entire island; it is as if people should not come ashore here."

"We're here."

"Yes," Peter said with a smile, "we are here."

The Forbidden Island was a large, lush island full of life. The shape was that of an asymmetrical cookie attempting to resemble a circle but with a bite missing in the northeast corner, where the shoreline was present. The surrounding perimeter consisted of rocky, sharp drops to the sea at cascading heights from 20 to 200 feet. The interior was covered in a thick forest with the exception of two clearings and a river that bisected the forest and the island in unequal parts and ended abruptly with a 50-foot fall to the ocean.

She picked more petals off the flower. "And the forest — what's its name?"

He looked back at her from the tracks. "Well, I don't think it has a name. What would you like to call it?"

"Deep Forest."

"I think that describes it well."

"And that red bird over there?"

"What about it?"

"What's its name?"

"I believe it is a robin."

"No, Ruby. And that spider?"

"He is a ground spider."

"Hugo," the little girl replied with wide eyes and a confident nod of the head. Peter looked at the girl and her serious face as she continued on, "And what about that bush?"

"That is a blackberry bush."

"He's Robertus. And that tree, Mabilia, and that tree, Wilma, and that tree, Ysac."

Peter laughed at the little girl. *She is making the forest her friend.* His smile faded when he heard something move in the bushes.

"Who's next to Robertus?" the little girl asked with inquisitive eyes.

Peter picked her up swiftly and hurried out of the area.

"What is it?" she asked as she looked back at the bush, attempting to see whatever animal was there.

"A cub."

"What's that?" she asked into his ear.

"A baby bear."

She gasped. "A baby? I want to see it!"

Peter waded across the shallow portion of the river with Annabelle in his arms. When safely on the other side, he set her down and explained, "No, Annabelle, because where there's a baby bear, there's a mother bear, and you don't want to meet her."

She looked across the river in curiosity. He offered his hand. Dropping her flower, she held on to his finger as she skipped to the cave.

The little girl's naming everything in sight went on for a month. Peter, at first, found it cute and childish, but his patience was tested with the constant personification of every animal, plant, and inanimate object. It came to a summit and standstill in one event.

"Shhhh, get down," Peter commanded, pulling on Annabelle's dress as he knelt down.

Annabelle crouched down, not knowing the reason for the sudden drop to the ground.

"There's a deer," Peter replied as he grabbed his spear.

"What are you going to do?" Annabelle asked.

"It will become our supper."

"No, don't kill it, please, don't kill it."

"Annabelle, there are too many deer on this island to begin with; they have free reign. Lowering their numbers will be better for them."

"Don't hurt it. Don't hurt Norman!" Annabelle cried with angst.

Peter sighed heavily as he picked up the girl and moved her over next to a tree. "Stand here and pout if you must. I will collect our food and clothing."

Tears fell from Annabelle's cheeks as she sat down and rested her head on her crossed arms atop her knees. *That deer didn't do anything to you. Don't hurt Norman. Leave him alone. He's just trying to live!*

She looked up when she heard the leaves rustling. Peter was on the attack with his spear in hand. She put her head back on her arms as she tried to drown out the sounds she heard.

Peter hung the deer up on a vine and cut it open with a rock as she tearfully watched. "Annabelle, you can't name everything. A wild animal is not a pet; it does not need a name. Your next meal is not a pet; it does not need a name. I want you to stop naming everything. Do you understand?"

Annabelle had never heard that tone from Peter. She knew he was serious. She nodded her head reluctantly as she bit her lip.

Rafts and Stories

"Can I get the eggs?" the bright-eyed Annabelle asked Peter. She was eager to show Peter her new skills by locating a nest by herself.

"Not this morning." It had been six months since the men had left, and a recent storm had laid some trees down. Peter thought it a prime time to try to build a boat of some sort. "Today we will search through the forest for fallen logs."

"What for?"

"For what," Peter corrected as he contemplated his answer. He did not wish to get the little girl's hopes up, for he knew it would take a while before any boat was prepared, but he did not wish to hide his plans. "My little one, I don't wish you to stay on this island evermore. We'll try to prepare a boat of some sort."

"I get to go home?" an excited Annabelle asked.

"Not yet, my little one. Not yet." She began to mope. "Come now, child. Let me see a smile. That face makes my heart break. Your joy comes from the Lord, so be joyful in all things."

"I should be glad while I'm here?"

"Yes. And you can be overjoyed when you return home. Now, come along. Let's find some logs."

"Will this do?" Annabelle picked up a foot-long stick.

Peter laughed. "Do you think that stick will hold you afloat? No, we are looking for downed trees."

"Oh! You could chop them down like Michael with his axe!"

"Michael, huh? Well, if I had Michael's axe, I certainly

could chop down some trees. But I fear all I have are rocks with pointy edges, and they will not suffice against large trees."

They searched the forest for hours and only found two downed trees of acceptable size.

"I'm afraid two logs will not hold you, yet alone me."

"You're coming?"

"That is a sea out there, my little Annabelle. You can't make your way to land by yourself, not at your present size. Besides, I could not live with myself if you did not make it."

"The wind could take me. Like the boats at sea."

"If it was a sail boat, indeed, but right now, my little one, it's not even a raft."

The little girl gazed at the ground as she concluded, "I'll have to grow bigger and stronger before seeing my family." Peter was amazed at Annabelle's problem solving, especially since the insightful solution required long-term planning.

Peter continued his teaching, and Annabelle continued her education as they walked about the forest searching for logs, berries, leaves, mushrooms, tracks, and eggs, and as they swam about in the river. Annabelle absorbed it all as she listened to his words and studied the island around her.

Peter and Annabelle embarked on a downed-tree-finding mission every day while the sun's light would cast its beams through the cracks in the towering canopy. Each week they would scour a different section of the island. Each day they did not find a log, Annabelle would sulk. Peter would try to cheer her: "It was not in God's will for us to find logs today."

"God doesn't want me to go home?"

"I'm sure He does, my little one, but not today."

Annabelle did not understand why, if God wanted her to go home, He did not just send her a boat.

As the season passed, Peter spent less time searching for

logs and more time preparing for the months to come: finding berries, curing meat, gathering sticks for fire.

When they had located six logs, Peter, believing it to be a sufficient number, started gathering vines to tie the logs together. He worked tirelessly on a raft that would be sea-worthy and safe. It took him many hours to make one spruce trunk acceptable — each limb had to be chopped off with his flint axe. When his makeshift axe would break, he had to prepare another.

The evenings turned colder, and the leaves turned vibrant colors of yellow, orange, and red. But the vibrant colors soon disappeared as the leaves fell to the earth.

Annabelle loved standing amid the tall trees with the canopy of color above her. When the wind would blow and leaves would descend to the earth, swirling around her in the wind, she felt as though she was a princess and the island was her kingdom, given to her by God.

Soon all the colorful leaves had fallen and only the barren trees were left in the tall forest. Annabelle did not mind this either; she could look up and see the sky, and at night, she could see the gems twinkling in God's blanket.

God made it all. How did He do it?

She did not remember such beauty at her home, a home that seemed more distant as she became comfortable with her new life on the Forbidden Island.

"Where's your boat, Peter?" the little girl asked as he tucked her into her moss bed one fall evening.

"My boat?"

"How did you get here?"

"Oh, my boat. My boat sank."

"Sank?"

"I released it into the ocean; it crashed upon the rocks."

"And your trunk?"

Peter looked over at his trunk. "It was safely on the sand when I pushed the craft into the ocean." He pulled the fur hide around her. "Now, my little one, no more questions. It's time for bed."

"Am I a princess?"

Peter was silent for a moment as he tilted his head and licked his dry lips. He took a deep breath, moved her hair away from her eyes, and responded with a smile, "Your Father is a heavenly king, so yes, you are a princess."

"You mean *God*?"

"I do."

"Wow." Her emerald eyes sparkled. "So, you're a prince?"

"You could say that," he said cautiously.

"Prince Peter!" The little girl beamed.

Peter's smile faded. "Please, Annabelle, don't call me that."

The little girl's eyes beamed. "You're an angel *and* a prince!"

Peter shook his head as he stood up. "You need to get some sleep."

The night's rest did nothing to quell her ideas. "Prince Peter, I am awake," she announced as she threw her arms around him in the morning.

What have I done? he thought to himself. "Annabelle, please don't call me that."

The little girl bit her lip as she thought and then decided, "You're right: you should be king! And this is your kingdom!" She swirled around. "King Peter the angel!"

"Why would I want to be king?" Peter asked as he stoked the fire.

"You could order people around!" she proudly suggested.

Peter looked over at her and almost laughed. "Tell me this, my little one, who am I to order around? You are the only other person on this island, and I already order you around."

She stepped back and pondered an answer. "The animals?"

Peter shook his head again. "No. God already gave man dominion over the animals; besides" — he leaned closer to her — "they're not very good at listening." He tickled her.

She giggled and moved closer into him. He cuddled her. Her young eyes looked up into his. "You're still an angel."

He turned her around and cuddled her again, her back to his chest. "Let me ask you this: What was Jesus?"

"God."

"Yes, and what else?" he asked in her ear.

"A man?"

"Yes. God became a man, not an angel. If becoming a man was good enough for God, shouldn't it be good enough for me?" He squeezed her, then released her.

The little girl pondered on his words. She looked up from the ground, "So you're a man, but you're *my* angel!" She burst into a smile and ran out of the cave.

"Will you tell me a story?" Their nightly tradition had been established.

"All right." He was silent for a moment. "Would you like to hear a story about a prince?"

The little girl's mouth dropped open. "Yes!" She climbed into his lap and yawned.

"Once upon a time there lived a prince, Prince Francis."

"That's my papá's name!" the girl said with excitement.

Peter smiled and nodded his head as he continued. "He had two best friends, Josephus and Mooey."

"Mooey? Was he a cow?"

Peter chuckled. "No, he was a boy. That wasn't his real name though. He shared his name with his father, so 'Mooey' was what his friends called him." He continued the story: "They snuck out of the castle often."

"His friends lived in the castle, too?" Her little head tilted as she looked up at him quizzically.

"Their fathers worked for the king; they visited often. Now, there was a secret passageway that the prince had discovered — a tunnel that led beyond the castle walls to a hollow tree."

She scrunched up her nose. "What?"

"It wasn't a tree in truth; it only looked like a tree." She tilted her head the other direction. He put up his hand. "This is my story; don't talk. There was a hollow tree that they used to escape from the castle. Now, the prince would always dress in servant's clothing when he would sneak out — he wanted to know how people really lived, what they did all day. His most favored place was the market. It was loud, crowded, and full of dirt — the opposite of the castle on a calm day — and the prince was caught in wonder at the sight of it all. He would stand back with his friends and watch the carts, people, and mice move freely through the market."

"One time, when the prince was about 10 years old, a farmer's cart was knocked over by some escaped pigs, who then sought to eat the newly fallen food. The prince and his friends scared the pigs away and helped the farmer to pick up his fruits. The farmer was so thankful for the help that he gave them each a shiny coin for their effort. It was not worth much, but it meant everything to the prince. It was his first, and only, pay for the work of his hands; he treasured it."

He looked down at Annabelle in his arms when she did not interrupt with a question; she was sound asleep. He lay her down on her moss bed and covered her with the fur blanket.

Little white flakes soon appeared. Peter told her to stay inside until it warmed up since her summer shoes were not sufficient for such conditions. Since he was spending so much time searching for logs, he did not have time to prepare proper attire for the young girl's feet.

Annabelle did not mind, at first, staying inside the mouth of the cave. Although it was a bit chilly, it was much warmer than the temperature outside. The furs kept her warm as she studied the wonderful array of rocks she had collected during the summer and fall. As the streams of sunlight found their way inside, she would look through a certain stone that colored everything green. She was particularly drawn to this rock because Peter had told her it was the color of her eyes. But she soon grew tired of studying the same rocks and remaining in the cave, not being able to explore the island, take in the fresh air, or feel the wind in her hair and the sunlight on her face.

"Peter, I want to go out!" she declared one day after throwing down her rocks.

Peter laughed. *You remind me so much of my Clare.* "All right, in the afternoon then, but only for a short while." She was so excited, she danced in happiness.

After lunch, Peter took her outside the cave. She ran wild in the white flakes, giggling and entertaining herself by chasing her own breath and playing in the snow. Peter stood back and marveled at her happiness.

Her delicate cheeks turned rosy, and she began to cough as she ran around in joy.

"All right, I think that's about all you need for today."

She did not want to quit playing, but she did not fight Peter as he picked her up, took her inside, and placed her next to the fire to warm herself.

"My toes are cold," she reported as she hugged herself tightly.

"I suppose they would be." Peter removed her socks and shoes. "Your socks are soaking wet."

The rosy-cheeked girl just smiled.

"What's this?" Peter pointed to a birthmark on the inside of her lower right leg. "Amazing," he mumbled.

"What?"

"The mark, on your lower leg," Peter stated, standing up to retrieve a warm fur blanket for the girl. "My daughter, Clare, she had one like it, but on her left leg."

Annabelle looked at her leg. "Mamá says that's where God kissed me before I was born."

Peter smiled and nodded his head. "Did she?"

"Did He kiss Clare, too?" the girl asked innocently.

Peter's eyes turned watery. "I suppose He did."

"Are you sad?" an observant Annabelle asked.

"It's a sweet bitterness," he replied, almost to himself, as Annabelle stared at him. "My little girl," Peter went on to explain, "was taken from me."

"You should go find her," Annabelle was quick to respond.

"No. I know where she is. She's in God's hands."

"God knows where she is?"

"God always knows where we are."

"Why doesn't He tell you then?"

He shook his head. "She's with her mamá and her brothers …" He could not get the rest of his sentence out.

"Why are you not with them?" Her emerald eyes seemed to stab his soul.

He shook his head. *I should be.* "God had other thoughts for me."

"God doesn't want you with your family?"

"I don't know or understand His ways." He knelt down and stared into the fire. He felt a little hand on his shoulder.

"I'm sorry, Peter."

"My Annabelle, you have done nothing wrong." He hugged her.

After a long moment of silence, the little girl asked in his ear. "Do you think Papá is looking for me?"

"Oh, there is no doubt in my mind that he is doing everything in his power to find you, and I'm certain your mamá has never prayed so hard."

As the bitter north wind blew in with the random blizzards, the little girl could not deny that fall was over. A momentary feeling of melancholy came over her. She associated the cold weather with her family's celebration of Advent and Christmas. She was sad that she would not make it home to celebrate the birth of Christ with her mamá and papá. But then she thought of Peter. She would get to celebrate it with him.

The cave was cleaned as well as it could be and a Baby Jesus was fashioned out of dried leaves and grass. On their appointed day for Christmas, Peter recited the Nativity story as Annabelle sat in his lap, holding the Baby Jesus.

She thought about her family: What were they doing? Were they attending Mass at that very moment? Were they thinking of her? She leaned back onto Peter's chest. She was so thankful for Peter, her angel.

Winter soon snuck away while spring slid in. With spring they celebrated Lent and Easter. Annabelle was amazed at how the forest seemed to emulate Jesus's Resurrection as it came alive — from flowers in bloom to baby creatures all around. She spent a good part of her days chasing baby rabbits and looking for baby birds while Peter, once again, focused on a way off the island for her.

Nearly a year had gone by when Peter declared the "boat" finished. All that was left to do was to check its seaworthiness.

It was no easy feat getting the raft to the shoreline from deep inside the forest. Peter belittled himself for the poor placement of the raft during assembly.

It took him weeks to move it through the forest. Little Annabelle just watched; he would not let her help. He would never forgive himself if she was crushed by the large and heavy raft.

The day finally came when the raft made its way to the shore. Peter held his breath as he pushed it into the water. He breathed a sigh of relief as he watched it float.

"Annabelle, come here." He held out his hand. The little girl stood with sand between her toes as the gentle water lapped upon her feet. (At the first signs of spring, she had tossed her uncomfortable shoes into the forest in a random location.)

Peter picked her up and placed her on the raft; it floated. *Yes! Yes!* But would it hold him as well? He climbed atop; it still floated.

"What does this mean, Peter?"

"It means, my little one, you will get to go home."

"Home …" The little girl was excited to see her family but did not want to leave her new friend. "You'll come with me?"

"I will take you to your family."

"And stay?"

"I can't welcome myself into your family, my little one."

"I don't want you to leave," she objected.

Peter hopped down and pulled her off the raft as he dragged it onto the shore.

"Annabelle …" What could he say? He could not stay with her indefinitely. "We won't be leaving for a while. We still need oars."

When they made their way back to the cave, a trip taking a few hours, Annabelle was still saddened and hanging on to Peter.

"You're my angel. You can't leave me!"

"Annabelle, I'm not an angel," Peter said with an irritated voice.

The girl turned her eyes to the ground. "You are to me."

Peter sat her up on a large rock so that they were eye to eye. "We must part with loved ones in our life. It's change, and that's what comes to pass. Do you understand?"

"I don't want you to leave!"

"Look. I will always be in your heart, and you will always be in mine. And I will pray for you, and I hope you will always pray for me. So, you see? We aren't really apart from each other at all. In the end, when both of our times are up, I pray we shall meet again with God and all our loved ones in Heaven. We might depart now, but God willing, it is only for a short time."

"But you could stay —"

"Your place is with your family, and it's not your welcome to give."

"But Papá would like you. I'm certain he would!"

Peter shook his head and smiled as he looked at the ground and repeated, "It's not your welcome to give."

Finding proper materials for oars proved much more difficult than finding downed trees. The task would have been much more successful if he had a stronger axe — or a knife or anything other than a sharp rock — with which he could form an oar of some fashion. But without such tools, he was forced to find pieces of sturdy wood with one part skinny but strong and the other broad and flat. After much searching, he decided no piece of wood existed upon the island and another solution must be found. He fabricated his own oars: a sturdy forked tree branch with a leather paddle. The summer was coming to a close when his oars were completed.

"Annabelle, I think it's time. We must gather food for our journey."

"How long will it take us?"

"Nearly a day on the water, but then there is the journey on land. Anchony is no small place."

Annabelle remembered that her father had made the same comment on the size of Anchony.

They gathered berries and meat and set out before the sunrise the next day, making their way to the short stretch of sand. Peter's eyes were transfixed upon the sunrise.

"It's so red," Annabelle commented.

Red, indeed. Not a good sign. He did not wish to worry her, so he said nothing.

The black clouds were rolling in by the time they found the shoreline. The wind had picked up, and it was a struggle for Annabelle to walk.

"We must retreat to the cave," Peter said, pointing to Annabelle's first hiding place on the island.

"We can make it!"

"No, Annabelle, we can't." He picked her up and climbed up into the entrance. They sat at the mouth of the cave watching the menacing clouds approach. When the large raindrops fell, they retreated farther into the cave. Sitting in the darkness, listening to the roar of the squall, Annabelle was not afraid, because Peter was there to protect her.

Hours later, when the wind was no longer howling through their shelter and the glimpse of the sunlight broke the darkness that surrounded them, they emerged from the cavern.

Peter's heart sank when he looked over at the shoreline. There sat — nothing. The raft had been taken by the storm, taken by the ocean.

Annabelle did not realize the sorrowful news as she hopped her way down the rocks. Leaving her footprints in the sand as she ran to where the raft once sat, she looked back at Peter when she could not find it.

He sorrowfully shook his head. "It must not be your time to return home."

A tear trickled down the little girl's cheek as she processed what that meant: Her parents, her brothers and sisters, they were lost to her again. She fell to her knees. Her tears dampened her hands as the ocean wet her dress. Peter did not know what words would comfort her, so he said none. He just picked her up and hugged her.

Peter was discouraged, as well.

All that hard work for nothing. Why? Do You not want her to go home to her family? Am I to give up on a raft?

Peter heard a reply in his thoughts: *"Work as if it it's up to you, but know that it is not."*

Why would You want her to stay on the island with me, Father?

"What can you teach her?"

Nothing that anyone else on Anchony could not give her. There are great teachers and her parents.

Peter suddenly had a flashback of his last moments with his wife and the surge of emotions he had felt: anger and guilt.

He swallowed with difficulty. *I understand what I am to do.*

Signs

The next day Peter introduced Annabelle to the hollow, an open field of wild grasses and flowers.

"Has this been here the whole time?"

Peter laughed. "Well, God did not now create it." He knelt down beside the 6-year-old — soon to be 7. "We're going to play a game. Do you see that rock over there?" He pointed to a rock across the valley.

She nodded her head.

"I want you to run over and touch it. I will hide, and then you run back and find me, do you understand?" She nodded her head. She had played such games with her siblings, but never with a grown-up. She took off.

Huffing and puffing, she touched the rock and turned around. She could not see him anywhere. "Peter, I'm going to find you." She ran back to where they had been. Peter was not there. "Peter?" She began to panic. "Peter!" She turned in circles searching for him.

"Do not fear; use what God gave you. Use your ears; follow my voice. Use your eyes; follow the trampled grass. There are signs all about you that will lead you to me."

She turned in the direction of the voice. Looking down at the grass, she noticed it was bent down where he had stepped. She ran to him. "I found you!"

Peter hugged her. "You did indeed."

Tears began to fall down her delicate cheeks. "Why did you do that, Peter?"

"You found me, did you not? And on your own?" She nodded her head along Peter's chest. "Then don't fret. You see, Annabelle, there are signs all around — you must not let fear overcome you but look for the signs that will tell you what you need to know."

"Why are we here?" Annabelle asked.

They were at the southwestern corner of the island.

"I wanted to show you something." He pointed to the horizon. "Over there is Anchony. If you were to leave from this side of the island, it would not take you long at all by sea. But since there are only cliffs along the bank, one can't leave from this side."

The little girl looked at the horizon. Her home was over there — somewhere. The life she once knew. The life that was slipping away, gradually.

"And while we are here, we can look for logs."

"Are you going to build me another raft?"

"Yes." *Even if it takes me years.* "Do you want to look with me, or do you want to sit here for a little while?"

"I'll sit here." She sat down on a little rock, looking out at the horizon, trying to remember more about her family.

A memory came back to her, not of her relations but of a visit to the sea she had made with her family. She was mesmerized by the large ships and their white sails; she waved to each and every one of them.

She was lost in her thoughts when she was jolted back to the present day. *What is that? Is that a boat?* She turned around to ask Peter, but he had gone farther into the woods. *Is it? Could it be?* She waited a moment as it got closer. *It is! It is!* She started waving frantically, using both hands. "Peter, look! Peter!"

He emerged from the woods in a full sprint. "What? Are you hurt? What's wrong?"

"Peter, look! It's a boat!" She continued to wave frantically. Peter looked at the boat and instantaneously stopped the girl from waving by pulling her back into the shadows of the trees. "Peter, what are you doing? It's a boat!"

"Yes, but you don't know if they are friendly."

"They were too far — I couldn't see if they waved."

"That's not what I mean."

"What do you mean?"

"They could be those that tried to seize you looking for signs of life."

She quickly lowered her arms as her chin began to quiver.

"Annabelle, it's all right. You didn't know ... and I won't let them harm you." His large, comforting arms surrounded the young girl.

Peter continued to take Annabelle to the hollow for a game of hide and seek. She became more and more proficient at locating Peter. After three months of games, he would purposely choose locations that would not easily give up his direction.

"How did you know I was here?"

"The grass wasn't flattened — you climbed the wall instead."

"Very good. I think we will have to make this harder for you." He pulled out a piece of leather from his pouch. "Turn around."

She did as commanded.

"Now, you will find me without using your eyes."

"Peter —"

"Listen to the valley, to all the creatures, to my breathing. They will all give you signs."

He guided her to the middle of the field.

"Count to 12 and then come and find me."

"1, 2, 3 ..." Peter took off. "... 11, 12." She stopped counting and listened. She could not hear anything. She began to walk around slowly. *Birds chirping, crickets all around, something at my feet — too small to be Peter. Wait — something changed.* As she took a step, the crickets near her went silent. And what was that noise to her left?

She placed her hand on Peter's shoulder. "There you are, Peter." She removed the leather to see if she was correct.

"Very good! How did you know?"

"The birds. You scared them away, so I knew you were over here. Then your breathing — I knew right where you were!"

"Very good, very good."

Annabelle soon mastered the valley; there was nowhere Peter could hide, even blindfolded, that she could not discover him.

Peter then took her to the woods for hide and seek. Annabelle at first thought it would be more difficult, with all the creatures and noises, but she soon realized that they were to her benefit. They helped her find Peter easier than in the valley, once she was cognizant of all the natural noises of the forest.

"So tell me, how many large rocks are there across the river right now — no, don't look." He stopped her head from turning.

"Peter?" Her forehead wrinkled.

"You must always be keenly aware of where you are, knowing what and who is around you, how far they are from you."

The 8-year-old looked at him. "I don't know, Peter." She closed her eyes. He thought she might cry from not having a correct answer. But she surprised him by saying, "But there are three loons on the other side of the river, one on our side, two cardinals, and four rabbits munching on grass by the rock."

Peter looked over at the rock. "I did not see any —" Four rabbits hopped out from behind the rock. Peter smiled the biggest grin he could give. "I'm amazed! You have learned well."

Annabelle smiled up at him and then looked over at the cardinal atop the rock. "And that bird is always there. May I name it?" she asked sheepishly. "How about Red?"

"I think that would be a good name, since he's *always* here." Peter, knowing the strength of her observation skills, wanted to test her other skills as well. Standing, he reached for her hand. "I've got an idea. Stand up. I want to show you some steps to a dance."

"A dance? Like at a fair? I think I might have a memory of one."

"It's not quite a fair. We don't have any music, but you can learn the steps just the same."

Besides teaching the little girl some dance moves, Peter had an ulterior motive: to test her coordination and see if the sweet Annabelle could physically pick up on fancy footwork and movement of the arms.

Annabelle stared at the outside of the cave. She studied its contours; it beckoned her. She wanted to climb it, to know if she could. She bravely gripped the sharp edges and pulled herself up. Hit by a powerful gust of wind as her head made it over the top, her breath was taken away. She smiled as she breathed it in and climbed up all the way. She sat down, cross-legged. One side delivered a view of nothing but the powerful ocean — miles and miles of the salty water. The other view was that of the island, now her home. At that moment, it became her favorite place to venture.

She became accustomed to sitting atop the cave to gaze upon the stars, feel the wind blow through her hair, and listen to the sounds of the ocean with the background sound of the forest. Peter would often join her. Her best education came in these moments with Peter atop the cave, surrounded by God's creation.

"What do you miss the most about Anchony?" Annabelle asked one evening as she watched the sunset glitter across the ocean.

"It is true that I miss my family, but there is something for which I ache more."

Annabelle was discombobulated. *Who or what could be greater to Peter than his family?*

"A few more years and you would be about the age when you could first receive Him. So, I ache for you as well."

Annabelle had no idea to what Peter was referring. She turned around to face him. "Peter, who should I ache for?"

"For whom ... Jesus."

Annabelle did not understand. "But Jesus is God and God is all around. How could I not have Him?"

"That is true, my little one. God is omnipresent — meaning being everywhere — but Jesus comes to us to see, to touch, to eat."

"Eat Jesus? Why would I want to do that?"

"Sacrifices that are offered up to God are eaten; that's why we eat the Eucharist — He is our sacrifice. Do you understand?"

The young girl shook her head.

"It goes back to our Jewish roots," he attempted to explain.

"I'm not Jewish, I don't think. My mamá and papá are from Anchony."

"I don't mean *your* Jewish roots, I mean *our* roots — as Christians. The first Christians were Jews. That's where we get many of our customs. In the Old Testament, the Jews steadfastly sacrificed animals to God. In the New Testament, Jesus sacrificed Himself for us and rose from the dead. And

He wants us now to eat and drink His risen and glorified Body and Blood."

She scrunched up her nose. "His living Body? Are you certain that's what He wants?"

"At the Last Supper He said, 'Do this in memory of Me.'"

"But how could it be Him? There are many churches, right? There would be nothing left of Him."

"Think of the feeding of the 5,000 — how was that possible? All things are possible with God." Annabelle pondered on that thought as Peter continued: "It is called the Real Presence of Jesus in the Blessed Sacrament when the ordinary unleavened bread and wine becomes the Body and Blood, Soul and Divinity of Jesus. Priests have that power through apostolic succession — meaning that it was handed down to them from the apostles — which is passed to the priest when he is ordained by the bishop in the Sacrament of Holy Orders."

Annabelle thought about the new information and then asked: "How do you know that's what He truly meant?"

"When Jesus told His followers they would have to eat His Flesh, many turned away from Him because they took His words to mean what He said. If He didn't mean it truly as He said, He would have gone after them, telling them, 'You misunderstood what I was saying,' but He didn't. That's how we know He truly meant one must eat His Body and drink His Blood — He let them leave."

"And if I was in Anchony, I would be able to eat the living Jesus?"

"The Body and Blood, Soul and Divinity of the Resurrected Christ. Yes — in a few years — but you must be confirmed first by a bishop. And then you could receive Holy Communion. The priest will probably ask you some questions first."

"Like what?"

"Not all people who receive Christ believe it is truly Him. The priest will want to make sure you are aware of the great marvel that you are receiving."

Annabelle looked across the ocean. "That is a wonder."

"A merciful wonder, but God's ways are not our ways."

"Why would He stoop so low as to have us eat Him?"

"'God so loved the world, He sent His only Son.' Why would He bother with us at all? We are His creatures and can only understand so much. We can't properly give Him His due, yet He loves us beyond everything. Our minds can't fathom that kind of love. Our hearts could not take it; they would burn to nothingness in awe. I hunger to return to Anchony for the Eucharist alone."

Starring at the glistening ocean, Annabelle ruminated on what truths she was able to comprehend from Peter's explanation.

Boats

Peter ran into the cave. "Boats have arrived."

"What?" Annabelle looked up from the rocks she was using as chalk.

The girl and Peter had lived quietly on the island for four years without visitors.

"They must have come to search for you again," Peter said as he doused the fire with water.

She did not know what to say or do. She had become comfortable with her life with Peter. The thought of being taken by those men frightened her, and the fact that Peter took down his important satchel of unknown contents and placed the strap around himself did nothing to ease her nerves.

Peter saw the fear in her eyes and instructed, "We'll not strike another fire until they have left. Stay close to the dwelling and within my hearing."

Annabelle nodded her head.

"It is all right, my child. God is watching over us."

"Peter, I'm afraid." Her chin quivered.

"I know, I know, my little one." He held out his arms as the young girl came to his embrace. The 9-year-old Annabelle stayed on his lap as the cold slowly crept its way inside. It was not long until she could see her breath. Peter retrieved the deerskin blanket and wrapped it around the shivering child. "We must stay close to each other, keep each other warm." Annabelle nodded her head. She placed her head next to his heart and fell asleep in his warm, comfortable arms.

"Wake up, Annabelle. You must rise."

Feeling the rocking of her shoulder, Annabelle's awareness awoke to the sound of distant barking dogs. "What? What is it?"

"Saint Hubert hounds, no doubt."

"Saint Hubert?"

"The best noses amongst dogs. We must get to the river."

"The river?" the girl asked as Peter guided her by her arm.

"To make them lose our trail."

Peter picked up the girl as they made their way toward the thick forest. Annabelle searched the forest line with the setting sunlight as Peter ran.

The barking of the bloodhounds increased as each moment passed.

"Oh, no ... Peter! I see torches," the 9-year-old informed him.

Peter increased his speed. *Lord, I don't think You would hand me this angel just to have her taken from me after four years. Please, Lord, make me swift and defend this child.*

They came to the river's edge. Peter followed the river up toward the roaring waterfall. "There is a little cave behind the waterfall. You must hide there. Climb on to my back." Peter easily moved the girl on to his back. "Hold on." Peter started climbing up the cliff behind the waterfall. He was about 15 feet up the wall when he bent his upper body into a hole. "Climb in." Annabelle did as commanded. He maneuvered the satchel off his shoulder into the haven. "Hide this."

Annabelle's eyes enlarged as Peter handed her his sacred satchel.

He started lowering himself down the rocks.

She stuck her head out of the hole. "Peter, what about you?"

"My child, there is not enough room for us both in there."

"Peter" — the girl's voice quivered — "don't leave me."

"Annabelle, I'll be back. Now is the time to trust in God, yes?"

She nodded her head, willing herself to be strong.

Peter looked her in the eyes and stated, "He is always with you. You are never alone." Pushing himself off the rock, he landed in the water as the dogs drew closer. She could not hear the voices over the roar of the waterfall, but she could see their distorted figures and torches.

She peeked out the cave. There was just enough light to see Peter swim to the side of the river. The torches and barking dogs stopped running, changed direction, and started following Peter. He took off into the woods.

Annabelle backed into the cave and hugged Peter's satchel and her knees as she shivered. *God, God, God, help us, help us, help us.* She rocked herself back and forth as the light from the torches faded into the night. Annabelle was left alone with her thoughts and the darkness. A calm came over her; she was still frightened and worried, but she felt safe. *Peter led them away from me. Peter is risking his life for me. Peter, my angel.* She laid her cheek upon the satchel and continued to rock herself, hugging herself for warmth. Sleep eventually overcame her.

"Annie, Annie, where are you?" Isabella was calling.

"I'm here. Can't you see me? No, you're going the wrong way!" Annabelle waved her arms as Isabella ran toward a fence. A horse fled in the opposite direction.

"She was taken! Will, she was taken!" Isabella screamed as she frantically ran toward her brother. "Annie! Annie!"

"What? Who? No!" William shouted in horror as he watched the dust cloud from the horse escape into the horizon.

"Where's Annie?" Thomas asked, short of breath as he came running to the screams.

Annabelle was on a horse. "Let go! Let go! Help! Help! Peeeter!" And Annabelle awoke.

She was still alone in the rock niche, but the sun's light was peeking its way through the clear, crisp water. She strained her ears; she could hear nothing over the amazing power of the waterfall — no voices, no barking. She saw no figures. *What should I do? What should I do?*

Her stomach growled. Her legs were cramped from being scrunched up all night long. She stretched them so they hung outside the cave. It felt better, but she did not know if she was putting herself at risk by showing her legs. She quickly pulled them back inside.

Peeking out of the cave, she searched for any signs. As she maneuvered awkwardly in the close quarters, she haphazardly knocked the satchel out of the hiding place. She lunged for it with no success as it fell toward the wet rocks. On its descent it caught between two rocks and sat insecurely three feet below. *Oh, no! Peter, your bag!* She reached for it — her fingers barely scraped the leather.

Determined not to lose Peter's bag, she lay on her stomach and inched herself out of the cave until she gripped a corner of it. As the blood rushed to her head, she swung the bag over her shoulder back into the niche. She stared at the rocks being pounded by the waterfall as she slowly slipped toward them, unable to pull herself back into the cave. *Oh, no! Please, don't let me hit them!* She had no control over her descent, but she would have sworn someone else did; she felt a gentle push just strong enough to put her out of danger of the precarious rocks.

The powerful waterfall wet her hair and pounded on her face. It forced her down, down, down into the cold water. She was sucked under into the swirling frigidness. Disoriented as she was, she knew she had to swim. She started swimming, though she did not know if it was to the top or the bottom of the river.

Emerging at the top, she gasped for air. The powerful river was moving her downstream. She started paddling toward the edge, but the current was too strong. She quickly grew tired. Her head started going under the water. Water, air, water. Her head bobbled up and down as she tried to stay afloat and the water pulled her against her will. Every cold blast of air brought a gasp from her lips.

She saw movement along the side of the water. Brown and black, large — a dog.

It was in the water, it had her clothing, pulling her toward the side of the bank. She did not know what to do: Should she face the men or stay in the freezing river? She struggled to get away from the grasp of the dog, but she could not. She no longer had a choice — she would have to face the men.

The dog pulled her to the edge of the river and up the bank. Coughing, she struggled to get a deep breath. She tried to crawl away on her elbows, but her long hair, dragging along the dirt, slowed her movement. *No! No! Peter, where are you?*

She looked up to face her kidnappers and saw — no one. No one but the dog standing over her. She rolled on to her back, rotating her arms so that the backs of her hands were touching the ground close to her head. The dog greeted her with a lick on the face. She turned to her side to get away from the slobber. *The men have to be around here somewhere. I've got to hide.* Turning onto her hands and knees, she crawled to the largest tree she could find.

The dog followed.

The sun disappeared behind clouds. It started to drizzle. A cold, miserable drizzle. Annabelle was wet enough the drizzle could not drench her clothes more, but the drops upon her face only led to more misery. She crawled up next to a large tree and grabbed her legs for warmth.

The dog watched her.

"Go away! You don't see me. Go away!" she yelled at the dog.

The dog moved closer to her and curled up at her feet.

Annabelle tried to move him off. "They'll be looking for you! You'll give me away. Go away!" The dog would not budge. "Go away!" Annabelle started to cry. "You'll lead them to me. Please go away!" The dog just stared at her. Annabelle fell on top of the dog, crying. *Don't lead them to me. Please, don't lead them to me.*

He was warm. Annabelle was thankful for that.

She stayed in that same area for a day, always close to the dog, picking berries from a close bush for sustenance.

"I haven't heard any voices. Do you think it's safe to get up?" she asked the dog. The dog leaped up and wagged his tail. "Is that a 'yes'?" Annabelle stood up — the first time she had done so in a day. Her muscles ached, and she was certain she would never walk normally again. "I need to find Peter. Do you know where he is?" The dog started walking through the forest, taking his time, smelling this and that. Annabelle followed him, though she did not think he was being very productive. "You could move a little bit faster."

She heard a twig break; the dog was alerted and took off running. Ducking down to hide behind a rock, she listened closer: breathing. She crawled to a skinny tree and slowly stood up, peeking around the tree from where the sound came. She did not see anything. *Did I make it up? Did I really hear breathing or am I only afraid?* She stepped away from the protection of the trunk.

Out of nowhere a tree branch came flailing toward her, stopped an inch from her face, and fell to the ground. "Annabelle!" Peter stepped out from behind another arbor.

"Peter!" Annabelle exclaimed, crying tears of relief.

"I went to the waterfall. I didn't find you. I thought they took you." His large hands embraced her head. "What are you doing outside of the cave?"

Her honest, emerald eyes looked into his. "I knocked the satchel out and I had to get it, but I couldn't get back in.

I fell into the river." He pulled her so close she could hardly breathe.

"How long have you been out here?"

"A day or so."

"In this cold?"

"The dog kept me warm."

"What dog?"

"One of the men's dogs."

"Annabelle, the men are gone. The boats are gone. They would not leave their dog behind."

"There was a dog! He pulled me out of the river."

"Where is he now?"

"He took off. You scared him."

"Whether there was a dog or not, you're here and you're safe."

"What do you mean?" She pulled away. "There was a dog! I named him Cuddles."

"Cuddles, huh?" Peter started to laugh. "Perhaps *that* was your angel, my little one."

Annabelle did not understand. She knew that the dog was real — as real as Peter standing before her.

"Let's thank God that you are safe."

"And you, too, Peter." She hugged him. "You will always be *my* angel," she whispered.

Findings

Two days later Annabelle was back to exploring the island — her usual occupation when not under the scholarly eye of Peter and his lessons. She liked to go to the waterfall and listen to the powerful roar. It reminded her of God's power and how He had saved her life that day.

Annabelle heard whining. She looked to the other side of the river. "Cuddles!" The dog took off into the forest. "Wait!" Annabelle looked around frantically for a way to cross the river that did not involve getting wet. She headed toward the rock wall that held the small cave that hid her from the potential kidnappers. She did not hesitate to climb on the thin rock ledge. Her tiptoes and fingertips gripped the rock wall as she slowly made her way to the other side. "Wait! Peter thinks you're an angel."

She made it to the other side, without consideration of the danger she put her life in to make it there. The dog came back from his trot, stared at her, and took off running again. She pursued him. She thought she was doing a good job keeping up, but she soon realized he was nowhere to be seen. She looked to her left for any signs. She looked to her right for any signs. Cuddles then barked. She took off in the direction of his noise.

"There you are." She found Cuddles sitting down waiting for her. "Ohhhh!" There before her, in the earth — where a large tree once was rooted — was a man lying still upon the soil. *Who is he? Is he one of the men that came? One who came to take me away from Peter? Is he alive?*

"Ohhhh …" the man moaned.

Annabelle gasped as she backed away. *He is alive! What should I do? What should I do? Peter will know.* She ran toward the dwelling, Cuddles followed her until she reached the river. She made her way along the rock wall and took off full speed toward Peter.

"Peter! Peter!" she yelled in a high-pitched voice.

Peter dropped the deer leather he was tanning to run toward her call. "What? What's wrong?"

"There … there …" Annabelle had to catch her breath. "There's a man in the ground."

"What?"

"And Cuddles is a dog!"

"Annabelle … breathe. Now, what are you speaking of?"

"I saw Cuddles, and he led me into the forest to a hole in the ground where there's a man."

"They must have left him to die," Peter muttered under his breath.

"He's not dead! He was moaning. But he's bloody."

"He's alive? Annabelle, you must take me to him."

Annabelle grabbed Peter's hand. "Follow me."

"Look! There's Cuddles!" Annabelle pointed to the dog sitting on the other side of the river.

"Well, I see it is."

The dog stood up and started pacing along the edge of the river.

"Annabelle, where are you going?" She was preparing to climb across the rock wall for the third time that day.

"He's on the other side."

"Did you cross this way before?"

She nodded.

Peter shook his head, stating, "There is a fallen log across the river not far from the top of the waterfall. It's much safer."

They climbed up the large, dry rocks on the periphery of the waterfall. When Annabelle reached the top, she spotted the fallen log Peter had mentioned.

Annabelle took off running once Peter set her safely on the ground. "Follow me." She fearlessly climbed down the rocks on the other side of the waterfall.

Cuddles greeted her.

"This way." She waved to Peter though he was right beside her. Cuddles took off running. The two followed suit.

They soon came upon the large crevice in the earth that trapped the injured man. "Down there!" Annabelle pointed, though Peter already saw.

Another moan escaped the lips of the fallen man. As he writhed in pain, Annabelle saw the mask around his face for the first time. She moved back in fright as all the terror she had felt at the time of her kidnapping tumbled forward into her awareness.

"Stay here," Peter commanded as he climbed down into the hole, lowering himself one root at a time, his muddy, worn-out boots digging into the sides of the earth. Annabelle did not move.

"Are you all right?" The man moaned for a third time.

Peter, noticing the man's injured ankle, removed the mask, throwing it across the hole without concern.

Annabelle looked to the man's face and spotted a slash across his left cheek.

Picking up the stranger, Peter threw him over his shoulder, and climbed out of the hole, relying on the roots to hold the weight of two.

The girl's eyes drifted to the mask. Appearing to be hide from a deer, the leather was further embellished with sticks and rocks fastened to it in such a design as to look angry.

Her heartrate tripled. Though she had not seen this particular mask before, every such mask spoke of the same meaning: a disregard of any decency.

Peter set the young man down on the ground to better inspect him in the light. "I think he'll be all right. He is shaken up and hungry, I suppose." Annabelle stood back, not saying a word, trying to calm her racing heart. Peter picked him up again and carried him to their dwelling.

She trailed behind, next to Cuddles, trying to calm herself. *He can't hurt me now. Peter's here. I don't need to be afraid.*

As they traversed the fallen log, Annabelle's fear of the mask had transferred to anger against the man that had worn it.

"Annabelle, fetch some fresh water, please." She stood watching the stranger breathe. "Annabelle!" She heard Peter's voice and turned her head toward him. "He needs fresh water." She picked up the leather water pouch and went outside as Cuddles followed her.

Annabelle watched as Peter pressed the water pouch to the man's lips and helped him drink. She watched as Peter tended to the man's slit cheek. She watched as Peter tried to set the man's ankle. She watched as Peter fed the man. She watched as Peter laid the man on his own bed of moss and used his own deerskin blanket to cover him up.

Annabelle helped Peter when he asked her to bring him a certain plant known for its healing properties. She helped Peter when he asked her to find some sticks that would hold the man's ankle straight. She helped Peter when he asked her to stoke the fire so the man's meat could be cooked.

When the young man was sleeping comfortably, Peter went outside, calling Annabelle along.

The stars were out, the sky as clear as glass. The forest was alive with crickets and owls. Annabelle wrapped herself in her deerskin blanket. "Peter, why did you give him your bed?"

"He needs a soft place to sleep."

"Where will you sleep?"

"On the floor." She was silent — unusual for her when she was around Peter. Peter noticed the absence of her chatter, and her requiring to be asked to help the stranger. "Annabelle, what's wrong?"

"I ..." She let loose, "I don't know why you are being so nice to him. He came to take me away from you! They took me away from my parents and you're helping him!" Annabelle viewed Peter's helpfulness to the stranger as a betrayal. Why was he helping someone who wanted to hurt her?

"Hush now, child," Peter said as he pulled her close. "I understand how you can feel this way but you must never let your feelings get in the way of your Christian duty." She intently listened as Peter continued: "When you look at the man, what do you see?"

"He ... he's hurt. His ankle and his cheek." She pointed to her corresponding body parts.

"Yes, but I also see a bruised and beaten Jesus who has been betrayed by His friends."

"Jesus?"

"Yes, my little one. I don't know why he was with those men; what made him choose that path in life that he was taking. So I will not judge his salvation. Perhaps he is following in his father's footsteps, and hatred and vengeance are all he has ever known. It's not up to me to judge."

"So, it's all right for him to take me?" A distraught Annabelle pulled back from Peter's embrace.

"No. No, my sweet child. Stealing a child from a loving

family is never good. I'm not saying he isn't wrong for seeking to take you. I'm saying that I don't know what presses on him to want to seize you."

"So, you're excusing him for what he tried to do?"

"No. He will have to fully account for all the choices he makes in his life."

"I don't understand."

"You judge what he does, not who he is."

"So, he is wrong to try to snatch me, but I can't judge him because I don't know why he wants to take me?"

"Right."

"And even if someone does something wrong, we have to see Jesus in them?"

"Yes. If they themselves are friendly and loving, you might see the resurrected Jesus, alive and in His glory. If they have been abused by the world, had a hard life, and act selfishly or hatefully, then you see the battered and bruised Jesus who died for them."

"Jesus did die for him, too," Annabelle said, talking to herself. She was silent for a moment and then sighed, concluding with a shake of her head, "Jesus wouldn't try to steal me from my parents."

"No." Peter chuckled. "He would not."

The next morning, the stranger opened his eyes to find a pretty girl with emerald eyes staring at him.

"Peter! He's awake!" the young girl yelled. Peter came inside the dwelling just in time to hear Annabelle inform the stranger, "You know, Jesus died for you, too!" Peter smiled.

"There is no truth to Jesus."

Annabelle was taken aback, and her smile faded.

Peter spoke up. "Annabelle, please go fetch some fresh water."

She got up without hesitation.

During the day, Annabelle sought out Peter. "Peter, what did he mean? He said there's no truth to Jesus?"

"Some people, Annabelle, do not believe that Jesus is the Son of God, or even lived."

"But ... there is a book about Him — the Bible."

"Some people do not have faith. Faith is a gift, you know."

Annabelle had never met anyone who did not believe in Christ. She was saddened. She thought about the stranger's awful situation. "Jesus is my best friend. I could not live without Jesus. Peter, who is his best friend?"

"I don't know, my little Annabelle. He might not have one."

No best friend? How sad is he?

Conversation

Annabelle's moss bed was moved to the opposite side of the dwelling. Sitting upon it, she observed Peter tending to the stranger's wounds. She had been told to stay on her bed, away from the man, and to leave the cave when Peter did.

"Why are you helping me?" the stranger asked, watching from the corner of his eye as Peter changed the medicated leaves on his cheek.

"Did you want me to leave you to die?" Peter answered back as he continued his task.

The young man, nearly still a boy, flared his nostrils.

Peter continued, "You're not yet ready to die. Where do you think you'll go when you take your final breath?" The young man turned his head away from Peter to stare at the cave wall. "You can't turn from the truth."

"There is no truth!" the young man yelled. Across the cave, Annabelle jumped, surprised at the man's anger. She looked at Peter.

"Annabelle, why don't you take Cuddles for a walk?"

She was ever so happy to get away from the man. His angry countenance seemed to suck the life out of her.

Climbing her way on top of the cave later that day, she sat down to look at the stars that were just awakening for the night as she listened to the crash of the waves upon the rocks 200 feet below.

He is so angry. Why? Lord, why is he so angry? Jesus, help him to be Your friend. Annabelle, with her warm blanket, reclined upon the cool rock, as she often did, to get a panoramic view of the sky.

"It's a lovely night, isn't it?"

She rolled over on the cool rock. "How did you know where I was, Peter?" she asked as her cloudy breath swirled around her.

Peter sat down, crossing his legs. "Cuddles gave you away. He follows you to the rock wall and waits for you there. And I know you like to come up here. The view is full of beauty."

She looked down toward the ground. "I wonder if that man can even see beauty — God's beauty?"

"His name is Stephanus. I got that much from him."

"Why, Peter? Why is he so angry?" She sat up on her legs in her passion to understand.

"I don't know, little one. He might have been raised without love."

"No love? But God loves him." She looked intently at Peter.

Peter nodded his head. "Indeed, but Stephanus doesn't know that."

"Did you tell him?" she asked with elevated eyebrows.

"It's not that simple, my little one. I wish it were, but it's not that simple." Peter stroked her face with his finger.

She shook her head. "What's not simple about it?"

"If you are raised to believe one thing," Peter gestured to the right; "and someone tells you otherwise," Peter gestured to the left; "will you easily believe him?"

Following his example, she spoke with her hand, pointing to each thing in turn. "About love? But, you said love is everywhere in God's creation — the twinkling of the stars, the roar of the ocean, a mamá bird feeding her young."

"You perceive love in all those places, because you have known it and have been taught it. He might not have been so blessed."

"So I think the way I do because you taught me to?" She sat up all the way.

"Well, yes, but you also have your own nature — your way of being — that shapes your view of the world."

She looked over her shoulder at the ocean and then turned back toward him. "Peter, if you had not taught me, what would I be like? You've shown me all of God's wonders."

"I'm certain your family would have done a fine and even better job than I."

"My family." She turned back toward the ocean. "I only see them in my dreams, and not very often."

"Come now, child, I'm certain you see them in your mind more than you are aware." He placed a comforting hand upon her shoulder.

Annabelle shook her saddened head. She was losing a little more of her family each day.

Living

Peter made an arrangement with Stephanus: He could have the land west of the river to himself as long as he stayed over there and did not bother Annabelle. Stephanus, seeing that this was his only choice, agreed.

Cuddles remained on the east side of the island with the people who cared for him. He was Annabelle's constant companion. They would go everywhere together. When Annabelle would fearlessly climb the side of a cliff to sit on top, he would patiently wait for her to descend, lying where her feet last touched the soil.

She was entertained with the way Cuddles would interact with the other animals on the island. Barking at squirrels, chasing rabbits, and — once or twice — going after small deer.

They got to know their half of the island fairly well: the caves, the hollows where she would race Cuddles, all the berry bushes, and the fruit trees. They had a wonderful time frolicking around together, and when it turned chilly, Cuddles was there to warm her.

Occasionally, when exploring along the river's edge, she would feel someone watching her. Looking across the river, she would find Stephanus cowering behind a tree. Quickly, she would turn away and head toward the dwelling, silently praying for Stephanus as Cuddles trotted beside her.

In the mornings, when she would wake, the first thing she would do was reach for Cuddles and feel him keeping her warm. When she was playing chess with Peter, he would patiently wait beside her.

Peter gave her the task of gathering firewood — sticks found along the forest floor. She loved this task because Cuddles would fetch the sticks she would throw. With each throw she would try to beat her last distance.

One morning, she threw the stick the farthest she had ever thrown. Cuddles went to retrieve it, but did not return.

"Cuddles? Cuddles? Come here, boy!" She became frantic when she could not find him anywhere. She could not hear him, and she could not find his tracks. She ran to Peter.

"I can't find him! I can't find him! Where could he have gone?"

Peter looked at her and noticed the absence of the dog. "You mean Cuddles?"

She nodded her head.

"I'm certain he's around. Come now, let's go to where you last saw him." She took him to the spot. They searched and searched. Cuddles seemed to have disappeared.

"Where could he be?"

"I don't know, Annabelle, but I think he knows this island as well as you. He'll come back. He knows where to find you." Peter stared across the river as he scanned the forest line. *What are you up to, Stephanus?*

Annabelle was not content waiting for him to return to the dwelling. She went in search of him.

Annabelle heard a whine from an animal, an animal she knew well — Cuddles. It came from across the river. "Peter! Peter!" She turned around and yelled as Peter appeared upon the path leading from the cave. "I hear him!" She pointed across the water.

Peter knelt down next to her and listened intently, eventually nodding his head. "Yes. I hear him, too." He closed his eyes and listened harder as Annabelle fidgeted in anxiety next to him.

"He sounds hurt!" a distressed Annabelle exclaimed.

Peter caught a voice uttering expletives in the distance.

He took a deep breath as he stood. "Annabelle, go back to the cave."

"What about Cuddles?"

Peter looked down at her. "I'll find him. You must go back to the cave."

She looked at him for a moment, wanting to protest, but finally turned away from Cuddles' cries to head back to the safety of their dwelling. Peter made sure she disappeared from his sight before he moved.

Peter came upon a frightful sight: a furry brown and black body, bloody and beaten, bellowing his moans by a blackberry bush.

"So, what did you think you would do? Lure her over here by killing her dog?" He spoke to the figure attempting to hide himself behind a bush. Kneeling down to examine the dying dog, Peter shook his head in disgust when he saw the animal would not survive. "So, what is your thought? You're so eager to take her, but what will you do then?" He looked through the bush at the young man. "How will you get her off this island?" The man looked away from Peter's gaze as Peter continued. "So who is it that gives you your orders? Which woeful noble do you follow?" Not receiving a reply, Peter spoke a name that had been churning in his mind for several years. "Sir Victorus?"

The man, shocked by the mention of that name by a wild man from a deserted island, wavered in his squat. Filled with indignation, he proudly stood and proclaimed: "Sir Victorus shall be king!"

"Hmm" — Peter answered with incredulity — "you think so?"

"I know so!" The man stepped out from behind the bush and shouted with indignation: "He has the support of all the nobles!"

"I doubt it," Peter said without a second thought.

"King Francis gave them plenty of cause — forcing the nobles to keep their word to care for their serfs!"

"Ah, yes — because nobles shouldn't be called to account for their treatment of people."

Stephanus, aware that he was being mocked, lurched at Peter. Peter quickly grabbed his arm and spun him around until he was on his knees in pain.

"Let me make one thing clear to you: You are not in Anchony now. Your shameful affection for Sir Victorus and the nobles will not help you here." Peter shoved him on to the forest floor with his knee upon the prisoner's back. "If you ever get off this island, you will not be taking her with you." Peter let go of him and walked toward the dead dog. As he knelt down to pick up the mortal remains of Cuddles, Stephanus ran toward him to attack.

Stephanus, not knowing what happened, found himself once again on his knees with Peter grasping his throat.

"I see our present understanding will not work." Those were the last words Stephanus heard before everything went dark.

Annabelle sat at the mouth of the cave, biting her lip, worrying about her dog. *Please let Cuddles be unharmed, Father. He sounded hurt. Please heal him if he is.*

How long must I wait? She stood up and looked out toward the path. *He told me to come to the cave, but he did not say to stay here.* She slowly inched her way through the cave opening and toward the path.

She arrived at the river in time to see Peter carrying the limp Stephanus over his shoulder as he stepped off of the fallen log.

"That's Stephanus?" she asked.

Peter looked down at her. "I told you to go to the cave!" he yelled with annoyance.

Annabelle gasped at his tone of voice as fear enveloped her body. *What did he do to him? Did he kill him?* She ran back to the cave, shaking and perplexed. Plopping down on her moss bed, she tried to calm herself, but nothing could quell her shaking hands and pounding heart. *He killed him! He killed him! Peter killed Stephanus! Peter! How could you? He is nothing like I thought. I don't know him. Who is he?* Her father figure collapsed before her. She was suddenly lost in a vast, unknown land.

"Annabelle."

She lifted her head at the sound of her name, called from outside the cave. She did not want to look upon him: the stranger. *How could he have done it? How could he?*

"Annabelle, come out here."

No! You're a killer!

"Annabelle, it's Cuddles."

Gasping as she stood, she cautiously made her way out of the cave. Her affection toward her dog outweighed her present contempt of Peter.

"No! No!" Her heart ached as she spotted the lifeless body of the dog in Peter's arms. She looked at Peter as tears rolled down her cheeks — she could barely breathe as her heart fell to her stomach. "Wha … wha … what took place?"

Peter shook his head as he laid him on the ground.

She fell upon the cold canine as her hair soaked up what little blood remained upon the body. *Cuddles … Cuddles is gone. My friend.* Her newly acquired disgust turned from Peter toward God. *How could You take him?! How could You?!* With such thoughts, her soul stumbled into a callousness it had never known.

Peter's heart broke at her saddened spirit. He knelt down beside her and petted her hair. She immediately pulled away from his touch.

Sitting upon a boulder as Peter dug his way through the soil, the last bit of earth was laid upon the animal as darkness fell.

Peter looked up at the forlorn girl. "Come, let's go inside. There's nothing we can do for him now."

An emotionally numb young girl slid off the rock and went into the cave. She did not take Peter's offered hand. She went straight to bed, facing the cave wall closest to her bed of moss. *God's not what I thought. Peter's not what I thought. All his preaching about doing what Jesus would do — Jesus wouldn't have killed Stephanus!*

God doesn't love me … He doesn't even care. If He did, He would have saved Cuddles. Everything is changed … or was I wrong in the beginning?

Peter started a fire. The shadow of the flames danced upon the wall. Annabelle closed her eyes as a single tear rolled down her cheek. Just the evening before, Cuddles was watching the shadows with her, keeping her warm.

Peter heard her sniffle. "Annabelle."

She did not even turn toward him.

"Annabelle, you'd better eat some meat."

She shook her head.

"You haven't eaten all afternoon."

She shook her head in rejection of anything he might say to her.

He brought some of the cooked hare toward her and knelt down to offer it to her. "Here, eat this."

She tried to move closer to the wall.

He placed his hand on the back of her head.

"Leave me alone, Peter."

His heart ached for the young girl. "It might not sound comforting now, but he was only a dog."

"He was my friend! My *only* friend!" *Because friends don't say one thing and do another. Nothing is as I thought it to be!*

"Annabelle, there was nothing I could do for him. If I could have, you know I would have. I would descend the deepest cave for you, walk the earth a thousand times, all to see a smile upon your face."

She shook her head and put her hands over her ears.

Peter did not understand why the young child was so angry at him, but he knew her well enough to know talking to her when she was that upset would do no good.

She closed her eyes and drifted off to sleep.

The chirping of the birds awoke her. She reached to feel Cuddles; he was not there. The reality hit her: He would never be there again. Her world was dark and dismal. *How can the birds chirp when my only friend is gone? How can the world go on? How can the birds be happy? They must not know that God doesn't care.*

Peter entered. "Ah, good, you're awake. I found some eggs. Would you go fetch some water?"

How can he smile after the awful thing he has done?

He glanced back at Annabelle with a "why have you not moved?" look. She slowly stood, grabbed the deerskin water pouch, and dragged it as she drudged out of the cave opening.

She took her time walking to the spring. She looked at the surroundings that once gave her such joy and filled her with such awe. The beautiful evergreens, the towering oaks, the rainbow of flowers — they had all lost some of their color, some of their splendor. The joyous sights depressed her since Cuddles was not there to enjoy them with her. *And Peter … who knows what Peter thinks about anything now.*

"Did you get lost? The eggs are getting cold."

She dropped the skin next to him and continued her way

to her bed where she hid her face in her arms as she cradled her legs.

"Annabelle, I know it must feel like someone has torn you apart and you will never be whole again, but you will only feel this way for a little while. 'This too shall pass.' Jesus is our hope —"

"How can you speak of Jesus?" she snapped.

Peter was shocked at the vileness in her voice. "Excuse me?"

"You are not like Jesus!"

"I know I'm not. I am far from it."

"So how can you say one thing and do another?"

"You're accusing me of being a hypocrite?"

"Well, if that's what a hypocrite is, then yes," she said saucily.

Peter was silent for a moment as he tried to ascertain from where she was getting her ideas. "Those are harsh words from such a young mouth. What is your evidence?"

"Stephanus — that's my proof!"

"I have my reasons for what I did to Stephanus. Do you know why he killed Cuddles?"

The perturbed Annabelle just stared.

"He tried to draw you across the river to take you again."

To take me again? She suddenly realized that he had done what he did to protect her. *Did he have no other choice but to kill Stephanus?* The more she thought about it, the more ashamed she felt for accusing Peter. As if infused by the Holy Spirit, the truth of all Peter had told her, hit her: She did not know why Peter had killed Stephanus and, although she did not approve of such an action, she could not judge him.

He felt a little hand on his shoulder. "I'm sorry, Peter." Annabelle realized at that moment that people do things for many different reasons. He hugged her, and she hugged him back. "We only have each other now."

Peter looked into her eyes. "When did you grow up?"

She shrugged her shoulders. She decided then that even if she did not like what Peter had done, she would still love him. And what of God? Certainly He was deserving of the same treatment. She might not like that God allowed her dog to die, but who was she to argue with God? She could not judge Him — His knowledge was far beyond hers. Maybe His loving answer to her prayers was to let Cuddles depart rather than to have him suffer on the island.

"The sunlight is wasting; we must search for logs."

Peter seemed to be in an extra hurry to find usable wood. He scoured the forestlands with a new vigor. He would often order Annabelle back to the cave where she was to prepare supper or tidy the cave. He would creep in late at night.

She observed his behavior and pondered: *Does he want me gone because I called him a hypocrite? It must have angered him greatly; he wants to get rid of me.*

She ventured one morning after prayer, "How's the boat?"

"It's coming along. I think I've gathered about half the logs needed."

She nodded her head, a new ache in her heart.

The days were becoming as cold as the fall evenings, and the evenings even colder. That meant only one thing: Winter was approaching.

Peter came in one evening dripping wet.

"Did you fall into the river?" a perplexed Annabelle asked.

"No."

"Why are you all wet?" she probed.

"I made a choice to go for a swim." He wrung out his shirt.

She watched the water and pieces of ice fall to the cave floor. "But it's freezing outside, Peter! You have icicles in your hair."

"Yes." Peter grabbed his blanket. "Annabelle, I need to borrow your blanket."

"But it's cold. How will I stay warm?" she asked from her seated position.

"We will build the fire nice and large tonight."

"What will you do with it?"

"There are other creatures, Annabelle, who need the blanket more than you."

Looking at him, she retrieved her fur as she replied, "Make certain the creature is warm."

He nodded his head and stated, "Stay here and build up the fire. I will need a warm place when I return." She nodded as she watched him leave and then proceeded to place more sticks in the flames.

Off to the Sea

The cold days were slowly fading away as the hollows, the woods, and the riverbanks were springing alive.

"Is the raft ready?" She stared at the meat she was cooking, afraid of the answer.

Peter was hesitant to reply.

Annabelle turned around and stared at him.

"It is," he finally admitted.

She looked up. "Why did you not tell me sooner?"

"Annabelle, the raft is not for you."

She felt a sharp pain in her chest that flashed across her emerald eyes. "What do you mean? You're going to leave me here alone on the island!? Peter, how could you?" She ran out of the cave before he had a chance to explain.

She climbed atop the cave and sat in the spring sunlight. *How could he do this to me? I thought he loved me. He said he wouldn't leave me alone.*

"You know you will never be alone."

"You took my best friend from me!" she shouted at the sea, as her ache was still festering deep inside.

"I thought I was your best friend. No matter what passes in this life, no matter how alone you feel, I am always here with you."

She suddenly felt so ashamed — placing a dog in the position only reserved for God. She was disgusted with herself. "I'm sorry. I'm so sorry," she cried aloud, as tears rolled down her face. She realized how wrong she had been about so many things. It did not matter that God did not save Cuddles, because God was there for her, He was her best friend, and nobody could take that away. And if Peter did leave her alone on the island, it would be all right, because God was with her. He would help her through any situation.

After drying her tears and sitting awhile amongst God's creation, she decided to find Peter and tell him that she would learn to accept him leaving her — she would be brave and try not to be upset. Climbing down from the rock, she looked inside the cave; he was not there. She wandered back outside; spotting his fresh tracks, she followed them. They led to the hollows. She looked around; Peter was not there. But what was that on the perimeter? *That's not Peter. Who is it?* She made her way closer. It was a man; he was tied to a tree. She soon noticed the scar on the face: Stephanus. Her heart fell to the pit of her stomach again as she was humbled by her ignorance.

"How are you alive?" she asked the bound man.

Stephanus looked up. "It seems I'm not worth killing."

"Annabelle." Peter walked into the hollows from the forest with fresh berries.

"Peter?" She looked from him to Stephanus, then back to him.

"It was best for you if you didn't know he was here." Peter untied the man's feet with his sharp rock. "He's leaving, today." Peter took him by the bound arms and led him north, the direction of the shore.

"The raft is for him?" she asked as she walked alongside.

"It is more important for him to get off this island than for you."

"Head around the island and then southwest — that will take you to Anchony." Peter cut the vine that bound his hands.

"You're letting me go?"

"You can't stay here on this island, and you're not ready to die; you must go."

Stephanus looked at Peter and then Annabelle. He jumped on top of the raft and took hold of the oar. Peter pushed him deeper out into the sea.

"Think of it as a second chance to turn your life around," Peter yelled at him as he paddled away.

Annabelle watched him paddle deeper out into the ocean. "He has been here this whole time?"

"We must pray for him, Annabelle. God is the only one who can save him," Peter answered, as he watched Stephanus paddle away.

She stared at the man she had so easily accused of breaking God's commandment. How easily did she conjure a lie? She was humiliated for her thoughts. In her humility, she begged forgiveness as she attacked him with a hug: "Peter, I'm so sorry! I thought you had killed him, and I thought you were going to leave me alone."

"Annabelle, it's all right. I would never leave you on this island alone by choice."

"I know, I really know that, Peter, but it didn't stop me from thinking —"

"Annabelle, calm your worry. You were confused, and I wasn't fully honest with you." He squeezed her into his chest.

"Will you forgive me, Peter?"

"Nothing could keep me from forgiving you, my little one."

They made their way back to the dwelling — Annabelle having a new appreciation for Peter, her angel. The rain let loose and the lightning started as soon as they were safely within the confines of the cave.

Lying on her stomach as she watched the rain pour down outside, her churning mind showed upon her countenance.

"What's wrong, Annabelle?"

"Although Stephanus is gone, not all traces of the men are."

"What do you mean?"

She rolled to her side to look at him sitting next to the fire. "His disguise is still in the hole where we found him."

Peter slowly nodded as he stoked the fire. "If he didn't move it, it would still be there."

"Can we burn it?" she pleaded.

He looked over at her sincere face. "Yes, we can do that."

Sitting before the fire, Annabelle watched the terror-causing mask catch fire, blacken, and disintegrate into ash. When there was nothing left, she took a deep breath and turned toward Peter. "There now, I'm free of them."

Revealed

The day after Stephanus's departure, Peter did not rise early to search for logs.

Annabelle did not know if she should question him about this. He had already made two rafts, neither of which were used for their initial intention. *Perhaps he's tired of making them. He deserves a break.*

Peter, however, soon revealed his plans: "We're to begin this morning."

"Begin what?"

"Your lessons."

"Lessons for what?" she asked with curiosity.

"The art of self-protection."

"What?" Annabelle raised her eyebrows.

"You don't know it, but this study started years ago."

She shrugged her shoulders. "Peter, of what are you speaking?"

Peter pointed his right finger. "You will learn to defend yourself."

"Defend myself from whom? Stephanus is gone."

"He may be gone, but there are other men like him in this world who would love to catch you."

"Catch me?" She looked at him quizzically. "You are the only other person on this island."

"Who says you will spend your whole life on this island?"

"This is my home now, Peter; I don't want to leave it — or you."

His voice became more insistent. "And what of your family? Have you forgotten them?"

"You are as much my family as they are, Peter. I've spent the same amount of time with you as I have with them," she said with a sincere face as she crossed her arms.

Peter shook his head in discontent. "I don't believe you. You speak as if you don't want to see your family. What's the *truth* behind your words? Why do you not want to leave this island?"

Uncrossing her arms as she released a breath, she revealed her true concern. "I'm safe here with you Peter. There are no men with hidden faces to cause affright." She looked to the ground. "If I never had to see another disguise again, I'd be blissful."

"You can't live your life in fear. You have a family, and you must return to them when God wishes."

She threw up her arms. "Well, He clearly doesn't wish it!"

"Not at present, but perhaps you have been brought to this island with me for this very reason," Peter replied.

"Brought to the Forbidden Island at the age of 5 to learn to defend myself? Peter, where do you get your thoughts?"

Peter shook his head. *God only knows.* After a moment of silence, Peter restated, "Your lessons have already begun; you only didn't know it."

She uncrossed her arms. "What do you mean?"

"You can walk into the hollows and know where each animal is. You can walk through the forest and spot any trail. These are needed to be able to defend yourself. You are keenly aware of all around you. And I fear, my dear one, that you will be a frightful thing to behold with the proper knowledge. Annabelle, you must allow me to do this, or else I will thwart God's will."

"God's will? You were here for me, Peter. You have been the best father I could have. You have taught me so much. How could you think you're not doing God's will?" She looked into his eyes.

"Annabelle, I want you to be safe no matter where you are, whether it is here or in Anchony, whether I'm with you or not." He sat down, and she followed suit. Peter's eyes began to get misty. "I want ... I want to tell you more about my wife. You've asked me several times over the past five years, and I always change the subject ... because it is so hard. You might wonder why I toss and turn at night and awaken trembling. It is because of her, because of what I *didn't* do for her."

Annabelle stared silently at his grief-stricken face wondering what he would say next and empathetic to his pained heart.

"I was a soldier once. I fought in the crusades and when I came back, I fought for the king of Anchony. I ... I did something my enemies didn't like, and they came after me through my family. You see, I was a knight, and I was feared by everyone. I never worried about my family because I always knew I would be able to stop anyone from hurting them — if I was home." He swallowed with great difficulty before continuing. "But one day Anchony's enemies came ... and I wasn't there. They weren't safe. They weren't safe at all. My wife had to watch our children die before they killed her. She barely lived to speak about what they endured." Peter closed his eyes as tears rolled down his cheeks and continued after a long silence: "I returned to a burned home and a broken life."

"And now, I have to live with the fact that I didn't even try to teach my wife, my pearl, how to defend herself. I will not make that same mistake with you, and I have not." He resolutely looked over at her as he stood.

"You have become aware of the sights and sounds all around you. Those are the base of what you truly need to know to defend yourself. There is so much more I need to teach you."

Annabelle could not get over his story. "Why would anybody be so malicious not only to your wife but also to your children, the most innocent?"

"Yes, my boys were my pride in life and my Clare — my dear Clare. She would be a couple years older than you. You bring her to my mind. When I look at you, I see what she could have become." Tears trickled down his face. He looked away. "Tomorrow we shall begin." He needed time alone.

Annabelle, with the greatest respect for the man walking away from her, stood stunned. *Lord, please don't let me ever thwart the hopes Peter has for me.*

She thought about Peter's story the whole day as she went about her daily tasks of gathering berries, carrying water from the stream, and observing all of God's creation. Later that evening she asked Peter further, "Who are Anchony's enemies?"

"Anchony's enemies?"

"You said that Anchony's enemies came after your family. Who are they?"

Peter took a deep breath and began, "The Demolites ... the ones who destroyed my family, and I'm guessing seized you as well."

"What? The ones that stole me from my parents? Who? Why, Peter? Please, tell me." She was not expecting to find out information about her kidnappers.

Peter sighed. "They are the disguised men that you fear."

Shaking away all the horrid memories of the masked men that came to her mind's eye, she pleaded for more information. "But *who* are they?"

Peter shook his head. "No one knows for certain. One could be a tiller from a county away, the miller from the market, your neighbor from a door away, or the lord in the castle. They hide their faces so the king can't arrest them."

At mention of the king, Annabelle stood in agitation. "The king can't stop them? What do they want?"

Peter was forced to admit, "I don't know for certain. No one knows."

"Did you ask Stephanus? He was one, wasn't he? What did he tell you?"

Peter shook his head. "Stephanus was only a follower. If he knew who the true leader was, he wouldn't say."

"So there's nothing that can be done? They can't be stopped?"

"I fear not," Peter said as he released a deep breath.

With pleading eyes, she looked at him. "No, Peter, there has to be a way! No one can truly live fearing everyone."

Her frightened countenance broke his heart. He wished there was some comfort he could give to her, but he had none to offer. The Demolites were a ruthless group of masked men that no one could stop.

Training

The next day her training began:

"Always remember that you are a lady; a fine flower, a prize to be won, worthy of only the most upright gentleman. You are worth defending and it is the man's duty to do so. If there is a man around to stand up for you, let him. Don't be prideful. Men should be stout and strong, so if you are stronger than a man, don't boast." Peter's voice grew louder. "But if someone puts you in such a place where you must defend yourself and no man is around, then do so out of honor for God. Your body is a temple of the Holy Spirit, and no one has the right to damage it. So, let us begin."

Annabelle stood out of obedience, unsure of this whole self-protection thing. "Peter, I don't see why —"

"Annabelle, we have already spoken about this. Each day is a day closer to someone finding you. And whether they'll be friend or foe, I can't say. You won't always be here. One day you will have to return to your family."

"You are my family, Peter. I don't want to leave you. If making it back to them means I have to leave you, then I'd rather stay here with you."

"You can't turn your back on your life. You must return to your rightful place."

"And what of you? You ran away from your life!"

Sitting down on a stump, Peter took a deep breath. "Annabelle, I didn't run away from life. I ran because I was afraid of myself. I was so angry, full of hatred. I wanted to destroy each person who had harmed my wife and I didn't even know who those men were. I was afraid I would go after everyone I *thought* was a Demolite — even if they had not harmed anyone. Annabelle, you should never do anything out of wrath. Vengeance is just another word for manslaughter."

"It was only by the grace of God that I came to the Forbidden Island. To repent of my sins and pray for my family." He stood.

"You must always do God's will, not yours, Annabelle. If God wants you to stay in this Deep Forest for the rest of your life, then so be it. But you must not close the door on the hope of returning to your family in case that is what God wishes."

Holding her breath for a moment, she finally spoke her fear: "But I'm scared, Peter. What if they don't think of me? What if they don't want me?"

Peter lifted her chin. "Don't doubt, my little one. No one could forget you."

Annabelle smiled weakly at the comment.

Peter stepped back. "Let us waste no more time. We must get started. First, you must know your body: your strengths and your weaknesses. Second, you must use your brain before your limbs. Study the place and people — how are your feet placed, where is everyone around you, what can work for your profit, how many are against you, will you be able to overtake or get away —"

"Peter," Annabelle interrupted, "this sounds —"

"A part of the second rule," Peter continued, "is to look ahead, think about what could come to pass next. My dear one, I will have you ready no matter how much you wish against it." She quizzically stared at him, shaking her head. "You are in fine shape. You shall be a force to reckon with, and you, being female, shall be unforeseen."

"Peter, I do not think I could —"

"This is for you to be safe, Annabelle, no matter how a Demolite tries to harm you. They have no code of right or wrong. They do what they please, and they live for the flesh. Not all men are God-fearing."

"But why would God allow it?"

Peter moved his right hand down quickly as if he was cutting a log. "I don't know His ways, but He wants you to help yourself. Learn to defend yourself and it shall never take place! You will not know who your enemies are. You will not know who to trust. You must trust no one but your family, close friends, and those who have gained your trust. The Demolites are everywhere." He took a breath and straightened up. "That is enough talk. We must not delay. Stand now — on one foot."

"What?"

"You must have perfect balance. Now stand on one foot."

Annabelle shifted her weight to her right and lifted up her left leg. She swayed slightly as she held out her arms to balance herself.

"Good balance comes from both seeing and feeling. First, stand with your feet on a hard spot — that rock over there." Peter pointed. Annabelle slowly walked over. "Good. Now, place the tips of your left toes next to your right foot without swaying, then hold up your left foot and count to 30, then close your eyes and count to 30 again. Then do the same with the right."

Annabelle dropped her foot back to the rock and her arms back to her sides. "Peter, this is foolish."

"Do it!"

Annabelle complied, not because she wanted to, but because Peter insisted.

He taught her how to feel her body, to understand how quickly she moved, how she fell, her natural reactions, how far to push herself, and when to rest. She learned to fight with her hands, with her feet, with weapons, and, most importantly, with her wit. He taught her how to read body language: the twitch of a muscle, the movement of the eyes, a change in countenance, signs that would aid her in anticipating the opponent's next move. Day after day, Peter insisted that she practice more, run longer, hit harder, and do it all quicker.

Change

Three years of intense training passed. Annabelle was well conditioned. She thrived at running, climbing, and swimming; they became her escape if Peter ever put her in a position where she felt he was getting the best of her.

One day she was not feeling particularly strong nor swift. They started their day of training next to the river in their usual pattern.

"Let's dance," Peter enticed with a nod of his head and a smirk.

"But I don't hear any music," she replied back with a nod of her head.

"Good." He would bow, she would curtsey, and then they were off.

Strangely, he took her down with ease that day. She pounded the ground twice, and he released her. She was so frustrated with herself.

"What's wrong?" Peter asked as he stepped back for a respite.

"I don't know," she said as she slowly stood up. "I am not myself."

"Do you want a break today?"

"No!" she insisted as her perseverance won over her aches. She took her position.

"You are slower today," Peter observed as he returned to his stance.

She grunted in frustration, fully aware of her defects.

He came at her; she was able to block his punches but could not return any with proper success. She relied upon a faithful trick: She waited until he bent down and used his back to climb a tree. She jumped at a tree branch; it took much more effort than usual to pull herself up. She barely made it. Once safely at the top, she shook her head in disgust.

"You are running away so early in the day?" Peter asked.

"I am weak, Peter. I don't think I can go on."

Peter looked at her with concern. He looked to the ground and calculated in his head. "You are 13, correct?"

"If I am not yet, I will be soon."

He nodded his head as he scratched his beard. "You are about that age."

"What age?"

"The age of change."

"What change?"

"The change into a woman."

She jumped down from the tree. "That makes me weaker?"

"No. Your body changes so that one day you will be able to carry a child."

"But I don't want to change. I like to be able to climb trees and move quickly."

Peter chuckled. "Just because you change doesn't mean you won't be able to climb trees — you might have to work a little harder to climb a tree."

She sighed and looked at the ground. "Is there anything I can do to stop it?"

"And why would you want to stop it?" Peter replied quickly, placing his hands on his hips as his smile faded.

She looked up shyly, "I don't want to change."

"Annabelle." Peter sat down and patted the ground next to him. She sat down. "That is the way God made you. It took place with your mother and to her mother and to every mother. It will take place to your sisters. It will take place with you — it will take place to your daughters."

She looked up at him as if he was speaking foolishly.

"You're not alone. It's a part of being who you are. It's part of being a female."

Three months later, she experienced firsthand what Peter had told her about becoming a woman. She had mixed feelings. She could no longer deny that she was changing, but a part of her wanted to stay young forever.

"I'm going for a swim," she stated as she dashed past Peter, who was gathering sticks along the riverside, into the water.

She dove down deep and touched the bottom, swam upstream, dove down again, and swam upstream. She repeated this cycle several times until she was tired.

Swimming back to the bank, she sat upon it, looking at the river and thinking about her life and her unknown future. She determined that if she must work harder to climb a tree, to swim quickly, to run like the wind, then she would do just that. She looked at the waterfall on her right; it beckoned her. Ever since the day she fell out of the niche, she had wanted to know what it would be like to go down the waterfall from the top.

She looked across the river. Peter was now hunting their supper. What would he say about it? Well, she was a woman now, right? At that moment, she did not worry what Peter would say.

Fearlessly, she climbed the cliffs on the periphery and stood at the top, looking over the edge. When she saw Peter's head turn toward her as his arms flew up in objection, she gasped and quickly jumped into the powerful liquid that pounded upon her skin, forcing her down, down, down. It forced her to the bottom and seemed to swirl her around. For a moment, panic began to infiltrate her mind — no matter how she tried to swim, she could not beat the swirling current.

Suddenly, a figure emerged and moved toward her — a girl, about her age. Peace filled her mind as an excruciating pain radiated in her left arm, shoulder, and eye. The girl placed her hand over Annabelle's eye and moved her left arm. The mysterious girl then smiled and disappeared into the darker water as Peter grabbed Annabelle and pulled her to the surface.

"What were you doing, Annabelle?! You jumped in on purpose. I saw you! Do not deny it!" He stood over her, wagging his finger with his fearful anger.

Annabelle touched her eye and shoulder as she stared into the river, searching for the girl. The pain, as quickly as it appeared, had dissipated at the girl's touch. "Did you see her?"

"See whom?" Peter yelled.

"The girl," she answered in wonder as she watched the river's crest, not believing the words that came from her own mouth.

"Girl? Annabelle!" Peter took a deep breath and stepped backwards. "Annabelle, why did you jump into the waterfall?"

Her eyes finally unglued themselves from the river, convincing herself she had made up whatever she might have seen in those brief seconds. "I ... wanted to."

"You *wanted* to?" Peter asked in disbelief.

"I ..." Her chin began to quiver. "I am ... a woman now." She looked away from him, not wanting to be chastised for her act of independence.

He sat down beside her and hugged her head. "My little one ..." He was not sure how to address the fact that she had experienced her irrevocable sign of change. He kissed the top of her head. "I am still here for you. Don't think that because your body is changing that you are a mature woman. And, please, please, don't feel like you're all alone."

She listened silently to his words as she squeezed his arm under her chin and stared into the forest.

"You could have hurt yourself, Annabelle. Please, don't do anything so dangerous, without proper teaching." She felt his tear upon her head. "You could have been killed."

She turned around and looked at him. "Peter, I'm sorry. I didn't mean to scare you." She hugged him in her sorrow.

After that day, Annabelle threw herself into the training, insisting she would listen to every word, practice every technique, and memorize every move until it became her second nature. She acutely listened to all of Peter's education in the art of self-protection.

"There are key points when it comes to taking someone down — such as below the nose and fingernails. Be aware: Wherever the thumb goes, the hand goes with it ..."

Show me and I will use them.

"Do not waste all your force in the swing, tense at the end for full power. Always twist your wrist during a hit to spare your hand from harm."

Teach me and I will learn.

"A little rock, well aimed, can be far deadlier than a large rock — think of David and Goliath."

I will think before acting.

She became proficient. Once she had mastered defending herself with sight, Peter placed a blindfold upon her. Then she learned with one arm tied behind her back, and then as if she had an injured leg. There was no situation that Peter did not account for. There was no situation Peter presented that Annabelle could not free herself from.

Every day of the week, except prescribed Sundays, Annabelle would push herself further, harder, quicker. Years of training passed until the student nearly overtook the master in skill and far surpassed him in swiftness. Her favorite pastime was swimming upstream, attempting to be quicker than the current; she was, more often than not, successful.

Annabelle took for granted her comfortable life on the island, including the training, the studying, and the observing of all of God's creation. But one encounter made her realize how happy she should be for her mentor, father, and angel, as well as her own life.

Celesa

Annabelle stared at the massive waterfall of the river that dumped into the ocean. She pondered at how the current seemed to double in intensity the last half mile of the river.

"Annabelle, come back from there," Peter said from inside the forest, looking at tracks, finding some bigger game to prepare for winter.

The 15-year-old dropped a flower into the water and watched as it disappeared over the edge within a second. She turned back toward Peter's voice. "I'm coming."

She walked casually toward Peter's position, studying the ground. But then her heart began to race at the sound of Peter's voice in distress alongside the horrid roar of a bear. She ran swiftly toward the noises and immediately halted when she spied the huge animal swipe at Peter's stomach.

"Peter!" She gasped and took a few steps toward him as the bear looked up at her.

"Annabelle! No!" Peter tried to yell as he held his core in the fetal position.

In a moment of horror, she heard the sound of a creature six feet away — a cub.

She turned her head back to the mother bear and read the twitch of its muscles before it started its run toward her. Swirling around, she was in a full sprint within five steps. She flew toward the river about 100 meters away. She did not dare to look behind her — that would only slow her down. There was no need to look behind her — she could hear the massive bear gaining on her. She jumped into the river as her leg muscles fired everything they had; pain seared through her back as the bear's claws ripped into her skin.

Agony engulfing her, her last image before going over the edge was the bear roaring along the side of the river, with the cub at its feet.

Focus. Focus. God, help me!

She instantly turned her attention to the feat that lay ahead: surviving first the waterfall and then the ocean. She crossed her arms and entered the water as safely as she could, according to Peter's instructions, as her back throbbed in its bleeding, injured state.

The salt immediately stabbed at her bleeding back. She swam with all her might, missing the rock bank at the end of the waterfall by an inch. Gasping for air as she emerged at the top, she was greeted with a wave that pushed her against a rock. Pain again erupted from her injury, but she pressed forward.

She swam with all her might while fighting the waves, fighting the fear, fighting the pain. She looked at the massive cliff of the island. Tall, so very tall.

Can I climb it?

She spotted a broken section of the cliff sticking out of the water, appearing as though it was a boulder about four feet tall: her new objective. She swam to it, relying upon the use of her right arm. Her left shoulder, being victim to the bear's ferocious claws, was still movable but painfully so; she did not wish to use it. A large wave pushed at her and forced her to gasp for air. Pulling herself up with her right arm, her feet gripped the cliff. It was much more difficult with one arm, but she managed.

Collapsing on the flat top out of fatigue, agony, and thanksgiving, her salty tears matched the water below her. She took a few deep breaths and courageously investigated the left side of her back. A crimson color appeared on her right fingertips as she touched her injury.

Father. Father. She sat down. She did not know what else to do. She looked at the ocean before her: massive, unending, dangerous. She twisted around and looked at the cliff. *Will I be able to climb it ... after I rest?* She turned back around as she closed her eyes and prayed. *Father, please, let Peter be all right. And help me. I don't know what to do.* She placed her head upon her knees and tried to rest.

After a small respite, she decided to attempt the tremendous climb up the cliff. Facing the cliff, she gripped it soundly with her right hand as she stood upon her tiptoes. Her left arm slowly reached for the rocky minerals. Cries of agony escaped her lips, but she pressed forward. She pulled herself up with a yell. Her left arm went weak in pain, and she fell back to the boulder in defeat. She slid her belly on to the rock and whimpered in crushed confidence and failure. *Am I going to die here? Father, help me!*

Either passing out from pain or sleeping out of fatigue, she drifted off into unconsciousness.

Annabelle awoke, hoping it was all a horrid nightmare, but tears came to her eyes when she realized she was really trapped upon a boulder, four feet above the wide, wild ocean.

"Why do you cry?"

She held her breath for a second. Did she just hear someone speak? She turned her head toward the voice that came from the ocean. There was a girl in the sea, effortlessly treading water. Annabelle's mind instantaneously relived her experience with the first waterfall and the girl who had appeared under the crest: They were one and the same.

Annabelle attempted to get away, scooting backwards, wincing in pain as her injury touched the cool rock.

"Why do you cry?" the girl repeated.

"Wh-who are you?" Annabelle finally muttered in disbelief after looking around.

"I am Celesa." She smiled.

Celesa? Annabelle did not know what to say.

"Why are you sitting there?" Celesa asked. Annabelle looked down at her boulder of refuge and back to the girl. The girl pointed to the cliff. "You live on the island, right?"

Annabelle heard words come from her mouth: "I saw you there. In the river."

Celesa only smiled.

"How were you there?" Annabelle asked in confusion. She looked at the girl presently in the water. "How are you here?"

Celesa continued to smile. "I like the water. It's safe for me." She looked into Annabelle's eyes. "Would you swim with me?"

"Swim where?" Annabelle replied in desperation.

"To the sand."

Annabelle shook her head. "It's too far. My back is injured."

"What came to pass?" Celesa raised her eyebrows.

"It's from a bear," Annabelle replied with a distressed memory of all that had transpired.

"Oh." Celesa looked at the water and then back up at Annabelle. "Well, you don't know if it is too far unless you try."

"Are you a good swimmer?" Annabelle asked.

"Are you?" Celesa shot back.

"I was," Annabelle answered pathetically.

"And suddenly you are not?" Celesa raised her eyebrows again.

"I'm hurt," Annabelle replied in both agony and agitation.

Celesa shrugged her shoulders. "So … you want to stay here always?"

"No," she said, almost crying again. "Peter. He … he will come for me." She said the words only out of hope.

"Peter? Was he harmed by the bear as well?" Celesa asked, tilting her head.

Annabelle lowered her head. She knew Peter could not rescue her, not this time.

"Then let's go." Celesa waved her arm as she swam backwards.

Annabelle moved forward and watched the figure move farther away. "Wait." She looked down and watched a powerful wave crash on to the boulder.

Celesa turned back toward Annabelle. "Are you coming?"

Oh, Father, I don't want to be alone ... forgive me. She stepped back toward the cliff and took a running leap back into the salty, foamy water. Every stroke of her left arm caused pain to burst in her back and radiate up and down her entire left side. She gasped with every movement.

Celesa swam next to her, looking her in the eye. "Do you feel that? The pain? That is letting you know you are still alive. Take it and use it."

I am alive. I have not drowned yet. Father, I do. I willingly take it. You take it ... use it ... unite it with Your Son's pain ... may it help someone. And help me to swim!

A new determination came over Annabelle — she would survive; she would find Peter and help him in his pain. She pushed through the physical anguish and forced herself to go as they followed the high coast of the island toward the strip of beach.

Hearing no noises, no animals around him, Peter sat up in agony as he held his stomach. Removing his tunic, he pressed it against his throbbing core.

He painstakingly crawled toward the water, looking for his adopted daughter's tracks. He saw the signs: The bear had chased her into the river. He saw the exact spot where her feet had left the soil — mixed with her blood.

Peter examined the bloody soil as he fingered it. *No. No!* "Annabelle," he said softly, pain erupting from his core. Tears filled his eyes as he crawled with one arm toward the edge of the waterfall. Did he want to look? Would he see her bloody remains? He did not want to, but he knew he must.

He slowly looked over the edge, his breath labored. He prepared for the worst and spotted — nothing. He could find no signs of her. He lowered his head as his tears fell to the ocean below. *The great sea has taken her body … Why? Why, Father?!* He backed away from the cliff and turned on to his back. "Why did you take her? Why?" he shouted at God, as surging pain erupted with each word.

Arms shaking in fatigue, Annabelle forced herself through the powerful waves as her pace began to slow. Celesa noticed the change.

"Don't wear out on me now. That would dash Peter's hopes in you."

Annabelle sprayed salt water from her mouth as she gave extra effort to speak back. "What do you know about Peter?" She struggled to get the words out.

Celesa took a few strokes before answering, "He's been helpful to me."

"What do you mean?"

Celesa only smiled and then changed the subject before increasing her pace. "You know … your mother prays for you every day."

"What?" Annabelle pushed herself harder to try to keep up and get more information. "Wait!"

The setting sun splashed colors upon the waves as Annabelle sliced through them, ignoring her pain. She had a new mission: to find out what Celesa knew of her mother.

She forced herself next to Celesa. "What do you mean? About my mamá?"

"Not a day goes by when she doesn't pray for you," Celesa said with her continual smile.

"How do you know?" Annabelle asked in confusion, bordering upon agitation.

"We're all joined."

"Joined?" Annabelle spat more water out of her mouth.

The distant beach, as if a dream, came into view as the light was slowly dying.

"We are all part of the Body of Christ. Look." Celesa turned ahead. "There it is." She sped toward it. Annabelle followed, her energy rapidly dwindling.

She crawled onto the beach, following Celesa's example. Completely fatigued, Annabelle collapsed. Her cheek rested upon the soft sand as she tried to catch her breath. She was so tired she hardly noticed her throbbing back. She closed her eyes for a second and then pushed herself over to question Celesa further.

A cry escaped from her lips as she rolled on to her back. She noticed the beauty of the emerging night sky; the stars were twinkling and becoming brighter with each passing moment. Escaping death, everything appeared with a new beauty, a new intensity.

"Celesa, I don't hear my mamá's prayers. How do you? Celesa?" She forced herself on to her right elbow and looked to her right. "Celesa?" She did not see her. She looked to her left. She was not there either. She turned back to her right, crawling upon her knees to investigate closer. But there were no signs of Celesa's presence. She looked at the imprint of her body in the beach, made as she had drug herself on to the sand; only one imprint was found.

What? Where did she go? In a confused state, she slowly stood and clumsily made her way into the forest to find some sustenance, constantly looking around to see if Celesa had somehow made it into the forest without leaving tracks.

The forest was alive with animals and their noises; she was never so thankful to hear them.

Needing food, she headed for a berry bush, but feeling the intense pain from her shoulder, she veered off course toward a willow tree. She pulled some bark from the branch and forced herself to chew the bitterness; she knew, in the end, it would help her.

After eating her fill of berries, she spotted a yarrow plant that she promptly picked, pulled into pieces, and attempted to place upon her open wound, though she could not reach the whole injury. Giving up in her struggle, she sat down against a tree. The natural aspirin — salicin from the willow tree — began to take effect. The pain decreased, and she was able to drift off into sleep.

She found herself in a room and saw a lady upon her knees. The lady's lips moved constantly, her eyes closed in powerful contemplation.

Celesa's words resounded in her head: "Your mother prays for you every day. Not a day goes by she does not pray for you."

She was so beautiful. Was that her mother? Annabelle wanted to touch her but feared to. She reached her hand toward the magnificent lady.

The lady opened her eyes and looked over at Annabelle and then turned her head straight toward the crucifix.

Annabelle fell backwards at the sight of the lady's clear emerald eyes — the color of her favorite rock — the color of her eyes. "My eyes! She has my eyes."

Suddenly, Celesa was beside her. She helped her up. The lady was gone. "Or is it that you have hers?"

Annabelle opened her eyes to the sunlight and the chirping birds. She sat up against the tree again. *What was that? Was that my mamá?* She shook her head. *She was so beautiful but ... I can't dwell upon a dream.*

She ate berries, tended to her wound, and took a piece
of the willow bark for later use as she set out toward the cave
that had been her home for many years. Her mind played over
the scenes of the previous day. She could not get the image
of Peter being ferociously clawed in the stomach out of her
mind. *Peter, please be all right.* She ignored the pain that pul-
sated with every step; it was nothing compared to swimming
the day before. She picked up her pace. The more she thought
of the injured Peter, the quicker she ran. She arrived at the
cave two hours later, nearly breathless.

"Peter?" she called. She entered the dark cave; there
were no signs he had been there. She checked the fire pit — it
was cool; it had not been lit in a while. She closed her eyes and
prayed. "Father, please let him be all right." She sat a moment
in silence as she drew strength and fortitude to seek him out.

She followed the river, searching for fresh tracks, searching
for fresh blood, searching for any signs of her beloved Peter.
Halfway between the cave and the river's freefalling end in the
ocean, she spotted him resting next to a tree as he applied aloe
to his wound.

Her hand flew to her mouth, overjoyed to see him. Tears
filled her eyes. For a moment she could not speak and when
she did, it was in a high-pitched shriek from a relieved heart:
"Peter!"

He immediately turned toward her voice — he could
not believe his own ears. He saw her standing there, crying
in happiness — he could not believe his own eyes. He painfully stood and watched in wonder as she dove into the river
and swam toward him. It was then that he noticed her injury.
First, by her altered swim pattern as she favored her right side.
Second, by the shredded leather dress that revealed red and
raised claw marks upon her back. As agonizing as it was, he ran

toward the river and met her near the edge in a foot of water. She ran into his arms and squeezed him as tightly as she could with her right arm.

His massive arms surrounded her and squeezed. She let out a moan when he pressed into her back. He lightened his grip immediately and cried into the top of her head. "I thought you were dead!"

She released new cries — cries of relief for finding herself safe in Peter's arms and cries of thanksgiving to God for both their safety.

He petted the back of her head as he pressed her head into his neck. He kissed her on the top of her head and whispered into her ear, "How did you live?"

Suddenly, she was overwhelmed with emotions of complete and utter pain, the shock of landing in the ocean, the wonder of Celesa's help, the survival of a bear attack, and the providence of God — still having Peter to guide her and protect her. She started to laugh lavishly.

He pushed her head back to see if she was really laughing. Her infectious giddiness was catching as she bent over in laughter. Peter attempted to copy her, but was halted by throbbing pain with the work of his abdominal muscles. He winced as he laughed.

Annabelle attempted to gain control of herself and to help Peter. Grabbing his arm, they mutually guided each other out of the water on to the bank where they sat down in the grass. She shook her head, attempting to answer his question. "Peter ... I don't know."

He took her head into his hands. "I guess, my little one, it was not your day to die."

She looked down at the grass. Her eyes caught a glimpse of his core, covered in leaves. She cautiously moved her fingers toward it.

"It's not as bad as it looks." He winced when she touched near one of the medicated leaves.

She looked up at him. "I don't believe you."

He released a held breath as he shook his head. "You know me too well. It is painful. But what about you? Turn around." He moved her right shoulder to examine her wound on the left.

She moved her hair in front of her and spoke over her shoulder. "I used the yarrow and willow, like you said, but I couldn't reach all of the wound."

"Well. That is easily fixed."

"What about you, Peter?"

"I am as fixed as I can be at present." He pointed to a rock sitting by a tree. "There is some yarrow by that boulder."

She looked back at him before rising, assurance in her eyes. "I know, Peter."

It was at that moment that he realized how good of a pupil Annabelle had become. She had listened, memorized, and used all the knowledge he had bequeathed to her. She was a survivor. She had survived a swim in the ocean, a 50-foot waterfall, and a bear attack. He had new respect for the little girl who had come into his life and grown before his eyes.

She handed the flowers to him and sat down with her back toward him, moving her hair over her right shoulder. He ripped her dress around the wound. She winced as he picked pieces of leather out of it.

"I guess this means I will need a new dress."

He held his breath for a second, trying to push away his own pain. "It will be awhile before I can hunt."

"Does this mean no more lessons?" She had become so accustomed to them that she was a bit saddened by the thought.

"No. This means more lessons — we will have to train harder to get back to the way we were." He held his breath for a moment and then continued, "Pain fades, wounds heal, but scars form. We must keep moving to make certain we can move." His thoughts turned to her survival. "How did you swim in the ocean with a wound like this?"

She thought about Celesa. She had tried to explain her the first time she met her in the river, but he had not believed her. Why would he believe her now? She gave the best answer she could, without mention of the mysterious girl. "I had to."

"Like you had to outrun the bear?"

"I didn't outrun the bear. We both know that."

Peter was silent for a moment. "No one can outrun a bear. You should not have run."

"So I was to lie down and have it swipe at me? Like you?"

He leaned closer to her ear. "Annabelle, that is what you do if a bear comes at you."

She held her breath. Would he chastise her? He did not say anything. She could not live with the silence, she must know: "Are you angry?" She attempted to look at him over her shoulder.

He repeated his earlier statement: "No one can outrun a bear, but" — he leaned in again toward her ear — "I'm certain that was the closest anyone has ever come to it."

"So, you're not mad?"

"My little Annabelle, how could I be mad at you — you're alive."

Questions

Three more years of daily and intense training flew by. Annabelle grew in her knowledge, reasoning, and justice along with her height and maturity. Her hair grew longer and fuller, her face more delicate, her figure more womanly. She trained harder, became quicker — better than she was before her freefall into the ocean. Peter noticed the primitive deer leather dress, the eleventh one he had made since her arrival on the island, was becoming too small.

Peter, full of insight and knowledge, thought it was time for Annabelle to start to leave the forest. To leave her leather dresses, with which she had become so accustomed and comfortable, for a proper dress that could be worn in society.

One evening, Peter returned from his chest and presented her with the fine dress it contained. "Your clothing is too small and not proper for your age. I wish I had some shoes for you."

"Peter, this dress is so fine — I can't wear it. I'll only get it ripped and dirty."

"Clothes are made for wearing. It does nobody any good sitting in this chest — especially when you're in need of it. Don't ever be too proud to take a gift. Receive it humbly, since it is God caring for you through the giver."

"But I could make a better leather dress. I wish it; I am at ease in leather …"

"No, Annabelle. I know you are at ease in the leather; that's the point. It's time that you were properly attired. You can't go back to Anchony dressing in animal skins."

"Back to Anchony?" Her brow furrowed.

"You must always remember, Annabelle, you are a lady.

And a true lady would want to present the beauty of God by how she presents herself."

She sighed. "I suppose if you demand, I will wear the fine wool. Besides, no one but you will see me in the dress when it becomes ripped and dirty."

"Present yourself in the best way. My pearl, my Sara made this dress. She was a great seamstress. I think she would want you to have it."

"Sara made it? Then I truly can't take it." She tried to hand it to him.

He pushed it back toward her. "No. You will take it, and you will wear it."

Annabelle was speechless. She could not remember such a pretty dress. Taking it from Peter's offered hand, she delicately investigated the beading and embroidery.

"Try it on. See if it fits."

She returned clothed in the soft, embroidered wool.

"You look like a diamond."

She petted the dress along her core. "It's so light. I feel as though I am wearing nothing."

"Yes, lighter than leather, which allows for longer length without the weight, but it's not as strong."

She shook her head. "Peter, how am I to defend myself in this? I do not wish to rip it."

"When you are around worthy men, you shouldn't have to defend yourself."

Annabelle looked down at the cave floor. "I have learned for so long now, Peter, I don't think I could not defend myself. It's like walking. It's like breathing. It's a part of who I am. I can't escape from it. Wherever I go, I am watchful of everything around me, what I see, what I hear, what I feel." She raised her head to look at him.

"Yes, and I pray that will never change. You should always be aware of the things around you — who is in the room with you, what their body language is saying. But if they need to be stopped from an ill course, that is not your duty."

She lowered her head. "I understand, Peter. I hope I never do anything to make you think ill of me."

He stroked her face with the side of his left pointer finger. "My little one, you will never do anything that would make me think less of you."

Annabelle looked at the floor at the sound of the affectionate nickname Peter had bestowed upon her. She looked up sheepishly. "I am not so little anymore."

Peter nodded his head as he patted her on the shoulder. "How true."

Overcome with thankfulness, she looked into his eyes. "Peter, thank you for all you have given me. If you would not have found me in the cave all those years ago, I certainly would have perished."

Peter smiled. "It was all in God's foresight. It is He who you should thank."

"And I do, I truly do." She smiled as she nodded.

"Is something bothering you this evening?"

She sighed as she looked up from the crackling fire she had been fixated upon for the last half hour. "I was only thinking. You have taught me what a true father is like, but what about a mother? I am sad to say I don't have memories of mine. What do you think she was like?"

"Well, you came to me with a base of principles and morals, and you are caring and loving. The first one to teach you that is your mother. So, I suppose she is as tenderhearted as you. And you must get your pretty eyes from her."

Annabelle's mind jetted back to the dream she had had years before when she saw the exquisite lady with emerald eyes, but she attempted to shake it from her thoughts. "And what of my father?"

"A God-fearing man, abiding in justice, a friend to all."
Annabelle turned her entire body toward him. "How do you say that? I mean, how do you know?"

Peter's smile faded and after a moment replied as he repositioned himself. "Rightful conduct is first taught by the mother, but the father teaches as well."

"And my siblings, how are they?" This question she asked more to herself than to Peter.

"Well, if they are anything like you, they are as sharp in mind as a dagger, as unwavering in conduct as a mountain, and as sweet in countenance and quality of person as the finest honey."

"Peter ..." She playfully pushed him.

I wonder what my children would have been like. His stare went to the distant cave wall.

Noticing, she figured what he was thinking. "Your children, Peter, would be like me, because you are my father, my teacher. Everything you said about me would be true of them too."

"Thanks, Annabelle." He squeezed her hand.

She squeezed back. "You would be proud of them, Peter. I know you would."

They both stared into the fire. Annabelle's remembrance of her dream stirred up thoughts about Celesa. She had never once mentioned her to Peter since her encounter in the river.

"Peter?" She looked at his face. "Who is Celesa?"

"Celesa?" Peter asked, shaking his head, at a loss.

"How did you help her?" Annabelle probed.

"I" — Peter thought hard and shook his head — "I know of no one named Celesa. What is this about?"

"Are you certain?" she asked.

"I am positive," Peter said with certainty.

"She has blonde, wavy hair. She likes the water." She tried to pull all she could from her memory.

Peter looked at her strangely. "Annabelle, what are you talking about?"

Releasing a breath, she decided to reveal all. "You know when I jumped into the waterfall and I said that I had seen a girl?"

"Yes."

"That was not the only time that I saw her." She turned her whole body to face his side. "After the bear clawed me, when I was in the ocean ..." Her eyes wandered over to the fire.

"Yes?"

"She was there. She swam with me to the shore. She pressed me to swim. If she had not been there, I likely would have stayed on the cliff." She looked back at him. "She told me her name was Celesa and that you had helped her and ..."

When she did not go on, he prompted, "And?"

Her voice went to a whisper. "She said my mamá prays for me every day."

Peter was silent for a moment. "And then what?"

"She made it to the beach, but when I turned around, she was gone."

Peter started laughing. "Could *that* be your angel?"

She was not amused; she wanted to find an answer. "But she said that you helped her."

"I'm sorry, Annabelle, but I have never known a Celesa." He looked back at the fire as his thoughts hazily attempted to connect dots that might or might not be there. He slowly turned his gaze to the satchel reverently placed upon the natural cave ledge. He shook his head as he turned back to the crackling fire.

Annabelle stared back at the flickering flames. The girl was still a mystery.

Unmasked

Squatting down to pick up a stick to add to the small pile in her arms, Annabelle caught an unusual sight from the corner of her eye. *What is it? Is it a bird?*

Turning to it, she set the pile of sticks down and used the branch in her hand to investigate. *It doesn't breathe.* Prodding at it, her mouth dropped open when she realized what it was: a Demolite's mask.

As her heartrate began to rise, she shook her head while her eyes searched around the area. *There aren't tracks.* Touching it again with the tip of the wood, a feather easily fell off. *It's old.* She sat back, unsure what to do. *It must have been left when Peter chased the Demolites away all those years ago.*

Taking a deep breath, she dropped the stick and bravely reached for the mask, confronting her fear. Staring at the worn leather with the loosened sparrow feathers molting from it, she curiously studied it in her perspiring palms.

As she easily picked off a feather, she spoke to the mask, "Even you, oh thing of nightmares, can't avoid the passage of time." A profound thought came upon her: *The Demolites too shall pass away, but God will remain.* With that realization, her heartrate decreased.

Turning the mask around, she felt the rough leather and slowly outlined one of the eyeholes. *What's it like to wear such a disguise?* She lifted it toward her face and looked through the eyelets, just to pull it away quickly. "What kind of man is behind the wearing of such a disguise?"

Closing her eyes, she shook her head as she pressed it into the ground with a prayer. "Father, I pray for the one who wore it. May he find You. You are what he truly needs." Releasing a deep breath with the end of her prayer, a peaceful calm came upon her.

Opening her eyes, she looked at the mask and said to herself, "He was only a man. And what is fear, anyway?" Looking to the canopy, she spoke both to herself and to God. "Why should I fear? You are always with me, and this ..." Picking the mask back up, she looked at it with a new perspective. "It's only a tool. A tool to cause fear." She stood, resolute. "And I will fear it no longer."

"Peter! Peter, look what I found!" She waved the molting mask around as she ran toward the cave.

"Annabelle, what is it?" Peter ran to her from the deer carcass he was dressing out.

She showed it to him with both hands. "I found one of the Demolites's disguises."

"Where?" Taking it, he examined it closely. "It's very old."

"From when they were last here, I would think." She pointed over her shoulder. "I found it north of here, where I was gathering sticks."

Peter knowingly nodded. "We can burn it."

"No! I don't want to." She offered her hand forward so he would return it to her.

"No?" he asked cautiously, uncertain he wanted to give it back.

"I'm not afraid anymore, Peter." Lowering her hand, she explained, "I've come to see that the reason the Demolites wear these is because of fear: They fear being caught and they wish to cause fear. And I'll not give in so easily any longer. I'll not *let them* have that power over me."

"Power?"

"Yes." She nodded matter-of-factly and lifted her hand again. "They don't have true power; only God does. They only have what we allow them to take."

He stared at her for the longest time, amazed by her revelation. "I've never thought about it like that before." He gave it to her this time.

Looking at the mask, she nodded and then smiled as she found his gaze. "When I was a little girl, I knew nothing of them but fear. Now I know better. Now I know they are only men."

"What will you do with it?"

"I'll keep it. It shall serve my memory of how much stronger I am now — stronger because God has opened my eyes to the truth."

He stared at her in wonder as he thought about her words. "*Only God has power.*"

She took the mask inside the cave and emerged a moment later. "I left the sticks where I found it, so I'll go gather them now."

He only nodded, for he could not find words to speak.

She'll not let them have power over her? Taken off-guard by her revelation, Peter walked into the cave, pondering how the girl he had raised became so wise, so brave, so strong, and how he had spent years running from himself. *Have I not been over-taken by fear all these years? Fear of myself?*

Seeing the mask next to her moss bed, Peter fell to his knees and spoke to himself, "What am I if not a coward — unable to face my faults?" As the painful memories of his burning home and his wife's body flashed before his eyes along with the surging anger he felt, he looked up at the sacred satchel sitting upon the rock wall. *I'll not let wrath have power over me any longer. It is only fear of myself that has kept me from looking.*

Rising, he approached the satchel, removed it from its perch, and untied the closures. Taking out the first item, wrapped in leather, he held it next to his heart and closed his eyes. "Father, give me strength to overcome all fear, strength such as you've given her."

A voice suddenly seemed to surround him: "They're on their way."

Jumping to his feet, he opened his eyes and found a girl with wavy blonde hair before him. "Who are you? Where'd you come from?!"

"You must give her the bag," the girl insisted.

Thinking of Annabelle, he suddenly made a connection. "You're the girl she saw?"

"She must get it home!" the girl said with urgency.

"Home? Why?" He glanced at the bag. "What's in —" When he looked back up, she was gone.

Without a wasted moment, Peter, quickly removed one item after another.

"Sorry it took me so long, Peter," Annabelle said as she entered with a massive pile of branches in her arms. "I saw a large branch and it took me some —" She stopped midsentence when Peter took the wood from her arms and threw it on the floor. "What?"

"Annabelle, come here." Taking her hand, he pulled her over to the satchel.

Noticing it not in its place of honor, she shook her concerned head. "What are you doing with that?"

"I need to tell you something. Sit down. Sit down." He pulled her towards the floor.

"What is it?"

"I've learned ... I've come to know ... a man named Sir Victorus is the leader of the Demolites."

"What?" She shook her head in perplexity. "How did you come by this —"

"I need to tell you a story. Many years ago, many years before you were born, there lived a servant girl — a servant girl full of such beauty. She worked beside her mother at a nobleman's home, the home of the queen's cousin, far away from the king's castle. You see, the servant's father died, and her mother was forced to find work. When she was old enough, the servant girl took up work beside her mother. They had been in the home for about a decade when the owner's nephew came to live in the house."

"This nephew — this Victorus — had been sent to the country to receive a respite from city life, where, by his adventures, he had made a name for himself in every corrupt way. He was comely by eye … but not in being. And the servant girl, just a few years younger, was the most striking sight in the land. The first moment he laid his eyes upon her, lust began to grip him and never released its grasp. The servant girl was not swayed by his looks, for she had a way of seeing the truth about people, and she knew him to be marred at his core. He tried his best to woo her, but she would not give in."

"The lady of the house and the servant's mother watched as Victorus tried to beguile the girl. The lady sent word to her cousin — the queen — who allowed the girl to become a servant for the sovereign household. They thought there she would be safe. But Victorus followed her to the castle where he was knighted. He was very sly and shrewd but a truly good fighter."

"The servant girl lived in fear of him. Every time she would enter a room, she would check to see if he was there. She would never go far from the queen alone. She lived like this for months; she thought of it as her own worry and not for the queen."

"Then the prince arrived home after finishing his work at the university. He was a friend to everyone, and he became friends with Sir Victorus, for Sir Victorus was a good performer. The prince too was overtaken by the servant's beauty, but instead of being lustful, he turned to God. He prayed that any lewd thoughts would leave his head so that he could see the servant girl for what she truly was — a daughter of God. Every time he would see her, he would pray for her. He soon began to love her with a rich, deep, *agape* love, which is a selfless, and self-giving love."

"The servant girl could see that the prince was a true gentleman and a godly man. She saw him as worthy of honor, but when he would try to talk to her, she would try to escape from his honest eyes. She, too, had been praying for her one-day king, and she, too, began to love him with God's love. But she did not think it proper for a prince to be speaking with a servant girl."

"Sir Victorus saw how the two looked at each other. He became jealous, and one day, he assaulted the servant girl when he thought she was alone, but the prince and his friend were close at hand. Sir Victorus was stopped before truly harming the servant girl. He then fled into the country where his anger against the prince, the prince's friend, and the servant girl boiled inside of him."

"When the servant girl and prince married, Sir Victorus' anger exploded into full hatred for the prince, his wife, all of Anchony, and God. He found others who were offended by the sovereign family for a multitude of reasons."

"Those are the men you know as Demolites. 'To demolish the tyranny' is their cry. But Sir Victorus' is a wrathful cry, only wanting vengeance for what he sees as dishonor done to him."

"Where did you learn this?" She looked at his bag. "Was it in the bag, Peter?"

He took her hand again. "Annabelle, the Demolites' desire is to wreak destruction upon all the people of Anchony, to make the sovereign appear weak so they can take it over and ruin Anchony by all of their wicked ways. This is why they have destroyed family after family. They want the sovereign to fall."

She pulled her hands away. "I was taken from my family because of an offended throng?"

"Yes," Peter said with a downward head.

"Because of this Sir Victorus?"

"Yes." His head lowered even further.

"Is there a book in there that told this to you?"

"Annabelle, I have ... for many years, suspected Sir Victorus, but I had no proof behind any claim."

"You knew him?" She backed away.

"I worked with him."

"And you have evidence now? There's writing in there that told you his story?"

"No," he shook his head as he picked up the satchel. "But you must take this bag with you." He placed it in her arms.

"What?" She looked at his esteemed satchel, which was fuller than usual.

"Wear it across your body. Only look at it when you're safely in your room at Aboly." Peter had a very serious and urgent look on his face.

"What? *Aboly?*" Annabelle had to recall the meaning of the word, and then she did. Confused, she asked, "Peter, how did you know I hail from Aboly? I don't think I've ever told you. I had nearly forgotten myself."

He dismissed her question for he had other matters on his mind. "Give me your word, Annabelle. I'm certain our time together is nearly over."

"What do you mean?" she asked with concern in her eyes.

He placed the strap over her neck and across her shoulder. "Keep it on you at all times. Do you understand?"

"Yes, but …" She shook her head, perplexed as to what had stirred him so.

"Pledge to me you won't look at it until you are safely in your room. No one but you must see the articles in this bag — no one. Pledge to me, Annabelle."

"You have my word," she answered, half afraid.

"And only when you are safe."

"When I'm safe," she repeated with a slight nod.

"Thank you, Annabelle. You know I love you like you are my own daughter." He squeezed her into him.

"And you are my father, my angel, my Peter." She looked across the cave at the rock wall. *What's going on?*

Peter hugged her harder than he had ever hugged her. While embracing her, he added, "I saw her, Annabelle. I saw the girl."

"Celesa?" She pulled away to look at him. "Did she tell all this to you?"

"Get it to Aboly. That's what must be done."

Annabelle was frightened by his words and actions. The fact that he seemed so unsettled distressed her even more. "Peter, are you all right?"

Rubbing his face, he knelt down with his back toward her. "I will be. I need to pray. Will you leave me for a time?"

"If you would like." Nodding, she walked out of the cave with the satchel hanging next to her hip.

She found herself sitting atop the cave with the sound of the waves crashing against the rock, the wind briskly blowing her hair away from her face into a tangle, and the distant call of a lonely loon.

Setting the satchel in her lap, she felt the leather with her fingertips. *What is in here? Has this made Peter that way or was it Celesa — whoever she is?*

Why must I wait until I'm in Aboly?
Aboly: What memories have I of it? She remembered gray stones towering into the sky — a cathedral, perhaps. *This island has become my home. But what have I missed?* Her brothers, William and Thomas; her sisters, Isabella and Cristine; what were they like now? And her parents? *Do they think of me? Do they wonder what I'm like? Or do they think me dead? Peter thinks I'm to go home? But what of him?* She suddenly gasped as she concluded that her angel must think he would not make it to Aboly with her. *Why?* A tear fell down her cheek as she tried contemplating a life without Peter. *Where will he go? What will he do? Does he not think he'll live?*

As an audible cry released from her mouth, her hand flew to it. *Father, Your will in all that comes to pass! Nothing but Your will. I am thankful for all the time You've given to me with Peter. I'm thankful for this island on which I've been allowed to run around and grow.*

"I will try to be strong, Father, but I need Your grace now. I am nothing but weakness without You!"

And if she felt this way, what was Peter feeling? Resolved to check upon him, she climbed back down the rock wall and peeked into the entrance of the cave, calling quietly, "Peter?"

Turning toward her, he held out his hand. "Annabelle."

Running to him, she sat down, leaning against him. "Are you better?"

"I have come to see how God has used my weaknesses for His will. I don't know what will come to pass tomorrow or the day after or the day after that, but I am certain His hand will be in all of it." Grabbing her hand, he squeezed it and kissed her forehead. "It always has been."

Peter's Request

Annabelle awoke early the next morning, somber and cautious, and had a longer prayer time than usual upon the top of the rock. "Dear Lord, although the sunshine is still bright, the water is clean to drink, there's plenty of food to eat, and the towering trees still provide us shade, I can't help but feel it shall all be lost to me." She closed her eyes. "But Your will, Father. You know best. Thank You, Father, for Peter, and help him in any way he needs help. Bless my family, Lord. Oh Father, give me the grace to do Your will and the strength for all You ask of me. Help me to endure all You wish for me to endure."

She spent extra time on her prayer spot, taking in the beautiful wonders God had created: the feel of the cool wind upon her cheeks and in her hair, the salty smell of the sea, the endless voices of the birds, and the dazzling glitter of the ocean. Peter's satchel sat next to her, the strap across her body.

Returning to the cave to prepare and eat breakfast, Annabelle observed Peter, remembering the conversation from the evening before. He did not appear any different than any of the previous mornings of the 13 years she had spent with him.

During Peter's prayer time, when Annabelle was quietly separating herbs, Peter stood up and hurried Annabelle out of the cavern, insisting that they needed berries.

"Berries? They are not in season yet."

"Strawberries. Yes, there are some early ones — 15 miles to the southwest near the giant redwood."

"I have never seen strawberries there."

"Don't argue, just go!"

Annabelle had never seen him act in such a fashion. Peter started moving her out the cave opening as he handed her a large leaf used for collecting berries, reminding her, "15 miles southwest, near the redwood."

"That is a far distance," Annabelle commented as she stepped outside.

"It is, my child, but many long journeys must be made in life."

As Annabelle made her way to the giant redwood, she examined how the once exquisite dress was faded and tattered. Shiny beads, which had once added a decorative touch, were no longer present. She noticed her feet: They were so callused and familiar with the forest floor that the twigs and rocks no longer slowed her down.

Reaching the giant redwood in the afternoon, she immediately began her search for the strawberries. She finally found a tiny bush and was successful at picking a handful of tiny red berries. *Well, this wasn't worth the trip. Did Peter know there would be so few?*

Annabelle headed back. It had taken several hours to journey there, and it would take several hours to journey back.

As Annabelle drew closer to the dwelling, she noticed the heavy, odiferous air — signs of fire. With a minimal amount of moonlight making its way through the foliage, she slowed her pace. She soon heard voices — not just Peter's, but other voices, too. She saw lots of little fires — torches. Many, many torches.

Her heart began to pound; she hid behind a tree. What was she to do? *Lord, what should I do? Where's Peter? Please, let Peter be unharmed!*

A twig broke to the right of Annabelle. She ducked down and looked to see the origin. There, two feet from her, a masked man removed his disguise. She saw a scar on the left side of his cheek. *Stephanus.* Annabelle no longer worried about her safety; Demolites were about, and Peter was in danger. Stepping out from behind a tree to search for any signs of Peter, she spotted him near the cave surrounded by eight masked men with swords. She gasped, afraid of what they might do to her angel.

A man grabbed her from behind. "Look what we have here, Snitz. So this is the reward for all of our trouble."

"I get her when you're finished," replied Snitz.

She instinctively elbowed the man in the stomach and swirled around, shoving her knee into his nose. "Peter!" she screamed as two more men came toward her.

Peter looked over to see two low-life brutes surrounding Annabelle. He remembered his Sara, his pearl, and the 13 years of life with Annabelle flashed before his eyes ... the unarmed man took on eight armed men as the tame lamb became a ferocious lion.

"I'm coming, Annabelle!" Peter yelled through the clash of swords as four men already lay on the ground moaning. Four more men joined in the fight and then six more joined in against one.

Annabelle, in complete horror, watched as Peter was overtaken by the numerous men and stabbed by a piercing sword. In his agony, he thought of his little one. "Fight, Annabelle. You must fight!"

Annabelle hardly felt her body fall to the forest floor as she was dragged to the ground, her mind numbed by the image of the bleeding Peter. Suddenly shocked back to the present, her mind processed Peter's words, and the art of self-protection came forth.

Reaching for a rock, she hit one man in the middle of his head, sending him backwards as she kicked the other man in the nose and then swiped the side of his knee; he yelled in pain as his ligament tore. Grabbing the satchel, which had fallen off during her tumble to the forest floor, she threw the strap around her body and sprinted toward her bleeding angel, stopping a short distance away.

Their eyes met in the briefest moment. He willed her strength; she willed him comfort. Her eyes slowly took in the whole, unreal scene; he was being punched and kicked from every side. She froze in fright as she watched the man who she knew as her father, take all the brutality on himself.

It was not until Peter took all of his energy to scream at her that she was jolted back to reality. "Run, Annabelle! You must run!"

"No." Annabelle whimpered as she shook her head. "I can't leave you." Two men started after her.

"Run, Annabelle!" Peter repeated. "Run! Forget me. I am in God's hands. Run!"

As if in slow motion, she watched all of the Demolites around him turn their attention toward her. She looked back at Peter; he lay on the ground, hardly blinking — she had no choice but to run.

So run she did — as only she could.

She quickly sprinted through the forest; her body knew the terrain — she did not need her eyes to see. She ran with her anger; she ran with her fright. She finally looked back — eight men with torches. But what was that behind them? The trees! The trees were aflame! *Oh, Peter!*

Far ahead of them, Annabelle knelt down to catch her breath and process all that had transpired. *God, why are You doing this?* Then she remembered Peter's words from that morning, a morning that seemed so distant. *"Many journeys must be made in life."* She remembered, too, her own prayer: *"Help me to endure all You wish for me to endure."*

Your will is for me to endure. So endure I shall!
Think. Think. How did all these men get here? Boats! They
must have boats.

She headed toward the seashore, though she still had a
couple miles to go until the trees started to thin. She prayed
that she could easily seize a boat and make her escape. The air
was chilly, but she was hot from movement. She felt the air
growing thicker. *Oh, Peter! Lord, forgive me for leaving him.*

She leaned next to a tree to catch her breath again and
relive the recent, horrifying events. She had left Peter —
injured Peter — to a posse of men and an inferno of the forest.
She was completely and utterly tired — her fast-twitch muscles
having been burned out, she had to rely upon her less conditioned slow-twitch muscles. Hearing a twig break, she opened
her eyes to see the men approach. One of the men's eyes met
hers, and the chase ensued again.

"Come here, little lady, I want to make your acquaintance." The other men started to laugh while another man
chirped up. "Yeah, me, too. And maybe we won't give you to
our patron; we'll keep you for ourselves."

You know these woods. Stop being the hunted. For the
briefest moment she paused, then she quickly made her plans
and positioned herself.

Six men passed by and as the seventh and eighth ran
after, she pushed over a half-fallen log. It caught the last two
men on its descent. The fourth, fifth, and sixth men heard
their yelling and came back to investigate.

"Look at that, Jallus, a tree fell on them!" The three men
began to laugh. Annabelle silently approached the men from
the back. She shoved the man on the right into the middle
man with a large stick.

"Why'du shove me, Warus?" the man said, as he shoved
back at him.

"I didn't, you fool. But you won't be shoving me and

gettin' 'way with it." Warus punched the man. Jallus struck Warus and fell into Osbertus. And so the men were distracted from the little lady whose acquaintance they wanted to make.

Annabelle traveled on toward the seashore, the two other men no longer in sight. *Dear Lord, please don't let them find me.* As quickly as she prayed, clouds appeared and darkened the moonlight.

She peeked out from behind a rock next to the cliff that ran along the seashore. The two men approached five other disguised men. There were questions asked, voices raised, and commands yelled. Daggers were pulled and soon two of the men were fighting.

It started to rain. Annabelle spied a boat and decided to use the men's prideful wrestling and the cover of the rain to work to her benefit.

Lord, I know that You are with me, and I thank You.

Sneaking out to the shore, she moved a boat into the water, and hopped inside. The men did not notice. She began to row with all her might. Row, row, row. The men shrank smaller and smaller as the distance increased between them and Annabelle.

When the entertainment was over and one Demolite was dead, the men began to look around. One noticed the missing boat and soon spotted her rowing around the island as the clouds moved to let the moonlight stream through. Running to the boats, they started their pursuit as raindrops suddenly poured down from the heavens.

Lord, I'm so tired and weak. Give me strength. I can't do this with my own power. Annabelle received a kick of adrenaline as she watched the men gaining on her. *Father, if only they couldn't see me!* She pressed forward, although her arms began to burn. The rain turned into a drizzle and the drizzle became a fog. It was not long until the men could not see Annabelle, and she could not see the men. Every once in a while, out of the dense clouds, she would catch a gruff voice — laughing and taunting her with what would happen if she was caught. Such commentary only made her row the harder in her wet, cold, and shivering condition. *Dear Lord, help me. I don't think I can go on.*

For hours and hours she rowed, not knowing from where the energy or fortitude came. The sun was starting to rise when she saw a ray of hope: a bird.

"Thank You. Thank You." Annabelle prayed with a truly grateful heart. *How much longer? How much longer?*

Suddenly, her boat came upon a rock and would not budge. She turned around to see how far she was from the land: about six feet. She looked in the direction she had just come and saw the tips of the men's boats come into view from the thick fog. She must jump.

She tried to stand, but her legs were so stiff that she could not move them in the chilly morning air. Though her arms were burning, she tossed Peter's satchel toward the shore. It landed on the beach, close to the water. She then fumbled over the side of the boat. Her right foot caught on the side, and she tumbled into the breathtakingly cold water. Moving her screaming muscles against their wishes, she finally made it to the shore and crawled as far out of the sea as she could go with her dwindling energy.

I need to keep moving! I need to keep moving! Her mind prompted, but her muscles won out: No matter how many times she tried to tell herself, her body would not budge. She collapsed on the seashore out of fatigue.

Annabelle lay on the wet sand, her dress plastered to her body with her legs still in the nearly frigid water. The outline of the fading stars burned into her vision — the same stars she had gazed upon safely atop the cave. Those memories seemed a lifetime ago.

"Are you all right?" A stranger approached. She could barely move her head to see who drew near. As the distance decreased between them, the stranger realized how much in need the wet, cold, young lady was. He quickly pulled her out of the water and took her closer to some rocks to block the wind. He removed his cloak and placed it around her. Then, cradling her in his arms, he easily carried her up a ledge.

You're not Peter. I don't know you. Annabelle was too wet, cold, and fatigued to resist his strength.

Stranger

Annabelle could not fight his strong arms. She was very, very weary and chilled completely. She looked back at the end of the sea and the beginning of Anchony — figures of men popped up above the ledge. She had no strength to say a word. She silently watched in horror as the Demolites drew closer, and the man took her across a meadow.

The man knew he was being followed. He increased his speed. He was soon in the stone structure; she was soon on the bed. As swiftly as he laid her down he picked up his sword, which rested upon his table. He stood outside the door, ready to engage in a fight if he must.

The small, dying fire in the fire pit crackled. It re-awakened the drowsy Annabelle, who was shifting in and out of consciousness. She caught a few of the exchanged words.

"You are trespassing upon my property, and I kindly ask you to leave."

"Well, you have something we want, and we want her back!"

"What is she to you?"

"She's our sister!" Laughter abounded.

Annabelle's rescuer was not amused. "You hide your faces when chasing after your sister?"

Another Demolite stepped closer to the man and in a rough, mean voice replied, "This is no worry of yours."

Annabelle heard metal clashing.

She shook her fatigued head in the bed. *They'll kill him and then get me. Peter, Peter, where are you?"*

She was on the island, the first day of training with weapons. "It shall be as if it was your arm." Peter handed her a stick.

She released it after the first blow. "But it's not my arm."
Peter picked it up and placed it in her hands. "You'll learn
to use it. It adds distance and wards off damage."
She was older, by two years. She knocked Peter off his feet
with a stick. "I do believe I like this, Peter. It gives me an edge for
an earlier escape — so when I am a distance ahead, I may stop
and laugh at you without the fear of being caught."

She opened her eyes again. The man was kneeling next
to her, feeling her forehead. She tried to swat his hand away.

You're not Peter. She recalled Peter's words: *"Trust no*
one unless they are family, a close friend, or they have gained
your trust."

"You're too cold." The man stood swiftly and built up
the fire in the middle of the dirt floor. He walked to a chest
and returned with a nightshirt. "You must get out of your wet
clothes." He moved the heavy blanket from under her and
rolled her to her side.

In her mind, she screamed at him: *Don't touch me! I don't*
know you! Leave me, please leave me! But in reality, her muscles
were limp in fatigue, and she could barely keep her eyes open.

As quickly and discreetly as he could, he removed her
clothing and pulled the nightshirt down over her, along with
a pair of wool socks and an extra blanket. His mind swirled at
the scars upon her back.

Hearing the sound of singing birds, she slowly lowered the
blanket away from her eyes. The dust particles flying through
the air were visible in the rays of daylight streaming through
the cracks in the shutters. She was in a stone structure. Whose
structure? She did not know. She vaguely remembered a man.
She sat up, slowly. Every muscle ached from stiffness. She
turned toward the wall and pulled herself up to the window.
She slowly opened the wooden shutter and felt the refreshing
breeze of the wind. The miniature keep lay in a meadow with

trees along the periphery. There was a man, a few years her senior, chopping wood.

Where am I? Who is he? She remembered her terrible flight from the Demolites. *Oh, Peter!* She stared at the man. Was he friend or foe?

Turning around with a pile of wood in his arms, he saw her.

She gasped, ducked, and turned around as her heart beat wildly. She heard the man drop his wood and run toward the door. *Where can I go? Where can I hide?* She haphazardly scrambled out of bed. She stood petrified next to the bedpost, leaning against it for strength as her legs ached. *What can I do? I can't fight! Help me, Father. Help me!*

The man opened the door and stopped. A smile broke forth upon his face with relief in his eyes. "You're all right." She shook in terror. He walked toward her. She backed against the wall, shaking her head. "It's all right." He lifted up his hand. "It's all right. I won't harm you."

She followed the wall down to the floor and pulled the nightshirt around her knees. She saw her dress folded up upon the table and began to cry. *Father, what has come to pass? What has he done?*

The man lowered his hand and stood up straight. "You don't need to worry. Those men who were chasing you are gone."

She looked at him. *Can I trust him or is he lying? Is he one of them?*

"It has been two days." He walked to the fire pit. "I suppose you must be starving." He ladled some soup into a bowl. She watched him closely. He took a few steps toward her, squatted, and held the bowl to her.

She looked at the brown pottery and at him. She was hungry, but she did not know if she could trust him. She did not say anything — she only stared.

The man gazed into her emerald eyes as he pondered over her current state. He shook his head and set the bowl down on the floor next to her. "It's hot now." Standing, he turned to a chair furthest from her, and sat. Leaning forward, he stared into the firepit as he watched her from the corner of his eye.

She smelled the soup and could no longer resist. Picking it up, she drank from it like a cup.

"So, did you know those men?"

Thinking about the men that were chasing her, Peter's death, and her narrow escape, she could not help but cry into her soup.

"I'm sorry." He sat up in alarm. "I didn't mean to upset you. I ..." Interiorly, he beat himself up for upsetting the strange young lady further. He shook his head. "My name is Nicholaus. Nicholaus Hunts." He looked back over at her. "What's your name?"

Why does he need to know my name? Father, help me. Where am I? She refused to speak.

"You do speak, don't you?" he asked curiously.

Let him think I do not! He'll not question me further. Let him think me less able. I will escape more easily, if need be.

"Well, um ..." He stood and unfolded her dress, showing it to her. "This is yours. I'm certain you want it." He placed it on the foot of the bed and left the miniature castle.

He stopped outside the door and listened. He heard her place the bowl upon the packed dirt floor and crawl on her knees to the dress. He peeked around the doorframe and saw her caressing the dress with tenderness. He was fascinated by the mysterious young lady with the emerald eyes.

Turning her head quickly, she saw him looking at her. He hastily walked away. She found a burst of strength and ran to the door and slammed it shut. Pressing her face into the dress, she melted into the floor.

Father, help me!
"Do you think I have forsaken you?"
She was struck by the words.
No. You have not forsaken me. You never would.
"Then be strong. Have faith. You are all right."

Energized by the soup, she donned the ragged, torn, but familiar dress. In it, she felt a little more like herself. Suddenly, she felt incomplete. She was missing something — Peter's satchel! Breathing quickly, she gazed around the room. She dashed to her knees and checked under the bed. It was nowhere to be found. She began to panic. Her eyes stung. She attempted to vanquish her sobbing, but it was not possible. She had lost the one thing Peter had given to her to protect, and she still had no idea of its contents! She had let Peter down, let him down in his death. *Where did it go? How could I have lost it?* Her fingernails dug into the floor as she cried in anguish upon her knees.

Nicholaus heard her cries from outside and ran to help her. "What's wrong?" She quickly turned on to her backside and crawled away toward the wall. He moved back, careful not to touch her, as she was obviously afraid of him. "What's wrong?" he asked again with great concern.

She looked into his eyes for a brief moment. That brief moment showed her strength and dependability, but could she trust her own judgment? Should she ask him for the location of the bag? *If it's not in here, he likely doesn't know. Did it not make it with me? No, it was with me in the boat.* Suddenly, she remembered she had thrown it when she exited the boat. It could be on the beach, if the waves or a Demolite had not stolen it.

She looked back into his kind eyes and then to the door. She spotted the ledge leading to the beach, she saw the distant sea, and she heard the crashing waves in the distance. Jumping up from the floor, she bolted toward the beach.

"Wait!" Nicholaus watched as she dashed from the castle and across the meadow. *Where is she going? Is she going out to sea?* He pursued her, running as quickly as he could, but he could not keep up. He was halfway across the meadow when she jumped over the ledge.

"Stop!" he screamed in fear. Fear that he would get there too late.

Jumping off the ledge, he ferociously searched the waterline; he did not see her. No movement but waves and seagulls. He ran out into the water searching desperately for any signs as he breathed quickly in fear, loss, and exasperation. "Where are you?" He heard something behind him; he turned.

There was the mysterious young lady standing, unharmed, with a satchel in her arms. "Oh! Thank God! Thank You, God!" He walked toward her with relief. She took a few steps backwards. He stopped. "I won't come closer." He bent over, placing his hands on his knees as he caught his breath. He shook his head. "I thought you jumped into the sea." He looked up at her from his bent position. She tilted her head, wondering why she would jump into the wild ocean. He looked back down at the beach, continuing to shake his head. "I have never seen anyone run as fast as you."

Annabelle nearly laughed. *You think that was fast? I am not even at my best.* Placing the strap around her neck and shoulder, she climbed up the ledge.

Nicholaus watched in amazement at how she easily scaled the ledge. *Who are you?* He followed her into the meadow as they were greeted with a strong, vibrant neigh.

Annabelle stopped and stared at the magnificent creature before her.

Nicholaus stepped out in front. "This is Cinny." He patted the horse on the neck. Cinny shook her head as if to say yes. Annabelle was transfixed. It had been 13 years since she had last seen a horse. She could not remember a horse so beautiful, with a shiny red coat and long mane. Annabelle wanted to touch her, with her intelligent eyes and strong build, but she was hesitant. "She is very friendly," Nicholaus said as he leaned against the horse, patting her shoulder.

Cinny? Annabelle slowly lifted her hand. Cinny stepped forward and rubbed the side of her head against Annabelle's hand. A smile broke forth on Annabelle's face as she nearly giggled.

Nicholaus watched the transformation; he smiled, too, as the mysterious young lady showed signs of contentment. "She likes you."

Looking at Nicholaus, Annabelle's smile faded. *Having a horse doesn't make him trustworthy.* She dropped her hand. Cinny took off running through the meadow.

Nicholaus stared at the young woman before him, his smile fading as well. He wished he could help her in some way. *Who is she? Where does she live? Where's her family?* Her emerald eyes seemed to pierce the deepest part of his soul; he was forced to turn away.

He watched Cinny run, so carefree. *At least I understand her.* He looked back at Annabelle; she was not there. He looked down at her footprints — they led to the forest. His heart began to ache for her well-being — had she run away?

It was not safe. He sprinted after her, following her tracks. He found her with her back toward him. "There you are. Please, don't run away. It's not safe. I will take you wherever you want to go."

She turned around as she placed a berry into her mouth, one of the many she was collecting in a leaf.

Nicholaus looked from the berries to the strawberry flower. "Oh. I'm sorry. I thought you were trying to leave."

She turned back to the bush, her heart pounding quicker as she stared intently at the berries. *Am I not allowed to leave?*

He saw her body tense. "Those men, I don't know how far they got. It's not safe for you alone." He felt as though nothing he could say or do would ever set her at ease. He lowered his head in defeat. "I'll take you to town. I must be getting on anyway." He walked away.

She watched him walk disheartened to his home.

Sticking the last item into his bag, he looked up when the sunlight no longer streamed through the doorway. He was struck by the paradox of the mysterious girl blocking the rays of light: In her dingy, ragged dress, and unkempt hair, the beautiful young lady with emerald eyes could run like the wind, but could not whisper into it. *Who is she? What has been her life? Why is she so afraid? How can I make her see that I am safe? Why can't she speak?*

Annabelle observed her shadow as it stretched toward the handsome young man who had kind eyes and strength, but she could not fully allow herself to trust him. *Has he proven he can be trusted? Peter, would you want me to? Father, what should I do?* She could tell he was distressed. Her body urged her to offer him some kind of comfort. She closed her eyes and stepped inside. She slowly placed the leaf full of berries upon the table and pushed it toward him, quickly stepping back.

He looked from his bag to the berries to her. "Thank you," he said genuinely as he took his hands off his bag and chose a berry. He placed it in his mouth and scooted the leaf back toward her. She took a small step forward and reached for a petite berry. He smiled. And what was that: the briefest sliver of a smile from her? She quickly looked away and then exited.

She sat down on a piece of wood abutting the keep's wall. She rested the back of her head against the stone and closed her eyes. *Father, what do I do? How do I find my family?* She opened her eyes and stood. She slowly walked through the meadow, feeling the tall grass as she wandered aimlessly.

Nicholaus exited the small stone castle, keeping a keen eye on the lady as he loaded his horse with supplies.

Wandering toward the ledge, she squinted her eyes to see if she was being deceived: there, in the far, far distance, was a little stream of smoke. She bit her lip as she shook her head. *I'm sorry, Peter, that I left you to the fire. Rest in God's peace. Thank you for all you did for me. I love you … until we meet again.* She wiped the tears from her eyes as she turned around and headed back to the castle. *I am in Your hands, God, as I always have been.*

Cinny was all loaded. Nicholaus waited patiently beside her as he studied the lady approaching. He sighed as he looked at the meadow, the trees, and the castle; he, too, said a private goodbye. When he looked back at her, Annabelle was petting the horse.

"I'm sorry I don't have a side saddle." He looked to the ground. "I've never had a need." His mind turned to some painful memories; he shook them away. "But if you don't mind, you may ride with my saddle." He offered his hand to help her up. She backed away. "It is a far distance to town. Please, get on the horse." He pointed with his hand to the saddle. She walked five feet in front of the horse toward the path through the woods. "Or you could walk."

They walked on opposite sides of Cinny for 30 minutes in silence, except for Nicholaus's occasional remarks to his rider-free horse. He finally broke the quietness between them.

"I am hoping someone in town will know you."

What town? Where am I? A lump was in her throat.

"I am hoping they will know where you need to go ... who your family is."

Aboly. I must get to Aboly. How far are we? Ask him. Ask him.

She opened her mouth to speak when she heard a distant, "Good day."

Nicholaus stepped out in front of Cinny to see who had addressed them as he halted the horse.

A man emerged from the trees. His cocky smile faded when he saw Nicholaus.

"What can I do for you, Bartlett?" Nicholaus asked with a somber tone as he stepped next to Annabelle.

The man did not answer — he spat on the forest floor, placed his hands upon his hips, and asked, "Who's your friend?"

"That's of no interest to you."

Annabelle stepped backward into Cinny as she studied the man — he was gruff and large, with cruel eyes.

The man swaggered closer. "She's of *every* interest to me!"

Annabelle gasped as she looked away from the grotesque male who thought himself a man.

Nicholaus stepped between them. "Move on, Bartlett. Your company is not wanted nor welcomed here." He placed his hand upon his sword handle.

Bartlett looked from Nicholaus's sword to Annabelle's profile. He spat again, "Not willin' to share?"

Nicholaus gripped the handle more firmly as he demanded, "Move on, Bartlett."

Bartlett moved away. "Of course! I must heed the famous Nicholaus Hunts' warning. We all know what he can do."

Nicholaus watched him until he disappeared between trees a distance away. He turned back to Annabelle; she was quietly sobbing. "Please don't cry. I won't let any harm come to you." He wished to touch her, to comfort her, but he dared not.

Annabelle looked up into his eyes. The man before her reminded her of Peter, a younger Peter. She cried more from the realization that God had sent her another protector than from the awful man's words. She looked to the forest. She could not see the man, but she knew he was still there. She dared not speak.

"If you do not mind, I will walk on this side of Cinny." She looked back at the forest as they resumed their journey. "Don't worry, he's gone."

No. He's not. Annabelle listened to the sounds of the forest, in particular the distant popping of twigs. Her senses began to decrease as she grew weary from the distant walking, only having awoken from her two-day bed confinement that very morning.

Her legs began to cramp, and her eyes became drowsy. They slowed to the slowest pace.

"You need to rest."

She forced her eyes open and attempted to walk forward at the sound of Nicholaus's voice. Her body won out when she tripped over a stick and lunged forward. Nicholaus caught her and picked her up. Closing her eyes, she fell asleep in his arms.

Town

"How does he know her?" a voice whispered.

"She just appeared," an older voice whispered in return.

Annabelle awoke to two female faces staring at her.

The older woman, Avilina, gasped. "Good heavens! Look at her eyes." She smiled largely. "I have never seen such eyes!"

The younger lady stepped closer to get a better view. She gasped, looked away, and stepped back. "Too bad she is a stray!"

"Rossa! Hold your tongue, child!"

Rossa, in her fancy dress and perfect hair, folded her arms. "Avilina, I am not *your* child. I am not *a* child!"

Who are you? Where am I? Where is Nicholaus?

Annabelle looked around the room — it was a small but comfortable stone cabin with a thatched roof and makeshift windows made of animal horns. She looked from the kind, elderly face next to her to the younger body who had turned away and was trying to open a bag.

Moving like lightning, Annabelle flashed toward Rossa and took Peter's bag. Rossa yelled out in surprise as she was thrust against the wall. Annabelle, breathing hard, squatted in the corner holding Peter's bag tightly, protectively.

Nicholaus and another man ran into the room at the sound of Rossa's scream.

"What is it?" Avilina's husband, Roland, demanded.

Rossa, attempting to recover from Annabelle's swift movement, pushed her loose hair back as she adamantly shouted, "She's mad!"

"What's come to pass?" Nicholaus stepped forward.

Avilina attempted to explain the best she knew. "I don't know. It was so quick. She was in the bed and then" — she pointed from the bed to the corner — "she was where she is now."

"She is mad, Nicholaus!" Rossa stepped to him for comfort, leaning upon him.

Nicholaus, moving Rossa away, stepped toward Annabelle and knelt in front of the strange lady. Studying the way she gripped the satchel, he looked over at Rossa, now standing by the door. "Did you touch her bag?"

Rossa grunted and stuck up her nose. "How do we know it's even hers? She could have stolen it."

"Hold your tongue!" Roland demanded.

Rossa turned toward Roland. "Let her deny it!"

"She does not speak," Nicholaus said, as he stared at Annabelle.

"A habit others should take up." Roland glared at Rossa.

Rossa, sticking up her nose, picked up her skirts and walked out of the bedroom.

Roland shook his head. "That girl has had everything handed to her." He turned toward Annabelle. "Is she all right?"

"Of course she is," Avilina replied as she offered Annabelle her hand. "Give us a few minutes and we will be out."

Nicholaus watched as Annabelle slowly took Avilina's hand and stood. Confident in her safety, he followed Roland out of the room.

"Nicholaus, Nicholaus ..." Rossa was again next to him, invading his space. "I did not mean to offend."

Nicholaus moved her an arm's length away. "Then you should learn to keep your hands to yourself."

"Nicholaus," Rossa said with her most loving eyes.

"Rossa Johansdotter, I believe it is time for you to leave," Nicholaus stated strongly.

"Ah!" She looked over at Roland. He opened the door. "Well!" She walked toward the door, dress raised along with her nose. Stopping when she got outside the doorframe, she turned back toward Nicholaus. "That dirty, speechless, deaf-mute will never bring you happiness."

"Rossa," Nicholaus said, as he turned his head toward the young lady. "She's not deaf."

"Ha!"

The door closed in her face. Roland, nodding in satisfaction, revealed, "I've wanted to do that for a while."

Nicholaus smirked as he looked at the floor. "My uncle would scorn such a deed, saying that a person shouldn't be treated with such little worth."

"The moment Rossa Johansdotter learns to show others worth, I will show her the same. Come now, we must not waver in our task." He stirred the stew in the pot, which was cooking over the fire pit.

Avilina pulled the stool out from the wall. "Sit there, child, while I work on that hair."

Annabelle stared at the chair. She watched as the lady picked up a comb from a table. *Peter would want me to.* She laid the worn leather satchel in her lap, placing the strap around her.

"I am Avilina. You met Roland, my husband; he is the master mason of the village." She sighed. "And that there malicious little piece was Rossa Johansdotter, the only child of Johan Merchant, the only merchant in the village. Her mother died when she was but a babe and her father has given her everything he could … to her loss, I must add." Avilina sighed as she took one of Annabelle's locks and went to work detangling 13 years of neglect. "She acts as if she is nobility." Avilina sighed, shaking her head. "The poor thing. Her dresses are bought from Anchelo, the 'latest fashion,' she claims. Her mother was a dear lady. I have tried to help the poor girl in whatever way I can, but I fear she has been corrupted by all that was bestowed upon her." She stopped for a moment to chuckle. "But then there is Squire Nicholaus." She leaned in toward Annabelle's ear. "That is one thing that she'll never have." She stood to resume her work. "Nicholaus Hunts — he is called to greater things. He comes from a good family. Good family. His uncle is bishop of the North, you know?" She leaned over to look at Annabelle's response.

Bishop of the North? A bishop? Annabelle shook her head slowly.

"He is the best hunter in the kingdom as well."

Hunter?

"I'm not just saying that because I am proud of him, which I am, but because he has won the largest hunting game of all." She brushed firmly as she continued. "He has been called to the service of the king. He is, in fact, on his way to be a knight. You could not have found a better man to bring you here."

Father! Annabelle started to shake with sobs. *Thank You! Thank You for Your divine care! Thank You for Nicholaus.*

"Oh! Hush now, child. No tears!" She knelt in front of Annabelle. "Why do you cry?" Annabelle looked down at her and smiled as she wiped away her tears. Avilina patted her on her hands. "It is a smile then?" She stood back up, returning to her occupation. "Tears of happiness we can allow." She was silent for a moment as she worked, "His father was an honorable man too. Little Jous — that's how I knew him. My mother was in charge of his meals when his father was away. And I, being five years older, saw fit to boss him around."

She chuckled with memories. "It angered him so, but his brother, the now bishop, always stopped him from taking his vengeance." Her smile slowly faded as she recalled the horrid memories. "It was a dreadful thing that came to pass." She sighed. "All that Nicholaus has been through and he's not bitter. It's a wonder. That takes a strong character."

What had he been through? What came to pass?

"But then, his story is not much different from other families, I've been told." She was silent before switching topics. "I have four daughters of my own. They are all grown, with children of their own. It has been awhile since I have combed anyone's hair, but I have done it enough in my day that I am wholly able; and from the condition of your hair, dear child, I'd say you have not done it in a while either."

If I owned a brush, I certainly would have. Peter would have made me.

Rossa and Avilina were the first females Annabelle had encountered — with the exception of Celesa, who Annabelle was not certain actually existed — in 13 years, and though Rossa's actions had not left a positive impression, Avilina's kind actions and constant chatter were warming her heart toward her own sex.

Rossa marched toward the mercantile.

"What has you so angry?" a voice said from the shaded side of the building corner.

She shook her head.

The man stepped out into the light: Bartlett.

"How could he choose her over me?" She looked at Bartlett with fury in her eyes. "He doesn't even know from where she hails. She's nothing but a stray!"

He took a step closer. "Who do you mean?"

"Nicholaus!" she said with reddened cheeks.

"Nicholaus Hunts?" he said with a grin. "And this stray, what's her name?"

"She does not speak!" she said, enraged. "He chooses a silent stray over me!"

"She doesn't speak?"

"She did not utter a sound."

Bartlett grabbed Rossa, pulling her into the darkness.

"Let go of me!" She tried to resist him, to no success.

Shoving her against the wall, he said, "I want you to bring her to me."

Rossa shook in fear as she pulled her arm away. "And if I don't?"

He cocked his head and said with a grin, "Tell me, do you love your father?"

She gasped in horror. "You leave him alone!"

He took a few steps farther into the darkness. "Send her to me or you'll be sorry."

"There!" Avilina exclaimed in accomplishment an hour later as she tied the ribbon to the braid in Annabelle's hair. "Let's see now." She took Annabelle's hand, helped her up, and turned her around. Avilina gasped as all of Annabelle's favorable facial features were revealed. "Oh, my child!" She shook her head. "You're a jewel!"

Annabelle moved the braid in front of her and marveled at Avilina's work. She turned to the beaming Avilina and hugged her.

"Oh, my child!" the older woman replied as she was squeezed and returned the hug.

"It's perfect! Thank you," Annabelle whispered into her ear.

Gasping, Avilina looked Annabelle in the eyes. "Did you just speak, child?" Annabelle nodded her head as she smiled.

"My heavens!" Avilina hugged her again.

There was a knock on the door, followed by Roland's voice, "Are you ladies all right in there? It has been *many* minutes."

Avilina opened the door. "We are ready." She stepped to the side so he could see her work.

"Avilina, I think you have outdone yourself."

She smiled toward Annabelle as she held out her hand. "It was easy with such a subject. Come, child." Annabelle took her hand, and they followed Roland into the main room.

Nicholaus stood when he watched the ladies enter the room. When he saw Annabelle, he dropped the wood he was whittling. She turned around so he could see the braid.

"I don't think he cares about the braid," Roland said, as he hit Nicholaus on the shoulder and sat down at the table. "Let's eat."

Annabelle's smile faded. She looked to Avilina.

Avilina rubbed Annabelle's face and squeezed her hand before walking to the pot and gesturing for Nicholaus.

Roland pulled a stool out for Annabelle. "Your seat, miss." Annabelle looked from Nicholaus — who retrieved his chunk of wood off the floor and then walked to Avilina — to Roland, who offered her the stool. She smiled as she walked over and accepted.

"Squire Hunts … Nicholaus …" Avilina whispered as she leaned close to him. "I must tell you …"

"What is it?" he whispered back.

"She speaks."

"What?" His voice grew louder as his eyes expanded.

"She spoke to me," she revealed as she stirred the stew.

Nicholaus leaned in closer. "What did she say? Did she tell you her name? What is it?"

Avilina stuck up her hand to halt his excitement. "She liked her braid. She said, 'It's perfect' and 'Thank you.' That's all she said."

He looked over at the breathtaking young lady. "She speaks."

"Yes. Now be a love and get me the bowls."

He retrieved the bowls and looked over the woman's shoulder, glancing at Annabelle.

"Staring at her will not help her to speak."

He looked at the bowl Avilina was filling. "It's ... why? Why has she not spoken to me?"

She handed him a full bowl. "Give her time, love. I'm sure she will." She filled another bowl. "Patience is a virtue."

He nodded his head as he took the second bowl. "I only wish I knew her name, where she came from, why she was being chased, where she needs to go?"

She looked at him with a grin as she handed him the third bowl. "Is that all?"

He shook his head and gave a slight grin. "I would settle for her name for now."

"Well, perhaps we can get that." She took a bowl back and turned toward the table. "The stew is ready."

Roland took the bowls from his wife, set them in their place, and pulled out his wife's stool. Nicholaus placed the bowl in front of Annabelle. She smiled up at him for a moment, then returned her eyes to the table.

After prayer, Annabelle carefully watched Avilina, sitting across from her, as she picked up her spoon and ate the soup. She followed suit.

"How is the bishop, Nicholaus?" Roland asked as he broke his bread in half.

"He is well. Very busy, but well," Nicholaus answered cordially.

"Will he be able to join you in Aboly?" Annabelle dropped

her spoon. She looked from Roland to Nicholaus. Everyone noticed her reaction. "You are familiar with Aboly?" Roland asked, as he shifted his weight.

Annabelle looked back at the mason and nodded her head.

"Oh!" Avilina exclaimed. "Are you … *from* Aboly?"

Annabelle stared straight ahead at the kind older woman and nodded her head.

Avilina nearly giggled as her husband responded, "Well, there you go, Nicholaus. She's going your way."

Annabelle turned her eyes toward Nicholaus and then, slowly, her head. He did not move; it appeared as though he did not blink. His solemn countenance did not change as he stared at her. He finally spoke, "What is your name?"

Annabelle swallowed and opened her mouth. "An —"

There was an urgent pounding upon the door. Everyone's attention turned toward the banging as Roland opened the door.

"I am sorry to disturb your meal, but there has been a malicious act!" The man shook his head as he looked to the ground.

"What is it, Albinus?" Roland asked.

"Actius Miller has been wounded. They are taking him to his wife." He looked over at Avilina. "Ma'am, if you don't mind —"

"Of course." Avilina grabbed her cloak and headed out the door.

Albinus looked over to Nicholaus. "Whoever did it is still loose." Nicholaus, without batting an eye, grabbed his sword and headed outside, followed by Roland.

"Annabelle." Sitting before the empty stools, she spoke her name into the air as people ran by the door toward a neighboring house. "My name's Annabelle."

The evening air shocked her senses as she left the warmth of the little stone cottage. She jogged toward the crowd at the miller's house, passing many people along the way. The miller lay outside, surrounded by his neighbors at a distance, as they pondered how they could help him, somewhat fearful of touching him.

Annabelle bravely made her way toward the man, ignoring all the other eyes. *Is it like Peter's injury? Can I help?*

"Do not remove that!" Nicholaus commanded one of the men, who was tending to the wound as the squire spotted Annabelle kneeling next to the injured miller. The neighbor did not heed the warning. Blood strongly spurted out from the wound, covering several people including Annabelle.

She shook her head as the blood ran down her face. She had never seen such a wound: The man would not make it. She watched as he was picked up and carried inside to his screaming wife and crying children, whom Avilina was attempting to comfort.

Turning away from the emotional scene, she wiped some of the blood from her face and looked at her hands.

"How wretched. You should clean that off your face." The perfect Rossa stood two feet away. "There is a river back there." Shaking, she pointed behind the houses.

Annabelle did not need to be pointed; she could hear it. She looked from the direction of the river back to Rossa who quickly looked away and ran toward her home.

Annabelle knelt beside the river's edge and stuck her hands into the crisp water. She splashed it upon her face. The alarming frigidity stabbed at her flesh like a thousand pinpricks. She worked quickly to eliminate all signs of the man's blood.

Her hands stopped their scrubbing; she stood and turned toward a figure four feet away — Bartlett. He laughed sadistically as he licked his lips, a bloody dagger in his hand. "I hear I don't have to worry about you screaming." He moved toward her.

In an effort to get around him, she tripped over a stone and landed in the edge of the water. The cold river brought a temporary numbness upon her legs. He came after her in the river. Breathing hard as he approached, she waited for the right moment. When his arm came within distance, she jumped up, spun around, and kicked it with all she had. The knife flew out of his hand as he fell into the water. Flailing his legs, he hit her and knocked her farther into the river. He grabbed her ankle and pulled her under; the coldness enveloped her whole body. She kicked at his hand as she fought to reach the surface for air.

"Who did this to you?" Nicholaus probed the dying miller.

Nicholaus put his ear close to the miller's mouth to make out what he was saying: "Bartlett."

No! He went the other way earlier in the day. He looked around the room for Annabelle, starting to panic. He found Avilina's face. "Where is she?"

"Who? Who, love?"

"The girl!"

Avilina released the miller's children from her comforting arms to search for the nameless young lady from Aboly.

She slowly released air, willing herself not to inhale. Suddenly, the bulky, flailing man stopped moving. His grip released and she burst to the top of the river, coughing into the evening sky, as the river continued to push her downstream. She swam to the steep edge, grabbing a tree's root. She held to it while she caught her breath and attempted to recover from her experience.

I ... have got ... to get ... out ... of ... the water. Shivering, she grabbed a root upstream and pulled herself against the current. Root by root she pulled herself toward her entry point. Her muscles began to shake violently; she lost strength in her hands, but still she pushed forward as her breath puffed out in front of her.

"Bring me light!" Nicholaus demanded as he searched for her footprints. A torch was handed to him. He squatted down and studied the tracks that headed toward the river.

No. Please, God. Let her be all right!

She made it to her entry point but had no strength to pull herself out of the water; she rested upon the river's edge.

"Miss!" She heard yelling from far away, muffled through the water in her ears. "Miss!" It was closer.

Nicholaus saw the lady lying on the river's edge. Face down. Pale. Not moving. *No, God! Please, no!* He sprinted.

Shoving the torch into the rocky soil near her head, he turned her over. She saw the young man's face as the torch reflected in his eyes.

"You're alive!" he said with greatest relief as he picked her up and sprinted toward the Masons.

"Annnnnaaaaa ... Annnaaa ... bellllle."

He gasped and squeezed her tighter. "That's your name?" he said with great relief that she finally trusted him enough to give him her name. "It's nice to meet you, Miss Bell."

She tensed. "Noooo. Annaaa —"

"All right, Anna." She had no strength to correct him. He squeezed her tightly as he ran toward the warmth of the Masons' fire. "Tell me, Anna, why is it that you intend to hurt yourself?"

Hurt ... myself? What ... does he ... mean? She tried to look at his face but could not see it.

"Norman! Run quickly and get Avilina Mason," Nicholaus ordered a boy of 10.

"Right away, Squire Hunts." The boy ran to the miller's house.

Nicholaus kicked open the Masons' door and placed Annabelle before the fire. Legs and arms at her chest, she sat shivering as Nicholaus ran for a blanket.

Avilina burst into the house. "What is — good heavens, child!" She knelt down beside Annabelle and started to undress her. "What took place?" she asked as Nicholaus hurried back into the room.

"Riiiivvvveeer."

Avilina took the blanket and nightgown from Nicholaus. "We need more wood."

"Of course."

When Nicholaus returned, Avilina was rubbing Annabelle's arms as Annabelle rested against her.

"It is a dreadful night for a swim. Why would you go into the river?" The woman's chin rested on Annabelle's head as she hugged Annabelle's arms.

"Peter ... would ... be ... thankful," she stuttered, nearly unintelligible.

"What's that, love? What does she say?" She looked at Nicholaus in her confusion.

Nicholaus turned his head from the fire pit. "It sounds like 'Peter would be thankful.'"

"Peter? Who is Peter?"

Why would he be thankful that she nearly drowned in the river? Nicholaus shook his head as he placed more wood on the fire. "I don't know." He turned around when a large fire was burning. "Her name is Anna. She did tell me that."

"Anna." Avilina caressed her face and then looked back at Nicholaus. "Be a dear, and bring me my cloak."

"Yes." He retrieved her cloak that had been haphazardly removed and tossed upon a stool.

"She is not shivering as badly now. Will you hold her?" Avilina crawled out from under Annabelle as Nicholaus took her spot. "I'm afraid my legs do not allow me to sit upon the floor for such a length of time."

"Avilina!" Roland flew into the room.

"I am here," Avilina replied as she added the cloak to the layers upon Annabelle.

"I didn't know where you wen — Why is she wet?" He looked from his wife to Nicholaus and Annabelle on the floor. He forgot all about his previous concerns.

"I found her in the river," Nicholaus said.

"How did she get there?" Roland knelt down beside her and felt her forehead.

"I wish I knew. But this is the second time I have pulled her from the water." Nicholaus squeezed her, wanting to give her his heat.

"The second time?" Avilina asked in disbelief as she pulled a stool close.

"Is she trying to kill herself?" Roland asked as he knelt upon the floor.

Nicholaus shook his head. "I don't know. I pray not."

"Through what has the poor child lived?" Avilina asked to the air as she made the Sign of the Cross.

They all bowed their heads and silently prayed.

Roland ended the silence as he remembered his previous concern: "Actius Miller is dead."

"God rest his soul," Avilina said as she made another Sign of the Cross.

"He could not have lived with such a wound," Nicholaus said knowingly.

"Who did he say did it?" Roland asked.

"Bartlett."

"Bartlett!" Roland stood. "And he is still out there?" He took a few steps toward the door.

"Yes," Nicholaus stated as he stayed steadfast on the floor.

"Then what are you doing in here? You need to go find him!" Roland became agitated at the whole night.

Nicholaus was torn. He did not want to leave "Anna," but he knew if Bartlett was to be caught, he would have to catch him.

"Calm down. Calm down, Roland," Avilina stated as she stood. She turned toward Nicholaus. "Nicholaus, she is doing much better. I will stay by her side."

He knew he must find Bartlett; he beat himself up for hesitating. Shaking his head at himself, he gently laid Annabelle upon the floor.

A posse of men banged on the door as he stood and donned his sword. "Roland, is Nicholaus in there?"

Roland opened the door. "Yes, we're coming."

Annabelle rolled to her side and saw Avilina asleep on a stool, with her upper body on the table beside her. She pushed herself up. Avilina awoke.

"There you are!" Avilina said with a smile.

Annabelle looked down at the huge nightgown she was wearing.

"Your clothes were wet. I had to remove them."

Annabelle turned around and looked at the blazing fire. "I was in the river." She turned to look at Avilina.

Shocked to hear a complete sentence from the young lady, she did not reply at first. "Ah, yes. Nicholaus pulled you out." She stood and walked behind the stool, placing her hands on the table "They went to … they'll be back. Can I get you a drink?"

Annabelle nodded as she pulled the blanket around her.

"It was a blessing he found you in time," Avilina said as she retrieved a cup and the leaves for the drink. "So ... a ... what were you doing in the river?" Avilina probed as she removed the pot from the fire.

Annabelle stared at the lady's face. "I fell in."

"You *fell* in?" Avilina did not know whether to believe her.

"Yes, well, I tripped," she answered honestly without revealing her capabilities.

"What were you doing so close to the river?" She stirred the tea.

"Washing the blood off my face," Annabelle recalled.

Avilina held the cup. "So you weren't trying to harm yourself?"

Annabelle looked up at her in shock. "No. Why would I try to hurt myself?"

Avilina shrugged her shoulders as she half laughed in relief. "We ... we were worried." She handed her the tea. "This should warm you right up."

"What is it?" Annabelle asked, letting the steam hit her face as she took in the aroma of the leaves.

"It's tea," Avilina answered in disbelief. "Have you never had tea before?"

Annabelle stared at the liquid before her. "Not that I can think of." She tasted it. It was unusual, but she liked it.

Avilina stared at the young lady as her mind pondered. "Anna." Annabelle looked up at her. "Where do you live?"

Annabelle did not know how to answer. "I ..."

The door opened. Roland and Nicholaus walked in as the frosty air billowed its way inside.

"Did you find him?" Avilina asked as she turned toward the door with great relief.

Roland nodded his head as he doffed his cloak. Nicholaus closed the door and looked over at Annabelle. He took a double look when he saw her sitting up.

"He has been arrested?" Avilina probed.

"No." Roland revealed as he sat down.

Avilina handed him a cup of tea as she gripped her husband's arm. "I don't understand."

Nicholaus sat down on a stool, staring at the fire. "He drowned."

Annabelle looked up at Nicholaus as Avilina gasped and made the Sign of the Cross.

Nicholaus's eyes slowly wandered to Annabelle's gaze. "I am glad you are doing better."

"Thank you," Annabelle replied quietly as she looked down quickly but then looked back up. "How ... how is the miller?"

"He ..." Nicholaus sat straight up. "He died."

"Oh," Annabelle said, not sure how to reply.

Roland looked as his wife. "So, she talks now!"

"I could always speak. I chose not to," Annabelle replied as she looked down at her knees.

"You chose not to?" Roland asked and then began to laugh.

"Who are you? Why were you on my beach?" Nicholaus asked with a serious face.

Annabelle's reply was not expected. "I escaped." Everyone turned toward her.

"Escaped from where?" Roland asked as he pulled his stool closer.

"The Forbidden Island."

"Where is that, dear?" Avilina asked when nobody else would.

"I ..." She looked at all the faces. "I ... don't know ... in the sea — northeast."

Nicholaus stood and asked, irritated, "Who held you?"

"I —"

"Was it the man you spoke of — Peter?" Nicholaus knelt down next to her.

"No!" Annabelle stood and backed away from Nicholaus. She looked back at him and responded adamantly, "No!" She looked at the Masons and at Nicholaus. "He ... he was a good man." She nodded her head to make sure they understood. "He raised me."

"Raised you?" Avilina walked toward her. "Child, how long were you on the island?"

Her chin quivered as she revealed, "13 years."

Avilina gasped and then grabbed and hugged her.

Nicholaus turned to the now standing Roland in disgust and then turned back toward the distressed lady. "You were taken from Aboly?"

Annabelle slightly nodded as an answer to his question.

"Child, how old are you?" the kind women asked.

"18," she said with a cracking voice as tears finally fell.

Avilina gasped. "You were but five." She looked back at her husband and Nicholaus as she guided the wailing girl into the bedroom.

"No wonder she chose not to speak to us," Roland said as he stepped next to Nicholaus. "It is a wonder she speaks now."

Nicholaus's fist tightened as his knuckles turned white. "A work of the Demolites — there is no doubt!" He turned toward the table and leaned upon it heavily as emotions bubbled up inside of him.

"Very likely, very likely," Roland agreed as he sat back down. "There is nothing you can do about it, Nicholaus." Nicholaus started to pace. "Sit down, Nicholaus. You are making me uneasy."

He looked at Roland, declaring, "I can't sit down!" He paused and then headed for the door. "I'm going for a walk."

Guided by the moonlight, Nicholaus made his way to

the riverbank. He sat down in disgust and rubbed his temples as he tried to forget the memories that were being conjured up inside of him. He could smell the burnt wood; he could feel the despair as the smoke hung in the air and the body wrapped in cloth lay before him.

"What took place?" a young Nicholaus asked frantically as he stared at the burnt remains of a foundation that held such happiness but would never be again.

The neighbors gasped and whispered amongst themselves, but they did not address him.

"Mamá?" He wandered around the gathered people searching desperately for his mother. "Have you seen my mamá?" He asked anyone who would listen. "Little sis?" He called for his sister. He feared for their fates, for no one would tell him they were safe. He collapsed upon his knees, not knowing what to do, what to think.

A wagon approached. A kind arm around him.

"Mrs. Mason, I can't find Mamá!"

"Come, love."

He sat up. "But where is Mamá and my sis and brother?"

"They are gone, love."

"Gone? Where did they go?" The little boy of 6 pondered through sobs.

"They have gone to meet the Lord."

"No!" He fell to the earth, gripping the grass as he realized he would never see his mother, his heart again.

"Nicholaus, please."

"No!" He swatted her away. "I will wait for my papá."

Avilina sat him up and caressed his face as she shook her head and tears flowed. "No, love. You can't."

"Papá?" New tears rushed down his face as he realized his rock, his protector, was gone.

The fears and insecurities of the 6-year-old child flowed down his cheeks, tears that had not flowed in many, many years. He had heard of many families being torn to pieces by the Demolites, so why did "Anna's" revelation bring up so much sadness from his own life? Perhaps it was because she was taken from her family at such a young age, just as his family was taken from him at a young age. He tried to shake it away. He wiped his cheeks upon his sleeve and kneeled upon the cold ground.

He grasped his hands together. "Father, I thought I was over the pain. But I fear I am not. Take my fear and give me Your peace. Take the despair and give me Your hope that I know is true, but do not feel. Father, I know that even as that scared child, You were there for me. I know You are here for me now because You gave Your word. I trust in You. I trust in You. All things work together for good for those who love and trust in You."

He sat down and tried to listen to God's words. He heard nothing, but he felt a smidge of peace, a settling of his heart. It would be all right; it would all be all right. Everything works together for good for those who love and trust in God.

Placing his hands upon the stiff ground to stand, his fingers sank into the nearly frozen, uneven soil. He moved to look at the impression in the moonlight: a man's footprint. He surveyed the soil further: a woman's footprint.

He traced the outlines in his mind and studied the movements. He saw the scene before him: Bartlett went after Annabelle.

He searched the shoreline for more prints. *They both must have fallen into the river. How did she make it? How did she make it for 13 years on an island? Her poor family. I have to get her home. I have to!*

Funeral

Nicholaus was up before dawn the next day, repacking his things for the journey.

"You are in haste."

Looking up, he saw Avilina wrapped in a blanket. "I'm sorry. I didn't mean to wake you." He looked back down at the blanket he was rolling. "She has been gone for 13 years. I'm certain her family is eager to see her."

"Eager? I doubt they think she's alive."

He thought about her words and turned back toward her. "All the more reason to get her swiftly home."

"Aboly is not a swift journey," Roland, newly awake, put in as he rolled to his side on the floor to look at Nicholaus.

"Yes, I know it's not," Nicholaus stated as he stared across the room.

Roland sat up. "A good deed, no doubt, but is it really good for you, Nicholaus?"

The squire tied the leather straps around the bundle as he thought about the man's words. "I have to." He turned back to the older man. "Who else could be trusted? She is so —"

"Yes. Her beauty puts everything to shame. But how is your heart, Nicholaus?" Roland asked.

Nicholaus looked down for a moment and then declared, "I have been called to be a king's knight, and that is what I'll be."

"Good morning, child," Avilina said to Annabelle, as she poured water into the cauldron. "You are up early."

"I heard talking." She looked around at everyone in the room. "I'm not used to so many voices."

Nicholaus stood. "We will leave after the burial." He left the house to check on Cinny.

"Is he taking me to Aboly?" she asked.

"Yes, love," Avilina said with a smile.

Annabelle breathed hard and was forced to find a seat. "I never thought I would *ever* see my family again." *But what is the price? The price of Peter's life?* Any joy she might have felt at the thought of being reunited with her family was interrupted by the pain of losing Peter. Sitting there with her longing, her hope, and her sadness, she could not smile, yet she could not frown.

"What's wrong, child?" Avilina replaced the ladle and caressed Annabelle's cheek. "Are you not joyous to go home?"

"I long to go home." Annabelle slowly smiled. "The sooner I get there, the better."

"It's not an easy journey," Roland offered.

Annabelle looked at him with a concerned countenance. "How far?"

"Around 400 miles. It's a three-week journey."

Annabelle gasped.

Avilina hugged her tighter. "Take care, love. You will make it home! It is only three weeks." She knelt down in front of her. "After 13 years, that is not so long, is it?"

Annabelle thought about the kind lady's words and nodded. "You're right. It's not that long when I have waited from the age of 5 to make it back home."

The town gathered around the grave. Annabelle stood nervously on the periphery, watching one of the neighbors speak kind words.

"Father Henricus was killed a month ago. There is a visiting priest that comes, but the body might be claimed by animals by the time he makes it back — if he makes it back."

Annabelle looked up at Nicholaus to see if she had heard his whisperings correctly. She did not need to speak; her concerned face said volumes. "Five-year-old girls are not the only ones who suffer from the wrath of hate." She made a saddened face as she stiffened. "I'm sorry, Anna. Please forgive me."

The funeral broke up and people dispersed. Annabelle looked around anxiously as the crowd came closer.

"Anna," Nicholaus said, offering his arm.

Looking around as the staring, pointing people maneuvered closer — wanting to get a better look at the strange young lady with fascinating eyes — she accepted his arm out of desperation. She felt safe with him; she could relax just a bit.

She pulled the green hood of the cloak Avilina had given her over her head. "Why do they stare at me so?"

"They have never seen eyes like yours before," Nicholaus whispered over his shoulder.

"What about my eyes?" she whispered back, almost inaudibly.

Does she not know? How could she not know? He looked back at her to see if she was serious — she was. "The color," he stated.

"What about it?"

"It is — they are a shade unknown."

"Does nobody else have green eyes?" Before he could reply, she squeezed his arm and asked, "Could you tell them to stop?" Her question was funny, if not ridiculous, but he looked into her eyes and almost felt her discomfort; he would gladly shout it to the world. "I am not a piece of land to be used for their fill of beauty."

"Anna" — he continued to gaze into her eyes — "*I* know that."

"Well, they don't!"

He turned around toward her. "Let us say our farewells and be gone then."

After hugs from the Masons, she found herself upon Cinny headed away from the kind couple, headed away from the staring eyes, heading toward her family.

Safely away from the town, the eyes, and the ears, Annabelle looked down at Nicholaus, whose gaze was plastered straight ahead. "Do you forgive me?"

He looked up at her, pondering what he was to forgive. He wondered whether she was talking to him.

"Do you forgive me?" she repeated, insistent for an answer.

"What is there to forgive?"

"For not speaking to you."

He looked up at her serious face and grinned slightly. "I am pleased you are speaking to me now."

"So you forgive me?" Her face was still serious.

"Anna, there is nothing to forgive."

"I didn't trust you. I didn't mean to dishonor you, or question your character."

"My character?"

"Your virtue as a Christian man."

His gaze turned forward. "You didn't know I was a Christian."

"I knew you weren't my enemy — your actions proved as much."

Thinking of all he had done for Annabelle, he knew, if asked of him again, he would do it all over in a heartbeat. He thought about the sorry state in which he had found her, and her story. "I would rather you err on the side of caution than to trust every man." He looked straight ahead at the small path cut into the endless forest.

It took courage for her to bring up Peter's name without tears, but she attempted bravely. "Peter. He told me not to trust anybody unless they prove themselves to me."

"He sounds like a wise man."

"He was. He taught me so much." She went quiet as she

stared at Cinny's mane and fought back the sting in her eyes.

Nicholaus's mind rolled. *How could I approach such a subject?* He fought himself for several agonizing seconds and then blurted, "Like how to make it out of a river?" He looked up at her.

Annabelle felt there was more behind his question, but she would offer no answers unless he asked the question. "He taught me to swim."

"Frigid rivers," Nicholaus stated as he looked ahead, not getting the true answer he wanted. He looked at the shadow of the leaves as they passed by tree after tree. Finally, he admitted, "I saw the marks of your feet. Bartlett went after you. He drowned. How did you live?" He looked up at her when she did not answer.

She saw him waiting for an answer. Was it ladylike to be able to defend herself? She offered the best explanation she could give without revealing her fighting abilities. "Yesterday, I suppose, God did not want me to die." Though her head was facing Cinny's ears, she looked at him out of the corner of her eye.

He turned from looking at her. "That is not the first time I have heard tidings such as that. So he taught you how to keep alive — in a river."

"And in a forest and in a cave; all of my learning I owe to him."

"Who was he?"

Annabelle smiled at her thoughts of Peter. "I called him my angel. He was always there for me, protecting me from the weather, wild animals, and the Demolites." Nicholaus looked up at her at the word "Demolite" as she leaned over and sobbed, remembering the last sight she had of Peter burned into her brain: bleeding, in agony, hunched over in defeat. She nearly fell off the horse as profound emotions somersaulted forward and violently shook her to her core.

"Whoa!" Nicholaus stopped Cinny.

"Anna!" He pulled her down before she fell off.

"I left him!" The tears trickled down as her throat became prickly, and the muscles in her chin fired randomly, turning her countenance into a pitiful sight. "He was wounded and bleeding and I left him!" She cried into Nicholaus's shoulder as her legs went weak. "How could I do that?"

He did not know how to comfort her — someone he barely knew. But his heart surged with compassion, and suddenly, she was an aching member of the Body of Christ, his sister. It was at that moment that *agape* love exploded within his heart. "Anna, shh." He petted her hair. "What could you have done?" He held her head in his hands as she melted toward the forest floor. "If what you have said about him is true, then he would've wanted you to live." Her deep aching brought tears to his eyes.

"He told me to run," she revealed as her head shook in his hands. She looked up at him with reddened eyes. "I left him! I left him to die! All alone." Her body hunched over on to Nicholaus's arm, a wet and sad mess. "I left him! My father, my friend, my angel. I left him … to die … alone!"

He could barely understand her, but her sorrowful sobbing made him gasp for air out of agony for her. "Shhhh." He rocked her gently as he supported her upper body with his arms.

As her sobbing decreased, she rested safely in his arms. Her guilt and anxiety slowly faded away and thoughts of what awaited Peter now entered her mind. *Have mercy on his soul, Father! May he enter into Your Kingdom. I offer this hurt, this pain for him. Take it. Unite it with Your pain. May it be of use for him! Thank You, Father, for Your mercy. Thank You for Your love.* She felt Nicholaus's arms holding her tightly. *Thank You for Nicholaus.* She set her cheek upon his arm for a brief second, and then she rolled off his legs and sat upon the ground. She slowly looked up at him, drying her eyes. "Thank you, Nicholaus, for being such a friend."

He had never heard gratitude so sincere. He was speechless for a moment as he looked at the amazing lady before him. *After all she has endured, she is still thankful? Father, may she find Your blessing in all of her past.* He was mesmerized as he watched her stand and pat off the dirt from her dress; it was at that moment he began to admire her for her strength and fortitude.

He stood and whistled for Cinny, who came trotting back from a nearby patch of grass.

Annabelle smiled at how the horse came at his beckoning. "I'd rather walk," she said solemnly as Nicholaus offered his hand to help her up.

Nicholaus looked down at the ground "It hurts your feet, doesn't it?"

"No," she stated as she wiped away her final tears. "It has been some time since my last pair of shoes. I don't feel the rocks and twigs."

"What's in the bag?" Nicholaus asked casually to break the silence that had fallen between them.

Annabelle looked down at the worn-out satchel hanging near her right hip. She slightly shrugged her shoulders as she answered, "I don't know. Peter gave it to me. I'm not to open it until I'm in Aboly."

"You don't know what's in it?" He looked over at her.

"No."

They walked farther in silence until Annabelle offered, "You are to be a king's knight?"

Nicholaus looked to the ground. "Yes."

"How did that come to be? I mean, it sounds like you were chosen?"

"Yes. The king chose me."

"You know the king?" A glimmer of a smile appeared upon Annabelle's face. All the stories Peter had told of the princely escapades, whether they were true or not, had piqued her interest with the idea of royalty a very long time ago.

"I have met him a couple of times."

"You have met him? How did you come to meet him?" She removed a piece of hair that blew into her face.

"I ..." He did not tell many people his connection with the king, but he wanted to bare all to her honest eyes. "My uncle witnessed the marriage of the king and queen."

"He married them?" Annabelle stopped walking with a joyful expression upon her face. "Well" — she started walking again — "I guess it is only right that they were married by a bishop."

"No." He looked at her as he shook his head. "He was not a bishop then. He had just been ordained a priest." He leaned in closer to her as if to reveal a secret. "No one else would witness it."

"Why not?" she whispered.

"The king didn't want the marriage."

Annabelle looked at him with confusion. "The king did not want the marriage?"

"The *then* king, King Xavier, King Francis's father."

"Oh." Annabelle looked forward. "Why was that?" Nicholaus bit his lip as he fought his thoughts that tugged against revealing and not revealing what was not common knowledge. "Was there a reason for his unease? Did they not love each other?"

"No, they loved each other very much." He chuckled at that thought. "My uncle says he has never witnessed such a holy union."

"Oh." Annabelle patted Cinny, confused as to why there was a problem.

"Queen Clara," he continued, as Annabelle turned her head toward his voice. "She's not of noble blood."

Annabelle looked ahead, unfazed. "Is that a bad thing?"

Nicholaus was not sure how to respond; he never imagined anyone would react to such shocking news so nonchalantly. "For the spouse of a sovereign, it is ... unheard of."

"Peter said nobility comes from character, not the blood. Are you, Nicholaus, of noble blood?" She looked him in the eyes. He looked to the ground, unsure how to answer with his present situation on his mind. She looked down at him. "Do you not know?"

He looked up, taking a deep breath, wondering why he was revealing everything to her. "My father, Josephus, was general commander of the king's soldiers in the crusade." He looked over at her.

Her countenance did not change much. "Is that King Xavier's or King Francis's soldiers?"

Nicholaus smiled. "It is Anchony's soldiers. He served under both kings."

Annabelle smiled, realizing how silly her question was. "So, does he still serve?"

Nicholaus's smile faded. "No."

She didn't know what to say. Had she offended him? How could she ask?

He spoke before she could question further. "My father was a great man, but the last few months of his life were a mystery. Some called him a traitor, some a lunatic."

Annabelle shook her head, not knowing how to respond. "But the king does not?" He looked at her. "If he wishes you to become a knight, he must not believe your father to be a traitor."

The truth of her words hit him with strength. He had made the connection before, but somehow, hearing it from her mouth made it much clearer. Despite the fact that he was the best tracker in the land and his uncle had married the royal couple, King Francis would not want anything to do with a traitor's son. A weight seemed to lift from his shoulders.

There was silence between them for several minutes. Nicholaus, not wanting to appear rude, asked, "And your father, Anna. What does he do?"

"Ah ..." Annabelle looked at her feet, attempting to arouse memories that were buried deep. "My memories are so few. I can't say for certain."

"You are from Aboly? Is he in service for the king?"

"I don't know ..."

"You have siblings?"

She met his gaze as she pondered the question. "Yes, or at least, I did."

Nicholaus was not sure how to respond to such an answer. He could not ensure her siblings were alive.

"Four." She continued, "Three older, one younger."

"Brothers and sisters?"

"Yes. Two older brothers." She looked away as a melancholy overcame her. "I have forgotten most of what I once knew about them." She gasped in remembrance and sadness. "The strongest memory I have is a selfish one: I took my younger sister's rattle and buried it beneath a window."

"You buried it?" He laughed at the image of a young Annabelle digging in the dirt.

"Yes." She chuckled with disgust. "I was so selfish."

"Why did you do it?"

"I thought she took Mamá away from me."

"Sibling strife." He smiled at a few of his own moments.

"My memory of the rattle is so clear. It was painted white with a flower upon it." She looked at him with great concern. "Why is it I know such qualities of a selfish act but the qualities of my family members have escaped me?"

He could not give an answer to her question, but offered what he could: "I lost a brother and sister when I was young. My memory of them is poor."

"Were they seized as well?"

"No." He looked at her. "No, they were not."

No further information was needed for Annabelle; she knew what his answer implied: They were killed. Annabelle studied the man out of the corner of her eye. *What wickedness has he seen? But yet he is unmoved, strong in character, steadfast. Thank You, God, for helping Nicholaus in his life.*

Confrontation

Annabelle was atop Cinny when she heard the distinctive sound of horse hooves and voices — both equestrian and human. They both looked up as the entourage galloped forward. Nicholaus moved Cinny to the side of the path as the horses and riders approached.

Annabelle spotted a lady in fine, embroidered linen and silks with a large, jeweled necklace glimmering in the sun's light. Her hair was perfectly hidden behind a wimple. She glanced over at Annabelle, lifting her nose higher. There were six men surrounding her in chain mail and different-colored tabards. The one man not in chain mail, who was riding beside her, halted his horse at the sight of Nicholaus.

"So, you are on your way and off my land." He smiled at Nicholaus. "Good. I think I shall knock down that feeble place strewn together by common laborers and turn it into a pig sty." Nicholaus swallowed hard as the man continued. "It's not worth much anyway, just a foolish reward for a serf with a stick."

"Lord Rackus," the lady, 20 years his junior, called as she looked back at Nicholaus and Annabelle with her upturned nose. "Let's not linger here any longer."

"You're right, darling." The lord sat up straighter looking at Nicholaus. "I shouldn't waste my time with one of such low form." He looked at Annabelle, donned in her dirty dress with her long braid, and then over at one of his knights. "Who is she?"

Nicholaus gestured Annabelle to get off Cinny so he could face the mounted knight on equal terms. Slipping off, she hugged Cinny's neck on the opposite side as the knight galloped toward them.

"Who is she?" a knight asked as Nicholaus climbed on to Cinny and faced the man. The knight looked Nicholaus up and down and smirked. "You decline to answer?" The knight shook his head and snickered. "The squire trained by a blind man — shameful." Though willing to throw insults Nicholaus's way, he was not willing to take a chance wielding the sword; he was fully aware who Nicholaus's father was, and he was not willing to test the son. Flaring his nostrils, he spat on the ground in front of Nicholaus as the group rode away.

Nicholaus pulled Annabelle on to the horse, and they rode off in the opposite direction. A quarter of an hour later, Nicholaus stopped Cinny and jumped down.

Annabelle looked down at Nicholaus's head as he looked in the direction they came from and swallowed hard. He could feel her staring at him. He turned around and spoke slowly. "That was Count and Countess Rackus of Basteel."

"Basteel?"

He cleared his throat as he led Cinny back onto the path. "We are in Basteel."

"Your land is in Basteel?" she probed.

He took another deep breath. "Yes." He stopped Cinny and turned toward her. "The fief was given to my great-great-grandfather for his service to Count Rackus's grandfather."

"He can't just take the land back, can he?" she asked as she dismounted Cinny.

He looked from the ground to her gaze. "Rendability. Yes, he can. It's when the land owner — whether king or duke — takes back the land he has given to another."

"Even though it's been in your family for five generations?"

He turned toward the path and walked forward, encouraging Cinny. "I'm not faithful to him, and he knows it. That's why he takes the land back."

"Not faithful toward your lord?" she stated with confusion as she looked at the path ahead.

"I have seen the way he treats people — without dignity, like common animals. It made me question my calling to be a knight. But my uncle, he told me how I could fight for a real Christian, for the king himself. He told me the king asked for me." He was silent for a moment but then continued, "A few weeks ago, I told Count Rackus I wouldn't be his knight. He told me he would take the fief if I did not fight for him; I did not take his bait."

She walked forward considering his words, and then asked, "What did the Count mean about the common laborers building your home? He said it as if it would harm you." She looked at his profile.

He swallowed hard and finally answered. "The keep was damaged the night my family was killed. Mr. Mason led the servants in rebuilding it. They removed all the old stones and took apart the fortress walls to build another."

"They must have thought well of your family to be so willing to help." She stared at his profile, but he did not reply.

Sacrament of Penance

It was three days of traveling until they came to the small town of Edgarton. Annabelle was both excited to see another town but also apprehensive about the many people who were within it. As they drew closer, they heard bells ringing. Annabelle's face lit up in excitement. "Are those from a church?"

"Yes. You see the stone steeple?" He pointed in the direction of the ringing.

Annabelle's eyes widened as she nodded her head. As they drew nearer, they saw a few horses tied up outside.

He offered his arms to lower her safely to the ground.

"Thank you," she replied as he helped her down.

He made sure he set her down quickly. He looked to the ground. "You're welcome." He took the reins to tie Cinny to a post.

Annabelle looked at the church across the street. How she longed to go inside, to celebrate the Sacraments. She looked down at her naked feet, her tattered dress. She felt unworthy to set foot in such a marvelous place that miraculously contained God.

"Do you wish to go in?" Nicholaus asked, observing her longing eyes.

"I do."

"It must be a special Mass, this late in the day. I suppose we should wait until it gets over."

Annabelle nodded her head.

Nicholaus offered her a place to sit on a fallen log.

"I have been sitting all day. I would rather not. But you, you should sit. You have done nothing but walk."

"I will stand," he said with a smile as he placed his hands around his belt, his sword secure on his left hip.

Annabelle looked over at the church and the few wagons and horses. "How many people do you think are in there?"

"Thirty or so. Are you all right?"

Annabelle took a deep breath. "It's only … will they point and stare?"

"I won't leave your side." He did not know if he should have offered that as a comfort. "If you wish it," he added quickly.

Annabelle looked at him. "Thank you."

"Think about all the great things that come to pass in that place. Will that help you to overcome your unease?"

"Peter told me about all the wonderful things I was missing. He said he longed to return to Anchony for the Eucharist alone. That and the Sacrament of Penance."

"I think my uncle would have liked him."

She turned toward Nicholaus with a sad face at the memory of Peter. "Yes, I think he would."

They stood silently beside each other across from the small church, patiently waiting.

"The doors are opening," Nicholaus observed as Annabelle's eyes wandered over the terrain of the land. She looked up toward the doors. "I see no corpse. It must be a wedding." Nicholaus pointed across the road.

They watched as the people exited the church and walked to an accompanying field. Food, tables, and musical instruments appeared out of nowhere.

They were spotted by the partygoers, who kept a keen eye on Nicholaus and his sword. The villagers, watchful and weary, had fallen victim to the Demolites a couple years earlier and were not eager to trust strangers. They offered no welcome.

"Do you wish for Penance?" Nicholaus asked Annabelle as she studied the villagers, just as wary of them as they were of her.

She looked at Nicholaus with large eyes. "Could I?"

Nicholaus smiled and bowed his head. "If I can find the priest." The dancing and music stopped as Nicholaus walked over. He offered his open hands to show that he was not intending to attack. "I want to speak to the priest."

"What do you want with him?" one man asked.

"I only wish to speak with him. It's about the Sacrament of Penance." They all eyed him suspiciously.

"Here." He heard a voice from the back of the crowd as a man in black walked forward. "I am here."

"Father —" A female villager begged him to be cautious. He put up his hand. "It's all right." He looked at Nicholaus. "You wish to confess?"

"Yes, but not only me. There is another who has never been." He looked over his shoulder to where Annabelle previously stood. She had sneaked over to the church step to escape the eyes of the crowd. He looked around quickly until he found her sitting in the shadows. "She is over here." He pointed with his hand. The priest looked but saw nothing. "Anna." Nicholaus encouraged her to show herself so the priest would not think he was trying to lure him over.

She nervously stood up and peeked around the corner of the church and then hastily retreated to her previous spot.

The priest, having more faith in the veracity of Nicholaus's words, walked toward the church. "I'm Fr. Davidson. I'm sorry for my distrust but" — he licked his lips as he thought about his words — "these are perilous times in which we live." He looked at Annabelle. "He said this is your first time?"

Annabelle stared wondrously at him: God's instrument before her eyes. She was speechless for a moment. After several seconds of silence, she finally mustered a word: "Yes."

The priest took a few steps toward the church doors. "You have been baptized?"

"Yes, as a baby, I believe."

"Is it Anna?" The priest looked at her. "Please, follow me." He walked up the steps and opened the door.

Nicholaus helped her to stand. "I'll wait for you out here," he said.

Annabelle looked at Nicholaus with half jubilation and half fear. She cautiously walked up the steps and stopped outside the doors, hesitant to walk inside without shoes. She looked down at her callused and dirty feet, not knowing if she should enter.

The priest noticed her hesitancy. "When standing before the burning bush, Moses was told to remove his sandals. Do not worry about entering such a holy place without shoes."

Nodding her head, she stepped inside as she pulled her hood over her head. The coolness of the sanctifying place engulfed her in peace. Through the wooden lattice separating the chancel from the nave, her eyes were drawn to the one flame left burning in the entire church: the flickering flame of the altar lamp telling of Christ's presence in the tabernacle. She gasped as she realized the Man who was viciously crucified nearly 1200 years before, her Savior, was silently waiting for her to come, to adore Him in a resurrected, miraculous form. Closing her eyes, she could almost feel the presence of the heavenly angels, on their knees adoring Him. It felt so real; she opened her eyes to see if she could see them, but the lone flame and simple cabinet next to the altar were all her eyes were permitted to view.

"So, why have you never gone to the Sacrament of Penance?"

Her eyes moved from the flame to the priest standing to her left. "I have been on an island for 13 years. I was raised by a good man. He taught me in all subjects, including the

Sacraments. Oh, to hear such words of absolution." Her eyes roamed around the room looking at the stained-glass windows, with the slowly fading light behind them, in awe of the whole place.

"Please just wait here, and I will be right with you." Annabelle did as instructed. She watched the priest disappear into the sacristy and return donned in a stole. He walked up to her and began: "*In nomine Patris, et Filii, et Spiritus Sancti. Amen.*" Annabelle signed herself. "I know this is your first time. Please name your sins."

Annabelle looked down at the floor as she thought through her memories and examined her conscience. "Bless me, Father, for I have sinned." Tears were brought to her eyes as she thought of all the times she had offended God in her life. "When I was a child, I was selfish; I would take my sister's toys, even though I knew it was wrong. I have doubted God's love for me at different times in my life; I have not trusted completely in His divine care." Annabelle recalled all the sins of comission and omission she could remember and ended with, "And for all the sins I have forgotten."

The priest spoke to her a little while about her sins, what she needed to work on, how she could do so, as well as asking her questions. He gave her a penance and asked her to say a prayer of contrition:

"My God, I am truly sorry with all my heart for all my sins I have committed against You." Tears trickled out of her eyes. "I've chosen to do bad, and I've failed to do good. Help me, Father, to always keep on the right path." In Latin she added, "*De profundis clamavi ad te, Domine,*" which means, "Out of the depths I have cried to thee, O Lord." She barely whispered, "Amen."

The priest put his anointed hands above her head. It felt as though he was pushing down on her, though that was impossible since he did not touch her. By the authority given to the apostles, the priest spoke the mysterious and miraculous words in the language of the Church, and she could feel the Holy Spirit come down upon her as he said: "*Ego te absolvo a peccatis tuis in nomine Patris, et Filii, et Spiritus Sancti. Amen,*" meaning, "I absolve you of your sins in the name of the Father and the Son and the Holy Spirit. Amen."

She felt as if a 20-pound weight had been lifted from her shoulders. Tears rolled down her checks — but they were not of sadness or regret, but tears of joy. *Oh, the mercy of God! To stoop so low as to forgive me. To stoop so low as to sacrifice Himself for me, to die for me, and to give His resurrected Self to me to eat.* She fell to her knees out of joy and relief and was so profoundly touched that she did not wish to move; she wished to kneel there in her clean state forever.

The priest opened the church door and addressed Nicholaus. "And you?"

Nicholaus looked over at Annabelle kneeling motionless and nodded. "Yes, Father." The priest walked outside.

"So, you experienced a Sacrament?" Nicholaus asked Annabelle as they walked out of the church.

Recovering from her experience with the divine, her emerald eyes sparkled. "Yes! It was powerful! Penance! And some day Confirmation and Holy Communion!" Her enthusiasm was bubbling over, and it could not help but excite Nicholaus as well.

They walked toward Cinny to camp for the night as storm clouds gathered.

Dreams

"Where are you going?" Standing next to Cinny, she had to yell to be heard above the thunder as her hair dripped in the sudden downpour.

"To find shelter."

Nicholaus ran across the muddy road. Annabelle watched as he knocked on the rectory door. Words were exchanged with gesturing and soon Nicholaus was running back toward her.

"Father knows a place for you to stay." Nicholaus talked into her ear so she could hear above the roar of the storm. "Elderly sisters, very hospitable, according to him. A couple houses down." He guided her down the flooding street.

He knocked upon the door and, within a few moments, she was inside a dry, quiet, homey cottage that was warmed by two kind smiles and a large fire. She looked back as Nicholaus turned toward the door. "Where are you going?"

"I will be back in the morning, Anna."

"Where will you stay?"

"I must find shelter for Cinny. I'll stay with her."

You're leaving me alone? She turned around; the two ladies were fixing a place for her to sleep. She took a deep breath. *I'm not alone.* Hearing the door close, she shut her eyes. *God is always with me.*

"Would you like any tea, dear?" Margery offered.

She opened her eyes. "No, thank you."

The other lady, Eva, returned from behind a curtain and handed Annabelle a cloth and a nightgown. "You're soaked."

"Thank you." Annabelle took it to ring out her hair.

"Put more wood on the fire, if you like," Eva stated as she disappeared behind the divider.

"Set your clothes by the flames, they'll dry during the night." Margery followed her sister.

"Oh ... all right." Annabelle was left to an empty room. Laying her head upon her arm after her prayers, she watched the fire dance until she fell asleep.

She was in a fancy dress, in a fancy room. It was crowded, very crowded. She was distressed at the closeness of the people. A man she did not know approached closely, uncomfortably so. She took a step sideways and he followed.

"Do you know who I am?" the man offered without decorum. "I am Edleton Haubson, count of Westcoast."

Annabelle spoke, impassioned, "I don't care who you are — kindly give me space." He grabbed at her wrist; she planted him on the ground before he could touch her. "Your birth doesn't set you apart from any other in this room. You are no more special than I, for we are all made in the image of God. However, wisdom can set a person apart, and that is where we differ — for I act properly and you do not." Removing her foot from his chest, she released his arm.

After a brief moment of recovery upon the floor, his face turned red, and he yelled for help: "Sirs!"

The conversations around the room ceased. The whole room became stagnant as they stared at Annabelle and the count.

She wanted to flee. She turned to her right and found a comforting arm: Nicholaus. Suddenly she was before a man sitting upon a throne.

"What is this about, Lord Haubson?" the king asked.

"He laid hands upon one of noble blood." He pointed to the man on her right, Nicholaus.

Annabelle shook her head.

"How do you plead?" the king asked Nicholaus.

He stepped forward in front of his Anna. "Guilty."

"*No*," *Annabelle countered behind him, shaking her head. She grabbed at his shoulder.* "*What are you doing?*"

"*Anna.*" *Nicholaus looked into her eyes.*

"*Why are you doing this?*" *Annabelle asked out of desperation.*

"*You don't know?*" *Nicholaus said with a flash of pain across his face.*

"*It was him!*" *The count demanded.*

Annabelle, closing her eyes, took a step forward, and found courage to speak. "*They are both lying, sire.*"

"*No, Anna!*"

She ignored his pleas. "*But one for noble reasons and the other for cowardly.*" *She lowered her head, for she did not know if she should have spoken.*

"*Go on,*" *the king demanded.*

"*It was not the gentleman who brought the count to the floor; it was I.*" *She could feel the air being sucked out of the room.* "*The noble man,*" *she continued,* "*is lying to spare me from the outcome of my action. And the count*" — *she raised her head slightly* — "*doesn't want it to be known that he was so easily overtaken by a woman.*"

Whispers abounded throughout the room. The king uneasily shifted his weight as he sat on his throne. The queen, princes and princesses, knights, and guests of the royal court all stood around waiting for the next move.

The king shifted his focus from the young lady to the two men. "*Is this true?*" *The count vehemently shook his head.*

Nicholaus, turning his gaze to the floor and then meeting the king's glance, nodded and said: "*It is true, sire.*"

"*Do you know it is treason to lie to your king?*"

Her movement awoke her with a swiftly-pacing heart. She looked around — she was not outside, there was no Nicholaus across from the fire. It was then that she remembered where she was. Sitting up for a moment, she looked into the blackness of the room. Realizing Nicholaus had not just been found guilty of treason, her heart slowly calmed. Laying her head back down, it took her some time to fall back asleep.

Nicholaus sat on the damp straw next to the resting Cinny. He thought about Annabelle's contagious smile after receiving absolution; the thought of her happiness made him happy. His smile slowly faded when he realized how attached he was becoming to the lady he was assisting. "Father," he prayed aloud. "Help me not to fall in love. I only wish to do Your will." Lowering his head, he closed his eyes. God's will, Nicholaus thought, was for him to become a king's knight.

He stood in front of his uncle, outside the church doors. His uncle patted him on the back as he pointed to Nicholaus's left. Nicholaus turned. There was his Anna, his beautiful Anna with her brunette hair up and thin curls cascading down the sides of her face from beneath her veil. Her emerald eyes sparkled. Her lips smiled. He took her hand and kissed it. He felt her hand; his lips felt her skin. It was real. He gently placed a ring upon her left finger and echoed the sacred words, "I, Nicholaus Josephus Hunts, take thee …"

Nicholaus sat straight up. The deluge was still hammering its song upon the roof. He rubbed his face with a pounding heart. *What was that?* He looked at the sleeping Cinny. *Is that Your help?* He was afraid to go back to sleep. *Dreams mean nothing unless sent by the Lord. Dreams mean nothing. Was it sent by the Lord? No! It could not be! I've been called to be a knight. I've been called to be a knight. Dreams mean nothing! Dreams mean nothing!* He scooted up against the wall, half afraid to fall back asleep.

Annabelle was up before the sisters. She donned her dry dress and sat next to the fire pit, still pondering over the significance of her dream.

He wouldn't do that, would he?

There was a knock on the door. She got up quickly, eager to take her mind off of her thoughts.

"Nicholaus." She automatically smiled when she saw half of his face through the crack in the door.

"I just wanted to make sure you were safe." He looked up at her.

She opened the door to let him in and whispered, "They're not up yet." She heard the birds chirping. "Is it a morning of beauty after the rain?"

He stepped aside from the door so she could see outside. "It is." She stared out the door. "Would you like to go for a walk?"

"I would."

He led her outside. "Did you sleep well?"

She thought about her dream and being in the lonely house. "As well as I could, I suppose."

"It was not restful?" he asked further.

"I slept … I only … I would choose to be around people I know."

"Were they rude?"

"No." She shook her head.

He turned her toward himself. "What's wrong?"

"I awoke in the night, and I didn't know where I was, and you weren't there." The statement jabbed at his heart. He pulled his arms back. She stepped away from him and then turned around to face him. "I have to ask you, you wouldn't lie for me, would you?"

"Lie?"

"To the king," she added.

Nicholaus looked at her strangely. "Bearing false witness is against the —"

"Eighth commandment. Yes, I know." She finished his statement as she shook her head. "It's only, I had a dream."

As did I. He stared at her for a moment. "What was it?"

She shook her head as she looked at the saturated ground. "Forget it. It shall not come to pass."

"Well," he said, not willing to admit that he, too, had had a dream that would forever tug at his heart. "I think we should head back now; Mass will be starting shortly."

Annabelle slowly walked through the massive frame of the heavy wooden doors to the church. Her eyes were delighted by the multi-colored sunlight streaming through the windows from the golden rays outside, a new experience from the evening before. She stood in awe of the mosaic glass with varied hues and the vibrant shades painted upon the walls and floors by the sunlight.

Amongst all the splashes of color, it was still that one flickering candle, suspended before the Sacrament House to the right of the altar, that trapped her attention, as it always would. It danced with the draft, drawing one's attention to the built-in wooden cabinet housing the Eucharist.

People moved into the church around her as she stood awestruck once again. When she did not move for a moment, Nicholaus leaned toward her ear and pointed to the holy water font. "Do you want to bless yourself?"

Annabelle's attention was taken off the wooden cabinet that held the precious miracle. She looked over at Nicholaus, smiled, and nodded. He guided her over to the basin where he stuck his right middle finger in the blessed water. She followed his lead by signing herself — as she had done so many times in the past — but with the addition of the holy water on her finger, she was reminded that she had been baptized into the Body of Christ.

Annabelle, holding tightly to Nicholaus's elbow, walked through the crowd and genuflected to Jesus in the tabernacle. *What a small action, for all You have done for me.*

The Introit was chanted as the priest walked toward the altar from the sacristy behind the wooden screen. Annabelle's eyes began to water; she was overwhelmed with such love. Thinking back on her life, she was so thankful for Peter. Though he was gone now, she was experiencing all the wonderful things he had described to her.

Father Davidson spoke the Latin words, his back toward the congregation. Though not able to hear all the words, she marveled at the interaction between the priest and the acolytes; like a cantor of a song, the priest spoke the verses and the acolytes responded with the chorus, with occasional interjections from the choir, the parishioners. And like a dance, they moved across the sanctuary in perfect harmony with the beat.

With the utterance of the words of consecration in the air and the ringing of the bells, the transubstantiated Eucharist was held high. Although already kneeling, she did not think that was adequate; honestly, nothing was good enough to be in front of the same Sacred Heart of Jesus that bled to death for her centuries before. She wished to prostrate herself, bury herself in a hole in the wonder, in the awe. Physical space, however, did not allow such actions.

She sniffled as tears fell down her cheeks. Nicholaus looked over at her and grinned. Annabelle looked over at him and smiled at his amusement, knowing that no one else in the church was crying at that moment.

What's wrong with me?

In her mind she heard a response: *"What is wrong with everybody else?"*

Annabelle grabbed Nicholaus's hand. He squeezed it gently.

She watched, transfixed, as the sacred Host was placed upon the tongues of the selected few who, having prepared themselves spiritually and physically, crossed the lattice wall to receive the Body and Blood of Christ. A hole of longing opened in her heart; she suddenly felt so sad for all those who had received their First Communion but, not properly prepared, could not receive Him on this day.

With this burden on her mind, the indescribable Mass was over and people were exiting the sacred place. She watched as others filed past in silence, cognizant of God's presence. Though the lattice dividing the nave and chancel was visually obtrusive, it was a great reminder of the Holy of Holies behind the screen.

She looked down at the still-praying Nicholaus, concentrating on the sublime within him.

"Are you all right?" Nicholaus asked as they stepped outside of the church.

She shook her head in distress. "I can't receive Him."

Nicholaus felt her longing, and it pained him; he offered the only words that could give comfort: "My uncle is traveling to Aboly."

"Your uncle? The bishop?" she said with hope as she looked up at him.

"Yes."

Her heart began to pound harder in anticipation, but then a cloud of doubt entered her mind. "When will he arrive? What if he doesn't make it?"

"Doesn't make it?" Nicholaus looked at her strangely.

"I'm sorry, Nicholaus, but you said the Demolites attack priests, and if they come for —" she spoke softly.

Nicholaus nodded his head as he interrupted to calm her anxious thoughts. "I did, but" — he guided her down the steps and toward Cinny, away from other ears — "my uncle …" He thought about his words. "My father was the first to teach me how to hunt, track, and fight, but my uncle continued my learning."

She looked from Cinny to him. "Your uncle taught you how to fight?"

He helped her up onto the horse. "Yes."

Tragedy

Two days later they came upon the village of Napala. This village was different; as they neared it, the first thing Annabelle noticed was the silence. It was odd enough not to hear human voices and noises from their daily activities, but there were no animal noises: no goats, no sheep, no pigs. The silence was eerie.

The closer they approached, the more desolate it became. She looked at the wattle and daub huts; there was no smoke emerging from the center of the roofs. "Where is everyone?"

Nicholaus knelt down and studied the tracks in the mud. He studied the hoof prints that emerged from behind the stick fences to the central path in the middle of the village.

Annabelle, looking to her right, spotted the church with its door cracked open. She dismounted and wandered over as Nicholaus went from hut to hut to search for any signs of life. As she pushed the door open, the light streaming in from the broken windows revealed the destruction: Nothing was left untouched. There was no candle glowing upon the altar; it was cold and shattered upon the floor. The tabernacle did not rest comfortably in its place of reverence on the altar; broken and empty, it had been shoved off its home and dropped upon the floor.

Her heart ached over such disrespect and sacrilege. Kneeling down in front of the tabernacle, she turned it upright as she heard Nicholaus enter. With tears in her eyes, she turned to him. "They stole Jesus." He knelt down beside her and helped her pick up the pieces. There was nothing they could do about it now but pray — pray for the ones who left such destruction, that their hearts of stone would be softened. They silently walked out of the church.

Annabelle looked at the church and village, shaking her head. "What took place?"

"They ran to the motte and bailey."

"The Demolites?" Annabelle stared into the distance, looking at the prints in the mud.

"No question."

"How long ago?"

Nicholaus shook his head as they walked toward the wooden fortress, the local shelter for the villagers in times of attack. "A day or so."

She gasped as she noticed the open doors.

"Anna." Nicholaus looked at her. "Stay here with Cinny." She watched him walk up the motte into the bailey as she petted the horse to try to keep herself calm. He knelt next to a body and then moved to another.

Hearing horses and people, she looked to the surrounding land. When she spotted their outlines, she immediately ran up the motte. "Nicholaus! Someone is coming!" He stood as she flew in beside him. He whistled for Cinny as he drew his sword. He moved Annabelle and Cinny toward the tower in the middle of the bailey.

Annabelle looked at the ground and gasped at the loss of life in horror: Bodies, old and young alike, were strewn everywhere as their blood had soaked into the soil. She knelt next to a body, a woman around her age. Her clothes were torn and disheveled. She spotted the marks in the mud where she had tried to escape from her captor. Annabelle closed her eyes as she shook her head in sorrow.

"They don't care about right and wrong." She recalled Peter's words as she felt his satchel against her hip. Opening her eyes, she moved a lock of shoulder-length hair away from the lady's face. Her fingers brushed the cold, bloodless fore-

head. She straightened the lady's dress. *Have mercy on her, Father. May she enter into Your Kingdom.*

As she prayed, the men on horseback entered the bailey and looked at Nicholaus and Annabelle. "Who are you?" the leader demanded.

Nicholaus eyed the throng cautiously. "Who are you?"

Annabelle, transfixed by the scene on the ground, looked around. *How many had met the same fate? Have mercy on them all.* She stood and looked around in despair, her thoughts turning to the Demolites. *Have they not been told of the sacredness of the human body? Or do they not care? Do they have no fear of God? Justice shall find them someday.*

As Annabelle stood with her back to the throng, the leader finally spoke. "We are from Agonen. When no one from Napala showed for market day, I sent my boy to check on them." The man looked around at the bodies. "He returned with grave tidings." His eyes returned to Nicholaus. "I ask again — who are you?"

Nicholaus lowered his sword. "I am Squire Nicholaus Hunts. We were on our way to Aboly when we came upon … this." He looked around, disgusted at the sight, and then glanced over his shoulder. "Anna, don't look."

Their leader spoke again. "We shall take care of them — we don't need help from others." Nicholaus nodded in understanding.

She turned toward Nicholaus, finishing her thought out loud: "If not in this life, then in the —" She stopped midsentence as the group of men looked at her, pasting their eyes upon her.

"We could always use more help." A man without a horse dared to speak as he stepped forward.

Nicholaus's blood began to boil. He stepped in front of her. "No, we'll be on our way."

"Another two hands are always good." The man continued to inch forward, slowly smirking.

"Saloman," the leader called to keep the man in check.

"I ... I ..." The man looked from his leader to Nicholaus.

"Anna, get on the horse," Nicholaus said over his shoulder. She could not have been happier to oblige.

Annabelle sat in front of the fire, emotionally drained. When she closed her eyes, she saw the bodies. She pulled Avilina's cloak around her as she tried to forget the horrid sight, but she could not. It was real. It was just one of the multitudes of villages attacked by the Demolites across the kingdom. She shook her head as she started to shiver, more from disbelief and disgust than cold. "Peter told me of the wickedness of the Demolites but I ... I had no ... Seeing it ..."

"I wish you hadn't."

She laid down on her right side. *I wish I hadn't.* She stared blankly at the fire. Nicholaus retrieved his wool blanket, which was strapped to Cinny. Unrolling it, he laid it on top of her. She turned her head to look at him. "How can they be stopped?"

He looked into her saddened eyes. "I wish I knew."

Her eyes turned toward the fire. "Has that come to pass in Aboly?"

Nicholaus knew there had been attacks in Aboly, but he did not have the heart to give her that information.

She turned her head back toward him. "Your silence tells me yes." She gasped. "Oh!" Worry overtook her. "What if they're dead? Where will I go?" Looking back at the fire, she gasped as uncertainty began to entangle her imagination. What would become of her? *Oh, Father!*

Nicholaus watched her silently praying. He turned away — he could take no more. What *would* become of her? Nicholaus could not stand to see her in need of anything. *Father, what am I to do? If her family is dead, what? I am to be a king's knight.*

"Are you?"

What? He looked around the forest in his confusion. *Of course, I've been called since I was a child.*

"Have you?" He stood up looking at the canopy of trees. The vivid marriage dream flashed before him. He shook his head, attempting to shake it from his memory; it did not work. He took a deep breath as he walked over to the horse. Cinny rubbed him on the shoulder. He turned toward her and, rubbing her head, confided, "I have never needed my uncle more."

Sitting down opposite the fire, he studied his companion, burying her face into her fists as she prayed with fervor. "Anna." She looked up at him, but he could say no more; he could give no promises. His heart ached for her happiness. He was beginning to realize how entangled his heart already was to his "Anna."

"We should come upon a broken keep in the next day or so." Nicholaus stared at the fire 10 feet in front of him with twigs in his hands.

"A broken keep?" She watched the fire dance in front of his face. It had been a few days since the awful sight at Napala. Since she could not rid her mind of the sight and smell, instead of trying to push it away, she accepted it and prayed for all those involved. In this way, she was able to cope with the horrid scene burned into her brain.

"Yes, well … it once was not so broken."

Annabelle shifted her weight as she sat on the cold ground. "Why is it in such a state?"

"The knight that lives there, Sir Machenus, figures it is not worth keeping in good order."

"Not worth keeping? No one will try to take it?"

Nicholaus bent down and picked up another twig. "He

thinks no one will attack it if it is not worth much." He stood up with his armful of twigs. "He's a king's knight."

"A king's knight?" Annabelle sat up. "So far from Aboly?"

"He's no longer on duty."

"Why is that?"

Nicholaus dumped the twigs next to the fire and then looked over at Annabelle. "His sight has failed him."

"Oh. Was that due to his service?"

Nicholaus shook his head. "He has never told me."

"You know him well?" She cocked her head.

"I was his page and squire."

"His squire? So, you didn't live with your uncle?"

Nicholaus shook his head. "My uncle was in charge of my learning."

She shifted her weight. "So why are you not a priest?"

Nicholaus smiled as he thought about his uncle. "My uncle knows it is not up to us, but up to God." He turned and looked at Annabelle as she picked a weed next to her. "It's a calling, and I am called to be a knight." Pushing away the disturbing dream that insistently crept into his awareness every time "a calling from God" was mentioned, he tried to ignore the quickening of his heart — the occurrence that followed every memory of the vivid dream.

"How do you know?" She looked at him and then at the flower.

"I wasn't there to defend my family, so I want to be there to defend another."

"You weren't there?" She looked at him quizzically as she tossed the flower aside.

Nicholaus was silent for a moment and then spoke softly, "I snuck out of our bailey to play in the woods. I was but 6. I was a grand knight amongst the trees; the forest animals became the Demolites. I chased them about with a stick. I had such joy, but on my way home, I got lost. I finally found my way back late in the evening." Nicholaus's chin began to quiver. "The keep was on fire. Everything was destroyed, including my family." Annabelle watched a sadness overshadow his face as he continued, "I returned to a slain family. I was playing in the woods while my family was slaughtered." He looked up at the night sky. "Mrs. Mason was there. She took me in until my uncle came."

"You were but a boy, Nicholaus." She shook her head as she looked from the fire toward his eyes. "There was nothing you could do. You would have been killed yourself."

Nicholaus closed his eyes and took a deep breath. "I know. But as I looked at the body of my mother, the spark, lit by my own father, was set on fire in my heart." Annabelle stared at the crackling flames as he continued, "A couple of years later, my uncle and I were in town when there was a tournament. I saw the knights ride so bravely toward one another with their lances. And they took the pain. I gasped when one brave knight was thrust to the ground, his lance splintering into pieces. And the crowd cheered, and then I saw boys, my age, helping the hurting knight off the field. 'I am to be one. I am to be a knight!' I told my uncle right there."

"So then you found Sir Machenus, and he taught you?"

"No." Nicholaus looked over at her with pain in his eyes. "A boy should not be taught by a knight who is losing his sight."

She shook her head in confusion.

For clarification, he had to admit: "None of the other knights would take me. 'A son of a traitor,' they claimed as they despised me." A shiver cascaded up and down Nicholaus's back as he recalled the bitter words.

"Why did Sir Machenus take you then?"

Nicholaus looked straight ahead. "He didn't want to at first — because he was going blind, not because of me. He knew my father, but my uncle; the head of the king's knights, Grand Sir Doey; and the king himself convinced him. I remember so clearly the king kneeling down and rubbing my face. 'He's already on the road to becoming a great knight. He only needs the proper teaching from a great knight. And who better than one who knew his father?'"

Annabelle's heart quickened as she listened to the words of the king. "So he knows you well?"

"Sir Machenus? Yes, I was with —"

"No, the king." Annabelle stated as the words spewed from her mouth. She was drawn to any words about the king.

"It's more like he knows *of* me."

"What's he like?"

Nicholaus looked over at Annabelle. "He's known as the most just king Anchony has ever known. He judges people by their character, not their birth."

Sir Machenus

"There it is." Nicholaus looked ahead with a smile at a sad-looking fortress planted in the quietness of the forest.

Annabelle stared in wonder; a paradox was before her eyes: the majesty of a miniature stone castle with a broken outer defense.

"Sir Machenus!" Nicholaus quickened his step as they entered inside the pathetic bailey.

A man emerged from the two-story keep with a sword secured in his grip. "Who's there?"

"It is I, Squire Nicholaus Hunts." He ran toward the stone dwelling.

"Nicholaus? My boy!" The knight dropped his sword and held his hands toward Nicholaus at the height of his head. Nicholaus placed the man's hands upon his face. "Nicholaus, how long has it been? How you have changed." He felt Nicholaus's face and then his shoulders. "You are a man before me."

Nicholaus hugged him. "It has been too long."

Annabelle slowly walked toward the castle. The old man's head turned when he heard the breaking of a twig. "You brought another?"

Nicholaus looked back at Annabelle. "Yes, this is Anna. Annabelle. I am taking her to her family in Aboly."

A slight moment of pain flashed upon the man's face before he shook it away. "Come in, come in." The man waved the young travelers into his lodging.

Nicholaus waited for a slightly nervous Annabelle to enter first. Grabbing her hand as she entered, he gave it a slight squeeze. The squire's eyes said it all: *Worry not; you're safe here.*

She smiled back at him and entered into the cozy castle. Her nose was bombarded with the smell of cooking deer meat as her eyes adjusted to the dim light. A form hunched over the fireplace, stirring a pot, emerged from the haziness.

"Lucinda, we have company. Squire Nicholaus and Annabelle." He turned back toward Nicholaus and Annabelle.

The lady turned away from her cooking, wiped her hands on her apron, and smiled, "It is a pleasure to —" She stared at Annabelle's eyes as she stopped midsentence.

"Is something wrong, Lucinda?" the old man asked, noticing her loss of words.

"No," she said as she turned back toward her meat. "Nothing."

"Nicholaus, you remember my sister, Lucinda," the old knight said as he pulled two stools out from along the wall of the grand room.

"Yes, Lucinda, it is good to see you again." He bowed toward her. She nodded her head in acknowledgment.

Lucinda jabbed at the fire and shook her head. "We are almost out of wood." She stood and headed for the door.

"I'll get more wood for you." Nicholaus was quick to offer.

"That is a fine thought." The knight patted him on the shoulder. "I'll take you to the stack." Nicholaus followed the man out.

Lucinda turned from the fire, shaking her head. "I love my brother, but sometimes it's so hard." Annabelle looked at her, not fully understanding. "He tries very much to do what he can't, and it worries me so, and tires me." She looked out the back window to Nicholaus preparing to chop the wood. "You see that? If I told him we needed wood, he would go back there and chop it himself." She shook her head. "And he might just get his leg instead. So I try to do it before he knows the wood is low, and it tires me so to do a man's labor."

"It's only you two who live out here?"

Lucinda nodded as she turned back toward Annabelle. After a pause, she said, "I wish it was not so. It used to be thriving with servants, and he had a family, a wife, and a young boy."

"Where are they now?"

Her eyes slowly made their way back to Annabelle's. "They were killed." Annabelle nodded her head, figuring it was another family victimized by the Demolites. Lucinda leaned in toward Annabelle. "It's not fair to him nor to yourself."

Annabelle stirred in her seat. "What's not fair?"

"He wishes to be a king's knight," Lucinda said without question.

Annabelle nodded.

"The king's knights are strongly advised not to marry. Some might say they are only thinking of themselves if they do."

Annabelle shook her head. "I don't understand."

Lucinda licked her lips. "There has not been a single knight whose family has not been harmed in some way. Their poor wives have all been slain. Have you met any other knights?"

Annabelle shook her head. "Not a king's knight."

"Most of the older ones … their families have already been killed. The young ones have joined with this under-standing — it is now like an unspoken rule, he has told me."

Annabelle contemplated the words. "That is dreadful, but what does it have do with me?"

"How long have you been with her?" the old knight asked as Nicholaus chopped.

Nicholaus took a deep breath as he prepared for a swing. "One week, six days and a quarter."

"You are on dangerous ground, my boy." Nicholaus held the axe in the air, listening to the wise man's words. "I might not have the use of my eyes, but there are some things that can still be seen."

Nicholaus dropped the axe and sat upon the stump. He could no longer hold in the truth: "I am already in danger."

"You love her?" the old knight asked.

"I have tried not to. I have prayed not to. But I think God wishes it. My mind is so unclear. I don't know what to do." He stood and faced the forest. "I have been called to be a king's knight my entire life, and when I was so close, she came along." He shook his head. "I don't know what to do."

"Anna, I'm going to go to town for Sir Machenus. Do you wish to go?"

She looked across the bailey and at the small keep. "I'll wait for you here."

Nicholaus was thankful for her answer. Maybe if he could get away from her, he could think clearly. "I should be back in the early evening." He turned and faced the old knight. "Sir Machenus, I place her in your care."

"And I shall protect her as if she were of sovereign blood." He offered his hand to Nicholaus. Nicholaus shook it and then hugged the man.

Annabelle watched him mount Cinny, exit the dilapidated stone wall, and ride off north into the trees. She turned toward the older man. "What was it like, sir?"

"What is that, dear?" the old man asked as he leaned upon his stick.

"Being a king's knight. I mean, you were willing to die for the sovereign family?"

"I still am," the man said stoically.

"Lucinda told me about your wife and son. I'm very sorry for your loss."

The man wavered in his stance and sat down upon a piece of wood. "That was many, many years ago. My son was but 3 years old, and my wife …" His face began to quiver as his mind took him to the moment he lost them.

Annabelle knelt before him and grabbed his hand. "I am certain the sovereign family is thankful for your sacrifice, and you will meet your family again someday, in Heaven."

He found the side of her face. "Sweet child, I see why he adores you."

Her brow furrowed, not understanding the meaning of his words. Her head turned quickly to the sound of hooves coming from the south.

"What is it?" he asked as he stood.

"There are horses coming, many of them."

"I know, but can you see them yet?"

"No."

"Stay here and I'll see what they want." The man walked toward the broken stone wall with his stick in hand.

Annabelle looked around. She was completely visible. She ran toward the woods, jumped over the two-foot high remains of the fortress wall, and quickly climbed a tree to see if they were friend or foe.

"Who's there?" Sir Machenus asked as the horses stopped outside his castle while Lucinda peeked around the door.

A man, donned in a green tabard, dismounted. "It is Sir Doey."

"Sir Doey!" The blind man held out his arms to his old

friend. "Michael, it is good to hear your voice!" He hugged him. "What brings you this far north?"

"An earnest matter: Princess Elizabeth has been taken!" Michael looked up at another man donned in purple, still upon his horse; Lucinda gasped from the doorframe at the sight of the man.

"When?"

"About two weeks ago. We've traced their movements to two miles southwest of here, but then the prints can no longer be found."

"Do you need water? Come in, come in."

"Thank you." The knight followed his old friend into the decrepit castle.

Michael tipped his helmet toward Lucinda. "Ma'am." She nodded.

"Have you seen any sign of her?" Sir Doey asked as he stood inside the not-so-grand hall.

"How old is she now?" Sir Machenus asked from his seated position.

"She is 7. Brown hair, looks like her sisters," he added in case Lucinda had seen a young, lost girl.

"No. I know of no signs."

Michael sat down for a moment's repose and a silent prayer. "We need help. The Lion's son, as you know, is to join us soon — and the sooner the better."

The old knight cut in. "He is here." Michael sat up as the blind knight continued. "I mean, he was here. He went to town; he'll be back. He's taking a girl to Aboly. He'll be back for her."

Michael stood, new vigor enveloping his body. "Send him to us — two miles southwest of here — as quickly as possible."

"I will do that."

Annabelle stared at the men in hunter green. Thoughts of her childhood began to swirl around — mottled, hazy, but swirling. Why? She tried to make sense of them. She was fascinated by the color, but frozen in fear as well.

There was one man who did not wear hunter green. He looked around at the tree line. He saw the mysterious girl in the tree. Dismounting his horse, he walked toward her, drawn to her as another knight, Sir David, dismounted and walked around the keep from the other direction.

A mysterious force drew her toward the handsome, regal young man. Jumping down from the tree, she slowly approached.

She was within a stone's throw of the regal man. He looked into her eyes, and it was as if he read her soul. She quickly ran behind the castle. Overcome with a thousand obscure emotions, she did not know what to do. She backed into Sir David.

Sir David tried to help her up, but she would not take his outstretched hand. He looked strangely at her when he saw her eyes. He watched, dumbfounded, as she bolted toward the woods and disappeared behind a tree.

"Did you see her, Sir David?" the man asked as he ran around the round keep.

The man stared at the woods, very much confused. "Yes."

"Where'd she go?" the man continued to question.

"She vanished," the knight stated as he stared at the last place he saw the girl run.

"She wasn't here." The man shook his head in confusion. Looking at the knight, he asked, "You saw her, didn't you?"

"I don't know what I saw. She vanished!"

"Prince William?" Sir Doey called from the keep's entrance and then walked around until he found the knight and the prince. "Squire Nicholaus Hunts is here. He'll meet us back at the prints."

Both the men ripped their attention from the woods and ran toward their horses.

Annabelle hid behind a tree, catching her breath attempting to recover from her encounter with that young man. When she heard the horses leave, she sprinted toward the keep. Swinging the door open, she stood in the frame not saying a word. She observed Lucinda crying.

"Anna," the gentleman addressed her. "We were visited by Grand Sir Doey. He comes with grave tidings: Princess Elizabeth has been taken."

She shook her head as her heart nearly pounded out of her chest. "Princess Elizabeth? How old?"

"She is 7."

She struggled to hold back her tears as her chest struck in and out. "No." *The poor girl. Help her, Father. Help her as You did me.* "Who else was with them?" Did she dare to ask?

"The knights."

"No. Someone not in green. Not with chain mail. Who was he?"

Machenus shook his head. "What did he wear?"

"Purple."

"That was Prince William."

"William?" she whispered.

Anna. Father, please let her be safe! Why am I worrying about Anna when the princess has been seized?! Because I love her! I can't deny it any longer. Father, what am I to do? Do I help find Princess Elizabeth and then give up any hope of knighthood for Anna?

Nicholaus had learned of the missing princess while in the town and immediately hauled himself toward the old knight's property. He flew through the forest and nearly fell off Cinny when he halted in front of the keep.

He flung open the door, and Annabelle ran into his arms. He looked around at the teary eyes and saddened faces. "You've heard?"

"Yes, Doey was here earlier. You can find them two miles southwest," Sir Machenus informed him. Nicholaus nodded his head as he continued to squeeze his Anna.

"Take me with you."

He shook his head. "Anna, Anna, you can't come with me."

"No!" She looked up at him. "Please, let me go with you!"

"Anna, it's too dangerous. There are Demolites out there."

"There are Demolites everywhere! I am safer with you." Tears flowed down her cheeks as she squeezed him tightly.

He wiped away her tears with his thumbs as he held her head. "Anna, I can't place you in any more danger."

"I am in danger no matter where I go. Please! Nicholaus, I want to go with you!"

"No. Anna, you can't. I'll come back for you." He pressed his cheek against her forehead. "I give you my word. I'll get you to Aboly."

He forced himself away from her embrace, on to his horse, and off into the woods toward the knights. He could not look back at her.

"Did you see her?" Prince William asked as he stared into the woods fresh from dismounting his horse at the last traceable tracks.

"See whom?" Michael responded.

"The girl."

"Which girl? We've seen several people today I don't know —"

"The girl at Sir Machenus's."

"His sister?"

"No! The girl!"

"I didn't see a girl, but Machenus did mention Nicholaus was taking a girl to Aboly. What about her?"

"Her eyes."

"Her eyes?"

Prince William finally took his eyes from the trees ahead to look at Michael. "They were emerald." A streak of pain flashed across the knight's face as the prince continued, "I know of no one who has emerald eyes but Mamá and —"

"Do not do that," Michael interrupted. "Do not try to dig up old wounds as a way to blame yourself for Elizabeth's taking."

The prince looked forward again and shook his head. "I wonder if she was even there." His look became distant as he pondered the possibilities.

When a twig broke, every man was on his feet.

"Who's there?" Michael asked into the early evening air.

"It is I, Squire Nicholaus Hunts." He emerged from the woods with his trusty horse at his side.

Every man took a deep breath. "It is good to see you, boy," Michael said as he slapped him on the shoulder.

The prince approached him. "Nicholaus Hunts, I hear you are the best hunter in the kingdom. Find my sister."

"Show me what you have," he said with a nod of the head.

"The prints." Michael explained. "We have traced them to here, but then we find no other." He waved Nicholaus over toward the trees.

"The prints may be lost, but the signs don't vanish — they only become subtler." Nicholaus followed Michael toward the last known track of the kidnappers.

Nicholaus studied the track — the moved dirt, the bent twigs — as he knelt upon the ground. He saw the scene before him. "The princess ran away. She slid down the hill." He examined the scratches in the dirt. "She pulled herself up, but the man did not." Standing, he looked over the edge. "And there he lies." They all peeked over the edge and saw the lifeless body of a Demolite who had thrown himself over the ledge attempting to catch the princess.

"My sister, where did she go?" the prince demanded.

"Sir?"

"Sir David, what is it?" Michael answered, stepping away from the prince and Nicholaus.

"I'm not certain, sir," the knight said as he shook his head.

Sir Doey looked at the confused young man. "What's troubling you, Sir David?"

"There was a girl at Sir Machenus's castle."

Michael stood up straighter. "What about her?"

"She had the queen's eyes."

Nicholaus traced the claw marks and broken twigs, and found a long hair caught in a bush. "She went northeast, toward Sir Machenus's." He shook his head. *Toward Anna.* He stood up quickly, disgusted by himself, as the knights and the prince surrounded him.

"Whom do you take to Aboly?" Michael asked with a serious face.

Nicholaus looked at all the faces. "I call her Anna."

"Anna?" The prince looked back at Nicholaus. "That's her name?"

"Annabelle."

The prince took off toward his horse, closely followed by Michael and the other knights. Nicholaus, finding that very peculiar, whistled for Cinny and dashed off toward the old knight's castle as well.

Identity

Annabelle squeezed Lucinda's hand. Thinking of the poor princess, and of her unknown future and lost years, Annabelle sat resolute, determined that, despite all the horror the Demolites had thrust upon countless families, her family would find happiness in the end with her safe return. When it came to her own life, the vile men would not claim a victory on her loved ones.

"That poor family," Lucinda said with a saddened countenance.

"What do you mean?" Annabelle asked, still not knowing her true identity.

Lucinda looked at her brother and stood. "That's not the first time one of their daughters has been taken."

"Not the first time?" Standing, she tilted her head toward Lucinda, who stared at her brother. "What? Who was the first? Sir Machenus?"

Clearing the sorrow from his voice, he said, "You share her name."

"What?" She looked at him, confused. The weight of Peter's bag seemed to triple and pull her toward the ground.

"Annabelle."

"What?" the princess could barely breathe. She sat down for fear of falling, as her heart beat wildly.

"That day is burned into my head. I was newly wounded; I could not search for her. She was the sweetest girl, with her mamá's eyes. Oh, the memory of those emerald eyes."

Lucinda gasped as Annabelle looked at her, her own eyes bombarded with blurriness from tears.

"What's wrong? Why did you make that noise?" the old knight asked.

"*She* has emerald eyes!" Lucinda stated.

The old knight stood. "Annabelle? What is your full name?"

Annabelle, breathing quickly, attempted to answer: "Annabelle ... of Anchony."

Lucinda sat down, nearly fainting.

"Annabelle! Annabelle!" He reached for her. She did not know what to do — she was in shock. "Annabelle, sweet girl!"

"I was taken 13 years ago. I lived on an island. I escaped. Nicholaus was taking me back to Aboly. I don't know who my parents are."

"You are the missing princess!"

"I ... I ... Are you certain?"

"You are the fourth child, second daughter, of King Francis and Queen Clara of Anchony — Princess Annabelle."

She pulled back from him, nearly hyperventilating. She looked at Lucinda, whose blood had drained from her face. "I ... I ..." She stood. Unsure what to do she ran out of the keep, across the bailey, and only stopped when she got outside the broken fortress wall. Sliding down the jagged stone wall, she tried to catch her breath and process everything.

Will? Was that you ... ? My brother? Am I a ... princess? Her whole body shook as she stared across the path into the forest.

When her breathing calmed and the shaking subsided, she was able to focus on the sounds around her. Particularly the sounds coming from the woods across the path, where a little girl emerged from in between the bushes. She stopped for a second, looked around, and ran joyfully toward Annabelle.

Annabelle slowly stood. *She looks like Isa ... but it can't be ...*

The girl ran into her core, hugging her and gripping her with all she had. Annabelle slowly placed her arms around her little frame and hugged her back.

The girl looked up at her, did a double take, and then stepped back. "You're not Isa!"

Annabelle knelt down and moved the hair back from the girl's face. "Neither are you." The rustling from the woods grew louder. Annabelle's eyes darted toward the forest as she realized the Demolites were about. "How many are there?"

The little girl looked back, about to cry. "I want Papá!"

Annabelle stood. "As do I." Grabbing her sister's hand, she ran back toward the keep. She spotted Lucinda, looking for her. "The Demolites are here!"

Lucinda gasped when she spotted the masked men running after Annabelle; she quickly ran back into the keep as Annabelle flew in behind her, carrying the little princess. Annabelle leaned upon the door, closing it quickly as she looked at Elizabeth.

"Who's there?" Machenus asked as he stood.

"The princess is here," Lucinda answered as she shook her head. "Both of them!"

"Who are you?" the little girl asked her older sister with a quivering voice.

"How many are there?" Machenus asked as he grabbed his sword.

"There's at least 10," Lucinda said, looking out the window.

"There are too many for you!" Annabelle stated.

Lucinda screamed as a torch flew at the castle door and lit it aflame. "It's on fire!"

"Out the back window!" Sir Machenus commanded.

Annabelle followed his directions and climbed out the window. She turned around quicky, pulled Elizabeth out, and helped Lucinda down. Lucinda fell out clumsily and injured her leg. Machenus followed as the men entered into the old keep.

They snuck into the tree line with Lucinda limping. Lucinda stopped against a tree, leaving a trail of blood. "No. No. I can't go on. Leave without me."

"No," Annabelle insisted. "We will not!" She looked over at Machenus as she still held tightly to her sister's hand.

Machenus put up his hand. "Princess Annabelle."

"I'm here." She took his hand.

"You must take your sister and hide."

"Hide where? I don't know this place." She looked around in the dying sunlight.

The Demolites, soon realizing the princess was not in the castle, started for the woods.

Lucinda gasped.

"What is it?" Machenus asked.

"They're coming!"

"Run, Annabelle. Take your sister and run. I'll hold them off as long as I can."

"Machenus —"

"Remember what I told you, Princess. I still am ... I still am." He ran from the tree line toward the men.

"Lucinda?" Annabelle looked helplessly at the bleeding lady.

"Go! Annabelle. Hide your sister." She waved her away frantically.

Annabelle looked down at her frightened sister, who listened to the words but could not quite process the meaning at that moment.

She looked back toward the keep. Machenus was engaged in a fight with six men. Four more spotted her. She turned, picked up her sister, and ran into the woods. Not knowing where to go, she just ran — like only she could.

Nicholaus, the prince, and the knights, sprinted into the bailey upon their horses. They immediately jumped down and ran to the burning and broken castle.

"Anna! Anna!" Nicholaus ran toward the castle skeleton as two knights held back the prince from entering the scorched building.

Sir David ran out from the building, narrowly missing the collapse of the roof behind him. He looked at his horrified cohorts, shaking his head. "No one was in there."

"Where is she?!" The prince wrestled his way out of the knights' hands and headed toward Nicholaus. "Where is she?!" the prince repeated as he grabbed Nicholaus's shirt and screamed into his face.

"Don't do this!" Michael yelled at the prince as he ran toward him.

Nicholaus shoved the prince back. The prince immediately unsheathed his sword. Nicholaus followed suit as he yelled, "I don't know where Elizabeth is! I have never met her!"

"Annabelle! I mean Annabelle!" the prince shouted with pain in his voice as he pointed his sword at Nicholaus.

Nicholaus lowered his sword. "Wh ... what?"

The prince lowered his sword as his face quivered in emotion. "Annabelle is my sister."

"Sister?" Nicholaus shook his head in confusion.

"She was taken so very long ago, and *this* very day, at *this* very place, I saw her. She was here. She has my mother's eyes. The lady you were with. *She* is my sister."

"Your sister? A princess?" Nicholaus shook his head in disbelief.

A knight yelled from behind the burnt remains, "Back here!"

The knights ran to where he knelt, holding the hand of an older man. The prince and Nicholaus looked at each other and then followed.

Nicholaus knelt down beside his mentor. "Sir Machenus. Sir Machenus."

"They ran. They ran. They ran. Where ... where ... is ... my sister?" He gasped as his last breath left him.

They looked around — he was surrounded by six fallen Demolites. They all made the Sign of the Cross.

"His sister is by the tree. She was stabbed in the heart," Sir Gregory reported.

"He said 'they.' Who did he mean?" The prince looked around at the faces.

Nicholaus looked with saddened eyes toward the forest. He spotted the tracks and rushed over to investigate. "These are Anna's, but they are deeper than normal. She carried more weight." He looked up and caught the prince's eyes. They ran into the forest together.

Hanging

Annabelle set the young girl down on a boulder as the setting sun cast colors through the trees. She caught her breath as she looked at the little girl before her — exactly as she had remembered Isabella.

The young princess looked at her with confusion. "You have Mamá's eyes."

Annabelle leaned in and whispered, "She is my mamá too. We are sisters."

"Sisters?" the little girl asked in wonder. Annabelle nodded her head. "Like Isa and Crisa?"

Annabelle's hand flew to her mouth at the mention of her sisters' names. She nodded as copious tears ran down her cheeks. Though not physically home, she had made it back to her family. Picking up the girl in front of her, she squeezed her with all her strength, grateful to be in the presence of a family member, though she had not even known of this sister's existence.

A spark of realization lit across the young girl's face as she whispered into Annabelle's ear, "Are … are you *Annie?*"

Annabelle cried harder into her sister's hair, remembering the name her brothers and sisters had called her. Hearing men approach, she forced herself to stop crying. She placed Elizabeth on the ground.

"What's wrong?" the little girl asked, surprised at her quick change in height. She gasped and looked nervously at the trees when she heard noises. She grabbed Annabelle's side. "Don't let them take me. Don't let them take me … don't let them …"

Annabelle knelt down before her terribly frightened sister, struggling against her own tears. "Elizabeth —"

"Liza!" the little girl corrected with fright.

"Liza, you have to have courage. We both have to have courage."

Annabelle searched the forest floor, the canopy, and everything in between for a hiding spot. She closed her eyes to listen intently to the noises of the forest — the birds, the squirrels, the bugs — and the very faintest sound of a waterfall. When the noises were enveloped by the racket of the Demolites stomping loudly on all the twigs, leaves, and rocks of the forest floor, she opened her eyes.

The kidnappers were three feet away.

In one fluid motion, Annabelle moved Elizabeth with one hand as she kicked a Demolite in the core. Elizabeth fell to the ground in surprise. She looked up to see her sister elbow another man in the stomach and flip him over on to his back; hit another man's knee into a nonfunctioning position; twist the opposite direction to punch a man in the face; and within the same 20 seconds, reach for her hand and pull her to her feet.

"Liza!" Annabelle screamed at her sister, as Elizabeth continued to stare at the spot where Annabelle previously stood. "Let's go!"

Elizabeth looked over at Annabelle; seeing her mother's eyes, she followed without question. She ran as quickly as her little legs could take her, but tripped over a rock and fell forward. Annabelle caught her before she hit the ground and picked her up. Annabelle quickly looked back to see two of the men getting up.

⁓⁓

The trees began to thin out as the sound of the waterfall grew louder. Setting Elizabeth down near a cliff, she peeked over the side. She looked back to the trees — the two men were coming. Kneeling down, she moved her satchel behind her. "Liza, I need you to climb on to my back."

"What are you going to do?" the little princess said in fright as she did as she was told.

"Climb the cliff," Annabelle said as she turned her back to the river.

Elizabeth gasped as she squeezed harder. Looking down at the river to her left and then to the right, she noted the massive waterfall and began to squirm.

"Liza, hold still!" Annabelle commanded as she descended the side of the cliff.

Elizabeth sobbed into her sister's hair and revealed, "I can't swim."

"You're not going for a swim," Annabelle whispered as she heard the men approaching. She moved herself to the left, where she was partially hidden by the cliff. "Liza ... pray."

"Our ... Our ... Our Father —"

"To yourself," Annabelle added.

The Demolites stood next to the precarious cliff and looked over it. Small rocks and dirt clumps bounced on to Annabelle and Elizabeth's heads and shoulders before falling into the wild river below. Annabelle gripped the rocks with all her strength, silently praying that the awful men above her would not discover them.

"Ya see 'em?" one man asked.

The other man, removing his mask, answered with a bloody mouth, "They either jump'd to the river" — he spat over the cliff — "or they're travelin' long the riverside."

"Not on the cliff?"

The man looked over the cliff for another sweep. His foot slipped on a stick, and he landed on his hind side as his cohort laughed. "Followin' the river," he concluded, as he stood up rubbing his backside, kicking the stick and cursing.

They followed the ledge downstream.

"Are they gone?" Elizabeth asked after a minute or two.

Annabelle listened for all the noises she could sense — she could not hear any footsteps. She carefully maneuvered her right hand and foot up the cliff.

The prince, the knights, and Nicholaus came upon the two fallen Demolites, groaning on the ground. The prince and Nicholaus looked at each other, both thinking the same thing: *Who did this? Did they fight each other?*

Nicholaus checked the tracks, and they continued on the hunt.

Annabelle ascended the cliff toward her original entry point. Her muscles, after half an hour of gripping, were beginning to quiver. Her head peeked over the ledge. The bloody-mouthed Demolite happened to look over at that exact time as her hair reflected the moonlight.

He pounded on his buddy.

"Wha'd ya want?" the man growled.

He pointed.

Annabelle was about to pull her sister and herself atop the ground when she heard the Demolites running toward them.

"Hold on!" she yelled as she descended the cliff farther — five more feet from the top.

"Ya think ya sneak 'way from me!" the bloodied man screamed through his disguise as he ran toward the cliff. He peered over the edge. "Where'd ya go?" He scooted himself further out as he reached with his arm.

Elizabeth began to shake and cry.

"It's all right, Liza. It'll be all right." Annabelle attempted to comfort the squirming, terrified girl.

"Take my legs, Odus, I won't let her be gettin' 'way."

Odus grabbed his legs as the man's arms descended closer and closer.

Elizabeth screamed at the top of her lungs as she squirmed more and more.

"Liza! Stop moving!" Annabelle screamed as her weakening fingers and toes fought with all they had to remain gripped to the edge.

⁓

"Liza!" William heard her scream as he, Nicholaus, and the knights ran out from the trees in full pursuit.

They pulled Odus back from the ledge, not knowing he held the other Demolite. Odus let go and was easily overtaken by a knight. The bloody-mouthed Demolite fell haphazardly toward the water, bumping Elizabeth as he plummeted to his watery grave.

Elizabeth began to slide down Annabelle's back. Annabelle instinctively reached with her right hand and grabbed Elizabeth's arm as her left fingers slowly slipped. She screamed in desperation.

She felt fingers around her wrist as pebbles hit her face. She looked up to see Nicholaus gripping her wrist as his legs were held by William.

Annabelle, relieved but still worried, looked into Nicholaus's eyes. "I can't hold her."

"Hold on!" William yelled. "Take his legs! Someone take his legs!" Two knights took hold of Nicholaus's legs and he joined Michael reaching for Elizabeth. "Liza, grab his hand!"

Elizabeth flailed about attempting to reach Michael's hand. "I can't!" She grabbed the one thing she could reach: Annabelle's satchel.

William looked over at his other sister. "Annie!"

Annabelle looked from Nicholaus to William. He stretched out his arm. "Give me your hand." She looked into his eyes — she knew that strength — it inspired her to give everything she had.

She let out a scream as she dug her feet into the rock and slowly pulled Elizabeth up inch by inch until the knight was able to grab her. Safe in the knight's grasp, Annabelle released her sister out of fatigue and fell limp against the rocks. She watched as Elizabeth was pulled up higher and higher; the satchel caught underneath Elizabeth's neck as she was pulled upward.

"Anna!" Nicholaus screamed in desperation. "Give me your other hand!" She was slowly being pulled out of his grasp as the satchel pulled her to the right.

William grabbed the satchel with one hand as he desperately reached for his sister. "Give me your hand!"

She reached up as her wrist was torn from Nicholaus's fingers. Grabbing the strap of the satchel, she fell down another foot.

William watched in horror as the strap seam busted loose and his long-lost sister plummeted down, down, down, into the raging river as Elizabeth was pulled safely to the top.

"No!" He was pulled back up, gripping the satchel. He watched by the light of the moon as she appeared to hit a rock and was swiftly taken over the waterfall. He looked over at Nicholaus, who was pale white in disbelief. He dropped the satchel next to Nicholaus and took off following the edge. "Annie! Annie! Annie!" he cried desperately into the night air. His eyes scanned the water frantically searching for any signs of life — or limb. Four knights positioned themselves along the ledge, systematically scanning the crest of the river.

Nicholaus fell to his knees as he watched the powerful water that had taken his love. He picked up the satchel and hugged it as he closed his eyes and relived the horrid scene, and how he had failed her.

"Annie?" Elizabeth looked at the river, at her frantic brother, and up at Michael, whose hand she held. "Where is she?" A tear fell from her eye; she knew the answer, but she did not want to believe it.

Michael squatted down next to her, caressed her head, and hugged her as he picked her up, watching helplessly as the prince ran frantically up and down the ledge.

After half an hour, William returned to the fateful spot, falling to his knees in surrender between Michael and Nicholaus. Michael knelt down with Elizabeth in his arms. He placed his hand upon the prince's shoulder. "No one could survive Angler Falls."

"I know that!" William snapped. "Don't you think I know that!" He broke down and cried.

Elizabeth crawled out of Michael's arms and into her brother's. She whispered to him, "That was Annie." He squeezed her tightly as he cried into her hair.

"We didn't see her body," Sir David reported as the knights returned from their self-appointed positions.

Nicholaus stood and in a trancelike state said, "I gave my word I would get her to Aboly."

Michael, anticipating Nicholaus fleeing southward along the river's edge to find her body, stepped in front of him. He placed his hands upon Nicholaus's shoulders. "It's too dark. You can't see tonight. We will search in the morning."

He looked back up at him. "I gave my word to her."

Michael shook his head. "I know you did." He patted Nicholaus's arms.

They all stared at the crackling fire, lips silent but minds somersaulting in what could have been, what had been, and why.

Michael threw pieces of a twig into the fire as he angrily beat himself up. *She was alive this whole time? Where had she been? How did I lose her again? My skills are waning, and I have no excuse.*

Nicholaus gripped Peter's satchel with all he had, wanting it to be his Anna. *Why? Why could I not hold her? Why did You send her to me only to be taken away? Why did I fall in love? Why ...*

Prince William held Elizabeth, who was fighting sleep as he leaned against a log. *Annie, oh, Annie. Now you are gone. How can I ever tell Mamá? And I could not save you ... again ...*

The first person to break the screaming silence was Elizabeth as she spoke softly to her brother. "I thought Annie was dead."

William placed his chin upon the top of her head. "So did I."

Michael threw the rest of his stick into the fire as he stood, angry at himself.

Elizabeth watched Michael and then turned toward her brother, "Annie saved my life."

William smiled briefly. "She did, didn't she?" He had to look away.

"Did she drown?" She looked at her brother for an answer.

He pulled her closer and shook his head, unwilling to answer.

Nicholaus's eyes moved from the fire to the young girl. He could see so much of his Anna in the little girl before him. He was touched by her sweet countenance. He observed the brother and sister in such a comforting embrace — it reminded him of what he had lost many years ago, as memories of a sister stolen from him flooded forward.

Elizabeth looked up at him with drowsy eyes. She pointed to the satchel. "Is that Annie's?"

Nicholaus looked from the satchel to the princess and then to the prince. He slowly nodded his head. "It is."

Elizabeth dropped her arm and turned her head more into her brother's chest, succumbing to sleep.

William petted his sister's hair to help sooth her as he looked at Nicholaus. "What's in it?"

Nicholaus looked down at the bag. "I don't know. She didn't know."

"What do you mean?" The prince tilted his head.

"Peter gave it to her," Nicholaus said as he looked at the fire.

"Who's Peter?" William asked as he felt his youngest sister breathing in her sleep.

"He raised her. The man on the island."

Michael walked closer to the fire from the tree he had been leaning against, arms folded. "What island?"

Nicholaus turned toward his voice. "The Forbidden Island."

Michael sat upon the same log the prince was resting against as the other knights sat up to listen. "Where's that?"

Nicholaus shook his head. "Northeast of Anchony."

"Who was this Peter?" William asked.

Nicholaus looked at the prince's face, figuring what he was really asking. "She spoke well of her childhood."

"Well?" Elizabeth stirred at her brother's raised and irritated voice. He quickly took a deep breath to calm himself.

"Was he a Demolite?" Michael asked.

Nicholaus smiled slightly as he shook his head. "She would cast you aside for such a thought." He looked around — every man stared at him. He clarified: "She ran away from the Demolites the moment she reached the island. Peter was … a hermit. He found her and raised her. She called him her angel, her father."

William shook his irritated head. *Father? Father? My sister … raised by a stranger? How will I ever tell Papá?*

Every man was up with the sun. Sirs Fredrickson and Underwood ran toward the dying fire with their report. "She's not within two miles down the river."

Michael looked to where Nicholaus previously lay. "Where's the squire?"

"Sir David is trying to sway him to come back here," Sir Fredrickson said, shaking his head.

"He's on foot?" Michael asked. Fredrickson nodded his head. "Well, he can't search the entire river without a horse."

Fredrickson shook his head. "I have a feeling he would try, sir."

"And I will join him," Prince William said as he stood up from repositioning a blanket atop his sister and belted his sword.

Michael stuck out his hand. "Prince William, that's not a good thought."

"She is my sister!" The future king's fiery voice came forth.

"She is dead, William," Michael stated bluntly. "You can't help her. Elizabeth is alive. Get her home safely."

The prince looked down at his slowly waking sister. He knew Michael was correct. He sighed heavily and looked back up at his head knight. "I failed her in every way."

"No!" Michael insisted, placing his hand on the prince's shoulder. "If anyone has failed her, it was the knights. It was *me*. Twice now, she has been taken under my command."

William shook his head. "No." Tears rolled down his face as he recalled that awful day years ago. "I led her out of the gates."

"You were but a boy!"

William stood, impassioned in his guilt. "I was her brother! I was supposed to defend her!"

"We were supposed to defend her!" Michael looked around at all the young knights before him. He shook his head as he pounded his chest. "It was *my* duty to defend her!"

"She didn't want to go! I led her out. If I wouldn't have, she never would have been taken," he yelled back, attempting to prove his point. "It is my fault!"

"Will?" Elizabeth looked at him with great concern as she hugged her blanket.

"Liza." He knelt down to her with open arms. She climbed into them.

Michael stared down at the royal siblings and repeated his earlier thoughts. "You can't help her now. We can't help her." Spotting Nicholaus walking back to camp with Sir David, Michael took a deep breath and looked at the squire. "You returned?"

Nicholaus shook his head in dismay as he sighed. "As quickly as the river is running, she could be three quarters through Anchony by now." He looked up. "I need my horse."

"You will return to Aboly whether you find her body or not?" Michael asked, looking into his eyes.

Nicholaus shifted his weight uncomfortably. "I told her I would get her to Aboly. I will keep my word."

"Nicholaus, we need you. Your skills at finding a trail, and fighting."

"The king demands it," William added as he stood with his sister in his arms.

"You want me to bring her back, do you not?" Nicholaus asked the prince, irritated that even in her death, he had to choose between his love and his destiny.

"I do, but —" The prince looked at his sister in his arms. "I have three other sisters. They need your skills now more than Annie." He turned away.

Nicholaus lowered his head. He knew the truth of the statement, though his heart swore he would never give up searching for his Anna. The depth of his being fought against the words that came from his mouth: "What shall it be, then?"

William looked to Michael.

Michael answered, "Two weeks. Wherever you are in two weeks, come to Aboly."

Nicholaus watched the knights quickly pack up their belongings. Holding his breath, he wrapped the strap of the satchel around the bag and stepped beside the prince, offering it to him. "It's only right that you have this now."

William looked at the offered gift, hesitant to accept it. He had studied how Nicholaus had clung to it. "Are you certain?"

Nicholaus nodded his head as he moved it closer to the prince's hands. "Its proper place is with her family."

Elizabeth, standing next to the prince, watched as her brother slowly nodded his head and accepted the package. Strapping it to his saddle, he then mounted his horse. She was hoisted up to her brother by Michael. She studied Nicholaus closely and asked her brother, "He's not coming?"

"No," William said as he watched Nicholaus say a silent prayer and then mount Cinny. Elizabeth sorrowfully waved good-bye when Nicholaus looked up at them.

Nicholaus was so moved by the little girl, he turned Cinny away, but quickly turned back. "Prince William." William looked over at Nicholaus as Nicholaus galloped over. "A sister is a precious thing." He looked down at Elizabeth. "Don't let that one out of your sight."

William nodded his head in agreement. "Until we meet again, Squire Hunts." He held out his hand, and Nicholaus accepted it. The prince and knights then sped off in the direction of Aboly as Elizabeth stared around her brother's arm at the new friend they were leaving behind.

Forty or so miles downstream, along the now calmly flowing Angler riverbank, a 10-year-old boy threw stones into the river as his jug filled with drinking water.

His eyes were drawn to something shimmering in the morning light, partially hidden by the tall grass next to the river. He tilted his head and looked to the left at his father and 12-year-old brother busily filling their jugs.

Curiously approaching the dirty white and green mass, he parted the grass and gasped as he stared at a beat-up lady with a bloody arm and shoulder blade. "Papa! Papa!" He looked over at his father.

"Artus? What's wrong?" his father asked as he came to him.

The little boy pointed. "What is it?"

His father immediately jumped into the river to reach the mass before his eyes. Turning her over, he pushed the hair away from her face. He gasped and stood with her in his arms when he felt air upon his hand and watched as she attempted to open her eyes.

"Papa? What is it?" the other boy asked as he watched his father turn toward him. He dropped his jug when he spotted a person in his father's arms.

"Atticus, run. Tell your mother to get blankets."

Atticus, without delay, sprinted toward their home, yelling, "Mama! Mama!"

His mother, Delfina, ran out of the cabin, wiping her hands upon her apron. "Atticus, what's wrong?" She looked around desperately for an answer. "Is it your father? Is it Artus?"

He stopped before her, catching his breath. "There's a girl!"

"A girl?" His mother looked at him curiously as his sister came out of the wattle and daub dwelling and met them.

"Blankets! Papa said blankets!" he managed to get out between breaths.

His mother looked at him curiously and then ordered her daughter, "Melody, gather up the blankets for your father."

"Yes, Mama." Melody did as instructed.

Delfina gasped when she saw her husband running with a bundle in his arms. She immediately ran inside the house and prepared a bed of hay and moss.

Mission

Nicholaus followed the Angler River, which gained intensity on the southern hills of Anchony. With a deafening sound and a spray the height of a man, the powerful Barstow River collided into the Angler in a rocky, watery tempest that then crashed on to jagged, dangerous rocks 50 feet below.

He stared at the robust confluence as he recalled the last several days, the cold, unwelcoming behavior of the serfs along the river, and the words of the one person who did speak with him, Doat Picker, and his scepticism.

"Are you a knight?"

"I am not."

"If you do not mind me asking, what do you intend to do with the body of a princess of Anchony?"

Nicholaus, distraught, shook his head as he dismounted the fidgety Cinny, who was very much agitated by the powerful convergence of the rivers. Sticking his hand in the water, he pulled up some clear liquid and drank. He watched as a four-foot log floating swiftly down the Angler was broken into pieces against the rocks and the powerful Barstow, and then, as quickly as it came, was flushed over the edge and disappeared.

He shook his head. *If she made it this far, she's in pieces now.* Squatting down, he stared across the mighty river.

Father, how am I to find her?

"Use the people."

They don't trust me. They will not speak to me, but they would if I were a king's knight.

A realization hit Nicholaus. What was stopping him from becoming a knight? At this point, only distance. With a renewed hope in his heart and a new vigor for his mission, he whistled for Cinny and headed north toward Aboly.

Annabelle opened her eyes. She could see the flickering fire from behind the thin dividing curtain and the shapes of bodies around the firepit.

"How's she doing?" Doat asked his wife.

"She barely eats. As soon as Markus and Gregory return, we must send for the surgeon. Her arm needs to be closed."

My arm? She did not have enough energy to look down at it.

"Why didn't you send the man for him?" a young voice asked.

Man? Annabelle's eyes opened and closed.

"There was a man? Was he looking for her?" the woman's voice asked her husband with hasty concern.

"I don't know for certain. He said he was looking for the body of a princess."

"A *princess?*" the women's voice raised.

Princess … me. Closing her eyes, she saw Nicholaus holding her wrist and William reaching for her. She shook her head and opened her eyes.

"… not a knight."

"Who could he have been?" said the woman's voice.

"He said his name was Nicholaus —"

All heads turned toward the curtain as they heard a repetitive word. The curtain was pulled back and Delfina was beside the agitated Annabelle. "Shhh … what's wrong?" She wet a cloth and placed it upon the princess's forehead.

"Nic … Nichol … Nichol …" She moved her head away from the washcloth.

"Do you know the man?" Delfina asked.

Annabelle pulled the cloth away with her right hand and attempted to sit up.

"Whoa, wait!" Delfina said. "You are not well enough to be out of bed." Delfina was surprised at Annabelle's strength.

Melody approached her mother from behind, wanting to help but unsure what to do as her brothers watched from their seated positions. "Mama?"

The door opened and the two oldest children, who had just returned from borrowing the village horse, entered. "We're home."

"Run for the surgeon, Doat. Go now," Delfina ordered as she attempted to hold Annabelle down.

She felt the presence of someone next to her and the smell of leather beside her head. She heard grunts and labored breathing. As her swollen hand rose by the strength of another, pain radiated up and down her arm and out to her chest as the man looked at her first injury.

"This needs to be placed above her heart. With some sewing and setting, the bone will heal itself." She felt her body being pushed on to her right side for the man to study her second injury. "The shoulder can't be fixed."

"What can we do?"

"Find the willow bark; boil it. Give it to her to drink. What's her name?"

Delfina, towering over the kneeling man with her arms crossed, shook her head as she raised one arm.

Annabelle felt herself being laid upon her back again.

"Miss, miss."

Slowly opening her eyes, she saw an elderly man staring at her with Delfina above him and every other Picker staring at her.

"Miss, I am going to sew up your arm. What's your name? Miss?" She was shaken again.

"Annabelle," she blurted out weakly as she turned her head in pain.

"There you go," the doctor said. "Can you bring me a stool and a light, and I will fix this arm the best I can." He looked at Annabelle. "Hold her down; this is going to hurt."

"Melody, Atticus, Artus, out now!" their mother ordered.

Annabelle grabbed the moss and hay, twisting them in her right fist, squeezing for dear life, as Doat, Gregory, and Markus held down her legs and unaffected shoulder.

The children heard her screams outside as the doctor placed the bone back together and stabilized it with sticks.

Annabelle, shaking with conjured strength, watched his face as he sewed up the open wound. "This took place when?"

"She has been here five days," Delfina said.

The doctor stopped sewing and looked up at her. "Five days?" He looked to Doat. "Is that certain?"

"Yes. She was found in the river five days ago," Doat answered as he stood in front of Annabelle's head.

"How curious."

"What is it?" Gregory asked.

"This wound has been open for five days, some of that time in the river, and it's not foul looking? I would say it is impossible, but I see it before me."

Annabelle's agony was significantly reduced after her bone was fixed into place and her open wound closed. As long as she did not move her left arm, she could keep the pain in check.

The elevation of her hand helped to decrease the swelling, and her bruises all about her body faded with time. Two days later, with her left arm in a makeshift sling, she was able to sit up. For the first time in a week, she stood and walked uneasily around the curtain toward a stool.

Delfina yelled and nearly dropped her ladle when she saw Annabelle standing next to her.

Melody ran in from outside. "What is it, Ma —" A smile broke across her face. "You're up."

Gregory entered in behind her.

Annabelle leaned against a stool. Feeling lightheaded, she started to fall to the ground, but Gregory caught her. Pain burst throughout her body as he jarred her left shoulder. "Melody, move the stool," Gregory said.

Melody pulled the stool behind Annabelle as she asked with sincere concern, "Are you feeling better?"

"Yes." Taking a deep breath, she accepted the pain. "I haven't" — she swallowed her discomfort — "stood in a while."

"You do too much. You must take it slow," Delfina said as she stirred her stew.

Annabelle nodded her head in agreement. She looked around the wattle and daub home. Where was she? From the Forbidden Island, to journeying with Nicholaus, and now without Nicholaus — where was she?

"I'm glad you're up," Gregory said.

She looked over her shoulder at him. "Thank you."

He stood. "Well, Mama, I'll go pick the apples now."

Annabelle watched him leave. Delfina smiled and patted Annabelle's hand. "We're all glad you're up."

"Me the most." Melody smiled. "Now I don't have to keep changing your clothes."

"Melody!" Her mother castigated her.

Melody turned red. "I'm sorry."

Annabelle looked at Melody. "It's all right. I'm sorry you had to do it in the first place."

"I didn't mind. I was just trying to be mirthful." The little girl looked to the floor.

Annabelle smiled. "It was mirthful. You are clever."

Melody looked back up and smiled at Annabelle. Annabelle smiled more at the little girl. Melody bit her lip. "You have pretty eyes."

Annabelle looked at the large cauldron on top of the

fire. "They come from my mother." Her eyes quickly darted around the room as she tried to hold back the tears. She stared at the other half of the home, where the animals were kept in the wintertime, thinking of the cave on the island, and Peter, and Nicholaus, and William, and Elizabeth, and her parents.

"Annabelle, what's wrong?" Delfina asked, coming closer.

"Where am I?"

"You are in the county of Lesseks."

"How far from Aboly?"

"Aboly?" Delfina stood up straighter, her mind rolling as she swallowed hard. Her tone changed as she answered: "Aboly is northwest of here, a five-day journey."

A tear trickled down her cheek. *So close. So close.*

Delfina observed her actions and returned to her cooking.

"I need to get to Aboly." Annabelle closed her eyes, having no idea how she would get there.

"Licking is but three hours northeast of here." Delfina stared at the injured girl. "Gregory and Markus have been allowed to take the apples there to market. How about it, Annabelle? How about you go with them?" Everyone looked from Delfina to Annabelle.

"Northeast?" Annabelle said with hope.

"Yes." Delfina smiled. "I'm sure they would be happy to take you."

"We certainly would!" Markus stated without hesitation and with, perhaps, a little too much enthusiasm.

Gregory reclined backwards on his arms as he sat on the floor and looked at his mother.

Delfina smiled at her son. "Gregory?"

He sat up and, after a moment of silence, responded, "Only if she wishes."

"But I don't want her to go!" Melody objected.

Delfina looked at her husband. "Do you have a word against it?"

He moved on the stool uncomfortably as everyone stared at him. "Does she truly wish to go?"

Annabelle nodded her head. "Yes. I do. I must."

"We can't keep you here against your will," Doat concluded.

Family

The storm clouds matched their moods, and after a wet and weary week of travel, the royal entourage finally reached the safety of the fortress walls.

"Papá!" Elizabeth reached toward her father as William lowered her into his arms.

"Oh! Elizabeth!" He hugged her with all he had.

"Francis?" the queen asked as she exited the keep with her daughters and youngest son. "William! You are —" She spotted her youngest daughter in her husband's arms. "Elizabeth! Elizabeth!" She ran toward her husband and daughter, smothering them both as only a wife and mother could.

"Mamá!" Elizabeth reached for her and was hugged tightly and rocked. Tears finally came to the young girl when she realized she had made it back to her mother's arms.

Isabella and Cristine hugged each other in happiness. Thomas picked up Eduard as he joined the hug with his sisters. Elizabeth reached for them, too. They ran toward her.

King Francis looked back at his eldest son who, morose, shook his head as he removed a satchel from his saddle. The king quickly looked at the other knights — everyone who had gone after Elizabeth was present, but they seemed years older, heavily burdened. He smiled at Michael. Michael looked at William and nodded his head at the king — his long-time friend — and walked his horse toward the castle stable.

"They are mirthless," the king said to William. "What's wrong?" He looked at Sir David as he approached to take William's horse.

Sir David glanced at the king and quickly diverted his gaze. He took the reins without saying a word.

"Elizabeth is back and unharmed. All the knights are accounted for. What has got you all so down?" he addressed the back of the crowned prince. When he did not answer, the king placed his hand upon his son's shoulder and turned him around.

He spotted a tear rolling down his son's cheek.

"What is it?"

The happy chatter of the royal family ceased when they realized William was crying. They all stared.

"Papá, I couldn't save her." He shook his head in failure.

Francis looked back at Elizabeth in his wife's arms. "She's safe."

William shook his head. "No. Not her."

The king looked quizzically at all the faces of his family. "Who?"

Cristine looked to Elizabeth. "Liza, why does Will cry?"

Elizabeth bit her lip for a moment and then said, "She drowned."

"Drowned?" Her mother looked at her youngest daughter and set the princess down as she slightly gasped for air. "Who, dear?"

"Annie," Elizabeth said timidly.

The world halted for the briefest moment.

"Annie?" her mother asked as pain flew across her face, and her heart began to race.

Everyone stared at the little princess and then at her oldest brother when she revealed no more.

"William. What is this about?" the king demanded.

"All these years, Annie has been alive," William finally revealed.

"What?"

Thomas shook his head. "How can that be?"

"Alive?" Isabella said with hope as she almost smiled.

Lightning lit up the sky as thunder crashed and a few droplets began to fall.

"She was," William said.

"She fell into the river," Elizabeth added, stomping her foot on the soaked ground.

"The river?" the queen gasped as she shook her head — Thomas helped her to sit as her legs went weak.

"Mamá." Cristine joined her mother in a hug on the ground.

King Francis shook his head. "This isn't reasonable. You're telling me Annabelle has been alive all these years and is only dead as of late?" His mind tried to comprehend the information. He shook his head in objection. "No. It couldn't be her. She couldn't have lived all these —"

"It was her!" William demanded.

The king attempted to find an explanation. "You have been very stressed lately —"

"No, Papá. It was her."

The king shook his head as he calculated in his mind. "She would be —"

"18," Queen Clara cried out from the ground.

"Yes, she was," William agreed, disgusted with himself.

The king shook his head. "No. This can't be. She would not look anything like the last time you saw her."

"She looked like Isa!" Elizabeth said as she hugged her mother's neck.

Everyone was silent for a moment as they stared at Elizabeth and then Isabella.

"Papá." William looked into his father's eyes. "Her eyes were emerald."

Clara gasped and began to cry. The king's stomach turned in a knot as he ran to his hysterical wife. And, as if the heavens themselves were weeping, the gray sky let loose and the cold rain fell upon the royal family.

Stunned for a moment, they remained in their spots as they let God's tears soak into their hair, their clothes, and their souls. When lightning began to strike, they were shaken out of their state. Thomas, still holding Eduard, guided his two older sisters into the castle. William grabbed Elizabeth as his father picked up his mother and carried her into the keep.

They all sat down in the foyer, safe from the lightning but still harmed by the recent revelation. The children stared at their crying mother; they could not remember seeing her so distraught.

"Thom?" a little voice whispered into Thomas's ear.

"Yes, Edus?"

"Who's Annie?"

Thomas sat Eduard down and knelt beside him. "She was our sister."

"Sister?" Taking Thomas's hand, they walked over to where their other siblings sat. William helped Eduard on to the bench and set him on his knee as Isabella hugged Elizabeth. Thomas sat down beside Cristine, putting his arm around her. She leaned her head against his shoulder and cried.

Ikus, the head butler, entered the foyer. He smiled when he saw Elizabeth, but his smile faded when he saw the faces of all the princes and princesses. He looked to the center of the room where the king and queen cried in each other's arms on the floor. Should he approach?

Beatrix and Alicia, two of the servants for the queen and princesses, entered as well. Distraught by all the royal faces, but spotting Princess Elizabeth with them, they, too, were perplexed.

"Sir Doey, what has come to pass?" Beatrix whispered when he walked down the hallway. "Princess Elizabeth appears unharmed. Why are they so sad?"

He looked into her eyes. "Princess Elizabeth is unharmed."

"I don't under —"

"We found Princess Annabelle alive, but … she drowned."

Beatrix gasped as her hands flew to her mouth. She quickly made the Sign of the Cross as Michael continued on his journey into the foyer.

Alicia watched him stand stoically along the periphery. She looked back at the shocked Beatrix. "Who is Princess Annabelle?"

Beatrix gained control of herself and pulled Alicia down the hallway to inform her about the kidnapped princess from years past.

※

"Where has she been? How did she live?" Clara cried into her husband's chest as he rocked her. "And now … she drowned. Oh!" A deep groan escaped the lips of the queen.

"Shhh." The king patted her gently on the head.

"Why was it by water?" A past ache crept up inside the queen, confounding her already pitiful heart.

"Shhhh … At least we know now that she is dead." Her husband attempted to calm her.

Queen Clara, swallowing some tears, nodded her head as she thought of the truth of her husband's words. "Yes … she has stood before the Father and has been judged." She looked up at her husband. Glancing to her right, she saw the pain on all of her children's faces. She shook her head, willing herself to be strong. She sat back on to her legs and kissed her husband.

He wiped away a tear from her cheek. "Are you ready to get up?" She nodded. He helped her to stand.

The queen forced a smile when she spotted Sir Doey. She held out her hands toward him. "Michael."

"Your Majesty." He bowed.

She wondered why he did not take her hands. She looked into his eyes. He turned away from the intense emerald hue that could pierce his soul. "Michael, it's not your fault." He shook his head. She could tell he did not believe the words. She took his hand and squeezed it. "It is *not* your fault."

"I think it is time that we all change," the king said as he looked from his wife to every dripping child.

His children obediently stood and followed their mother up the stairs as she took Elizabeth's hand, lifting her dress with the other.

Watching his family ascend the steps, the king then looked at Grand Sir Doey, his long-time friend. "Where has she been? What became of her?" His mind swirled at all the fates she could have had. "Don't hold anything back. Give it to me plainly."

"Nicholaus Hunts told us —"

"Hunts? Nicholaus?" the king asked in disbelief. "What does he have to do with this?"

"He found her on his land."

"On his land?" The king turned directly in front of Michael. "How'd she get there?"

"She arrived on his beach after escaping off the Forbidden Island," Michael said as he spoke to his friend.

"The Forbidden Island?" the king demanded quizzically.

"None of us had ever heard of it. It is northeast of Anchony. Nicholaus was bringing her here when we found him, and he joined us to find Elizabeth. While he was helping us, the princesses found each other. The Demolites went after them and they ran. They ended up clinging to a cliff. Annabelle fell in the Angler River and down Angler Falls."

"She was … well?" the king asked, holding his breath.

"She looked well, sire. And she must have been quite strong for the amount of time she clung to the cliff."

"My daughters taking safety on a cliff!" He shook his head as he turned to the wall and, with controlled anger, banged upon it slowly with his fist.

"My children, my children! God, help us! How can we stop the Demolites? Those cowardly fiends! Hiding behind those masks! What can we do? They come out of nowhere and vanish just as quickly!" The king turned around and looked toward the ceiling. "Father, we need help." He put his fist to his mouth and slid down the wall.

"Francis." Michael's heart ached for his friend as he put his hand upon the king's shoulder.

"What can we do, Michael? What can we do?"

Michael sat down beside the king, shaking his head. He could find no words to comfort him. "If only we knew who they were and where to find them."

The king put his head up and stared across the foyer. "Could we plant a spy?" He looked at his friend.

Michael shook his head slowly. "I don't know. Who would we send?"

"How about Hunts?"

"Nicholaus?"

"Michael, who did we trust more than his father? Certainly he is as trustworthy."

Michael's thoughts churned. He had to speak about what was on his mind. "Not everyone feels the same."

"I don't care what jealous nobles think!" the king said as he stood.

Michael stood, sighing. "Those nobles help to keep you in power."

"You speak of a riot as if it is a breath away."

"Sometimes it feels that way, Francis. When I am out there" — he pointed his head toward the door — "the people don't know who to turn to. They are losing trust in their king because they are undefended."

"How can I defend my people when I can't even defend my family?"

They had questions but no answers.

The king turned toward the staircase. "Where is Hunts?"

"He is looking for Annabelle's body. He told her he would bring her home, and he intends to keep his word."

"Even in her death." The king nodded his head as he studied the stone staircase. "He is our man, Michael. He is our man."

Hope and Despair

Staring at her reflection in her crude mirror, Isabella watched her chin quiver as a tear rolled down her cheek. She was so entranced in her own sadness that she did not hear the servant approach or speak. It was not until the older servant, Beatrix, touched her that she was aware of her presence. The princess's reaction was severe and sudden as she bolted off the bench, grabbing her chest to try to slow her racing heart.

"My lady, I didn't mean to cause a fright."

"Beatrix." Her chest heaved as she tried to catch her breath.

"My lady, the queen sent me in here to help you change."

A new fright enveloped the princess. "Send Alicia in."

"Alicia is with your sister."

"Then I'll wait! It must be Alicia!" she said protectively as she grabbed her dress near her neck.

"You do not wish me to help you?" Beatrix lowered her head as if she had done something wrong.

"It's not that. It's — I need Alicia." Her knuckles turned white from grasping the dress so tightly, further distressed that her request was making Beatrix feel hurt.

Beatrix curtsied. "Yes, my lady."

William set the satchel down beside him on the chair. As thunder shook the window, he looked at the cold fireplace. Shaking his head in disgust at himself, he closed his eyes for a brief moment and then found the courage to rise and change his clothes.

247

There was a knock on the door as he stood before his armoire. He turned his head to the servant, Timothus, who held logs in his arms as he bowed. "Prince William, I am to start your fire."

William consented as he pointed with his hand toward his fireplace.

Timothus set the wood down as a lightning bolt splattered up toward the heavens and the green glass shook. "That is some weather, aye? I think it has rained off and on the whole time you have been gone. The rivers are taking on their own character — wild and mean."

"What?" William asked with anger as he halted from doffing his surcoat. Timothus looked up at him, not sure what he had said that upset the prince. "I will do the rest," William said.

"Your Highness, I —"

"Out! Now!"

Timothus looked to the floor as he bowed. "Yes, Your Highness."

William walked to the window without changing. Through the sheets of rain, he could see the Barstow River, nearly twice its size and three times its speed, rushing down the landscape. Closing his eyes, he saw the Angler River in all its fury, just after it had taken his sister.

"It's cold in here," Thomas announced as he entered. He looked to the fireplace. "Why is your fire not lit? Did Timothus not come?"

"I sent him away," William said as he continued to stare at the distant river.

Thomas went to the hallway and returned with an oil lamp. Heat was soon spreading throughout the bedroom. He returned the lamp to its spot and entered back into his brother's room, sitting in one of his brother's oak chairs, contemplating all the events.

"Will, are you certain it was her?"

He turned from the window. "It could be no one else."

"Are you certain she is dead?"

William walked behind his other chair, placing his hands on the back. "She fell into the Angler River. She was swept down the Angler Falls."

Thomas took a deep breath. "Angler Falls? Forty-five bodies have met that fate; not one has lived to tell the tale."

William looked at him before returning to his armoire to change his clothes.

Thomas leaned forward. "How did you find her?"

"Nicholaus Hunts found her," William said as he doffed his tunic. "He was bringing her here."

"Nicholaus? Really? I saw him when I was at the university." Thomas turned around to look at his brother. "How did he find her?" He sat back in the chair as he waited for the answer.

William changed his linen shirt and removed his hose. "He found her on his land. She just escaped from an island." He stuck his legs into a dry pair of hose.

"An island?" Thomas asked as his brother walked back to his chair and slumped down into it.

"The Forbidden Island." William spoke to the fire as his right elbow poked at the satchel. He sat up and grabbed it. "And this was hers."

Thomas studied it. "May I see that?"

William handed it to him.

Thomas felt the ties and leather design.

"What is it?" William asked.

Thomas leaned forward. "You see the make of the bag? The sewing and the place of the ties?"

William placed his feet upon the floor. "What about it?"

"This is a soldier's bag, issued 20 to 30 years ago, only to the officers of the highest honor in the crusade."

"Let me see that." William took the bag back.

"How did she get it?" Thomas asked.

"There was a man on the island who raised her," William said as he studied the satchel. He then looked up. "Peter was his name."

"What's in it?"

William shook his head. "She wasn't to open it until she made it back safely to her room."

"She isn't coming back," Thomas said as he looked into his brother's eyes.

William nodded as he looked at the satchel and untied it.

Cristine, in her dry clothes and wet hair, looked down the long hallway toward the servants' wing as she stood outside her father's public chamber abutting the Hall of Justice. "Papá?"

The king, hearing his daughter call, turned away from his fireplace and walked toward the door. "Cristine, is that you?" He pushed the heavy oak door open. "What are you doing?"

"Papá, do you not find it odd that most of Prince Phillipus's men are here at the castle while he is not?"

"He only went to the market, Cristine, to learn any tidings about Johannes Fletcher." He stepped aside so she would come into the room.

"And why has he taken such an interest in the missing man?" she asked as she walked inside.

"He wishes to show how helpful Sethel can be."

"To be *worthy* of Isabella?" she asked with great sarcasm.

The king shook his head. "Cristine, I don't want to hear about this again."

"But why does he have so many men, Papá? His knights are nearly as many as ours!"

"I told King Henrard what it's like in Anchony; he wanted to make certain his son was safe!"

"Did he leave any for himself?" she mumbled under her breath as she folded her arms.

"What's that?"

She finally let loose of the real concern she had — the one he was tired of hearing about: "I don't like him, Papá."

"Well, it's a good thing *you're* not marrying him!" He turned toward his fireplace, trying to distance himself from the conversation.

"Isa shouldn't have to marry him either!"

"Have to?" He turned back toward his daughter. "She agreed to it!"

"She agreed to it for Anchony, not for herself. She knows how it will make Anchony stronger. How could she not when we are daily confronted with the horrors of the Demolites?" She defiantly held back the tears that wanted to fall.

King Francis shook his head and, with a lowered voice, said, "You're not to hear those tidings."

"Well, we do! We know how badly Anchony is in need of help!"

Compassionately, he stepped forward and took his daughter's hands. "Cristine, do you have proof of Prince Phillipus being malicious in any way?"

"No," she was forced to admit.

"Then you need to stop speaking ill of him."

"But —"

"It's all set! King Henrard, I'm certain, is on his way here by now."

"With more knights?" Shaking her head, she stepped away. "This isn't right!" She marched out, more frustrated than when she entered, passing by Sir Michael.

"What disturbs Princess Cristine?" Michael asked as he entered.

"It's Cristine. She always has words about something."

Michael looked at the paper in his hands. "I fear I've got

words to say, too."

"What's that?"

Alicia silently pulled the dress over the fading bruises on Princess Isabella's back as the servant swallowed hard.

They both nervously jumped when the door opened. Seeing it was Cristine, Alicia took a relieved breath.

"Oh, Alicia, I didn't know you were in here."

Finishing her task, Alicia stepped away. "I'll leave you now, my lady."

Isabella silently nodded as she held back tears and walked back to her window.

Cristine followed her. "Isa, have you been crying?"

Isabella turned away, finding a seat on the bench in front of the mirror.

"Although I have no memory of her, I, too, feel like I lost her again. Lost a sister I never truly knew." Cristine looked at her sister's reflection. "I'll lose you, too, when you marry and move to Sethel."

Gasping, fresh tears rolled down Isasbella's cheeks as her hand flew to her mouth.

Cristine sat down beside her. "I know you must feel her death worse than I for you have —"

Isabella could stand no more. "I don't cry because of Annie."

Cristine looked at her sister's reflection. "Then why do you cry?"

Standing, Isabella walked back toward the window. "I can't tell you."

"Why not?"

"Because it would only make things far worse."

"Make what worse? Isa, you're scaring me. What's going on?" Cristine straightened. "Is this about Prince Phillipus? You know I've never liked him."

"Stop! Stop speaking like that! I've agreed to marry him, so marry him, I shall!"

Cristine stepped away in annoyance.

"Papá says an alliance with Sethel would be most helpful to Anchony. They could send in more men to figure out who the Demolites —"

"Well, I don't like their men, either!"

Isabella pleaded for understanding. "Crisa, please! Tell me what I'm doing is right!"

"You don't love him, Isa! You hardly know him! You agreed to marry him after exchanging letters and he's only been here a few weeks!"

Isabella turned toward the green glass in her window. "The one man I loved is dead."

Cristine, stepping closer, stroked her sister's hair. "Isa, please. I only want what's best for you."

"And I want what's best for Anchony."

William opened the satchel and removed a leather scroll lying on top of other items wrapped in leather.

"What is it?" Thomas asked as he sat back in the chair.

William looked at his brother. "It has Annabelle's name on it."

"She could read?"

"I suppose," William said as he untied the thin leather strap.

Thomas leaned forward in his chair. "What does it say?"

William read aloud: "'My dearest Annabelle, if you are reading this, then you safely made it home.'" William looked up at his brother and shook his head as Thomas frowned. William cleared his throat and continued, "'I thank God for your safe return. Do not worry about my lot, for I am in God's hands. Please, however, keep praying for me and my family, and I will keep praying for you until we see each other in Heaven.'"

"'My sweet child, this I want you to know — I never told you a lie, but I also held back the truth. My dear princess, I know your true identity — Annabelle of Anchony, fourth child of Francis and Clara, King and Queen of Anchony.'" William looked up at Thomas in shock.

Thomas moved to the edge of his seat. "Who is he?"

"Nicholaus said he was a hermit by the name of Peter," William stated, shaking his head.

Thomas waved him on. "Read on!"

William looked back down at the leather. "'My child, do not be angry that I hid this from you, for it made no matter upon the island and I'm certain it was all a part of God's care. You are ready to take your place as a princess of Anchony. You have learned well all that I have taught you and your ability to reason astounds me. Your use of justice and mercy in every matter has sailed past my hope for you — the scholar has indeed eclipsed the teacher —'"

"Who is this man?" Thomas asked.

William shrugged his shoulders as he looked back at the leather and continued: "'I think back on my life and see how God's hand has been leading me to this point. It was my family's slaughtering that led me to the Forbidden Island, which led me to become your teacher. I am honored that I was chosen to bring up a leader of Anchony. For you shall be a leader: Your love, your openness to God, your wisdom, and your understanding are too sharp not to lead something. You shall not be forgotten by Anchonians in ages to come.'"

William's voice changed as he read the next line: "'Alas, my child I must tell you — I was acquainted with *your father* —'"

"What!" Thomas shouted as he sat up so straight he nearly jumped out of the chair.

"Shhh!" William put up his hand. "Let me get to the end. 'Enclosed in this bag is a gift for your father. Give it to him yourself — place it in his hands to be certain he gets it.'"

Thomas grabbed the satchel and removed a parcel that bore his father's name. William continued as Thomas pulled out another package. "'There is yet another gift for Fr. Dominicus. I am aware that you don't know who this man is, but put faith in God that He will send him to you.'"

Thomas held up the package. "Father Dominicus? Is that Bishop Dominicus?"

"It could be," William said as he read the rest of the letter. "'I must close now, my princess, my child, my little one. Never forget to do all things with humility, for you are a wonderful woman of God. With all of my affection, your Peter.'" William looked at his brother.

They spoke at the same time: "We must tell Papá."

Together they ran out of the bedroom.

Michael walked farther into the king's public chamber. "The queen has me figured out, sire." He offered the king a paper.

"What is this?" The king took the paper and opened it.

"A letter for the release from my duty as commander of the king's knight."

The king stood and stared at Michael. "Release from your duty?" He shook his head. "No. You are not released!" Turning toward the fire, he attempted to read by the light. Tears filled his eyes. He could not finish it. He looked back at Michael, seething with anger and hurt. "Are you trying to betray me?!"

"No!" Michael said adamantly as he grabbed his belt.

"Why? Why would you give this to me?" The king crumpled it in his grasp.

"I don't think — there must be someone better than

me." His voice cracked for he could not hold back his own emotion.

"Better than you? I trust no one more than you, Michael! You have been there for me and for my family through it all!"

Michael nodded his head. "Yes, I have been here. I was in command when Annabelle was taken the first time. I was in command when Elizabeth was taken. I was there when Annabelle was lost for a second time."

"Michael, you weren't *here* when they were taken! If you had been, they wouldn't have been taken! Has your memory failed you? You were looking for that Demolite castle when Annabelle was taken, and you were following more tidings of the Demolites when Elizabeth was snatched away. You have spared my family harm a multitude of times! Have you forgotten when Cristine was 5 and she wandered away while we were at Mass? When William and Thomas insisted they spend a night in the woods and Thomas got lost in the trees? Or when the wild man from Bethel tried to lure Isabella away? What about those times? You were there for us, and there is no one I trust more with my family! You are the best knight I know!" The king shook his head as he chucked the paper into the fire. "Whether you like it or not, you are a part of this family." The king fell back into his chair.

Michael sat in the chair opposite the king's. "She was in my sight and ... she slipped away." Michael looked down at the floor. "I have never felt so unskilled. If only we would've arrived a minute earlier. She had held on for so long. She had no more strength. Your daughter was right *there*." He quietly remembered and then cleared his throat. "I'm sorry, sire."

The king studied his friend. "Michael, my family *is* your life. You've given your wife, your children. My family is all you have left."

Michael nodded. "Yes, that's true."

"Laura was a great lady," the king said as he recalled her kindness and smile.

"She was," Michael agreed with a brief smile.

The king shook his head. "All that you have endured; all that the knights have endured; all that Jous endured."

Michael, taking a deep breath, sat up in the chair. "I miss him."

"As do I."

Michael began to chuckle. "I think I miss his lessons the most." He shook his head. "How he liked to beat me up. 'You can't learn without feeling it.'" Michael recalled the words of his old friend.

"Where would we be if he was here?"

"You would be better defended," Michael said with confidence. "Don't look at me like that. You know it's true. Jous was always more skilled and quicker. He didn't earn the name 'the Lion' for nothing."

The king took a deep breath. "Yes, it seemed to move through his blood. When will his son be back?"

"I told him to return here after two weeks — no matter if he found her or not."

The king turned to his friend, irritated. "I want my daughter found."

Michael put up his hand. "I know. I know. But I also know that you want — we need — Nicholaus, so I gave him a timeframe. When he returns, we will send others to look." Standing quickly, Michael unsheathed his sword as the door burst open.

He replaced the sword and looked at the king when he spotted the two princes.

"Why do you not knock?" the king asked as he looked at his sons.

Both princes spoke at the same time: "There's no time for that." "This is a great matter!"

"Whoa! Calm down." The king extended his hand. "What is this about?"

Again, they spoke at the same time: "Gifts." "Peter's bag."

"One at a time. One at a time," the king demanded.

"Annabelle's bag?" Michael asked.

"Yes," William answered as Thomas enthusiastically nodded.

Thomas placed the package bearing the king's name on Francis's lap. "What's this?"

"It was in her bag," Thomas said. "Read the letter. Read the letter," he told William.

"We opened her bag to see what was in it — she didn't even know. The man who raised her — Peter — gave it to her."

"The man who raised her?"

"But he knew who she was!" Thomas cut in. "And he claims to know you, too!"

"He knows me?" the king asked incredulously. He looked at Michael. "I don't know a Peter."

"Let me read the letter. Listen to this …" William read the scripted letter. Michael sat down in the chair again as Thomas leaned against the fireplace.

"Oh! And the bag … look at it!" Thomas pointed toward William. "It was issued to officers of the highest honor 20 to 30 years ago."

"An officer in the crusade?" the king asked as he looked at his sons and his longtime friend.

"Open the gift, Papá!"

The king looked at the package in his lap and the package in Thomas's hand. "And the other is for Fr. Dominicus? Is that Bishop Dominicus?"

"We wondered the same thing," William said.

The king turned the package in his lap over and untied it. He cleared his throat and read: "'To my dear and faithful friend, Francis …'" The king looked up at Michael, who shook his perplexed head.

The king continued reading: "'You are probably wondering about this unknown letter and how your precious daughter, Annabelle, came to have it. It is God's will that she get this home — I know it is! I will give her my bag with the demand that it not be opened until she is safely home.'" He stopped and swallowed hard as he realized his daughter would never be safely home.

Sighing, he continued: "'I was blessed when God called me to a small cave on the Forbidden Island. In that cave I found a scared and shivering child hiding from a multitude of men. She made me think of my Clare. I took her to my dwelling and began to teach her how to live well in our harsh world. My dear friend, your precious daughter became mine, and she began to put light back into my life. I thank you for allowing me to have a part in bringing her up.'" The king looked up. *Allowing?*

Thomas and William read their father's face; they knew he was not happy with their sister being reared by a stranger or — worse — a stranger who pretended to know the king.

The king continued, after tilting his head. "'Her awareness of right and wrong is well placed, and her sense of justice without fault.'"

"'Every day, I watch her grow into a young lady more full of God's beauty than she was the day before, marked with her clear, emerald eyes — no doubt from Clara.'" The king stood as he read his wife's name. He continued, his voice wavering, "'She makes me think of Clara in her grace and in all of her form but her jaw, which, without doubt, comes from you.'" The king looked up from the letter. "Who is this?!" He looked at the faces around him — they were just as clueless. He shook his head and continued reading: "'I hope you do not think me wrong for teaching her the ways of fighting, but after seeing what my dear Sara went through, I feared what could pass if I did not.'"

"Fighting?" Michael asked. He looked at William.

The king stared at his friend and eventually continued, "'My dear friend, I realize now I have written all this to you and have not said my name: I am ...'" The king's mouth dropped open; he could not speak the name.

"Who?" William came closer as did Thomas.

"Josephus Peter the Lion." Crashing into his chair, the letter fell from his hand and fluttered to the stone ground.

Michael retrieved it and continued, "'Josephus Peter the Lion, your childhood friend. Your daughter does not know me by that name — only by 'Peter.'"

"'I hope you did not think me dead, or worse, a betrayer. Let me tell you what took place. After my whole family was massacred by the Demolites, I fled to the Forbidden Island for three reasons. One, I wished to escape from my memories. Two, I feared I would turn to violence if I remained in the kingdom. Three — the highest of them all — I believed God was calling me to do so. I now understand why God called me to this desolate island — to take care of your Annabelle.'"

"'Now, the true reason for my letter — I have given Annabelle a gift for you. I need to account for it, for I fear it was what brought about the destruction of my family.'"

"'The day I entered the Demolite castle ...'" Michael looked at the king as his reading slowed. "'... my men most likely did not see me return for I snuck out an unknown way. How did I know about it? I found a drawing of the castle.'" Michael, glancing at the king again, turned his attention back to the letter and continued. "'I heard the Demolites coming and I gathered all I could. After 16 years, I looked at what I had taken. Francis! I wish I could have given it all to you sooner! You will find a book containing a list of Anchonians with affection toward the Demolites as well as a list of Demolite spies, which contained a few names I know.'"

The king opened up the other packages hastily as Michael continued reading:

"'I also came upon the Demolite Manifesto. It is Sir Victorus! Sir Victorus is their leader!'" Michael shook his head. "Is this true?" He looked at the king.

"Is that the end? Keep reading," Thomas insisted.

Michael looked back to the letter. "'The Demolites knew I was in the castle. They knew I took things, and they wanted their books back, I can only hope that by my leaving Anchony, the Demolites will have forgotten about the missing articles or think me dead and the articles lost forever.'"

"'I hope no other families suffer from my deeds.'" Michael's eyes began to sting. He sniffled as he continued. "'Your sweet daughter will be returning shortly, so I must close. Send my love to Clara and the children as well as to Michael and his family.'" Michael took a deep breath as he tried to push back the tears. "'Do not worry about me, for I am in God's hands, and may God's will always be done.'"

"'The gifts I provided to Annabelle for you contain the articles I took from the Demolite castle. May my family's suffering not be in vain. With deepest friendship and goodwill, Josephus Peter the Lion.'"

The four men stared at each other in shock.

"… and I've never seen anyone move as fast as she did!" Elizabeth said with astonishment as she told her mother the tale of her rescue.

"What's that, dear?" Clara asked in confusion as she held both her youngest daughter's and youngest son's hand as they walked down the upstairs hallway, Elizabeth fresh from a bath. Spotting Alicia, she called out to the servant.

"My lady?" the servant replied as she turned toward the queen and curtsied.

"Beatrix tells me Isabella asked for you to dress her. Do you know why?"

Alicia suddenly became nervous; the queen noticed. "My lady, the princess must have her reason … and that reason is hers to tell … only hers."

"I see." She looked over at Isabella's door. "Is she in her chamber?"

"I believe," Alicia said with great anxiety.

"I see. Alicia, will you take Elizabeth and Eduard to the parlor? I'd like to talk to my daughter alone."

"Yes, my lady," Alicia said nervously as she took the prince's and princess's hand and curtsied.

As she took the children downstairs, Alicia passed by the king, who was on a mission to find his wife.

"Clara!" he called out when he saw his wife about to knock upon Isabella's door.

"Francis?" She turned away from the door.

"Clara, you're not going to believe this!"

"What?"

"We know who started the Demolites," he said with a smile.

"Who?"

"Sir Victorus."

Mouth dropping open in shock, her head shook as she thought about the news. "Because of me? Is all their doing because of me?"

"No, my love, it's because of Sir Victorus!"

Seeing the smile upon his face, she said, "You don't seem angry?"

"Clara, we have answers! I only hope it is all truth."

She studied her husband's face. "You know more?"

He took her elbow. "I'll tell you everything, but we must go to the Hall of Justice. All the servants are being summoned."

"Whatever for?"

"Princess Isabella, Prince Phillipus is here and is requesting you meet him in the parlor," Ikus announced after knocking on the princess's door.

"Well, I must go," Isabella said to her sister as she stood stiffly.

Cristine, following behind, watched her sister exit the bedroom and walk towards the stairs. "I'll go with you, Isa."

Isabella turned around sharply. "No! I mean … Alicia will be with me."

Cristine, slowly following behind, rounded the stairs with folded arms as her right shoulder rubbed against the rough stone.

"Prince Phillipus." Cristine heard her sister speak. "You're back. Have you any tidings of Mr. Fletcher?"

"None today. We're on the lookout though."

As Cristine walked down the last few stairs, stopping three steps behind her sister, Phillipus grinned at her; she did not return a cordial smile.

"I wish to speak with you, Princess Isabella."

Isabella looked to the king's knight. "Find Alicia."

"Your Highness, all of the servants have been summoned to the Hall of Justice," the knight informed her.

Phillipus, in a near panic, turned toward the knight. "What for?"

"For business of the king," Sir Underwood said.

"Of course." Phillipus shook his head and offered his elbow toward Isabella. "Shall we go down there?"

Cristine suspiciously watched her sister take the prince's elbow and walk down the hallway, followed by the eight men who had accompanied him while at the market.

Queen Clara held out her hands to her two youngest children, calling them to herself as she stood inside the Hall of Justice; Alicia gladly released them as the servants looked around in confusion.

Taking their hands, the queen looked back at Alicia; the servant looked lost and fearful amongst the whisperings of the servants. She gladly ran to Beatrix and Ida.

"Donaldus Lands!" the king called with anger in his eyes.

"Sire?" the landworker said, stepping forward from among the other servants.

"Come here!" the king demanded. He slowly stepped forward, breathing hard. "Tell me" — the king stepped up very, very close to him — "are you a Demolite?"

Whisperings erupted throughout the room.

"No," he said, almost laughing. He looked around at everybody in the room; no one else was laughing. "Why would you accuse me as such?"

The king held up the journal. "This book was taken from the Demolite castle. It contains names; one of which is yours."

The man gulped and shifted his weight uneasily. "Where … where did you get that?"

"Does it matter?!" William stepped forward.

The king stopped him from advancing. "If he is not, now is the time for him to deny it." He looked back at the landscaper. "It is from General Commander Josephus Peter the Lion."

The man swallowed hard and looked to the ground. "I have served this castle for 22 years." He shook his head as he looked up at the king. A smirk slowly emerged. "And it took you 22 years to figure that out!"

"Arrest him!" the king yelled as William tried to grab at the man but was stopped by his father. "And don't let anybody leave! Markus Smith, Lucas Mason, Timus Baker — arrest them all!" The king walked toward his wife still barking commands. "Call upon General Hoskins — reassemble the soldiers. I want all these rats arrested!" Clara picked up her son and moved to the wall with her daughter in her other hand.

"They are all Demolites?" she asked the king when he was right in front of her.

"I think" — he dared to smile — "our prayers have finally been answered." He kissed her and hugged her. Taking his son into his arms, he kissed his head.

Cristine, Isabella, the foreign prince, and the posse of men from Sethel — Sethelians — walked toward the Hall of Justice but were greeted by a closed door with yelling inside.

"What's going on?" Cristine looked at her sister. Isabella shook her head, clueless. The doors opened, and the knights marched out with four servants bound.

"Michael, what has come to pass?" Cristine asked.

"Spies among us."

"Spies?" Isabella said with concern.

"Prince Phillipus." Clara stepped into the hallway. "You're back from the market?"

"Yes, Your Majesty." He bowed his head, working tirelessly to not make eye contact. "I was wondering if I could speak with Isabella in the parlor. Is that Alicia around?"

"Yes. Alicia," the queen called, waving her forward.

Clara watched the servant lower her head and hesitate the moment she realized the reason for her summoning.

The queen stared at the tapestries on her chamber wall as she helped Beatrix to take down her hair.

"Beatrix?"

"Yes, my lady?"

"Do all of Prince Phillipus servants remain when he is away?"

After a moment of silence, Beatrix answered, "They do, my lady."

"Is there something you're not telling me, Beatrix?"

"No, my lady, not for certain."

The queen looked at her servant. "Your meaning?"

"I don't know, my lady. Everyone seems off with the Sethelian servants here."

"Off? Why?"

"They are *always* around."

"Yet, Prince Phillipus has been here very little, hasn't he? I've scarely spoken with him."

"And the times you've seen him, my lady?"

"I haven't seen him long enough to say anything about him." *Does he avoid me?* She looked over her shoulder at the servant, "Have you seen anything going on between Isabella and Prince Phillipus?"

"What do you mean, my lady?"

"Isabella does not seem herself, though she hasn't ever been the same since Annabelle's taking. If you see anything, anything at all, let me know."

Beatrix looked at the queen's reflection, pondering on her words. "Yes, my lady."

The queen's hair cascaded down her back after the removal of the hair threads. The queen looked over at the door and saw the king enter.

"Beatrix, will you leave us? Thank you." Beatrix put down the brush and curtsied before exiting.

"Francis." The queen turned toward him as he doffed his belt with his sword. "Something is off with the servants, especially Alicia."

"They've found out they've been working side by side with Demolites for years," the king offered.

Standing, she moved toward the bed. "It was even before that. I think it might have to do with the Sethelian servants."

"What about them?" he asked as he removed his embroidered tunic.

"I don't know. I wish I did, but I don't." She sat down on the edge of the bed.

Sitting down next to her, he took her hand. "Have the servants said anything to you?"

"No. I wish they would."

"Not even Beatrix?"

"She doesn't know anything."

Staring at her hand, he offered, "Do you wish to have another meeting?"

"I'm certain the one today shook them up well. I can't do that to them. We'll see if she's better with the Demolites gone." She leaned her head upon his shoulder. "I shall add it to my prayers." She made a face. "If my prayers do any good."

Sliding off the bed, he got in front of her. "What's that to mean, my lady?"

"I have prayed for Sir Victorus for years — for his heart to change." A tear ran down her cheek. "And hearing he started the Demolites ... and because of *me*!"

"No, Clara! It's not your fault! It is the fault of malicious men."

As tears streamed down her face, her heart spoke. "Why can't he change?! Why can't he find God?" She shook her head. "I fear my prayers have fallen on deaf ears."

"No. No, my queen." He hugged her. "God always hears our prayers."

Isabella sat on the floor in front of her fireplace as her tears soaked her gown. Distraught and sinking into despair, her desolate self saw no hope, no chance of escape. She had no reaction to the knock on the door; no signs of life but the bare essentials.

She felt a hand upon her head; she saw her sister's hair; she felt her sister's cheek upon the side of her skin; and then her view of the fireplace rotated as Cristine moved her head into Cristine's lap.

"Isa! Tell me what's wrong. Please!" Cristine did not know what words to speak that could bring comfort; she did not know the overwhelming cloud of tribulation and gloom her sister felt. She held her sister among the sounds of sobbing as her tears — tears from not knowing how to help Isabella — found those of her sister's.

With the sunrise, a ray of hope emerged over all of Anchony as an army was beginning to assemble. A number of men were arrested during the night for crimes against the king. A spark of hope lit in many hearts across the land. A precious hope to so many, though to two princesses, it did not come.

Word spread through the Demolites as well: The journal stolen by the Lion was found, and the army was coming to arrest those labeled as Demolites. Fear enveloped them — this was a long-awaited retribution. Their fear turned to panic, their panic to chaos, and their chaos to attack. The Demolites, however, did not fall into total despair, for their greatest plan was still at work.

Visitor

"Excuse me." Nicholaus addressed the guards at the gate. "I am Nicholaus Hunts. Could you tell Sir Doey I am here?"

The guard eyed his sword and then moved his head to the other guard, signaling him to find the knight.

Nicholaus leaned against the wall. He was tired, so very tired. He patted Cinny as she, too, rested.

"Sir," the guard addressed Michael. "There is a man at the gate asking for you."

Michael turned from the pile of weapons being cleaned and sharpened as all eyes went up. "Who is he?"

"He said his name is Nicholaus Hunts."

William turned toward the guard, away from his brother, whom he had been instructing in better fighting techniques. "Nicholaus is here?" He sheathed his sword and ran toward the gates.

"He's early," Michael said as he followed the prince.

"Your Highness." The guard bowed toward the prince as he approached the gate.

"Squire Hunts."

William could see the head of his horse, but that was it. He did not know for sure if he wanted to see the bundle he thought the horse would carry. Nicholaus stepped away from the wall toward the gate as Cinny, too, moved closer. William looked around desperately from Cinny's saddle to Nicholaus's arms. When he found nothing there, he searched the ground.

"I didn't find her." Nicholaus saw the disappointment in the prince's eyes, and he suddenly felt ashamed for returning empty-handed. "I thought I would profit if —"

"Let him in," William ordered.

"Your Highness, he is armed."

William looked at the guard again. "Let him in."

The guard looked to Grand Sir Doey as he approached. "Let him in," Michael said firmly.

The guard opened up the gate and held out his hand. "Your sword."

"No," William replied.

"It's all right," Michael echoed the prince's sentiments.

The guard looked at the prince and knight as if they had both lost their minds.

"You want him armed on the castle grounds?" He watched the prince shake the arm of the armed man in shock.

"You did not find her?" Michael said as he looked at Cinny's back.

Nicholaus looked at the man. "I came to the castle so I could fulfill my duty. So many did not trust me. I figured the only way they would speak to me was if I was a knight."

Nodding his head, Michael stuck out his hand and shook Nicholaus's. "Nicholaus Hunts, it would be an honor to fight beside you."

Nicholaus looked to the ground, exhausted. "If I may take my horse to the barn."

"I will have Sir Martinus take it for you," William said as he waved to a knight from across the yard.

"No. She has treated me well; I will do the same for her."

The prince and head knight watched a man with so much conviction walk toward the stable.

Prince William looked at Michael with a smile. "Sir Hunts it is!" He nodded his head, looking at the castle. "I will tell my father he's here."

He brushed down Cinny as she drank. He had not slept in two days, and the fatigue was overwhelming. He laid his forehead upon her neck for a second.

"Nicholaus."

He slowly walked out of the stall. There stood his Anna. Anna, alive. Before him. Unharmed, in a beautiful dress — a princess before his eyes.

He reached for her.

She slowly shook her head as his hand drew nearer and nearer, but never close enough to touch.

Jerking his head back, he woke with a startle. He looked around, disoriented for a moment. Out of his periphery, he spotted an inch of skirt and long hair leaving the barn. Was *that* his imagination? A walking dream? He followed it.

He looked in wonder at the back of a lady, the same height as his Anna, the exact build. The hair the same length but a slightly different shade. There was another lady present. Distressed and in tears, Nicholaus heard the other whisper, "They say —"

"Anna?" He did not mean to interrupt, but he had to know.

Both ladies jumped at the voice. The one closest to him had fright upon her face, but no emerald eyes.

Taking a few steps backward, she defensively backed into the crying woman.

"I'm sorry. I didn't mean to scare you both."

Isabella quickly gasped as she tried to act as if she had not been scared out of her wits by the unknown man.

"Are you all right?" He moved a step closer with his hand out.

She looked around and then back at him. "Who ... who are you?"

He looked to the ground. "Forgive me, I … I am Squire Nicholaus Hunts."

Glancing at the crying servant behind her, the princess took a step away from the wall, breathing hard. "Nicholaus, did you find my sister?"

"Sister?" Nicholaus stood straight and then bowed. "Princess, I'm sorry; I did not mean to dishonor you."

Isabella's concerned eyes diverted to the stable opening. "Where is she?"

Nicholaus looked at the princess before him. "You are the closest thing I have found to her." He shook his head. "I'm sorry." He turned away as his voice cracked. He cleared his throat. "I have not found her."

Isabella openly cried as a new despair pressed against her heart. She turned away from him to look at Alicia.

"It is only right that you mourn your sister. Is it … Princess Isabella?"

He saw her head nod from the back.

"She spoke of you."

She turned around, gasping. "She spoke of me?"

He nodded his head. "She spoke of all her siblings — lovingly."

Her eyes seemed to dance for the briefest moment.

Nicholaus looked at the distraught servant. "Is she all right?"

Alicia lowered her head as she tried to conceal her cries.

Isabella, gasping herself, said, "Please leave us, Squire Hunts."

"Can I be of service?"

"Leave us to ourselves," the princess said adamantly.

"Yes, Your Highness," he said and cautiously returned into the barn.

Isabella, watching him go and certain he was out of ear-shot, turned toward her servant. "Alicia, what have they done to you now?"

Moving her collar and an extra cloth to absorb the blood, she revealed the start of a laceration. "They say what the king has done means nothing. Anchony still needs the men and if you dare to back out of the wedding, they will go deeper with the dagger and kill me the next time. And they won't stop with me — they'll go for all the servants!" Shaking her head, she dropped down to the ground. "There's so many of them, my lady! I think they could and I think they would!"

Isabella joined her on the ground with her own tears. "Why are they like this? I want nothing to do with Sethel! Nothing to do with them at all!" She leaned against the side of the barn. "What am I going to do?"

Walking toward the castle, Nicholaus was greeted by the royal family at the east entrance.

The king and queen had been informed of his unsuccessful mission, but Elizabeth had not.

"Where's Annie?" the girl asked as she looked up from his feet.

He knelt down. "I haven't found her yet. But I give you my word, she'll get home. I'll bring her home."

She wrapped her little arms around his neck. He picked her up and hugged her. Looking at the people before him as they descended the steps toward him, everyone in some small way reminded him of his beloved Anna … and the queen's eyes … he could barely look at her, for the resemblance was uncanny.

The king approached. Nicholaus bowed with Elizabeth in his arms. When he realized he still held the young princess, he set her down, his face reddening.

Shaking his head, the king hugged Nicholaus. "You look so much like your father."

Nicholaus did not know what to do — the king was hugging him.

"Nicholaus." The queen stepped forward with outstretched arms. He was forced to look into the queen's sparkling, clear, emerald eyes — he found strength and clarity. Taking her hand, he bowed. "Your Majesty." He let go and looked away. "I'm sorry, but your eyes." He could not finish.

"We've been told," the king said. "Squire Hunts, I don't believe you have met everyone. This is Prince Eduard." He patted on Eduard's shoulders, who now stood before him. "You have met Princess Elizabeth and Prince William." William nodded as he picked up Elizabeth. "This is Princess Cristine, and Prince Thomas is coming."

"We have met!" Thomas said as he descended the steps. "We met at the hunting competition in Anchelo." He extended his hand as Nicholaus bowed to him. "Old acquaintances do not bow."

Nicholaus stood up and took his hand. "Yes. And you won an award for your studies, if my memory serves me."

Thomas nodded.

"Oh, here comes Isabella," the king said as he looked toward the barn.

Nicholaus looked back to see the princess and servant walking forward with lowered heads. "Yes, we've met."

"Come! There is much to speak about," the king said, patting Nicholaus on the shoulder.

"Sire, I will willingly go, but at present … I would only like a bed."

"A bed?" The king had important information to give him.

"Francis, he has not rested in a while. Look at his eyes. Any words can wait until after a sleep," the queen suggested lovingly.

"Of course, you're right. Nicholaus, Ikus will take you to your room."

Ikus, looking over at Alicia, stepped forward. "I'm at your service, Squire Hunts."

Nicholaus followed the man into the castle.

"Isabella," the queen called to her daughter. "Isabella, I want to speak to you."

The princess, hurrying up the stairs, looked to the steps. She did not want the queen to see her reddened eyes. "Mamá?"

Glancing over at Alicia, Clara noticed that the servant, too, had been crying. "Isabella, I want to see you in your chamber. Alicia, join us. Cristine, you, too."

"Mamá?" Cristine asked as she watched her mother walk up the steps.

"I want to know what is going on and I want to know now," the queen spoke firmly as she looked at her two seated daughters and then turned to the standing servant.

Cristine nodded her head. "If I knew, I would tell you, but I know nothing!" She stood up to turn toward her sister. "Isa will not say! I'm worried about her, Mamá!"

Isabella gasped as she forced herself not to speak a word.

Her mother knelt down in front of her. "Isabella, tell me, please!"

The princess looked away.

The queen, standing, approached the servant. "Alicia, I know you know. Tell me."

Alicia pinched her lips together as her chin began to quiver.

Clara stepped back. "If you will not tell me, I can't help you." Frustrated, Clara walked out as she shook her head.

Cristine sat down next to her sister. "Isa, why won't you tell Mamá? I'm certain there's nothing she can't make right."

A torrent of tears rolled down Isabella's cheeks. "Not this time, Crisa. She can't make it better this time. No one can. Too much could be lost."

Nicholaus awoke from his restful sleep with the full realization that he was in the castle. His Anna was still lost, but he would soon be a knight.

The heavy wooden door creaked as he opened it. Stepping out into the stone hallway, he noted the intricate tapestries, the oil lamps lighting the path, and the knight standing at the top of the stairwell. He nodded to him; the knight nodded back. Nicholaus descended the spiral stone staircase quickly.

"Ah, Nicholaus!" The queen was walking past the stairwell at the perfect moment with Cristine beside her. "Will you join us for supper?" She smiled briefly.

Nicholaus bowed to her and followed her toward the hall.

"Four men, you say?" Thomas listened with disbelief to his youngest sister as they walked out of the parlor. "And quickly?"

"Yes, but two got up!" Elizabeth elaborated. She turned to her other brother. "Didn't you see, Will?"

"I didn't, Liza," William said in truth. "But I did see two men on the ground."

Elizabeth, catching Nicholaus's sight, ran to him. "You were there. Didn't you see?"

"See what?"

"Annie! She took down the men like that!" She snapped her fingers together.

"Anna?" He shook his head in confusion.

"She saved my life, you know?"

"Yes. I do know that." Nicholaus smiled as he recalled how Annabelle had given her life for the child before him; Annabelle's sisterly love had known no bounds.

Elizabeth suddenly gasped. "Are you to eat with us?"

"I will."

Elizabeth grabbed Nicholaus's hand. "Sit by me!"

"Elizabeth," the queen corrected her, "Nicholaus will sit where your father wishes."

Her brow furrowed, then, as if a marvelous idea had entered her head, she dropped Nicholaus's hand and ran down the hall to try to find her father. "Papá! Papá!"

"Elizabeth!" her mother chided, shaking her head. She looked back at her other children; they were all smiling — thankful their little Liza was with them and able to make such a ruckus. She could not help but smile, too.

William stepped forward, offering his hand. "How are you doing — truly?"

Nicholaus took his hand and looked at him and Thomas. "I wish I came with my duty done."

"You will. You will," William said, squeezing his hand.

"If anyone can find anything, it's you," Thomas proclaimed.

Nicholaus closed his eyes and shook his head. "I wish there were prints to track."

A silence fell between them.

"The princess demands that you sit next to her."

Nicholaus turned around to meet the eyes of the king; he bowed.

"And has her demand been granted?" the queen shot back.

The king looked at his wife and then at Elizabeth out of the corner of his eyes. "It has."

"Yes!" Elizabeth jumped and grabbed Nicholaus's hand again. "Let me show you where you sit." He was dragged inside the Great Hall.

The young princess skipped ahead. "This is my seat, and here's your seat."

"You're giving him my chair?" Thomas said, pretending to be upset.

"I don't wish to take your seat," Nicholaus said.

Thomas shook his head and smiled as he waited for a reply from Elizabeth. "Well ..." She did not have a solution.

Thomas pulled out her chair for her, and she sat down, still thinking.

"You go ahead and sit there." Thomas nodded to Nicholaus as he walked around to the other side of the table and stood across from Elizabeth, to the right of William. The men sat down when the queen and princesses were seated.

The king made the Sign of the Cross as everyone followed. They all bowed their heads as the king prayed, "Father, we thank You for this day and all of our blessings. Thank You for the arrival of Nicholaus. Bless him in all of his duties." His voice cracked; he cleared his throat, and it was a good 10 seconds before he concluded, "Thank You for the food You give us this day. Amen."

Nicholaus looked up as he signed himself. Everyone had a distant sadness in their countenances. Even the previously happy Elizabeth was burdened with far too much for such a tender age.

He closed his eyes and silently vowed to all of them, to himself, and to God: *I will bring her back to her family!* It was no longer just a promise or a mission, but his life's purpose. *I will never stop looking. Father, with Your guidance, help me bring her home.*

Thomas was first to suggest the topic they were all wanting to speak about, but that no one dared to mention. "So, you were with her for two weeks?"

Nicholaus felt every eye plastered upon him, waiting for every word he had to say. He nodded. "I was."

"What was she like?" This from Cristine, sitting two chairs down on his right.

He thought about his Anna; his eyes stung. "She did not like crowds." He swallowed and nearly laughed in sadness.

"She did not like people staring at her. She appeared to be so keen about everything. All she wanted" — he looked around at the downcast faces — "was to get home."

Sniffles echoed throughout the room.

"Did she have memories of us?" Isabella echoed the question she had brought forth earlier in the day.

Nicholaus looked at her, sitting across from Cristine, and nodded. "She did."

Isabella covered her mouth to lessen the sound of her crying.

The food was brought into the hall and set upon the table. Everyone just stared as the servants cut the meat and set it on their trenchers, the stale bread that was their plates.

"She liked berries best of all." He broke out with a smile and laughter. "She said it was easier to catch than meat. It just sits there and waits to be picked."

"She ate berries?" Elizabeth asked.

Nicholaus nodded as he looked at the little girl. "She grew up in a forest. There was a man on the island, Peter, who taught her which berries were safe."

The older princes and princesses glanced nervously at each other, their mother, and then their father at the mention of "Peter." The king knew what everyone was thinking because he was thinking it, too — but it did not seem like the appropriate place for such a conversation. He cleared his throat. "Let's eat." He picked up his knife and fork and forced himself to eat.

Sitting around the fireplace in the parlor, they recalled all they could of their beloved sister, daughter, and friend.

The queen brushed away a tear as she recalled, with a bit of laughter, "She was so jealous of Cristine." She looked at Cristine and smiled. "She took one of your rattles, but I could never find it. It was like it vanished!"

Nicholaus turned from the fireplace to look at the queen. "Was it painted white with a flower on it?"

The queen tilted her head as she sat up straighter, slowly nodding her head. "Yes. How did you know?"

Nicholaus swallowed hard. "She buried it underneath her window." William and Thomas sat up and looked at each other as Nicholaus continued, "She recalled it with sadness." Nicholaus looked up as Michael walked in.

Michael brought in the satchel and gave it to the king. Nicholaus sat up straight, recognizing the bag. His eyes asked a thousand questions. An awkward silence fell through the room as every eye turned to look at him.

"Nicholaus, we have to tell you something." Nicholaus swallowed hard as the king opened the bag and pulled out two leather letters. "Annabelle's 'Peter' ... was your father."

Nicholaus tilted his head and looked at the king in disbelief.

The king presented the letters to him. "Before you say anything, read these."

Taking the letters cautiously, he looked from the king to Michael to the princes to everyone else in the room, who sat silently listening to the crackling of the fire. He unrolled Annabelle's letter and read the best he could with his heart pounding and his eyes stinging. He shook his head when he read his father's words recalling the tragedy that was thrust upon their family. He looked up at the king when he finished the letter as a tear rolled down his cheek. He quickly brushed it away and unrolled the second letter — written to the king.

He gasped when he read his father's name written by his father's hand and then mustered, "He thought I was dead," when he read about the demise of Peter's family. He looked up and dropped the letter when he was finished. He did not know what to say.

The queen grabbed his hand as she knelt before him. "You don't have to say anything."

He looked into her emerald eyes. "I never knew what became of him." He did not know if he should cry tears of sadness or joy. The queen hugged him — she could not help but mother an aching child.

He felt the king's strong hand on his shoulder. Then he, too, was kneeling next to him and hugging him.

Nicholaus numbly walked to the chapel; he found himself kneeling before a shiny, golden tabernacle. He needed strength and clarity.

Could it be true? My father was alive all this time? He left me for an island.

"He did not leave you. He loves you."

Nicholaus suddenly recalled Annabelle's words: *"He prayed for his family every day."* Tears wet his hands.

Father, what am I to think?

"It is the truth. Take it and be thankful."

Be thankful? Thankful? He was suddenly enlightened. *I should be thankful. My father was there for Anna. He might not have been there for me, but I had my uncle, and Anna had a father. She wouldn't have lived without him.*

He looked up at the majestic tabernacle, a new happiness within his heart as he spoke his newfound truth. "That short life she was able to live was, in part, due to my father." He looked down at the base of the tabernacle and studied it as his eyes elevated to the golden cross on top. "And now, I am to bring her home." Nodding his head, he stood, and was permeated with the strongest conviction and calling.

He rejoined the royal family in the parlor as they sat in a circle staring at a very old and dirty rattle that had just been retrieved by William and Thomas. They could not get their sister back, but they could find the one thing she had buried before that tragic day.

Michael nodded to Nicholaus as he stood at the entrance to the room.

Cristine was the first of the royal family to notice Nicholaus's presence. "Look, Nicholaus! They found my old rattle."

Thomas stood up. "There can be no doubt now — she was Annie." He looked at Nicholaus.

Nicholaus nodded his head and turned toward the king. "Sire, I wish to continue my search for her body."

King Francis stood and studied the man before him, slowly nodding his head. "Michael." He looked past Nicholaus to the grand knight guarding the entranceway. "Gather the knights." Michael obediently bowed before him before exiting the room.

Nicholaus knelt before the king as the knights surrounded him. The king unsheathed his sword. "Nicholaus Hunts, do you swear to defend the sovereign family from all harm, foreign or known, man or beast, your duty demanding your life if needed, as God is your witness?"

Nicholaus looked up at the king and adamantly declared, "I do."

"Then" — the king tapped Nicholaus on the shoulders with the sword — "I knight thee, Sir Nicholaus Hunts. Now arise and join your brothers in arms." The king offered his hand and helped to pull Nicholaus up.

Applause erupted as Nicholaus stood and Fr. Robertus, the castle chaplain, robed him in the familiar hunter green tabard with a prayer for protection and right judgement.

Licking

Annabelle, in a new brown dress and the green cloak, found herself waving goodbye to Melody as she walked between Gregory and Markus. Melody had no idea she would not be returning. The village horse pulled the cart full of apples as they walked beside it.

Every step rattled Annabelle's arm, but she pressed forward, determined to find her family. She offered up her pain and eventually grew accustomed to the rhythmic jabbing that cascaded from her shoulder.

Three hours later, they arrived in Licking. They headed toward the market where many other carts, horses, and people were congregated. She immediately began to feel uneasy.

"Is something wrong?" Gregory asked as he glanced at her.

She looked around and noticed all the other eyes that were looking at her. She shook her head. "I'm sorry, but I can't stay here. Which way is it to Aboly?"

"Aboly is a few days away," Gregory said.

"The count doesn't allow us to travel there," Markus added, almost laughing.

"But I must get to Aboly."

They stared at her blankly, unable to offer assistance.

She ran down the middle of the street toward the end of the market. Stopping in a quieter section, she leaned against a post. She was away from the staring eyes, but she was not closer to knowing the whereabouts of her hometown.

"Can I help you?" a blacksmith journeyman, catching sight of a person from the corner of his eye as he shaped a horseshoe, asked between swings. Finally looking up, he did a double take, and then quickly shook his head, returning his attention to his anvil.

She watched him take a couple of swings as she pondered, *Can I trust him? I have to trust someone — I need to know how to get to Aboly. I must know!* As she stepped closer, only one word came from her mouth: "Aboly."

His hammer stopped mid-swing at her word. He looked at her again as his arm lowered. "What did you say?"

She looked behind her as a group of noisy villagers were passing by. "I need to know how to get to Aboly. That's all. Can you point me on the way?"

The blacksmith shook his head, incredulously. "Aboly?"

"Yes." She studied him, wondering why it was so difficult for him to believe her.

"The little lady needs to go to Aboly?" Annabelle looked to her left to find a plump middle-aged man in a bloody apron and missing some teeth staring at her. "I'll take you right where you need to go."

"Mr. Butcher, why don't you return to your meat?" The blacksmith set down his hammer.

"Meat's all cut," the butcher insisted as he, smirking, gawked at Annabelle. "I'm free to take you anywhere."

"Then return to your wife," the blacksmith insisted, picking up a cloth to wipe his face, and walking closer to the fence that marked the perimeter of the blacksmith shop.

The butcher eyed him and then, disgusted, turned around and headed back toward the market.

Annabelle looked back at the smithy, unsure what to say. *He defends me? What is his reason?*

The blacksmith, returning to his anvil and hammer, glanced back up at the princess. "You say to Aboly?"

She stepped closer, pondering why it was so difficult for him to believe she would want to go there. "Yes, to Aboly."

Whack. The hammer contacted the horseshoe. He looked up at her again and shook his head as he looked toward his work, mumbling to himself.

"Excuse me? Did you say something?" She was not sure if he was speaking to her.

The blacksmith looked back up at her. "It can't be," he said to himself, trying to convince himself of something.

She inched closer to the fence, trying to understand what the man was pondering. "What can't be?" She studied his stance: Though looking her way, he did not gawk at her. He *was* different, somehow. She took a few steps backwards as words burst out of her mouth with no previous thought. "You have not always been a blacksmith."

He stopped mid-swing and looked back up at her.

She did not know why she had spoken such words, but she felt them to be true. She found herself staring at him, wanting to flee, but resolved to stay and discover his secret.

Lowering her head, she was just about to turn and leave when he said, "And you are not a commoner."

Her heart nearly jumped out of her chest. "Wha —?" She walked toward the wooden fence in wonder.

"You look like a princess," he said as he walked closer to the fence to get a drink from a barrel of water. "Princess Isabella, to speak the truth." She fell against the wood, in shock, unable to utter a word. "But with the eyes of the queen."

The princess gasped. "You have seen the queen?" Her hand flew to her mouth as she stared at him in disbelief.

He looked around hesitantly and then returned to his anvil. Picking up his hammer, he added, "I was about 10 years old when I was told of the taking of Anchony's second princess. Annabelle — that was her name." *Whack. Whack.* His hammer made contact as sparks flew. "I had never met her, but they said she looked like her older sister." *Whack. Whack.* "But with her mother's eyes."

Annabelle made a slight noise as she attempted to move closer, though the fence prevented it. "How did you hear of such things?"

Whack. Whack. "It's like you said" — *whack, whack* — "I have not always been a blacksmith."

Annabelle stared at him, frozen in wonder. Somehow, she felt her head nodding, bewildered at the man before her mentioning the names of her loved ones. Her eyes began to sting. She was so tired of running; she wanted to be home. Home with her family.

Stepping closer to the fence, he spoke in a lowered voice: "Listen, Princess Annabelle, I will take you to Aboly."

She shook her shocked head. "But who are you?"

Lowering his head, he answered, "I'm one that knows you need to get home."

Home? She shook her head again as she fished for more information to decide if she should truly trust him. "But why? Why would you do that?"

He looked at her resolutely. "It is my duty to the kingdom."

Duty? He knows who I am and he wants to get me home. She looked up toward the heavens as a tear rolled down her cheek. *Father, did You place him here for me?* Looking back down at him, she leaned against the fence. With all sincerity, she looked into his eyes. "Thank you."

Annabelle sat in the shadows of the shop as the blacksmith busied himself with the horseshoe. She watched how diligently he worked as his muscles flexed with every swing of the hammer. "What's your name?"

"Sy."

"Your whole name with title," she said swiftly from the darkness, unable to accept the simple name offered.

He looked back at her quickly and then returned to his work. "Lord Symon, duke of Gemmeny."

"A duke? How can this be? Why aren't you on your land? How did you become a blacksmith?"

He took a deep breath. "You ask a lot of questions."

"You don't give many answers," she shot back quickly.

He looked in her direction. His stern face turned to a smile as his head nodded. "Cristine's character."

Annabelle moved forward, her heart quickening. "Crisa? How do you know her? How do you know my mother and my sisters? Please, tell me."

He looked ahead as he heard laughter in the street and horses go by. "Princess Annabelle, this is not the time nor the place. Get some rest. We shall leave on the morrow."

They set out before the sun's light had completely evaporated the morning dew.

Annabelle, already upon her horse, studied the man as he mounted his. *Is he truly trustworthy? I have no choice.* She looked back at the little shop. "You can just leave your shop so quickly?"

He looked over at her. "This shop is owned by the master blacksmith. I will have to find another to work under."

She shook her head. "You stay. Tell me how to go, and I'll get there."

He quickly shot down such an idea. "Princess Annabelle, never."

She looked at him, shaking her head. "I have never claimed to be the princess."

He said with certainty, "You don't have to." The discussion was ended. Riding out of town, they headed along the northwest path.

Annabelle's mind pondered over the life of the handsome duke, acting as a blacksmith journeyman now escorting her to her home. "Where is Gemmeny?" She finally ended the silence between them.

"Northwest of Aboly."

"How did you end up in Licking?" she asked.

He looked to his horse's mane. "My home was taken from me. I fled to save my life."

"Taken from you?" She tilted her head. "By whom?" He did not answer. She shifted in the saddle. "Why don't you take it back?"

Silent for a moment, he finally stated, "I wish it was that easy."

She looked into his honest, bright, and strong eyes. "You have met my family?"

He was forced to turn away from her intense emerald eyes. "I was once close to your sister."

"Which one?" she shot back quickly.

He glanced at her. "Isabella."

"Isabella? Isa?" she said with hope.

He nodded once.

A smile spread across her face. "What's she like?"

He looked at her in surprise, saying, "You haven't been home since you were taken, have you?"

"No, I have not," she answered with a cracked voice.

He stared at her silently and then answered, "She is the sweetest, most open-hearted person I know." His eyes began to water. "Though, I fear, her understanding of duty leads her to poor choices."

"Poor choices? What do you mean?"

He looked at her profile. "Do you not know?"

"Know what?"

Because the reality of his words were hard to speak, he was forced to look down at his horse. "Your sister is betrothed. She is to be married the day after St. Celestria's Day."

"Betrothed?" Annabelle thought about his previous words and concluded, "You don't favor the man?"

He swallowed hard. "I've never met him; I don't know about his character."

She studied Symon's profile. "You mean that she marries out of duty and not for love?" He would not look back at her. Annabelle watched his body language; he was holding back tears. "*You* ... are in love with her?" Unable to admit without crying that his heart had been stolen by her sister long ago, he did not answer.

A selfish shadow of sadness fell upon Annabelle as she thought about her sister's situation. "If she marries him, she'll not stay, will she?"

Symon looked at her and saw the concern written upon her face. "She will live with him in Sethel."

"Sethel?" she said in a near whisper. "Where is that?"

He looked at her distressed state. "Sethel is the kingdom to the west."

"How far?" She stared straight ahead as she held back her own tears. Was she to lose her older sister for a second time?

"It takes a week to get to the coast in Anchony and then two days on the sea, and then it's halfway through Sethel." He watched a tear roll down Annabelle's cheek. "Princess?"

"Does she have to leave?" The words came out in a complete whisper as her reddened face turned toward Symon.

Symon was so stunned by Annabelle's sadness that he could not speak. He swallowed hard. "Yes. She'll have to live with him." As the words came out of his mouth, he felt such emptiness as he realized in just a few days Princess Isabella would no longer be in the kingdom — he would never have a chance to see her again. He took a shallow breath as his heart felt as though it was plummeting into a deep, dark hole.

Rescue

Sir Hunts pounded upon the large wooden door of the count of Lesseks.

A hunched old servant opened the door fully when he saw the hunter green. "Can we be of service, sir?"

"I wish to speak with the count."

"The count is ill."

"It's of high interest to the king; it's about one of his daughters."

The old servant slowly opened the door and stepped out of the way. "We shall see if he's able to speak. Follow me."

"Thank you." Nicholaus followed the slowly moving servant down the cold, dark hallway. He wished to just ask for directions and run ahead, but he knew he must be patient.

He followed him down the long hallway, up a spiral staircase, and down another long corridor. The old man finally stopped outside a door. "Wait here, and I will see if he is up to seeing you."

"Please, ask him if he has heard any of his people mention a body being found, pulled from the river. A female with emerald eyes."

"He has been ill for a while, but I'll ask."

Nicholaus's heart sank. *Why did I shift from the river's course? Have I wasted three days?* He was tempted to leave the dank castle and fly back to the river, but his conscientiousness held him bound; it would be impractical to come all this way and leave without an answer.

Nicholaus waited and waited and waited. Thirty minutes later, the old servant walked out of the room, shaking his head. He said nothing to Nicholaus as he walked down the corridor mumbling to himself.

"Excuse me?" Nicholaus asked.

The servant turned around and looked with surprise at Nicholaus, and then the blanket of a tired and old mind lifted from him. "Oh, I forgot you were out here." He shook his head. "The count is dying." He said no more as he turned around and continued on his slow journey.

Nicholaus closed his eyes and shook his head. *Idle time!*

"Are you the one looking for the body?"

Nicholaus turned back to the count's chamber door as an older gentleman wiped his bloody hands upon a cloth.

"Yes." He tilted his head. "Have you heard something?"

The man took a deep breath and shook his head. "I know of no *body,* but" — he continued to shake his head in remembrance of an extraordinary case — "I did come across the most confounding circumstance. A young lady, shattered shoulder, broken and cut arm, but the most amazing thing — there was no blackening or reddening! No odor after five days, can you believe it? Very odd." He shook his head in disbelief.

Nicholaus, certain Annabelle was dead, half-heartedly listened to the man's story as he thought of his best excuse to escape from the man's self-described fascinating tale.

"And part of that time was in the Angler Ri —"

"River?" Nicholaus's full attention suddenly leaped upon the man in front of him, daring to hope that maybe — just maybe — she could have survived.

"I know! No change in color after being in the water."

"The *Angler* River?"

The man nodded as if it would clarify his words. "She was pulled from the Angler River."

"What did she look like? Where was she?"

The man put his hands upon his hips as he held the bloody cloth. "Let's see. Well, she was very bruised." He twisted his mouth as he thought. "Probably late teens, long, brown hair. She said her name was —"he looked up over Nicholaus's shoulder as he thought hard "— ah ... Annabelle. That's what it was."

The blood drained from Nicholaus's face. "Annabelle? She *said* ... she *said* ... you mean ... she's *alive*?!"

"I know! It was a miracle she was not at death's door with a wound that large! Truly amazing."

Nicholaus's knees went weak. He grabbed the man's arms. "Where? Where? Where is she?"

The older man looked at the knight before him, "Who are you, sir?" He guided Nicholaus to a bench and helped him sit.

"Hunts," Nicholaus stated in shock.

"Well, the girl I spoke of ..." He suddenly recalled her most telling feature. "Yes, she did have green eyes ... more like an emerald in truth." He looked back at Nicholaus. "She was ... let's see, where was I? Yes! That's it!" he spoke to himself out loud. "She was at the Pickers' place. That is ... let's see ... about five miles south of here."

"Five miles? Five miles? Five miles?" Nicholaus looked up at the doctor as a spark of hope lit his heart and bubbled forth in uncontrollable laughter.

"Are you all right?" the doctor asked with concern.

He shook his head. "I have never been better! Thank you. Thank you!" He squeezed the doctor's still slightly bloody hands. He flew down the hallway, the staircase, the other hallway, and out the door.

Nicholaus's bubbling joy turned to anger when he recognized the land before him. *That man! He lied to me! Anna was here! She was here and he lied to me!*

Doat Picker opened the door after three loud knocks.

He recognized the man before him as the one who had stood across the river several days prior.

"Where is she?!" Nicholaus demanded before the man could speak.

"I don't know what you're talking about." He started to close the door.

Nicholaus placed his foot in the door and pushed it open while pulling his sword. Gregory and Markus jumped up from their seats. After kicking Gregory and Markus swiftly to the ground, he grabbed Doat's tunic, pushing him up against the wall as parts of the thatched roof fell upon them. "I know she's here! I'm not going to ask you again!"

"But she's not! Look around. Only my family's here." The man shook in fear.

Nicholaus scanned the room — from the terrorized young children to the embarrassed older sons — he did not see Annabelle. "The surgeon told me she was here." His eye caught a familiar material lying on a corner table. Letting go of Doat, he walked to it. He picked up the cloth that had been lovingly mended by the saddened Melody and pressed it against his nose as he knelt down. Annabelle's fading scent. *She truly is alive!*

Nobody in the room dared to move except the young Melody. Observing his peculiar behavior, she approached him while her family froze in terror. "Are you her friend, sir?"

He looked at the young girl. "Yes."

Melody smiled. "She went to Licking."

"Licking?" he stated with a gasp. He looked at the other faces in the room for information. When they did not speak, he turned to the young girl. "Did she go by foot?"

Melody nodded her head as she pointed to her brothers. "Gregory and Markus took her."

He stood, tucking the dress around his belt. He approached the two eldest sons who had just found their feet.

"Where is she now?"

Markus looked at his brother and back at Nicholaus as he shrugged his shoulders. "She's not our worry."

Nicholaus tilted his head as he walked toward Markus. Markus's apathy turned into a grin; Nicholaus sent him to the floor with a bloody nose from a well-placed and quick punch. "Do you know what you've done?" he screamed at the man on the floor and then looked up at the rest of the family. "She is a princess of Anchony, and you sent her on her way alone!"

Doat shook his head as he attempted to explain his actions. "We didn't know, for certain, if she was the princess."

"I did," Delfina spoke. Nicholaus looked indignantly at the mother as she continued, "I sent her away."

"What?" Doat replied in shock.

"She asked where Aboly was. I knew that she, being a princess, would only bring trouble to my family." The wife looked around the room. "And I was right."

"Mama?" Melody looked at her mother. "How could you?"

Delfina stood straighter. "I did it for my family."

Nicholaus, approaching her, looked into her eyes. "You are heartless." Glancing around in disgust, he exited the cabin.

Enraged, he climbed upon Cinny.

"Wait!" Gregory ran out of the wood and clay structure. He looked to the ground for strength. "I saw her with Sy the blacksmith."

"A blacksmith?" Nicholaus shook his head as he rode off into the evening sunset on Cinny.

Travel

They finished their simple forest meal and nestled among the grass for their nightly rest.

Annabelle stared into the vast and majestic canopy of pinpricks of light. "May I ask you something?"

"What is it, Princess?" the voice answered from five feet away.

"How do you know?"

Symon's mind churned for the meaning of her words. At a loss, he inquired, "How do I know what?"

"How do you know that you love her?"

He was silent as he thought about his Isabella, his beloved.

"I mean, we are to love everybody. So how is it different?" Her words shot toward the twinkling stars. He did not reply; she pleaded for a response. "I really want to know."

Hearing the ache in her voice, he was compelled to answer. "When your thoughts, no matter what they are, always turn to her and you would do anything to see her smile. When you pray for her to have joy, even if it doesn't mean you are in her life — that's when you know."

Annabelle's memories turned through her mind. She thought of Lucinda's words and her unusual dream, and she thought of Nicholaus. Memories of Nicholaus and all he had done for her, all he had said. Did he do it because he was a friend or did he do it because of more?

He is my friend. I will always pray for him. Where is he now? Is he safe?

"The hardest part" — Symon continued with a shaky

voice — "is the inner call to marry her, the deepest desire you have ever held, and you know it will never come true."

Annabelle turned toward him. "Why are you so certain it will not come to pass?"

"She is to wed another," he replied almost in annoyance.

"But if it is God's will, it will come to pass," she said with certainty.

Symon was speechless as he looked into her emerald eyes and then up at the glorious night sky. He had never heard a statement spoken with such faith. He attempted an explanation: "Circumstances do not always follow God's will."

"Does she love you?"

He shook his head, unknowingly. "I thought she did." He swallowed the lump in his throat. "But love is a choice, and she does not choose me."

Annabelle chewed upon his words. *Love is a choice. Love is a choice. Who do I choose? Do I choose Nicholaus?* A fear suddenly overtook her as she remembered Isabella's inevitable departure from the family — her fate, too, would be the same. *Even if I do, I could not marry him. I would have to leave my family. I miss my family and I don't wish to depart from them. I choose my family — but is that all I choose?* She drifted off to sleep with her confusing and worrisome thoughts.

"How far are we from Aboly?" she asked as Symon helped her on to the horse.

"A few days," he said as he mounted his horse.

"And if the horses ran?"

Symon looked at her. "Princess, I know you want to get home, but the faster the horses run, the greater the chance of harm. And if they are hurt, the longer it will take."

Annabelle sighed heavily.

"Take heart; in a few days' time, you will be with your family."

"And you, Lord Symon, duke of Gemmeny? Will you be with my family, my sister?" She smiled.

He replied quickly, "Lord Symon is dead."

Her smile faded. "Dead? But you are not ..." Her head tilted. "Does Isa think you're dead?"

He aimed his horse toward the path. "Daylight is burning."

She trotted up next to him. "She thinks you're dead?"

He trotted ahead, not answering.

She caught up with him. "Tell me, Lord Symon: How is she to choose you when she doesn't know you're alive? Lord Symon —"

A red-faced blacksmith turned toward her. "The duke died in a fire!"

A wave of compassion came over Annabelle. "Symon, I don't know what you have been through, but you can't run from the truth." She looked down at her horse's head and took a deep breath as she trotted forward.

"Princess, I'm sorry. I didn't mean to yell at you. It's only, I fear that after all this time she does not love me, or worse, she has forgotten me."

"Forgotten you?" With the greatest of concern, she looked over at him. "How long has it been?"

"Five years."

"But love endures," Annabelle said, staring into the woods.

Symon took a deep breath as his mind pondered over memories. "The last time I saw Princess Isabella, I gave her a rose. It made her cry, in sadness." Annabelle looked at him. "She said it would only die." He shook his head in confusion. "Some divine foretelling?"

"No." Annabelle insisted, "It was a kind deed. I'm certain Isa was just thinking of the flower, how it had to be torn from its roots to be given to her." There was silence between them until Annabelle added, "Would not an abiding flower be better for her?"

Symon looked at her strangely. "An abiding flower?"

"Yes, one made of stone or wood, one that would last through all of time."

"An abiding flower." His mind swirled with the concept.

She looked at him with a smile. "That could be your new foretelling. But of course" — she looked at him with a grin — "you'd have to give it to her."

They stopped next to a pond to rest for the night. Annabelle stared at the water glistening in the moonlight, reflecting the starlight, as she sat next to a boulder. She sighed heavily, with thoughts of Nicholaus on her mind. *Where was he? Was he a knight now?* She smiled at that idea.

Symon looked up from the small fire to catch her smile. "Does this night give you delight?"

"A knight — with all hope, yes. Although this night is wholly lovely."

Symon, baffled by her meaning, shook his head.

She looked at him. "Squire Nicholaus Hunts. He is my friend. He was taking me to Aboly. He was to become a knight. I don't know if it has come to pass."

"Nicholaus Hunts? Is he the son of the Lion, the general commander?" She peeled her eyes from the glistening glass of the lake to look at him as he continued, "There are fables about his father."

"Fables?" She turned toward him.

"He was courageous; his skills were far beyond those of any other knight then, now, or ever." Symon leaned against a smaller rock. "I know of a story where he, himself alone, stopped 12 men from charging at your grandfather."

"My grandfather?" Her forehead wrinkled. "But Nicholaus said his father was a soldier. Does Anchony have a lasting legion?"

"No. He was friends with the prince — your father. He was in Aboly at the castle at that time. He was but a teen."

"He took down 12 men while in his teens?" She looked at Symon in disbelief.

"So the story goes. He became a knight, and during the holy war, he was appointed as the leader of the Anchonian knights."

"Nicholaus's father, Josephus?"

Symon licked his lips and nodded. "I don't know his name. I only know of him as the Lion." He took a deep breath and added, "His brother they say was as skillful, though he chose another path."

"The bishop." She nodded his head. "Nicholaus said he could fight."

Symon shook his head. "He was not always a priest."

Annabelle thought about that statement, then her mind turned to Nicholaus. "It was the bishop who raised Nicholaus, taught him how to track and fight along with Sir Machenus."

"His father started, and his uncle and others built upon what he already knew."

Annabelle looked at the small fire, placing her chin upon her knees. A silence fell between them as the crickets, owls, and forest creatures behind them made a harmonic choir to the rhythm of the night. Annabelle broke the human silence. "What is St. Celestria's Day?" Symon looked at her. "You said Isabella was to marry the day after."

He slowly nodded his head, his mind succumbing to thoughts of Isabella; he shook them off long enough to answer her question. "It is the feast day of St. Celestria."

"But who is she? I don't have a memory of that name."

He moved himself into a side-lying position. "She is the patron saint of Anchony."

"Who was she?" Annabelle dropped her knees into a side-sitting position.

"It was about 150 years ago when the Helvanites, pagans as they were, arrived in Anchony seeking the destruction of the Church. They traveled along the coasts killing priests, burning churches, slaying believers."

"The story goes that St. Celestria, a faithful 15-year-old at the time of her death, was placing fresh flowers at the foot of the altar at the Church of Mary, Mother of God in northeast Anchony. The only remaining priest for 100 miles, Fr. Thomas Long, took out the Host from the tabernacle and, placing it in a shrine, was shot through the heart with a flaming arrow. With his dying breath, he gave it to her, telling her to defend it with her life."

"She ran as fast as she could. She ran into the river, her right hand held high with the Holy Host, so careful not to let any water touch the shrine. They shot at her for 30 minutes without an arrow touching her, and then they pulled back and waited for her to come to shore. She treaded the waters of the Angler River for three hours, the whole time with her right hand held high."

"What came to pass after three hours?" Annabelle lowered her body toward the grass to try to understand his words better, intrigued by such a story.

"A monk, who had been summoned by an inner calling, spotted her in the river. Wearied, she swam with her left arm toward the edge of the river. She placed the shrine holding the Holy of Holies into the monk's hand just before being shot with several flaming arrows. She fell into the river and died."

"She died? After all she had done?" Annabelle stated, a bit saddened.

"One must be dead to be a saint."

Annabelle slowly nodded her head. "Her reward is in Heaven."

A day and a half later they found themselves next to the Barstow River, waiting for the ferry. Annabelle fearlessly washed her face in the swiftly moving water with her good hand. Symon watched her in wonder.

She looked up at him. "Is something wrong?"

"You're not afraid of the water?"

"No." She stood. "Am I supposed to be?" she asked with a light laugh.

Symon thought about his words. "Your sisters don't know how to swim."

"They were never taught?" She wiped her right hand on her brown skirt.

"They weren't allowed."

"Not allowed?" She looked at him with confusion. "Why is that?"

"My father told me once that it was because of Queen Clara. Her sister drowned saving her from the water. She is afraid it will claim the lives of her loved ones. She doesn't allow your sisters near the water."

"There is a river next to the castle, is there not?"

He nodded his head and gestured to the river. "It's the Barstow; this very one."

She turned toward the raging river. "That's not reasonable to live so close and not know how to swim."

"I agree, and that's why your brothers were given a few lessons."

"She agreed to it?"

"The king demanded it."

"But he did not with my sisters?"

"I'm certain he did, but he couldn't handle the pain in your mother's eyes."

"Are you waiting for the ferry?" a man asked as he

stepped off a floating wall of wood, and they both turned toward his voice.

"We are," Symon answered. "How much is it?"

"One pence each." The man looked at Annabelle as he took the money.

They climbed aboard with their horses and were pulled across with ropes as the man guided their course with a long tree branch. "She is a handful with our recent rains," the man said from the back of the ferry.

When they reached the other side, Symon helped Annabelle over the riverbank.

The ferryman tapped Symon on his arm. "You be careful. There was a group of men up to no good who crossed a few hours ago. Keep a keen eye open."

"Thank you." Symon nodded his head as he guided the horses over the bank.

Annabelle became uneasy when she noticed the multiple horse prints in the mud. She had heard the ferryman's remark to Symon. "How far are we?"

Symon looked over at her. "A few miles, that's all."

A few miles. A few miles more and that's it. She swallowed hard as she was suddenly hit by a few large rain drops. The few turned into a downpour, and they were suddenly soaked.

Symon pointed to an overhang of rock to the left a few hundred yards away. "Let's get out of the rain." She did not want to stray off course. She watched him trot over to the shelter and dismount. When he noticed she had not moved, he looked back at her. "What are you doing? Come on."

"It's only a little rain." Her words were drained by a lightning strike and the instantaneous thunder that sent the horse into a rear, flinging her to the ground. She landed hard on her left side as the hores took off in a wild flee. Numbed with pain, she could not move. She felt Symon lift her from the mud and carry her toward the overhang.

"Princess, are you all right?" Symon set her down in the dryness as he attempted to inspect her left side. "It doesn't look like you're bleeding."

"The horses." She pointed pathetically with her right hand as she watched both the horses flee.

"Don't worry about the horses." Symon attempted to comfort her.

When the deluge turned to a drizzle, they stepped out from underneath the protective overhang. Symon's attention turned south at the distant dot of a black animal. "I see one of the horses." He started toward it.

Annabelle looked toward the north as her heart began to beat wildly, realizing how close she was to her family. *A few miles. Only a few miles.* Her longing beckoned her forward. Her rational mind could not dampen the calling. She spoke over her shoulder: "I can't wait."

Symon turned around, unsure of what she had said. "Pardon?"

She faced him, 10 feet away. "I can't wait."

She did not give Symon time to reply; she spun toward Aboly and sprinted. "Wait!" Symon took off after her. A few yards later he realized he could not keep up with her on foot. As he stopped to catch his breath he turned back toward the distant horse — the only way he stood a chance of catching her.

Fire

Annabelle's heart fell to her stomach as she looked upon the castle and the columns of smoke billowing up into the cloud-covered, angry heavens. She could not escape the memories of her last day on the island when the smell of burning wood rudely bombarded her senses.

Assuming the worst, her ever-nagging fear raged inside her — she was alone. Peter was gone. Now, the castle on fire, her family was all dead as well. In a daze, she stumbled through the wide-open gatehouse as injured servants were escorted to the church. She collapsed into the cold mud on to her knees. Removing her hood, she felt the cold, large droplets upon her skin as if they were penetrating the loneliness in her soul. She glanced to the left and marveled at the majestic cathedral standing paradoxically near the fallen, wounded castle. She could take no more: Replacing her hood, she cried into her knees as they sank deeper into the mud.

Elizabeth, peering out a window from the southern wing of the cathedral, did a double take. She watched the girl with emerald eyes pull her hood over her head and bend toward the ground. "Hey!" She looked around; who else had seen her? No one. She pounded on the stained glass, trying to get the lady's attention.

"Liza, stop!" Cristine ordered as she hurried over from tending to the burned and wounded servants by offering them water and what comforts she could.

"It's Annie!" Elizabeth looked at her older sister with large eyes.

Cristine shook her head. "Liza —"

"I'm not lying! Look! The lady in the green cloak!" She pointed out the window.

Cristine glanced out the window. "Liza it's only a servant."

"It's her! I saw her eyes!"

"Liza" — Cristine took a deep breath — "Annie's dead. Now, we've all been through enough. Stop this foolish talk!" She walked away agitated.

Biting her lip and angry that she was not believed, Elizabeth turned back to the window and stared down at the green mass. *I know it's her! It has to be her!* Determined to find out the truth, she ran toward the church doors.

"Whoa, whoa, whoa! Where are you going?" Michael grabbed her by her core and swung her around just before she touched the wooden doors.

"Liza!" Cristine yelled at her determined sister as she marched over. She took Elizabeth's hand. "I'm sorry, Michael, but she is seeing things."

"I am not!" she rebutted with a stomp of her foot and fisted hands.

"And what do you claim to see?" the head knight asked.

"I'll show you!" Grabbing his hand, she led him to the window.

"He has greater things to do, Liza!" Cristine said, shaking her head as she refused to look out the window again.

"Do you see that lady?" She pointed. Michael followed her finger, looking at the scene with all the moving people, trying to ascertain about which person the young princess was speaking. "It's Annie!"

A disheartened Michael knelt down beside the youngest princess as he took an extended breath. "Princess, you were there. She fell into the river, she went over the falls. Elizabeth, I'm sorry, but it can't be her."

"I told her that!" Cristine joined the conversation again from five feet away, water pitcher in hand. "But she will not listen."

"I know what I saw!" Elizabeth demanded as she turned back to the window away from the naysayers.

Michael stood. "And there will be no going to check, do you understand?" He stared at the top of her head.

"Yes, Michael," a defeated voice said as it breathed on the glass.

Nicholaus breathed hard as he sat upon Cinny. Bewildered, he stared at the smoking furniture on the castle grounds. In disbelief, he dismounted, never taking his eyes off the castle's skeleton.

"Sir Nicholaus?"

Nicholaus looked back as Sir David approached with ash upon his face. "What has come to pass?"

Sir David shook his head as he looked at the ground — he could provide no answers.

"The family?"

Sir David looked up. "They're safe. They're inside the church." He pointed with his head.

Nicholaus took a shallow breath.

"You return empty-handed, I see." Sir Martinus approached, he, too, covered in soot.

"Leave him alone, Martinus," David replied. He looked at Nicholaus. "Sir Doey is in the church."

Nicholaus nodded his head. He turned back to his faithful horse for a prayer of thanksgiving for safe travels as the rain droplets continued to pound him. His eyes caught a puddle formed in a footprint. He knelt down to investigate further — it was the perfect size. His fingers sank into the mud.

It has to be.

He looked to see from where the footprints came: They followed the riverbank as far as his eyes could discern from a distance. He quickly turned the other direction; they led to a green mass kneeling in the mud.

His heart beat wildly as he dared to approach. "Anna?"
She put her head up and held her breath. Did she hear what she thought she had heard?

"Anna."

The voice was much closer. She turned and looked to her left as she finally breathed — swiftly. There, before her eyes, was her long-lost friend, Nicholaus, but three feet away. She attempted to stand, but she finally succumbed to the pain of her ankle, which she had twisted on her sprint to Aboly, as she tumbled toward the mud.

He caught her and held her so tightly.

Tears filled her eyes. "Nicholaus." She placed her head against his chest as she shook it. "My family —"

"They're safe," he whispered down into her ear as he held her tightly. "They're in the church." He petted her hair.

She released a moan of glee as her knees went weak at the joyous, unbelievable news. He picked her up. She touched his chest with her right hand. Was he really there? Was her family really alive? Was she about to meet them? She was so weary from running, weary from being ever vigilant, weary from the constant and throbbing pains all over her body. But she was finally safe — safe in Nicholaus's arms.

Elizabeth moved her head closer to the window as she leaned against the windowsill. "Ah! It's Nicholaus! It's Nicholaus!" She looked back at Cristine. "Crisa! It's Nicholaus!"

Cristine squeezed the cloth in the water basin as she shook her head. "Liza, what is it now?"

"Nicholaus is here!" She turned back to the window as Cristine scurried over. Elizabeth gasped. "He picked her up!" She followed him with her eyes as he headed toward the southern entrance used by the royal family. She gasped again. "He's coming!" She ran toward the doors.

"Wait, Liza!" Cristine searched the view from the window — she saw nothing. No green mass. No Nicholaus.

Symon slowed his horse when he came upon the frantic scene. He looked around in disbelief. *What has taken place? Did the castle catch on fire? Where is the princess? Did she make it?* The moment before he was about to go into a complete panic, he spotted her green cloak in a knight's arms being carried up the cathedral steps. He took a deep breath: She was safe now. He lowered his head in gratitude. *Thank You, God.*

He looked back up at the large cathedral as Annabelle disappeared into the building; he was happy that she would be meeting her family soon. *Her family. Her sister.* He stared at the massive church. *Behind those stones and mortar is Isabella.* He looked down at the mud. *She should be with her sister now.* He looked toward the scurrying city people and slowly led the horse down the main street.

Nicholaus entered the church with a green bundle in his arms. A deafening silence fell upon the church in its entirety while, for the briefest moment, nothing moved from man to molecule — everyone knew what he held.

The king, near the sactuary, slowly walked forward and then, convinced Nicholaus held his daughter, sprinted as his footsteps echoed among the tall arches. The queen was forced to sit as her worst fear was presented before her. Michael swallowed hard from the back-left corner of the southern wing.

Elizabeth's frustration was instantly turned to joy as she viewed the muddy, green mass in Nicholaus's arms. A smiled erupted upon her face.

Cristine's heart quickened. *Could it be true? Was Liza right?*

Isabella's heart sank to her stomach as she looked upon the bundle in Nicholaus's arms; her self-blame from that fateful day, those many years ago, cascaded down her entire body as she physically felt weaker in the presence of her failures.

"Annie!" Elizabeth yelled five feet away from Nicholaus.

Dread filled every heart as they listened to the little girl's hopeful cry. Did she not know Annabelle was dead? That Nicholaus was returning the lifeless body of the princess he once escorted?

Annabelle turned her head toward her name and reached for her sister. "Liza!"

At that very moment, the air, the beating hearts, the miserable minds, stood still as the dolefulness encompassing all emotions was lifted. The crowd passed from an initial shock to all-out glee. Isabella dropped the rags with which she was binding burn wounds; the king halted his movement; Thomas stood from helping an injured servant; the queen crawled on to her knees before struggling to stand, nervous with excitement; William, he, too, in a stupor, offered his hand to his mother, never taking his eyes off the green mass — the living, breathing, speaking, green mass.

Nicholaus lowered Annabelle so she could reach her sister. She pressed her sister, whose fate she had never known, into herself with her right arm. "You're all right!" Annabelle kissed her sister on the side of the head as tears of joy fled from her eyes. *Thank You, Lord, for letting her be all right.*

Elizabeth, suddenly overcome with the realization of how Annabelle really had saved her from the awful men several times, cried into Annabelle's ear as she gripped her with all her strength. "Only because of you!"

Annabelle looked up through blurry eyes to see her parents approaching. Her mother was held erect by her father and eldest brother. Eduard trailed behind in confusion.

Thomas helped Isabella to stand as she fumbled over from the right side of the wing, tripping over the injured servants lying upon the makeshift beds.

Clara knelt before her daughter as she called out from her soul: "My child!" She gently rubbed her daughter's face. *Is it really her? Alive? Before me?* Tears fell from the queen's eyes as she stared into the green hue before her.

Annabelle looked into her mother's emerald eyes with all their love. She felt her mother's gentle touch, and the deep ache of a young girl growing up without a mother cried out for all it had lost: "Mamá!" The long-separated mother and daughter embraced one another with uncontrollable crying. The years of longing melted away as they held each other.

"How?" The king knelt down, still in shock. "Can it be true?" He looked at Nicholaus for confirmation as he placed his hand on the back of his daughter's head and petted her hair. *My Annabelle? Truly? Before me, alive? After all this time?*

Annabelle looked up from her mother's shoulder and gasped as she spotted the man before her. "Papá!" She reached for him with her right arm that still embraced her mother.

He held her hand and pressed it against his cheek as his salty tears fell onto her fingers. "My daughter!" His right hand wiped away a tear from her cheek as her chin quivered against her mother's shoulder.

The queen, crying yet nearly laughing, pulled herself away so her husband could see his child. The king took his living daughter from Nicholaus's arms and hugged her in his lap. The queen, now giddy with happiness, laughed as tears rolled down her cheeks. She squeezed Elizabeth into herself.

"Annie?"

Annabelle turned in her father's lap to her three older

siblings and Cristine staring at her. She was so overcome with emotions she could not speak. Her hand traveled from her quivering chin to an open arm for their embrace as they all fell to their knees to hug her.

Eduard walked over to his mother, very much confused. Clara pulled him over and hugged him too.

Nicholaus, at first, remained on his knees. Staring at his beloved and thrilling in her joy at meeting her family. He soon realized he was the only one so close to the royal family during their personal moment. He stood up and backed away.

Michael walked up beside him, shaking his head as a smile erupted, and he slapped Nicholaus's shoulder and then hugged him. "You did it. You did it ... and she's *alive!*"

Nicholaus shook his head. "She found her way home; I found her in the bailey."

Sir Martinus stuck out his hand. "Well done. Well done."

"She was on the castle grounds," Nicholaus tried to explain.

"But you wouldn't give up," Sir David added.

Nicholaus looked at him and Martinus, and Martinus's hand. He accepted it with a shake. Looking back at Annabelle — safe with her family — he walked to the church doors.

"Sir Nicholaus, where are you going?" Michael asked.

"My horse, sir, is out in the rain. Are the stables unharmed?"

"They are," Michael nodded.

Nicholaus nodded back as he caught a glance from Annabelle's eyes. She smiled at him. He smiled back and bowed before exiting the church.

"Where's Nicholaus going?" Annabelle looked with concern at her family as she attempted to stand, her smile fading. It was at that moment, surrounded by her family, that she was overwhelmed with love. *I choose both. I do choose Nicholaus. I choose him with all my heart.* As soon as she felt the love and thought the words, confusion took over — would she have to choose between Nicholaus and her family?

"Michael, where has Nicholaus gone?" William asked.

Michael walked over, still in awe. "To put up his horse," he answered as he stared at the princess. He half-laughed as he said, "No one has ever lived to tell the tale of Angler Falls."

Annabelle smiled as she looked down. "I suppose it was not my day to die."

Michael looked at the king as they both noted the influence of their long-time friend from his main mantra.

"Where did you go, Annie?" Elizabeth asked as she hugged her sister.

"Down the river," she said truthfully.

"And this?" Her father pointed to her arm in its sling.

She looked at her arm and then up at her father. "You expected me to go down Angler Falls without harm?" She smiled weakly as she fought the pain from her shoulder.

He pulled her head to him and kissed it.

"Oh!" Clara exclaimed in happiness. "All my children are home!" There was a massive hug with Annabelle in the middle.

"Ow." Annabelle finally voiced the pain arising from her crushed scapula and throbbing left side. Everyone pulled back and mumbled apologies.

Her ankle began to throb again. She raised her foot as her father picked her up and carried her to a blanket. Surrounded by love and a comfort not found in possessions, she was completely at peace and fell into a restful slumber.

Cathedral

Annabelle awoke to a throbbing left side and an aching ankle. Reaching out, she touched the cool stone wall that vibrated with every colossal ring from the tolling cathedral bells as she closed her eyes and thought about the events of the recent past. *Did I truly make it home?*

Sitting up, she turned to face the open church. Looking toward the high altar, she studied the beautiful woodwork cascading up toward the arched ceiling, interrupted only by the tabernacle with the altar candle's glow falling upon it, the eight-foot crucifix, and the occasional candles and flowers. She bowed her head, fully aware that in that little box Jesus was waiting, waiting for her, waiting for everyone. She shook her head at the unbelievable awesomeness of God's love.

Thank You, Jesus, for becoming one of us. Thank You, Father, for giving us Your Son. Thank you, Mary, for your "yes." Where would we be without your fiat? *You were the first tabernacle.* She looked back up at the altar. *And there could not be one full of more beauty.*

Turning her head toward the nave, looking between the legs of the knights guarding her family, she saw the injured servants all around. She stood, balancing upon her left foot. The startled knights turned around and instinctively bowed to her. She looked to the ground, unsure how to answer such formalities as she slowly placed weight upon her right ankle. She grimaced as she stood taller. *I can do this. I accept it. It lets me know I'm alive.*

"Annie!" Elizabeth stood from playing with Eduard and ran into Annabelle's left side. Annabelle gasped as her left arm, slumbering in its sling, was tussled further. "Oh!" Elizabeth pulled back, afraid of the injury her surprise hug had caused.

Annabelle, forcing a smile, pressed her sister closer, to hide the pain. "It's all right." Elizabeth squeezed harder at her sister's reassuring words. Annabelle bit the pain back.

"You're up."

Annabelle looked up to see Thomas standing beside her. She smiled and held out her arm. "Thom."

He gently squeezed her as he spoke into her ear. "A thousand prayers answered right before my very eyes." He shook his head. "I still can't believe it's truly you."

"And I" — tears fell from her eyes — "I can't believe I made it home."

He pulled back to look at her as a large and satisfied smile spread across his face.

Annabelle looked from her brother to the injured servants. "What came to pass?" She stepped forward with a limp.

Thomas grabbed her arm. "Wherever you wish to go, I'll take you."

She shook her head. "I only wish to see." She looked around as she held tightly to his left arm.

"The castle caught on fire," Elizabeth answered.

"Caught on fire? How?" Annabelle looked down one column of injured persons to the other.

Thomas shook his head. "We're not certain, but the good tiding is that the fire is out and only half of the castle was damaged. Our sleeping quarters are unharmed."

Annabelle turned from the injured to her brother's profile. "What was harmed?"

Thomas pointed with his head. "Mainly the servants' quarters and the hospital chamber."

"Up so soon?" William walked up beside his brother and sisters.

Annabelle smiled when she spotted him. "Will!"

"But I suppose if Angler Falls can't stop you from coming home, weariness would only slow you down." He kissed her on her left cheek. "I thought I lost you," he whispered into her ear as he hugged her head and then released her.

Isabella and Cristine, just realizing their sister was awake, arose from tending to the wounded and joyously scurried to their siblings.

"I did lose you." She looked around to all the faces. "I lost all of you." She caressed Elizabeth's cheek and hugged Isabella and Cristine. "But by the grace of God, I have made it home."

Eduard walked up to Thomas and leaned upon his leg before Thomas picked him up.

William shook his head. "You've not made it all the way home yet."

Thomas cleared his throat. "Annie, this is Eduard."

"Eduard?" Annabelle asked as she looked closer, and a smile slowly appeared across her face. "It's nice to meet you." She held out her hand toward him.

Eduard eyed her suspiciously and then declared, "I've never met anyone who's dead before!" They all erupted in laughter. "What?" Eduard stated as Thomas put him down and he looked around at everyone.

Annabelle attempted to placate his curious mind: "Neither have I, Eduard —"

"Edus!" Elizabeth called out.

Annabelle smiled as she looked to her youngest sister and then back to her brother. "Edus." She knelt down in front of him and placed his hand over her heart. "Do you feel that?" Eduard slowly nodded his head. "That is my body telling you I am as alive as you."

Eduard looked at her curiously. "They said you drowned."

Annabelle leaned in closer, widened her eyes, and answered back, "I swam."

Eduard's hesitancy turned into a smile of acceptance as he hugged his sister who he never really knew existed.

"What's this? A family meeting without your father and mother?" The circle opened at the king's voice.

"Annie was telling Edus that she isn't really dead." Elizabeth explained as Annabelle stood and turned toward her parents.

"Is that so?" the king asked as he watched his daughter stand. "How did she live?"

"She swam!" Eduard yelled out.

Clara looked with fright at Annabelle.

The king looked at his youngest. "She swam down Angler Falls, is that it?" Eduard bit his lip and looked up at Thomas for help. The king disheveled Eduard's hair as he answered his own question. "She lived because that's what she does." He looked at his daughter's emerald eyes. "She overcomes all hardships. She lives."

Annabelle looked away. She did not like being given such characteristics when she knew it was only by the grace of God that she stood where she did.

Clara gasped as she found her way to a wall and sat down.

"Mamá?" Annabelle, along with the entire royal family, watched the queen collapse in emotional distress. Annabelle hobbled her way to her mother and sat down beside her. "Mamá?"

"They said you had drowned," the red-eyed queen commented. "My sister ... my sister ..."

Annabelle grabbed her hand. "I know. I know, Mamá."

Clara looked up with a new resolve in her eyes. "Annabelle" — she tenderly touched Annabelle's face, below her right eye — "you're not allowed near the water."

Annabelle looked at her mother with confusion as she shook her head, trying to defend her position. "Mamá, I can swim."

"No. No, Annabelle." The queen adamantly shook her head.

"I am a good swimmer." Annabelle attempted to plead her case as she sat up tall.

Clara rubbed Annabelle's face again. "I lost you once to the river; I'll not lose you again."

Annabelle stared into the eyes of her mother as she realized she would never be as free as she was on the island. A part of her wanted to protest: "I love to swim. It's what I do," but she looked past her mother's shoulder at the crucifix hanging above the tabernacle. She closed her eyes. *Father, if that will make my mother merry after all she has been through for me, then I shall keep it.* Opening her eyes, she nodded her head in acquiescence. A small part of herself died at that moment, but she rejoiced that she was able to give something up that brought her joy to make another happy.

"The smoke is out of the castle. It's safe for your return," Michael informed the king as he walked straight into the church from the newly secured grounds. The king nodded as he stared at his wife and daughter seated on the floor. Michael followed his eyes. "Have you told her yet?"

The king shook his head and looked to the floor before looking up at Michael. "I think Nicholaus should tell her." Michael thought about the king's words and slowly nodded his head.

"Where is he now?"

"He's looking at the rooms, trying to determine how the fire started." Michael turned toward the church doors, ready to strike any intruder, as Prince Phillipus burst through.

The king looked from Prince Phillipus to his eldest daughter, who grabbed Cristine's hand. He thought nothing of it as he finished his conversation with Michael. "Tell him to meet me in my chamber next to the Hall of Justice before supper."

Michael bowed his head.

"I came as soon as I heard!" the visiting prince exuded as he hurried toward the royal family. "Oh! Isabella, you're safe!" Isabella, swallowing hard, released Cristine's hand as the Sethelian prince, with outstretched arms, embraced her head and kissed its side.

He turned toward the other royal family members. "Your Majesties, I heard the castle was on fire, and I came as quickly as I —" He stopped speaking when he spotted Annabelle.

"Prince Phillipus," the king addressed him as William and Thomas helped their mother and sister to stand, "this is Princess Annabelle."

He bowed toward her as he studied her injured arm, her limp as she walked, and her mysterious and perfect emerald eyes that matched those of the queen.

"It was good of you to check upon all of our safety," the queen replied as she walked to her husband's side.

Only Annabelle noticed the uncomfortable length of time he looked at her; she turned to the side to hide herself behind William.

"You're too late," Cristine stated bluntly as she folded her arms. "The fire's out."

"Cristine," the queen objected to such a tone, "don't be without manners."

The prince finally peeled his eyes off Annabelle and addressed Cristine with a smile. "I ran my poor horse as quick as he could go."

His smile did not warm Cristine's heart.

"Have you come upon Johannes Fletcher?" Thomas asked.

"No," he answered quickly.

"No damage was done in the living quarters." the king explained. "We were about to return —"

"I offer my hand and those of my men in any way we can be of service." He bowed to the king.

The king patted him on his back. "That's good of you."

Anxiety

William carried Annabelle up the steps and through the castle doors. A vague familiarity enveloped her as she looked with wonder at the colorful and warming tapestries against the large but steady grey bricks. The massive foyer contained an expansive candle chandelier that welcomed her warmly home and revealed the majesty of the castle. A spiral staircase pointed the way to the additional floors, and multiple halls jetting off from every direction gave great opportunity for exploring.

"Where do you want to go?"

Annabelle looked up at William. She was so overwhelmed, she did not know what she should do.

"Let's take her to the second floor." Her mother came to her rescue. "I'll have Ida draw a bath for you."

William followed his mother up the stone steps.

Prince Phillipus watched the figure in the prince's arms ascend the steps. "What's been her lot?"

"She was on an island, then she swam down Angler Falls," Elizabeth explained the best she could as Isabella turned away from her fiancé.

Prince Phillipus grabbed Isabella's hand. "Your Majesty, may I have the privilege of speaking with the princess?"

"Of course." The king guided him to the door on the right with a gesture from his hand.

Cristine shook her head in disgust as she watched her sister walk toward the library with the awful prince. She fidgeted and swallowed hard as she looked to her father and brother.

"Crisa, what's wrong?" Thomas asked, noticing her agitation as Alicia and one of Prince Phillipus's manservants followed them into the room.

"I don't think she should be alone with him."

"She's not alone with him." The king took a deep breath, shaking his head. "We all know you have never liked him. Give him a chance, Cristine." She tried for a rebuttal, but he cut her off. "He has been nothing but courteous. Now leave them be! Leave them be, Cristine!"

She jumped at her name; she knew by his tone she must not press the issue any further. She bit her lip as she breathed quickly. Elizabeth and Eduard grabbed their father's hands, not wanting to get chastised like their older sister.

"Come on, Crisa." Thomas held out his elbow toward his sister.

She looked hesitantly from the door to his elbow. Feeling as if she was doing something wrong, she turned from the door and took her brother's elbow.

As soon as the door closed, the prince shoved Isabella into a bookcase. "Who is she?" he yelled.

"Stop —" Alicia called out but was grabbed and silenced by Phillipus's servant's hand over her mouth. The man whispered threatening remarks into her ear as she shook in fright.

Isabella, shocked by the shove and feeling her bruised ribs, nervously and painfully gasped for air. He picked her up roughly by her arm. Spit fell upon her as he yelled in her face, "Who is she?"

"Sh-sh-she is my sister," she mumbled out through her terrified tears.

He released her quickly and spun around, running his fingers through his hair. "Where has she been?" He agitatedly paced in front of the fearful Isabella. "You have been hiding her from me!"

"No." Isabella shook her head as her body quivered in terror. "We thought she was dead." She glanced quickly at her servant, held tightly to the point of pain by the prince's servant.

He rushed back toward her, an inch from her face. "And I thought you were a beauty." He took a step backwards, slightly grinning. "No, I didn't mean that ... you are." She flinched as he brought his hand toward her and rubbed her cheek, and then stepped back. "But she is more."

Isabella thought about his words as she stared at his feet. Was her sister her savior? Did he not want to marry her now? Her heart sank for Annabelle. She swallowed hard and bravely surrendered her thoughts: "You don't wish to marry me now?"

He chuckled sadistically as he turned toward her. "You'll not back out on me now!" He smiled. "Do you see what comes to pass when you cross me?"

Isabella looked up as the blood drained from her face. "The fire? That was you?"

"Your servants were beginning to talk." He walked toward Alicia. "It seems they were growing worried about this one."

"Leave her be!" Isabella called out.

Running back toward Isabella, he grabbed her shoulder and pushed her into the wall. "If you scream, she will die right here!"

The princess watched the prince's servant pull out a dagger and hold it next to Alicia.

"Now, I need your pledge that there will be no more talk from anybody."

With a quivering chin, Isabella looked at her terrorized servant, and nodded her head.

"Say it!"

"I give you my word."

He shoved the princess into a small table, knocking its contents onto the floor. "I'm warning you — don't cross me. The last man that did ended up in the river."

Her shaking, terrorized body melted into the floor. She felt less than dirt. Wailing, she collapsed onto the fallen books.

Cristine heard the library door open. She slipped out of Thomas's grasp. "I don't want to look at the damage."

Thomas looked at her and shrugged his shoulders. "You don't have to if you don't want to." He continued down the hall.

She ran back to the corner of the hall to peer around the foyer. Watching Prince Phillipus and his servant cross the hall and head her way, she stood up straight and looked at the other side of the corridor.

"Where has your father gone?"

She pointed down the hall, not saying a word.

"Will you come with me?" He extended his elbow with a smile.

She shook her head.

He stepped closer, but took a step backwards as two Anchonian knights came into the foyer from outside. "All right." He smiled again and bowed before walking down the hall.

Cristine immediately flew toward the library. She spotted her sister in a pile on top of some books, trying to muffle her cries. "Isa? What are you doing on the floor? What's wrong?" Receiving no response from her sister, she looked at the pallid servant, who was breathing quickly and leaning against a wall.

Isabella's chin quivered as she attempted to sit up and straighten the massive pile. "The books, from the monks in Anchelo." She could hardly get the sentence out as her tears wet the precious vellum pages.

Cristine knelt down next to her sister, "Forget about the books, Isa. Did Prince Phillipus hurt you?"

Isabella looked at her sister. No words could be forced

through the ferocious tears that were released at the sight of her sister's eyes. Her head fell into her sister's lap.

"What did he do?" Cristine demanded. Receiving no response, she again looked to the servant. "Alicia?"

Alicia, shaking her head, wiped away her own tears.

Not getting a reply from either, Cristine began to cry herself as she rubbed her sister's back. "Isa, tell me what's wrong!"

Isabella jerked when Cristine's hand rubbed her throbbing shoulder.

Cristine, pulling back Isabella's collar, spotted the handprint. "What is this?!" She jumped up, ready to dash out the door, but before she could, Isabella grabbed her hand.

"You can't tell!"

"Why would I *not*?" Cristine demanded.

"He set the fire!" Isabella screamed through copious tears.

Cristine stepped back in shock. "What?"

Tears fell upon the books as Isabella, unable to look at her sister, kept her head lowered. "He and his men set the fire."

"What?" Cristine adamantly shook her head. "He can't get away with this!"

"But he has."

"What do you mean?"

Isabella finally raised her head to look at Alicia. "Show her."

"My lady?" Alicia said in fright.

"She needs to see or she will go and tell!" Tears streaked down the princess's face.

"I need to see what?" Cristine demanded.

Cautiously walking over, Alicia wiped away a fresh tear as she said, "Yes, my lady." She pushed up her sleeve to reveal black, blue, purple, and green bruises — all in different stages of healing — up and down her arm.

Cristine's mouth dropped open in shock. "Who did that to you?"

Returning her sleeve, Alicia lowered her head. As a tear fell on to her dress, she revealed, "That's not half of them, my lady."

"And he's given his word" — Isabella pleaded for her sister to keep silent — "if I break off the engagement or speak a word to Papá, or Will, or Thom, or the knights, he'll kill Alicia and the other servants."

Cristine folded her arms in rejection of the idea. "He can't get away with this! I don't care if he's a prince!" She pointed to Alicia's arm. "Using threats and fear to —"

"They're not threats!" Isabella revealed as she shook her head. "He had Elizabeth taken."

"What? Why would he do that?" She knelt down in shock. "*How* did he do that?"

"And he's killed a villager."

"What?"

"He said there's a man in the river." Isabella shook her head. "I don't know what to do! I have to marry him! How many others will he kill if I don't?"

"He's a brute!" Cristine said as she petted her sister's hair.

"You can't tell. Please, Crisa, you can't tell."

"You can't marry him," Cristine insisted, finally aware of the depth of fear her sister was carrying.

"I have to!"

A plethora of tears ran down Cristine's face. "Isa, why did you not tell me sooner? Why have you carried this burden alone?"

Isabella laid upon her sister's lap. "Give me your word you won't tell."

Against everything in her, Cristine looked across the room and promised, "I will not speak of it."

"Thank you, Crisa. Thank you!"

From the corner of her eye, Cristine watched Alicia bend over in relief.

The queen guided her two children into the bathing room. "Set her there, William." She pointed to a stool in the corner.

William set his sister down. "All right. I'll be by the door," he stated as he turned around to leave.

"That's not need —" Annabelle leaned forward.

The queen put her hand up to stop her daughter from finishing. "Thank you, William." They both watched him exit the room and close the door.

Annabelle turned to her mother. "He doesn't need to wait on me."

She rubbed Annabelle's cheek with a smile and a nod. "I think he does."

Annabelle tilted her head but was stopped from questioning by Ida with a large bucket of steaming water from the adjacent room. "The first of the water, my lady."

"Thank you." They watched as Ida poured the steamy water in the tub.

Annabelle untied her cloak and struggled out of her sling. Her mother helped her with the painful task of undressing. The queen looked with wonder at the claw marks upon Annabelle's back, but she did not mention them; she silently prayed for her daughter, who had endured so much.

Annabelle carefully scaled the side of the tub; it was painful, but she weathered it. The warm water was so relaxing she nearly fell asleep until her mother poured a pitcher of water over her head.

There was a knock on the door. Beatrix entered with a fresh dress; she placed it on the stool and helped the queen.

Annabelle could not help but listen to the whispered dialogue between her mother and Beatrix, attempting to figure out whom they were speaking about as they scrubbed away days of dirt.

"Have you seen anything out of the ordinary?" Beatrix looked up at the queen and then back down at the water, not answering. "Beatrix, do you find anything?"

After a few seconds of continued questioning, Beatrix finally spoke. "My lady, the servant's rooms were burned."

Clara, a bit annoyed, nodded her head. "Yes, Beatrix, I know that. Neither you nor the other servants will go without bedding. Have you seen anything?"

"My lady, I did as you said. I had a close eye on Prince Phillipus and *my* room was burned."

"Beatrix, I am sorry about your room, but I need you to answer me."

The servant shook her head as her eyes began to water. "My room, my lady. Our rooms."

Clara shook her head in annoyance, sighing heavily. "Beatrix" — she pointed to the door — "thank you. That is enough. Ida will finish up."

The servant stood and bowed her head. "Yes, my lady."

When the door closed, Annabelle asked, "Who were you talking about?"

Clara poured another pitcher of water over Annabelle's head. "Oh, dear, you don't need to worry about it."

Annabelle stared ahead as she thought about all the questioning. "But you are worried about it?" She looked back at her mother.

"You have markings on your back. Where did they come from?" Her mother changed the subject.

You don't need to worry about that. Annabelle sighed, shaking her head. "I was in a forest, Mamá, with animals." She did not finish. Her mother did not need to know that a bear had chased her into the river and she had taken a swim in the ocean.

"Have you come upon anything?"

Nicholaus stood and faced the king as he bowed. "It had to have been set on purpose."

"Why do you say that?" The king stepped next to him and looked at the charred remains of furniture.

Nicholaus knelt back down and pointed. "The fire had to come from somewhere in the room. The only place I see that it could are the fireplace and the candles, but neither were lit." He looked around the room. "And it's not only here; it has been the same in the last six rooms." He took a deep breath and shook his head as he stood. "Unless there are a multitude of cases of wood and bedding bursting into flames themselves, this was set willfully."

The king looked toward Michael. "Who would've set it?"

"What's 'willfully' mean?" Elizabeth, standing just outside the door with Thomas and Eduard, looked up at her older brother as Thomas held both of his siblings' hands.

"It will be time for supper soon. Let's go get ready," Thomas said hesitantly as he guided them down the hall toward the main staircase.

Evening

Nicholaus looked at the king, sitting in his chair and staring at the fire, from the doorway. He knocked on the doorframe, but the king did not stir. He hesitantly entered the room and cleared his throat.

The king looked back. "Oh, Nicholaus. Good." He pointed to the chair across from him. "Have a seat."

"Sire, I am still looking for any signs that would give away —"

The king put his hand up. "This is not about that." He took a deep breath. "This is about Annabelle." Nicholaus finished sitting, slowly, at the mention of his love. The king picked up the famous leather satchel that was lying next to the leg of the chair; he removed two scrolls from it and held them out to Nicholaus. "I think it is only right that you should tell her that Peter was your father."

Nicholaus looked at the leather scrolls. "Are you certain?"

"Are you questioning your king?" he said with a slight grin.

Nicholaus shook his head, and he accepted the scrolls. "No, not my king, only Annabelle's father." The king tilted his head as Nicholaus continued. "You knew him better than I. I was but a child."

The king faced the words as they came from his mouth. "But she knows you better than any of us."

Nicholaus thought about the words and the weeks he had spent every day with Annabelle. He could not argue; he nodded his head. "I will tell her, sire."

"Where does that lead to?" Annabelle asked her brother about a spiral staircase that seemed to disappear into the ceiling as he carried her upstairs after supper.

"That goes to the highest tower," he said as he readjusted her in his arms.

Annabelle's heart quickened. "Let me down."

"What is it?"

"Let me down, please."

He set her feet on the ground as he repeated his question. "What is it?"

"My ankle is much better." She placed more weight on it — it was improving. She looked at the staircase. "I want to go up there."

"I will take you." He leaned in to pick her up again.

"No!" She moved away and onto the first step. "I can do it, see." She pointed to her feet. "Will, I'm thankful for all you have done, but I need some time alone."

"Are you certain?"

"Yes!" she said adamantly.

"Oh." He took a step backwards, feeling a bit hurt. "You don't want me to help you."

"Will, please." She took his hand. "I grew up on a large island with only one other person. I'm not used to being carried around. Please, let me do this alone."

William took a step backwards and bowed his head. "If you wish it. But I will be right here, waiting for you."

Annabelle smiled before facing the steps and making her way up them. "Thank you."

"Prince William." Nicholaus found him sitting upon a bench next to a spiral staircase. "Have you seen Anna" — he shook his head — "Princess Annabelle?"

William stared at him for a moment. "She will always be Anna to you, won't she?"

Nicholaus looked at his feet.

William pointed to the staircase. "She's up there."

Nicholaus looked with shock. "Up the stairs?"

William nodded. "She wanted to be alone." He looked up at Nicholaus from the stairwell, sighing. "I think she only wanted to get away from me."

Nicholaus grinned. "Smothering her with brotherly love?"

William chuckled as he nodded his head. "I suppose."

Annabelle stared at the distant Barstow River, longing to swim, knowing she never would again. The sun was slowly setting behind her, and she was marvelling at how the stars randomly popped into the blanket of darkness to bring beauty to the sky. The night wind occasionally blew her hair wildly and left her with a small chill, but she did not mind. Being up so high with the full view of the sky and the sounds of the river reminded her of the Forbidden Island, and for the briefest of moments, she felt that she was home.

She shook her head at herself. *This is my home now. That island was the dream, a play yard for a little girl who must grow up now.* She sighed heavily as she heard footsteps approaching.

"Will, I really am fine —" A smile broke forth on her face when she saw who stood before her as her heart began to pound a little faster. "Nicholaus."

He bowed to her, and then placed the torch in its holder.

"I thought you were Will. He seems not to be able to leave me alone." She slightly sighed.

"Can you blame him?" he asked as he stepped closer. "He wants to make certain you're safe. No doubt he feels guilty for you falling into the Angler River."

She shook her head. "He needn't."

"As do I."

"You, Nicholaus?" She touched his arm. "You have done so much for me; you brought me to my family."

He lowered his head, his heart beating wildly. "I'm sorry I can't do more, as your brother does."

She looked up at him, pondering his words as the wind blew, and she shivered slightly. He removed his tabard and placed it around her.

"Thank you." She examined the hunter green cloth. *I choose you, Nicholaus. I do choose you, but what does that mean? I don't want to leave my family.* "I never got to praise you" — she looked up at him, a foot away — "on your knighthood."

He opened his mouth, but no words came out.

She turned toward the river and night sky. "I suppose we both got what we wanted." He stepped up behind her; she spoke over her shoulder. "You got your knighthood, and I found my family."

"Anna, I have to tell you something," he whispered into her ear.

She turned around as he nervously pulled out two scrolls from his pocket. "What is that?"

"These came from Peter's bag."

Gasping, the blood drained from her face. "Peter's bag! Where is it? I don't have it. I don't know what became of it. How could I have forgotten?!"

"Anna, Anna, it's all right." He tried to calm her down. "William brought it here. He opened it —"

"He opened it?!" Panic and failure enveloped her body as she shook her head. "No one was to open it but me — by Peter's words! I've failed him!"

"No! No, Anna!" He pulled her close and hugged her, trying to calm her panicking body, petting her hair. "It's all right. There was a letter for the king."

She pulled back and looked into his eyes. "The king? My father?" She shook her head. "How would Peter have known?"

"And a letter for you." He held the scroll out to her.

She looked at it and then up at him. "That letter is for me?" Nicholaus nodded his head.

Taking it, she headed toward the torch. She slid down the stone to sit. Through watery eyes she read Peter's letter.

Tears trickled down her face at the words from her beloved Peter, as if he had spoken them to her himself. She looked over at Nicholaus, very much confused; he was now sitting next to her. "He knew I was a princess?" She shook her head. "How could he have known? She looked back at the letter to see if she had read it correctly. "And he knew my father? I don't understand. And who is Fr. Dominicus?"

"Father Dominicus is my uncle," Nicholaus said.

"Your uncle?" She looked back down at the letter and then up to him, shaking her head. "How did he know him?"

"Anna" — he turned toward her — "Peter was my father."

"What?! I don't understand!"

"Read the other letter written to your father."

She tried to open it, but she was shaking so much she could not. Nicholaus took the scroll and opened it for her as she wiped tears away with her wrist. He handed it back to her.

"You read it," she said as she pushed it back to him.

When he had finished, she placed her chin upon his arm as she looked at him. "Your father, Nicholaus — he didn't know you were alive."

"I know." He nodded his head as he moved his arm around her and pressed her closer.

She wiped away another tear with her right wrist. "So, he gave my papá things from the Demolite castle?"

"Yes," Nicholaus said with a chuckle. "And they have been very helpful."

"What did he give your uncle?"

"I don't know. He's not been here to open it."

She stared at the letter, thinking of all of her time with Peter. "He was your father."

Nicholaus began to tear up. "I know."

She sat up and faced him. "He was a good man. The best father." She grabbed his hand. "And he died defending me." She squeezed it.

"I know." He looked into her eyes, as the reflection of the torch danced amongst the emerald green. "Anna, when I thought you were dead, I wanted to die, too."

She tilted her head, afraid of the words he was about to speak, not because she did not want to hear them, but because she did not want to leave her family. "Why would you say that?" She sat back on her legs, shaking her head. "You have a destiny before you." She stood, continuing to shake her head as her heart beat wildly and fresh tears came to her eyes. "Why would you say such a thing?"

He stood up and faced her. "Anna, I love you."

"No." She shook her head. "You can't tell me this!" She did not want to face such a decision when she had just made it home. She hopped backwards until she touched the stone. "You can't!" She looked up at him as she breathed heavily, unsure what to do.

"Anna." He reached out to touch her.

"Don't touch me!" She took a step sideways. If he touched her, she just might melt. She slowly moved her way toward the door, shaking her head as her heart nearly beat out of her chest. She could not face such turmoil. "I can't leave my family!" She bolted down the steps, each step making her ankle throb a bit more.

"Be careful! You're going to hurt yourself! Anna!" He called as he chased after the fastest person he had ever known.

William stood and walked to the bottom of the staircase when he heard the quick footsteps and voices.

Her ankle gave out on the last step, and she fell into William's arms. "Annie?"

"Take me to my room. Take me to my room, please." He picked her up as he stared at the helpless-looking Nicholaus. "I will," he said, looking at Nicholaus with confusion.

She looked back at his figure but could not look him in the eyes. She loved him, but would she have to leave her family whom she had just found? She could not imagine such a horrid, cruel fate.

"Mamá, where will Annie sleep?" William asked the queen.

Clara looked at her distraught child. "With Isabella. What's wrong?"

William shook his head, as Annabelle could not find words to speak. He pushed Isabella's door open with his foot; Isabella and Cristine jumped two feet and grabbed each other, fearing an unwanted visitor. He set his sister down in a chair.

"What is this about?" Clara asked further as Annabelle gasped in distress.

William shrugged his shoulders. "She was up on the tower, and Nicholaus went up there, and then she came flying down the steps."

Clara sat next to her daughter and took her hand. "Did Nicholaus tell you about Peter?" Annabelle nodded her head. Clara took a deep breath. "Thank you, William. I'll take it from here."

"Are you certain?" He looked from his mother and Annabelle to Isabella and Cristine.

"Yes." His mother smiled.

"Well, good night. I love you all." He walked to Isabella and Cristine and kissed their foreheads.

They answered back, "I love you, too."

He walked to his mother; she stood and hugged him as he kissed her, and she replied, "I love you more than the stars at night."

"And the rainbow after a shower?" he teased.

He knelt down to Annabelle. "Annie, I love you." He kissed her forehead; she grabbed his hand, refusing to let go.

"Annie? Annie, what's wrong? I need my hand."

"I can't choose," she whispered to herself and then to God. "Don't make me choose."

"Choose what?" William looked up at his mother for assistance.

Clara rubbed her daughter's head. Annabelle released her brother and grabbed her mother's wrist. "Mamá, I can't choose."

"Choose what, dear?"

Annabelle looked to the floor. "How cruel."

"Mamá?" William asked, unsure what to do.

"Thank you, William. I'll speak with her."

William looked at Annabelle one last time and left the room, closing the door.

Nicholaus was waiting outside. "Is she all right?"

"In earnest, I'm not certain. What did you say to her?" He looked at the knight, stripped of his hunter green.

He took a deep breath. "I told her I loved her, and she ran away."

William started laughing.

"I'm glad you find joy in that," Nicholaus replied awkwardly.

"No, it's only … she wouldn't tell me she loved me, either." He took a deep breath. "Give her time. Time heals all, right? Do you know where you're to sleep?"

Nicholaus nodded. "I do." He took a deep breath. "But I'll stop at the chapel first."

"Annie?" Isabella and Cristine crawled their way to their sister and sat beside her. Cristine offered her hand.

Clara rubbed Annabelle's head as she knelt on her left. "Are you thinking of Peter? I know it comes as an amazing revelation, but I'm certain Peter hid the truth for a reason."

"This is not about Peter," she said as she stared at the floor across the room. "It's a cruel fortune, that's what it is," she said to herself while her mother and sisters were listening.

Clara looked at her two other daughters quizzically. Cristine shrugged her shoulders. Isabella sat stoically, concerned about her sister, but with her mind churning over her own problems — she knew too well about cruel fates.

"Fortune? This is about Nicholaus?" Clara asked.

Annabelle nodded her head. "Yes. I treated him poorly."

Cristine, confused, looked from her mother to Annabelle. "So this isn't about Sir Nicholaus losing his father while Sir Josephus raised you?"

"How did you treat Sir Nicholaus poorly, dear?" Clara asked.

Cristine squeezed her sister's hand. "Whatever you did, I'm certain he'll forgive you. *He's* a good man."

Isabella pathetically whimpered beside her while their mother took note of the behavior.

Annabelle finally tore her eyes away from the floor to look at her mother and sisters. "He said he loved me, and I love him."

Clara could not help but giggle over her daughter's perceived condition. Isabella's focus suddenly centered on her sister at the mention of love.

"Well, did you tell him? How'd you treat him poorly?" Cristine, more confused, wanted answers as she shook her head. "What did you say to him?"

"Nothing! I ran. I'm a coward!" She shook her head as she swallowed the lump in her throat. "Is this the bitterness of life I must now face?"

"What?" Christine squeezed her hand harder. "I thought you said you loved him, too?"

"Bitterness of life?" Clara embraced her daughter's face as she shook her head. "Love is not bitter. Love is sweet and nothing of which to be afraid."

Annabelle, through stinging eyes and a forlorn face, attempted to look at her mother. "I'm now home. I don't want to leave!"

"Honey!" Clara stood next to the chair and hugged her daughter's head. "Why would you have to leave?"

Hope filling her, Annabelle looked up at her mother's smiling face. "I wouldn't have to leave?"

Clara giggled again as she pushed Annabelle's hair out of her face. "I wouldn't want you to."

I don't have to choose between the man I love and my family? Annabelle hugged her mother again. She took a relieved breath and then sat straight, grabbing Isabella's hand. "Does that mean Isa's not leaving?"

Isabella removed her hand and stood, looking around nervously.

Clara watched her behavior. "No. She'll leave with Prince Phillipus."

"Then there is still bitterness. I don't want her to leave either! I return to lose her again?"

Isabella gasped, holding back her own emotions; she knelt down before her sister. "Annie, I will always be your sister, no matter the distance!" She hugged Annabelle as Annabelle hugged her back.

Annabelle's mind churned as she embraced her sister. *Where's Symon? Why hasn't he come? Is he still alive?* A wave of fear infiltrated her thoughts. *If he is dead, what good would it do to tell her?*

"Well," the queen sighed, "I'm glad the strife bothering Annabelle was made clear." She held out her hand. "Cristine, let us go to our own chambers."

Annabelle stared at the fire as she removed the hunter green cloth. She held it tightly and smelled it; it reminded her of Nicholaus. "I was such a fool," she announced to Isabella, who was quickly changing into her nightgown with Alicia's help. Alicia stared silently at the bruises. Annabelle turned toward her sister right as Isabella's bruises were hidden by her hair. "How can I ever face him?"

Isabella approached her sister. "Annie, I don't know much, but I do know this: if you love him, you should tell him." She turned away as tears fell.

Annabelle looked at her sister, attempting to ascertain what the tears meant. Were they tears of joy or tears of sadness?

"Princess Annabelle," Alicia called.

Annabelle set the tabard down and headed toward Alicia for her to help her with her dress. "Thank you," she said when finished. She turned back to her sister; Isabella was kneeling next to her bed in prayer as tears still fell.

Annabelle watched Alicia leave and close the door. She joined her sister with her own prayers. They climbed into the fluffy bed. Annabelle could not go to sleep without knowing; she looked over at her sister, already lying down. "You must really love him?"

Isabella could handle no more. She adamantly shook her head. "No."

Annabelle plopped down on to her right side beside her, shaking her head. "What?"

"I don't love him. I don't even like him. I ... I *loathe* him!"

"But you're marrying him?"

Isabella turned from her sister to stare stoically across the room.

Annabelle stared at the candle burning on the nightstand, observing its dancing shadow against the brick walls. "You have loved another?"

"It doesn't matter; he's dead!" Isabella said with anger.

Annabelle moved to the head of the bed to sit next to her sister, stroking her hair. "Don't marry the prince, then."

"I have to!"

"Why do you have to?"

"Because I do!"

"But why?"

"You don't understand."

That's for certain. She stroked her sister's hair until Isabella fell asleep.

"It was only the servants' chambers that were burned, right?" Thomas, standing in his father's public chamber next to the Hall of Justice, asked William, Sir Michael, and the king as they secretly met to discuss who the arsonist could be.

"Yes," Michael replied, as he walked away from the door.

"Why? Why only the servants' wing?" Thomas asked.

"Who would want to harm the servants? And why?" William asked.

The king straightened up tiredly. "I can't help but think Cristine might be right. There are an awful lot of Sethelians here."

"You think one of the Sethelians did it, Papá?" William shook his head. "Have Prince Phillipus's servants not got along with ours?"

"Michael," — the king looked to his friend — "have you heard any talk?"

"No, sire." He walked closer, thinking about the whole situation. "If there is worry among the servants, they have not shared it with your knights."

"And Prince Phillipus? Have you found anyone to speak poorly of his character?"

"No, sire. All word has come back praising his worthiness and character."

"He's certainly worked eagerly to find Johannes Fletcher. I don't think there's been a day he has not gone in search for him," Thomas observed.

"He was gone when the fires were set," the king said as he folded his arms and leaned against the table.

"Are there more Demolites among our servants? What if the others found out and were going to tell?" William suggested with a new passion.

"No body was killed. If he wanted to silence a person, wouldn't the Demolite have killed the servant?" Thomas shook his head. "I don't think it was intended to be a threat against one servant."

"You think it a threat against all?" Michael asked as he approached Prince Thomas.

"Who would be threatening the servants?" The king looked at his second eldest son.

"Who do we know the least about?"

The king shook his head. "You are saying the Sethelians are to blame?"

"All it takes is one," Michael suggested.

"What am I to do with this? Ask Prince Phillipus if one of his men can't be trusted? King Henrard is on his way here. Isabella is to marry in a few days time. I can't accuse a Sethelian with no proof!"

"What if it wasn't *one*?"

Everyone turned toward Thomas.

"What do you mean, Thom?"

"Can one person threaten every servant?"

The king shook his head. "I don't like this, Thom."

"But what if it that is what's taken place?"

Disgruntled, the king turned away.

Hearing a curtain move from around the bed, Queen Clara turned toward the light. "Francis, is that you?"

"Yes. Did I wake you?"

"I can't sleep." She pushed the blankets away.

"I doubt I'll be able to either," the king said as he sat down on the edge of the bed for a moment and then lifted his legs up to the mattress.

Moving over to him, she took his arm, leaning against his shoulder. "What was learned about the fire?"

"It was set wilfully."

"Who would do that?"

"That's the worry." Finding her hand, he squeezed it.

"What does Michael say?"

"There is to be a meeting in the morning."

"Meeting with whom?"

"The Sethelians."

She pulled herself away. "You think one of them did it?"

"We have no proof of anything. Michael has placed guards outside their chambers."

Clara shook her head. "And yet our daughter is to marry their prince." She moved away to sit up against the wall.

"Clara? Where'd you go?" Reaching out, he could not find her in the dark.

"This isn't right. Something isn't right. Between Alicia and Isabella and now even Cristine."

Giving up on his search, the king dropped his hand. "What about Cristine?"

"She has fallen silent! I haven't heard her speak an ill word about Prince Phillipus in hours!" Clara adamantly nodded. "I think I shall have my own meeting in the morning."

"Very well." He sighed heavily.

Hearing his distressed sound, she moved back toward

him. "Francis, I'm sorry. I'm here." Setting her head against his chest, she said. "Would you like to hear some good tidings?"

"Please," he said as he hugged her.

"Nicholaus loves Annabelle, and Annabelle loves him back."

"He's a good man," the king said as he rubbed his wife's arm.

"He is." Her smile slowly faded when her thoughts jumped from Sir Nicholaus to Prince Phillipus. Her mind wandered to the conversation with Beatrix earlier. *"Our rooms were burned." What if she was answering me?* "What if the fire was because of Prince Phillipus?"

"What do you mean?"

"I don't know for certain. I have seen him so little. Is it not odd that he seems to always be gone?"

"He is working to find Fletcher. He knows we need arrows to fight the Demolites."

"Yet he's had no profit from all of his searching? Is that not odd?" Sighing, she concluded, "Something is not right, indeed."

Requests

Hearing a noise, Sir Michael looked to the door as he sat up in bed. Grabbing his dagger, he moved toward the small slit of light coming in from an oil lamp in the hallway. As he approached, he noticed something on the floor. Picking it up, he opened his door and looked both ways down the hallway. Walking to an oil lamp, he read his name upon the outside. He broke the wax seal and read: *A man is in the river.*

He stepped southward, looking both ways down the hall; he saw no one.

Walking north down the knights' hall, he spotted a king's knight standing guard outside the Sethelian knights' chamber. "Sir Underwood, has any man passed by you?"

"No, sir."

"Did you see anyone near my chamber?"

"The light is poor down there, sir."

"Indeed," Michael agreed as he squeezed the paper in his hand.

Annabelle was up before the first rays of light colored the horizon. She stared out Isabella's window as the light slowly filled the room. *I have to find out if Symon is alive! I have to!*

She looked down at the castle grounds and then to the right as Aboly began to emerge from its sleepiness. She took a deep breath as she thought of Nicholaus, unable to get him off her mind; she placed her hand upon the green glass. *I'm sorry, Nicholaus. I do love you. Will you forgive me?* She turned around when she heard footsteps.

"Oh!" Ida jumped at the sight of Annabelle next to the window. "Pardon me, Princess." She bowed. "But I was going to check the fire. Would you like to dress?"

"Yes."

Ida smiled. "I'll be making you some dresses shortly. I don't have anything to measure with me at present. I didn't know you would be awake."

"That's all right. You can find me when you are ready."

Ida took out a dress. "Will this one do?"

"It does not matter to me," Annabelle said as she looked out the window.

Ida then noticed the knight's tabard lying on the back of a chair. "Would you like me to take that, Princess?"

Annabelle looked to where Ida was gazing. "No." She nearly whispered, "I'll return it. Where are the knights?"

All the knights froze at the presence of the princess. She bravely hobbled toward the unsheathed swords and daggers. Nicholaus swallowed hard as he watched her approach with his tabard draped over her arm.

"Princess Annabelle, is everything all right?"

She looked with a smile at Michael, who had run over to her. "Yes, thank you." Her eyes diverted toward Nicholaus's direction. "I would like to speak with Nicholaus."

He bowed to her and jogged over toward Nicholaus. "Sir Nicholaus, she would like to speak with you. And, oh, get the princess out of our training yard."

"Yes, sir." He bowed as he headed toward her, fearful of what she would or would not say. He had thought she would never speak to him again.

"Princess Annabelle, you really shouldn't be out here." He took her right arm and guided her out of the training area. "It's not safe."

When he let go, she turned around and looked back at the knights who had only just begun to return to their prior activities, and then down at the ground. "I'm not allowed to step within the rocks?" She looked up at him for his reply.

"The rocks are there for a reason."

She studied the small rocks purposely placed amongst the green grass; she followed the line back toward the stone perimeter wall and then left to the plentiful fruit trees in the corner. Her eyes slowly made their way back to Nicholaus as she shook her head in hopes of shaking away the present conversation for another that she wished to discuss. "Nicholaus, I'm sorry for running away."

He shook his head. "No, Princess. I am the one who should be sorry. I should not have been so forward." He looked at the ground. "I have no right to —"

"Nicholaus, I ..."

He looked up at her.

"I ..." *Tell him. Tell him!* She closed her eyes and took a breath; she did not have the courage. "I wanted to give this back to you." She smiled as she extended her arm. She held her breath at her weakness.

He scooped it up, the back of his hand touching her arm. "Thank you, Princess."

Annabelle nearly screamed. *If he calls me* princess *one more time ... Why? Why does he do that?*

"Are you all right?" He looked at her with concern. He could tell she seemed agitated.

She looked down. "I'm fine."

"All right. Well, good day." He started walking away.

"Wait!" She stepped toward him.

His heart began to flutter as he turned around. "Yes?"

She looked into his eyes. "Nicholaus, I ..." She could not force the words out. "Could you do something for me? It is of great matter to me."

"Anything." His heart spoke.

How could she explain? "I need you to find someone for me." She shook her head. "I don't know if he's still alive, but I pray he is."

"Who?" Nicholaus stood up straight.

"Symon." How could she describe him? "He's a black —"

"Blacksmith?" Nicholaus cut in.

"Yes." She nodded her head with a smile.

"Sy the blacksmith?" Nicholaus clarified as his heart was stabbed with a dagger.

"Yes. Do you know him?" She looked quizzically at him.

"I do not, Princess."

Annabelle took a staggered breath at the name of "princess." She closed her eyes. "Could you find out if he is alive for me, please?" Opening her eyes, she looked at him.

Are you sending me to find your love? Are you trying to wound my heart again? But I will, for you. "I will check with Sir Doey after our morning lesson to see if it is all right. I can't give you my word for there is to be a meeting this morning."

"Oh, well, thank you for checking." She turned to go inside.

"Do you need help?" He looked at her ankle.

She turned around. "My ankle is better now, thank you."

He watched her slowly walk to the entrance and then turned around as his heart deflated to nothingness.

Walking down the upstairs hallway with Beatrix behind her, Clara called out: "Alicia."

"My lady?" The servant turned toward her, about to enter Isabella's room.

"Bring Cristine in here."

"Yes, my lady." Alicia curtsied as the queen and the older servant went into Isabella's room.

"Mamá? I'm not dressed yet," Isabella called out as she

hid under the blanket.

"Yes, and I hear you don't wish for Beatrix to help you."

Isabella lowered her head and, fixing her hair so that it covered her shoulders, got out of bed.

"Mamá, do you wish to see me?" Cristine asked as she walked through the door with Alicia behind her.

"Yes. And you, too, Alicia."

Alicia froze as she quickly looked at Isabella.

"Mamá," — Isabella walked toward the younger servant — "what is this about?"

"I want to know what is going on and I want to know right now. I will not take silence this time." She stared at her daughters, who looked away, and then the servants.

"If someone does not start speaking now, I shall be forced to do something I do not wish to do." She waited, and waited, and waited; no one spoke a word.

"Is this the way it is to be?" Not one eye dared to look at her. "All right. Alicia ..."

The servant stepped forward. "Yes, my lady?"

"Your service is no longer needed. Gather your things and leave."

Horror passed over everyone's face.

"No!" Isabella objected as Alicia threw her hand in front of her mouth and stepped backward.

"Mamá, you can't!" Cristine pleaded.

"And why can't I?"

Cristine lowered her head with a frustrated whimper.

"My lady," — Beatrix stepped forward — "Alicia has no where to go."

"She'll be killed!" Isabella immediately covered her mouth.

"Killed?" Clara turned toward her daughter, studying her acutely with her emerald eyes.

"I mean, Mamá, she has no where ... no place ... no one

… it's not safe…" Isabella looked at her sister, unsure what she should say.

Clara looked at the younger servant. "If she does not wish to leave service here, she must speak to me. Otherwise, she must be gone by this evening."

Alicia, sobbing, ran out of the room.

"Mamá, you can't!" Isabella begged as she began to shake in fear, breathing quickly as she fell to the floor.

Clara knelt down next to her daughter as Cristine stood silently in shock. "Isabella, tell me why you cry!"

Isabella only shook her head.

The queen looked up at Beatrix. "Go to Alicia if you must."

"My lady." She bowed her head quickly and scurried out of the room.

Watching her daughter cry for a moment, Clara stood up and walked out.

Cristine, gasping, shook her head. "What will they do to her? Will they kill her so she can't speak?"

Fresh tears streamed down Isabella's face. "This is all my fault! It's all my fault!"

Annabelle's attention was caught by a portrait set outside the Great Hall. She was mesmerized by the young girl in the picture with wavy, blonde hair — a face she knew. Her heart rate increased. *Celesa?* She looked around, wanting to question anybody about the portrait.

Hearing footsteps descending the stairwell, she waited for whomever would appear.

"Thom!" She ran to him.

"Annie, what's wrong?"

Grabbing his hand, she pulled him over to the portrait. "Who is this?"

"The painting?" He looked at her as he went on to

explain, "It was painted in 1050 by a monk from Anchelo, Brother —"

"Who is she?" she interrupted.

"That is St. Celestria."

Annabelle gasped and covered her mouth. In wonder, she stared at the picture.

He looked from the picture to his sister's profile. "It's a painting of St. Celestria," he continued, "painted 20 years after her death by the same monk who took the Eucharist from her before she was shot and fell back into the Angler River. Are you all right?"

"I think I need to sit." He helped her over to the stairwell where she sat down. She swallowed hard, staring at the floor. "So that is what she looked like?" She shook her head in utter disbelief. *Celesa? Saint Celestria? A saint?*

"Princess Annabelle." Ida stopped three steps above her. "I'm ready for measuring, if you are."

Annabelle stood, in a haze, and turned toward the seamstress. Unable to speak, she just followed.

Thomas watched her ascend the steps as he looked back at the portrait, not understanding his sister's behavior.

"Thom," Cristine, with a deterimed countenance, rounded the spiral staircase. "Are the Sethelians to meet this morning?"

"How did you hear about that?"

"Is it all of them? Servants and knights?"

"Yes," he answered as she walked past him. "They're being summoned now."

"I'm going."

"Crisa —"

Adamantly, she cut him off. "I'm going."

He watched her, with great curiosity, walk toward the Hall of Justice.

Nicholaus walked through the bustling market filled with a variety of voices, dancing dust from carts gone by, people purchasing produce and packages, children chasing one another, and occasional rodents. A small boy peeked around a cart and watched the hunter green uniform pass by, looking with awe. Where would he look? Whom should he ask?

"Excuse me," he addressed a man at a stand. "I'm looking for a blacksmith by the name of Sy."

The man pointed down the market. "Smithy shops are down there."

"But he is not from Aboly."

"Smithy shops are down there," the man repeated with another point.

He walked amid the busy market toward the guild section around the corner. There were several blacksmith shops in Aboly. He stood at a distance, not knowing whom he should speak to.

"I told Doey it would be ready Friday."

Nicholaus approached the man who addressed him. "I'm not here on that matter."

"No?" The man spat upon the ground. "Then why are you here?"

Nicholaus looked at the man, who stood colored by his labor: dirty, blackened, covered in perspiration. "I am looking for a blacksmith by the name of Symon, or just Sy. Have you heard of him?" The man began to grumble as he went back to work shaping metal on his anvil. Nicholaus stepped closer. "Have you heard of such a man?"

The man looked up as he continued speaking, now grumbling audibly, "… and you can tell that Fulco he can keep his young blood. I won't be outdone."

"Fulco?" Nicholaus asked as he tried to understand the man's words.

"Are you looking for Smithy Fulco?" A man closer to Nicholaus's age asked as he held a saddle in his hand.

"Perhaps," Nicholaus said as he looked at the muscular man before him.

"I am going that way." The man eyed Nicholaus's uniform. "You are a king's knight?"

"I am," Nicholaus said as he followed the man.

The man stopped walking. "Forgive me, but I must ask: Princess Annabelle, she is safe?" His eyes plead for an answer.

Nicholaus studied the man before him closely as his mind churned. "Are you the blacksmith named Symon?"

The man nodded his head with a brief smirk as he looked to the ground and then returned his gaze. "Sy, I am."

Nicholaus swallowed hard as he stared at the man before him. *He looks hardy. Why wouldn't she love him?* "Princess Annabelle sent me to make certain you were alive."

His face lit up as a burden was lifted. "She is safe! Oh that's good tidings!" He walked over to a fence and swung the saddle on top of it. "So, she has met her family after all these years? Wonderful!" He looked at the shop before him before turning around.

"Is there a patron, Sy?" a voice from an injured blacksmith called from inside the shack.

"Do you need to speak with Fulco?" Symon asked.

"No." Nicholaus shook his head. "Only you."

Symon nodded his head. "No, no patron." He turned back toward Nicholaus. "I went to the gate this morning, but they would not let me enter." He shook his head staring across the yard. His eyes found their way back to Nicholaus. "Her family is merry? I mean" — he shook his head — "of course they are." He really wanted to know about Isabella: How was she? Was she happy? Was she still to be wed? He took a deep breath as Nicholaus was about to say his goodbyes. "Could you give the princess something?" He moved toward the gate.

Nicholaus moved uncomfortably. He did not like being the message boy between the princess and the mysterious blacksmith that knew too much about her for his liking. Symon returned with a metal rose. "Your timing is great. It was readied before getting the saddle." He offered it to Nicholaus with a smile. "It should make her merry to get it."

Nicholaus looked at the metallic rose before him as his heart pounded wildly. *There is no question now! He is courting her!* He wanted to punch Symon, break the rose in half if possible, and throw the remains at him. But, instead, he closed his eyes, praying for strength and humility. He accepted the rose, which felt as cold as his beaten, barely pumping heart. He swallowed a lump as his voice cracked. "Any message?"

Symon's breath quickened as words finally escaped his lips in a whisper. "I hope her sister is well."

Nicholaus looked up. "Princess Elizabeth has been home for two weeks now, with no harm to her."

"And Isabella?" he asked quickly.

"Princesses Isabella and Cristine are fine," Nicholaus stated, tilting his head pondering why the blacksmith was taking such an interest in the princesses.

"Sy! We have paying patrons. That saddle will not mend itself."

Symon turned back to Nicholaus. "I am glad they are unharmed." He held out his hand. "Thank you for the tidings."

"Sir Nicholaus," Nicholaus replied as he forced himself to shake his hand.

"Oh! Nicholaus Hunts?"

Nicholaus nodded.

Symon increased his grip and shook more. "It is very nice to meet you. Very nice indeed!" he said with a smile.

Nicholaus nodded as he pulled his arm back and watched the blacksmith pick up the saddle.

"Crisa, what are you doing here?" William asked in disbelief as Thomas walked in behind her.

Stopping, she folded her arms and looked around the room. "Where is Prince Phillipus?"

"Crisa, what are you doing here?" William asked again in a harsher tone.

"Where is Prince Phillipus?" she asked back, louder.

"Princess Cristine." Michael, hearing the raised voices, approached. "Prince Phillipus is searching for a body in the river."

"How does he know about a body in the river?" she spoke so loudly, the men around her stopped talking.

"I received a note this morning," Michael looked around curiously as all the men stared at Cristine.

"And who sent it?" she said loudly.

"Unknown. It was unsigned."

"Then someone who knows the body is in the river had to have written it." She looked around the room. "So it was either a scribe or a knight. Someone in this room."

All the Sethelians began to look at one another.

"Cristine, you were not summoned here," the king said as he walked in.

"I'm leaving."

Thomas watched his sister curiously as she walked out without an argument.

"Princess Annabelle."

She had watched Nicholaus enter the room over the top of the scroll as she sat in the window seat with the parchment of poetry she was not reading, her mind still pondering over Celesa or St. Celestria, whoever she was.

She was not sure how she should address him. Should she be offended that he was calling her by her formal title again? It was her name, but it felt cold, impersonal, as though he wanted to distance himself from knowing her, from their shared time together. She was disappointed but maybe he was required to use such formality — though he had not the previous night.

She put down the document, assuming she had pinpointed the reason. "Did you find him?" she asked with hope, holding her breath.

"I did."

She gasped as she covered her mouth with her hand. "He is alive?" She stood up. "That is a wonderful tiding!" she said with an infectious smile. Her smile faded when she saw pain in Nicholaus's eyes. Her heart sank. "Nicholaus … what's wrong?"

He held out the metallic flower. "Your rose."

"My rose?" She looked at his face and then to his hands. A smile burst forth upon her face; a shiver of despair enveloped his body. She took it in her right hand and examined it in the sunlight through the window. "Symon made this?" She smiled up at Nicholaus. "It is a marvel, is it not? It is the perfect image of a rose!"

He could no longer avoid her gaze. He looked into her eyes as the happiness exuding from her countenance put a flutter back into his heart. He dared to smile at her contentment. "It is a marvel." He watched her as she further examined the gift. *She is joyful. At least there's that.*

She looked back at him, with the biggest smile. "Do you know what this is? This is an abiding flower, to show that love is lasting, endless." At the mention of love, her eyes turned back to the rose. She could not meet his eyes after how she had treated him.

I thank You, Father, that Symon gives her joy. Nicholaus

took a deep breath. "I pray," he dared to whisper, "that he shall always give you such merriment."

Annabelle looked at him quizzically. "Who?"

Before he could reply, Sir Gamel stepped into the room. "Sir Nicholaus, the king wishes your company."

Nicholaus bowed to the princess and backed out of the room as she was left, mind spinning, chewing on his words, attempting to decipher them.

Nicholaus walked into the king's empty public chamber. He looked around as the king came through the door from the Hall of Justice. "I heard my daughter sent you on an errand."

"Yes, Your Majesty," the knight said, at attention.

"I hope it was not too hard."

"No, Your Majesty," he said, hardly blinking.

"Good." He knocked upon his table quickly. "The Sethelians are still in there, but in truth, I'm glad not to be." He pointed his head toward the Hall of Jusitce.

"Has anything come from the meeting?"

"Not as of yet. Cristine seemed to make them start talking among themselves, but to us they haven't spoken." Shaking his head, the king spoke to himself. "What is going on in my home?"

"Your Majesty?"

The king looked over at him. "Nicholaus, your father and I were great friends; do not call me by my sovereign title when I do not call you by your title."

Nicholaus's nerves jumped to an unprecedented level of discomfort.

The king leaned against the table, taking a deep breath. "I still can't believe what your father did. Taking those articles from the Demolites and giving them to my daughter." He shook his head. "I don't know if I should be joyous or full of wrath. What would they have done if they caught her with it?"

He stared across the room. "I suppose I should thank God she wasn't found with it." He looked back at Nicholaus. "What do you think of all of this?"

Nicholaus shook his head. "She didn't know what was in the bag. It was for the best, I deem — my father's keen wits in play. I think it's why he never told her who he was, who she was. She would've been in *more* danger if she had known."

"*More* danger?" The king sat forward.

"Your Majesty —" The king looked at him, annoyed. "Sire," Nicholaus corrected. "Anna — Princess Annabelle — was in danger no matter where she was, not because of her title or the bag, but because of her beauty." His heart quickened and his palms began to perspire. Should he have spoken so bluntly?

The king sat up straight. "Yes." He looked past Nicholaus and then at him again. "She was blessed to find you."

Nicholaus lowered his head at the compliment.

"A person's character, not one's blood, shows the true colors of a man." He looked at Nicholaus. "Do you agree?"

"Yes, wholeheartedly," Nicholaus said as he shifted his weight.

The king stood up straight. "Most look at my daughters and think some fine matches could be made."

Such as Isabella and the prince of Sethel?

The king shook his head. "My children are given the same freedom I took, to marry for love. My daughters" — he looked into the knight's eyes — "are free to choose any man, no matter his station."

That does not appear to be the case with Isabella. His mind then turned to his Anna as he released a depressed breath. *Like a blacksmith?*

"So long as there is a quality of character — humble, courteous, full of honor and proper conduct."

He appears to be.

"Am I understood?"

Wholly. He nodded his head though he wanted to vomit.

"Good!" The king nodded. "Now, as to why I really summoned you. You may choose to welcome or decline, but I dare say you will welcome."

Nicholaus shifted his weight again.

"Bishop Dominicus is on his way here. We received a message of distress an hour ago. He is in Darlum, and the people are in fear from a Demolite uprising."

"I shall leave at once," Nicholaus said, ready to hurry to his uncle's aid.

The king put up his hands. "I wouldn't commonly send a knight for this duty, but since he is your uncle, I give you leave. But I can't spare any extra men. If you go, you must go alone. There is talk of the Demolites assembling. I give you the choice, Nicholaus. He might even be on his way here by now. You know how slowly tidings travel."

Nicholaus was secretly thankful to escape from the castle walls where he was constantly reminded of his emotions that rolled like the hills with the finding, losing, finding again, and final loss of his beloved Anna. It was his chance of escape, to clear his mind. "Yes, Your Maj — Sire."

"Isa?" Annabelle knocked upon her sister's door. Not hearing a reply, she let herself in. "Isa?!" Finding her sister rocking herself on the floor, weeping uncontrollably, Annabelle went to her, dropping the metal rose beside herself. "Isa, what's wrong?"

"It's all my fault! It's all my fault!"

"What?"

"She'll be killed, and I'll still have to marry him! But I will because you're here."

"Me?" Annabelle lifted up her sister's head. "Isa, what are you talking about?"

Another wail escaped her lips as the eldest princess held on to the younger. "It's only right. It's only right."

"You don't have to marry him!"

"Yes, I do!"

Annabelle picked up the rose. "Look! It's a gift!"

Isabella shook her head in confusion. "What is it?"

Shaking her head, Annabelle revealed, "I'm sorry I didn't tell you last night. I wasn't certain if he made it."

"Who?" Isabella shook her head at a complete loss.

"Lord Symon."

"What?" Isabella's face tightened as she began to breathe hard.

Annabelle nodded her head. "Duke of Gemmeny," she added for clarification.

Isabella shook her head. "No, he died. His castle caught on fire."

"He's alive, Isa!" She offered the metal rose to Isabella. "And he made this for you. It's an abiding rose. He wants you to know he still loves you."

"What?" She stood up, very much angered.

"He's working for a blacksmith now. He made this for you!" Annabelle held out the rose.

"Stop!" Isabella put her hands on to her ears.

"He helped me get here," Annabelle tried to explain, standing with the rose in her hand.

"Did Crisa send you in here?!" Isabella looked around frantically.

"Crisa? No. Lord —"

"Stop!" She shrieked with her hands over her ears.

"Isa?"

"Get out!" Isabella screamed in furry.

"What?" Annabelle stepped back in shock.

"I can't stand to look at you! I wished you'd never returned!" Her shaking body dropped to the ground.

"What?"

"Get out!" Isabella, hunched on the floor, screamed again as she stared at the gray stones.

Placing the metal flower on the floor, Annabelle backed out of the room as her sister continued to scream. Out in the hallway, looking through the doorframe, Annabelle said, "Isa, you don't have to marry Prince Phillipus."

Grabbing the rose, Isabella flung it at her sister. It never made it outside the room. "I *hate* you!"

Turning away, Annabelle took a deep breath as fear crept into her mind. *Why does Prince Phillipus have such a hold on you, Isa? Symon loves you. Why won't you believe me?* Suddenly getting an idea, she hobbled toward the spiral staircase.

Nicholaus rolled his clothes into tight cylinders and placed them in his bag. He looked up when he heard someone burst through the door.

"Nicholaus!"

"Anna? I mean Princess Annabelle."

"I need you to tell Isa that the —" She looked at his bed. "What are you doing?" She stared at the rolls and bag. "You're leaving?" She stiffened. "You're leaving because of me?"

He did not deny it.

Shaking her head, she walked back out of the room.

"Anna?" He caught her in the hallway. "Anna, I go because my uncle needs help."

"And because of me?"

He lowered his head.

"Well —" walking away, she spoke to herself, "— it seems everyone wants me gone."

"Anna, what do you need?" Nicholaus pleaded as he watched her disappear up the steps.

"Sir Nicholaus," a squire informed him, "your horse is ready."

Revelation

Clara, on her knees in front of the tabernacle, turned toward the door. "Annabelle?"

"Mamá?" The princess knelt beside her mother. "Do you think everyone would be better off if I had not come back?"

"What?!" Clara grabbed her hand. "What are these words that you speak?"

"Isa wishes I hadn't."

"Oh, Annabelle." She pulled her daughter into herself. "Isabella is hurting and I don't know why."

Her mother's loving embrace, which had brought her so much comfort years ago, was now beginning to tear down the pain from her recent rejections.

"Sweet child." Clara hugged her.

"Mamá, she said she hates me," she said with confusion. "I'm worried about her."

Clara shook her head as she assured her daughter. "Isabella does not hate you." Petting her daughter's head, the queen revealed, "She has not been the same from the time you were taken."

Annabelle laid her head against her mother's neck as she felt her mother's touch stroking her back. She listened attentively to her words.

"She is upset about something." Clara took a deep breath, shaking her head. "And she will not tell me what it is. But, Annabelle, my dear child, I love you, your whole family loves you so much; your taking pained all of us." A tear rolled down the queen's cheek. "Annabelle, I never stopped praying for you. On your 10th birthday, I settled with the thought that you were gone." Clara gasped for air between a sob. "I yielded you to God's care, though I never halted my prayers; and now, He has given you back to me!"

Annabelle looked at the queen's crying countenance. "Mamá! I'm sorry you hurt because of me."

Clara smiled as she rubbed her daughter's cheek. "It was a good hurt. I'd rather hurt from losing you than to have never known you at all."

The princess scooted closer to her mother, and they embraced each other again. The tight pressure of her mother, willing love into her daughter, fulfilled a lost need of a small child. Annabelle relished it, despite the pulsating pain from a shattered shoulder.

Annabelle looked up at the crucifix — a visual reminder of how much God loved her, what He was willing to do for her, what He would do just for her, if needed. She recalled the words of the mysterious Celesa, who bore the uncanny appearance of the painting of St. Celestria. She whispered into her mother's ear, "Celesa told me you never stopped praying."

"Who's Celesa?" Clara whispered back.

Annabelle looked into her mother's emerald eyes, shaking her head. "I think she might be St. Celestria."

"What?"

"I don't know. She was a girl on the island. I only saw her twice, but" — she looked at the floor — "she looked like the painting of St. Celestria." Her gaze fell upon her mother again as she whispered, "She knew that you prayed for me every day."

Clara chuckled at the revelation as her hands flew to her mouth. "Dear, when I prayed for you, I prayed for St. Celestria's intercession."

A shiver cascaded down Annabelle's back as she broke out in tears, laying her head upon her mother. They were not tears of sadness or loss but tears of an awesome realization —

the realization of God's unconditional love and the awesome power of the Body of Christ, spanning all times and all states. She suddenly remembered the rest of Celesa's words as her head tilted. "But she also said Peter had helped her?"

Clara took her daughter's head into her hands and kissed her forehead. Then, thinking about her eldest daughter, the queen asked, "What was it that made Isabella so angry?"

"Duke Symon of Gemmeny."

Clara tilted her head. "How do you know that name?"

"I met him. He's alive." She followed her mother as she stood up.

"Met him?"

"When I was traveling home I met him. He knew who I was; he called me by name!"

Clara tilted her head. "Is this like St. Celestria?"

"No." Annabelle shook her head adamantly as she stepped forward. "He's in Aboly. He's working for a black-smith. He made Isabella a rose — from metal — and I gave it to her. And that's when she became so angry." Her voice cracked.

"He's alive?" Clara looked over her daughter's shoulder at the flickering red flame.

"Yes!" Annabelle said clearly.

"My dear" — Clara stepped forward and took Anna-belle's hand — "Are you certain?"

"Yes! I'm positive!"

Clara pulled her daughter close and hugged her. "This could be the answer to my prayers!"

"What do you mean?"

"I can tell Isabella doesn't want to marry Prince Phillipus, but she always says she does."

"She told me she *loathes* him," Annabelle said honestly.

Clara covered her mouth as she shook her head. After a moment, she sighed deeply. She moved her daughter's hair back behind her shoulder. "At least I know you love Nicholaus."

Annabelle turned away.

"What's wrong?"

She turned back around to face her mother as her chin began to quiver. "He's leaving because of me. I ran when he said he loved me ... and now he doesn't want to be around me." She sat down on the stone floor.

The queen sat down next to the blue princess. "My dear, the first time your father told me he loved me, I ran away, too."

"You did?" Annabelle looked into the loving emerald eyes.

"Yes," Clara said while remembering. "Your father tried to get away, too. I was a servant here at this castle, and he, of course, was the prince."

Annabelle diverted her gaze to the stone floor as connections were made from conversations gone by. She looked at the queen, the servant Peter had spoken of. "It was you?"

"What was me?"

"The prince and the servant, and Sir Victorus?"

The queen sat up stiffly. "How do you know that name?"

"Peter told me." She stood up and stared at the shiny tabernacle, reflecting the glow of the red flame. "He told me everything." She turned back to her now standing mother. "The Demolites were started by Victorus. He tried to assault you."

"He told you everything?"

Annabelle forced her thoughts to her mother's words, "Yes, he told me about the prince and the prince's friend." She stopped and her mouth dropped open as another revelation emerged.

"What? What's wrong?"

"The prince's friend ... it was Peter! That's how he

knew!" Her face changed from enlightened to serious as more of his stories were recalled. "All the stories he told me of the prince and the prince's friends. They were of Papá and him and *Michael*? Mooey?"

The queen chuckled at the name she had not heard in quite a while. "Mooey, yes, Michael Doey. It was your Peter that started that one, I've been told."

"They were all the truth," Annabelle spoke to herself as her mother walked toward the door.

"Pardon me, Annabelle, but I'm going to go find out why Isabella *loathes* Prince Phillipus."

"How? When she won't say?"

Clara nodded. "I have my ways of finding out."

When her mother left, Annabelle turned back to the tabernacle and knelt down.

Watching the Sethelians about to fight each other, William rubbed his head as he looked at his brother. "This is going nowhere."

A Sethelian stepped forward. "You need to find the scribe that wrote the words, that's what you need to do!"

Sir Gamel entered, whispering into Sir Michael's ear, who then spoke to the king. King Francis stood, shaking his head and looked at his sons. "I wonder, if we stare at them long enough, if the guilty party will come forward."

To turn against one another, Thomas thought.

"I must attend to your mamá. William, I leave this to your care." He walked away from his throne as William walked closer to it, leaning against it.

"You're not here because of the note that was left," William announced above all the whisperings.

But it certainly has helped. Thomas walked toward Michael. "May I see the note?"

"Then why are we here?" another Sethelian called out.

"Because our servants were attacked and we believe one of you — or maybe *all* of you — have something to do with it."

Taking the note from Michael's hand, Prince Thomas examined it and then handed it back. "I'll be back."

"Where are you going?"

"To find the one who wrote it."

As he walked down the hall, he heard men entering from the main entrance. "Prince Phillipus, did you find the body?"

"We did not." He looked around. "Where are my men?"

Thomas pointed down the hall. "They're in the Hall of Justice."

"And why are they there?"

Thomas turned toward him. "Do you know of one of your men who would want to harm an Anchonian servant?"

"No. Of course not. There must be some kind of error."

"Must be." Thomas slowly nodded. "I shall be joyous when it is cleared up."

"Yes," Prince Phillipus said, watching the other prince astutely. "Well, if there is an offending man, I shall find him."

Thomas watched the prince and his plethora of men walk down the hallway. "You do that." Shaking his head, he turned toward the spiral staircase.

"What is this about Lord Symon, duke of Gemmeny?"

Annabelle, turning toward her father's voice inside the chapel, stood to tell him all.

Beatrix, hugging Alicia's head next to her heart, tried to give comfort as the younger servant cried, "They'll kill me as soon as I'm out of the bailey."

"And who are 'they'?" Clara asked as she stepped around the corner.

"My lady," the sniffling servant stood and curtsied as Beatrix took a few steps away. "I'm going to leave, I was —"

"Tell me, Alicia, do you truly think I would turn you away from the castle?" Clara walked deeper into the chamber until she was a few feet away from Alicia.

Alicia looked up at the queen in surprise and then looked at Beatrix for confirmation that she had heard what she thought she had heard. "My lady?"

"We have much in common, Alicia. I was once where you are."

"What do you mean, my lady?"

"I know what it's like to live in fear." Looking around the room, the queen's eyes found Beatrix's. "Sir Victorus was his name." The queen, walking in front of Alicia, stepped closer to Beatrix. "I was a servant once in this castle, too."

Wiping away a stray tear, Alicia shook her head, certain she had heard the queen incorrectly.

"Tell her, Beatrix."

"My lady speaks the truth. We worked beside one another here."

Alicia's mouth dropped open in shock as she backed away. "No, my lady."

"That's why I knew what it takes to make a servant talk."

Alicia looked to Beatrix as if she had been betrayed.

"Do not blame Beatrix. She was only doing what I commanded her to do. If she had known the full truth, this would not have been needed. Now, does she need to tell me, or will you?"

Staring intensely at the orchard trees from her chamber window, Cristine did not flinch when her door opened after a quick knock.

"Crisa," Thomas said as he entered. "Prince Phillipus is back with his men. They didn't find a man in the river."

She breathed upon the green glass, not speaking a word.

"Your words have the men nearly fighting down there." He walked in closer to her. "I know you wrote the note, Crisa. These are your letters. I taught them to you myself."

She took a quick breath.

"Say something, Crisa! It's not like you not to talk."

"Why is it, do you think, that Prince Phillipus didn't find the man in the river? Why is it, do you think, I told his men what I did?" She turned sharply from the window. "Why is it, do you think, I wrote the note praying you would figure it out, Thom?!" Angry tears flooded down her cheeks. "I gave my word I would not speak about it, so I found the only way I could tell someone!"

"Prince Phillipus or one of the Sethelians killed the man and you have made them question whether there is a traitor among them? My word, Crisa, you are clever!"

"He has done more than kill a man." With those words spoken, she turned back to the window, refusing to say more.

"Crisa?" Shaking his head, he grabbed the hilt of his sword and ran out of her room.

As copious tears of both fear and relief ran down her cheeks, Cristine ran to Isabella's room. Finding it barricaded, she pounded on the door. "Isa, it's me. Let me in! Thom knows. Thom knows, Isa!"

"You told him?!" With fury in her eyes, Isa shoved the furniture away from the door to face her sister. "Did you tell Annie, too?! Did you tell her about Symon?!"

"What?" Cristine looked over her shoulder as she heard footsteps ascending the stairs.

"There they are," Clara said in relief as she held Eduard in her arms with Elizabeth in tow, hurrying up the steps.

"Everyone in the chamber!" the king yelled as Alicia and Beatrix followed after.

Ida, cautiously walking up the steps, looked back down them when she heard shouts.

"Ida, over here!" the king yelled.

She scurried over to Isabella's chamber, clueless as to what was taking place. Once inside the room, she looked at the door being barricaded by the king. "What's going on? Prince Thomas told me to come up here."

Eduard hugged his mother. "Why's Papá yelling?"

"He wants to make certain we're safe, that's all." Clara tried to calm her child.

Meeting

"Lord Ghent!" Michael stood outside the blacksmith shops. "Lord Symon Ghent, duke of Gemmeny!"

The hammering stopped in every shop. The blacksmiths all looked at each other as they shared a thought: *He's asking for a duke?*

Smithy Fulco addressed his recent journeyman as he hobbled out of the building. "Is he batty? He thinks there's a duke present?"

Michael spotted the young blacksmith and approached. "Lord Symon?"

Symon's heart sank. His secret could no longer be hidden.

"The king orders you to come to the castle."

Symon stepped closer to Michael, addressing him in a near whisper, as Fulco watched, befuddled. "I can't face the king; I have been a coward."

Michael shook his head. "I don't care what you've done. You are coming to the castle, whether you want to or not." Michael stepped closer. "The castle is in a state of strife and if I am right, it has to do with you."

"Strife?"

"Yes. Princess Isabella —" Michael shook his head, he did not even know how to describe her; he had never seen her so distraught.

Symon stared at the ground, closed his eyes, and then removed his frock.

Nicholaus heard a unique whistle. He halted Cinny in her tracks and looked to his right. A man emerged upon a horse. Nicholaus turned Cinny toward him and looked around curiously. "You ride alone? Where is your protection?" Nicholaus watched as the older man exited the woods completely and joined him on the path. "It is not safe for you to be alone out here."

The man shrugged his shoulders. "I suppose that's why we have angels to watch over us."

Nicholaus shook his head as he grinned.

The man continued, "My protection is still in Darlum with dysentery, as are the Demolites."

Nicholaus extended his arm toward the man. "It is good to see you, Uncle."

The bishop took his hand as he touched Nicholaus's shoulder. "It is good to see you, a knight before my eyes."

Nicholaus looked at his hunter green tabard. "Uncle, there is so much to tell you."

"I demand you let me and my men go!" Prince Phillipus addressed Prince William as he walked into the Hall of Justice. "My father shall hear about this."

"My father already has. Your men have threatened our servants! And they are all under arrest!"

Chaos broke out as the Sethelians — servants and knights alike — unsheathed swords and hidden daggers.

"You can't arrest my men!" Prince Phillipus screamed over the clink of metal.

Outside, Thomas pounded upon the door. "Let me in!"

William, hearing his brother, unbarred the door.

"Arrest Prince Phillipus!" Thomas yelled as he entered.

William was suddenly shoved into the brick corner as Phillipus, unsheathing his sword, ran toward Thomas. William grabbed his foot, tripping him as Thomas kicked Phillipus' sword away and placed his sword upon Phillipus' back. "You are under arrest."

As William stood, the Sethelians pressed toward the exit.

"Take him to the dungeon, Thom!" William yelled before shuting the door and barring it so the other Sethelians could not escape.

"Get up," Thomas ordered. "Slowly."

Rising, Phillipus grabbed his dagger and threw it at the Anchonian; Thomas deflected the dagger with his weapon as Phillipus found his sword on the floor, and ran down the hall.

"Stop him! Stop him! Sirs!"

"Where's Thom and Will?" Eduard asked with concern, staring at the metal rose on the floor, as he waited on Isabella's bed.

"They're making certain you're safe," his mother tried to assure him.

Elizabeth, pulling herself away from her mother, looked around the room. "But where's Annie?"

The king, stepping away from the door, suddenly turned back to it. "Oh, no! She's in the library waiting for Lord Symon." He shoved the furniture away from the door with a passion. "Stay here!"

"Sire?" Sir Gamel, keeping watch outside the chamber, asked when he saw the king.

"To the library! Annabelle's down there!"

Sirs Markus, Dyonisius, and Fray unsheathed their swords at the sound of Prince Thomas's yell. When they saw Prince Phillipus emerge from the hallway, they looked at one another.

"The prince of Sethel?" one asked.

Phillipus, seeing his exit blocked, ran to the one door he saw open — the library.

Slamming the doors shut, he shoved a chair under the door handles as he tried to come up with a plan. His eyes darted around the room.

"What are you doing?"

He jumped two feet; his eyes eventually focused on Annabelle. His breathing began to calm as a sly smirk emerged with his newfound scheme.

Annabelle's eyes darted toward the door as she heard banging and yells from the knights, her father, and her brother. Her heart quickened; her eyes dilated as she held tightly to the book in her possession.

"You're coming with me!" he barked as he neared her.

She shook her head and walked backwards to the window. "I will not."

He tilted his head and laughed. "No? You'll be sorry you said such a thing!" He lunged at her with his unsheathed sword.

She held up the book — his sword cut halfway through. Pushing her back onto the bench, his sword broke the window. Shards of green glass speckled her face as she swatted the sword away from him to the left and struggled to stand. His left arm shoved her against the stone corner. Agony escaped her lips as her shattered scapula was further jostled. It took all her strength to stand.

His surprise at her swift response quickly cascaded to full rage as he realized he had been resisted by a female. He attempted to pick her up by the top of her dress. As the air slowly returned to her, she grabbed at his neck with her right hand. He gasped for air and transferred his grip from her clothing to her hand. Grabbing her arm, he shoved her through the window as her face and left side felt the sharp bite of the already broken glass.

Blood filled her vision as she felt warm liquid rolling down her stinging face. Disoriented, she felt herself being dragged off the bench and pulled to the floor. Her right hand fingered for anything; it found a leg to a table. She held firmly. When he bent down to remove her hand, she took full opportunity and gathered up all her strength as she quickly kicked him in the ribs with her left foot; he collapsed onto the floor as his fractured rib bruised the sensitive lung tissue.

She slowly turned on to her stomach and crawled away, leaving a trail of blood from her face and her eye on the stone floor. Her dress soaked up the redness as she moved across the floor.

The knights burst through the door as the awful prince, hardly able to breathe, clumsily climbed to the bench and fell onto the shards of glass camouflaged in the grass.

"He's out the window!" Sir Markus called as he followed the prince's footsteps.

"Annabelle!" Her father ran to her and turned her over; he gasped at the horrid sight. Her bloodstained face was peppered with glass bits, including a long sliver through her left eye.

"Annie?" Thomas knelt down beside her, afraid to touch her.

Sirs Fray and Markus dragged in the despicable prince; he moaned in pain as he labored to breathe. They laid him on the floor in the foyer.

Michael, with sword drawn, and Symon walked through the open castle doors as the king, with Annabelle in his arms, exited the library.

"Good heavens! What's come to pass?" Michael looked from the princess and king to the prisoner moaning on the floor as he gripped his unsheathed sword.

"Annabelle?" Symon, paying no attention to the man on the floor, ran toward the king.

Looking at Lord Symon in utter disbelief, the king did not say a word. He flew up the steps followed by his son.

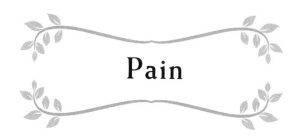

Pain

The queen nearly fainted when she spotted the bleeding Annabelle. She held herself up by the bedpost. "What on earth?" she finally managed to ask as the whimpering Annabelle was laid on the bed.

The princesses jumped down from the bed and backed up to the wall. Their mother ran to them. They hugged each other tightly, fearing for Annabelle's life.

"Papá! The Sethelians are secured. It seems they turned on one another." Running into the room, William looked to the bed. "Annie? What took place?"

"Prince Phillipus got to her," Thomas said as he began to pick glass from his sister's skin.

Ikus brought in some clean cloths and placed them on the bed. The king picked them up and pressed them against her face as a moan escaped her lips.

Symon watched the scene before him, shaking his head. He looked to his left and saw his Isabella and the other princesses clinging to each other. He felt so out of place.

"Get her to the light," the barber-surgeon said as he hurried through the doors with Michael on his heels.

The queen watched through teary eyes as the doctor ran in; she noticed the blacksmith standing by the door, unsure what to do. She squeezed Isabella's hand and looked straight ahead for a moment, glancing back at the man to see if he was still there. "Symon?"

He took a step forward as Isabella stepped away from her mother to see whom she was daring to call the duke's name. She gasped as her shaking hands unsuccessfully held back her cries. Symon did not know what to say as he viewed his frail, disheartened love before his eyes. Isabella shook her head and ran out of the room.

"Isabella! Isabella!" He ran after her and caught her in the hall.

Her tears released years of sorrow, years of pain. Her mind swirled through her recent interaction with her sister; she was suddenly so ashamed. She pulled back, shaking her head. "No! You're dead! You died! You aren't here!"

"I'm sorry. I'm so sorry." A lump caught in his throat as his heart ached for all Isabella had had to endure while he gripped her sleeves, stopping her from fleeing from his sight.

"I blamed Annie! I blamed Annie!" She pulled back her arms and began to pace, unsure what to do, where to go, as she hit her chest with her fist. "I said I wished she hadn't returned! She was trying to help me. And now" — she fell to the floor in her emotional agony — "he assaulted her!" Her traumatic words rolled out of her mouth to bounce throughout the castle. "And she might die!" Symon sat down beside his bereaved beloved and dared to place his hand upon her head; she collapsed on to him.

Cristine, Elizabeth, and Eduard, ushered into the hall by Alicia and Ida, clung to one another.

The surgeon was leaning on her face, attempting to stop the bleeding.

Clara watched as the color faded from her daughter's face. She stepped next to her husband. As he put his arm around her and kissed her head, she asked, "Will she make it?"

The surgeon looked up from the patient to the worried queen. He slowly shook his head. "Not if the bleeding doesn't stop. If pressing doesn't stop it, her wounds will have to be burned." His eyes wandered over to the castle chaplain, who had followed the sound of wailing into the room as William removed his dagger and headed for the fire. "She might not make it."

Father Robertus did not hesitate: He pulled out a small vial of blessed oil and anointed her head, her hands, and her feet, praying the sacred healing words. The queen cried into her husband's shoulder — seeing Extreme Unction being bestowed upon her young daughter only made plain the gravity of Annabelle's condition.

The physician removed the cloth — blood oozed out everywhere. He quickly replaced it. Looking into the king's eyes, he articulated the horrid truth: "Bring the metal."

"No!" Clara cried as the king had to hold her up.

"Thomas, take her!" the king commanded.

Thomas escorted his wailing mother outside as the physician, who took the dagger from William's hands, looked at the king, Michael, the prince, and the priest. "Hold her down."

The men moved around her; they saw the gaping hole in her eye that the glass had previously inhabited. Their stomachs sank; they had to will themselves not to vomit.

When the red-hot metal touched the delicate tissue of the eye, she screamed until she nearly choked on her own blood rolling into her mouth as she twisted and contorted in pain.

The queen clung to her son just outside the room as her other daughters held each other. They all held their breath as they listened to Annabelle's horrific screams.

Inside the room, the horrid sight of the simmering tissue, the sound of her tortured cries, and the smell of burning flesh was difficult for any of the men to take.

As the steam rolled off her eye, she finally passed out.

Bishop

"What's going on here?" Nicholaus, with sword drawn, tiptoed into the foyer, staring at the prisoner prince moaning on the floor. "Who has assaulted him?"

"You mean whom did he assault?" Martinus said as he squatted next to the writhing man, having no pity.

"Why is the physician not here?" the bishop asked, kneeling down beside the man.

"He's with the princess," Sir Martinus said as he looked into Nicholaus' eyes.

"Anna?" Nicholaus said with fear. He did not wait for a response; he flew toward the stairwell.

The royal family, minus the queen and injured princess, sat silently outside Isabella's room.

Nicholaus breathed heavily as he looked at the grieved faces. "What's taken place? Where's Anna?" He looked over at Symon sitting next to Isabella, holding her hand. He did a double take as his mind did not understand what he saw.

William stood up. "She is not well."

"What's taken place?" he asked again as he went closer to the door.

William stepped out in front of him. "Her eye had to be burned closed."

"Burned closed?" Nicholaus stepped back as he thought about the pain his Anna had to endure — it physically sickened him. He slid down against the stone wall.

The bishop stepped forward. "Has she been anointed?"

"Yes," the king said as he stood and hugged the bishop. "Sir Gregory, retrieve the bag in my chamber." Sir Gregory nodded as he headed down the stairwell and the king sat back down. The king turned to the bishop. "Nicholaus has told you about your brother?"

The bishop bowed his head. "He did."

"Will Annie get better?" Eduard climbed on to his father's lap.

The king could not answer — he could not face the answer. He had failed to protect his daughters from danger — danger even from within the castle walls.

"Where's Prince Phillipus?" Elizabeth asked whomever would answer.

"Down the stairs as of right now, soon to be in the dungeon along with all the other Sethelians," William answered with disgust.

"I hope he rots," Cristine said to the air.

The bishop shook his head. "No. You must forgive. We all must forgive."

Cristine knew the bishop was right, but she did not feel it.

Nicholaus stared at Isabella and Symon sitting next to each other; he could not comprehend what he saw.

"How will Sethel take the tidings that their prince has been imprisoned?" Thomas asked his father as he leaned upon his knees.

The king shook his head, a new burden on his mind. "Let me worry about that."

Thomas knew he should not press at that moment — especially in front of his sisters. His father would not want them to worry.

"What was on the floor?" Eduard asked, looking at Isabella. Isabella did not know to what he was referring, so he turned to Cristine. "You know, Crisa. What was on the floor in there?"

"Oh." Cristine took a deep breath and sat up. "It was a metal rose or something."

Isabella squeezed Symon's hand as Nicholaus's attention zoned in. Symon answered since Isabella was unable. "It is a metal rose I gave to Isabella." He shook his head and corrected himself. "I gave to Annabelle to give to Isabella." He smiled briefly as he looked at Nicholaus. "I gave to Nicholaus to give to Annabelle to give to Isabella."

Nicholaus's insides collapsed. *What a fool! What a fool I am!* He wanted to run away from himself, but, alas, he could not.

Sir Gregory handed the auspicious leather satchel to the king, who took out the package and passed it along to the bishop.

The bishop unravelled the scroll and read it to himself, gasping in disbelief as he grabbed at the package accompanying it.

"What does it say?" Thomas asked.

The bishop quickly handed the letter to his nephew. Nicholaus stood to read it. "Read it aloud." He untied the carefully wrapped package as Nicholaus began:

"'My dear brother, let me tell you where I have been and why. After the slaughtering of my family, I fled to what I called the "'Forbidden Island.'" I had to. I feared I would take vengeance if I did not. Plus, God called me to it — how did I know it would lead me to the sweetest little girl? God works in unknown ways, right?'" Nicholaus shook his head as he choked back tears.

"Keep reading!" his uncle instructed as he turned that newly untied package over to unwrap it.

Nicholaus took a deep breath and continued: "'But, alas, the real reason for this letter is to inform you of the reason my family was slaughtered. I secretly snuck into the Demolite castle, without orders from Francis, and took some articles that, I believe, should be helpful. However, the books and papers were not the reason for the covert deed — it was for you, for your parish, and for all believers in general. I went there to retrieve the precious relic that was stolen from your parish —whose first theft grieved the kingdom. Since all is in God's hands, I take it that now is the right time and place for this to be returned to you. I hope you suffered no ill deeds from the wickedness of the Demolites. May God bless you and keep you — I will see you again someday, God willing. With love, your brother, Josephus.'"

Nicholaus looked up from the letter to see his uncle holding a very old and brittle bone about an inch and a half in length. All eyes stared.

"What is it?" Eduard asked as he moved off his father's lap to stand next to the bishop's knee.

"This is the missing relic of St. Celestria. It was stolen 20 years ago from Mary, Mother of God Church."

"I thought it was destroyed," the king replied.

"Jous has had it for the past 15 or more years," Michael responded in wonder.

"My brother ... he never ceases to amaze me." The bishop shook his head as he smiled.

"Did Annabelle know Jous had this?" the king asked.

"I don't think he would have told her," the bishop replied.

"She carried it — all the articles — the entire way?" the king said in amazement.

"No wonder she didn't want anyone to take her bag," William responded.

"I must inform the pope," the bishop said.

"You are welcome to keep it here for protection until it is placed elsewhere," the king said.

The bishop's mind swirled. He stood up, but instead of

going to his bedroom to write a letter, he walked toward Isabella's bedroom. The princes and princesses, briefly looking at each other, all quickly followed the bishop.

Anna, all you did for my father, and I reward you with harshness. Nicholaus slid back down the stone wall.

Symon squatted down beside Nicholaus as he sat upon the floor. "Sir Nicholaus" — Nicholaus looked up at him through red eyes — "she spoke highly of you."

Nicholaus shook his head at himself, disgusted. *Why did I leave her like I did? My love, my heart.*

"Lord Symon," the king said, "I believe you have some explaining to do." Symon nodded his head. "But not now." The king followed his children to the doorway.

The bishop placed his hand upon the queen's shoulder. "How is she?"

Her red, puffy eyes looked up at him; she stood. "Bishop Dominicus." She hugged him and then turned back toward her daughter, shaking her head as she bit her lip in worry. "She only moans." New tears rolled down the queen's tortured face as she sat back down.

The bishop presented the relic and its protective leather covering. "Do you know what this is?"

The queen looked at it through her stinging eyes. "No."

The bishop kneeled down beside her. "Do you have memory of the relic of St. Celestria that was stolen from Mary, Mother of God Church?"

She looked into his eyes. "Yes."

"This is it."

The queen shook her head. "How did you come to have it?"

The bishop shook his head, nearly laughing. "I didn't have it; Annabelle did."

"What?" She looked back at her miserable daughter, lying prone. "How —"

"It was in my brother's bag."

"How did it get there?" the queen asked with a forlorn expression.

"Jous took it back from the Demolites."

Her hand flew to her mouth as she recalled her daughter's words, and hope filled her. "'She said Peter had helped her.'" The queen grabbed her daughter's left hip. She looked over at the bishop as she laughed with joy at God's providence.

"What?"

"Annabelle …" The queen shook her head, unable to answer coherently. "Saint Celestria."

"Queen Clara, will you allow me?" He held up the relic.

"Of course!" She stood up and moved the chair away, Standing back three feet. Her children and husband rushed to her from their position of observation in the doorway.

They all watched as the bishop placed the first-class relic below Annabelle's bandaged eye and the third-class relic — the cloth it was wrapped in — upon her shoulder. Bishop Dominicus stepped back and addressed the royal family. "Let us pray." They all signed themselves. "Father, we thank You for the protection You provided for Annabelle as she went down Angler Falls and made her way home. Father, if it is Your will, heal Your child. Saint Celestria, we ask for your prayers. This faithful sister of yours has delivered your relic so it may, once again, be treated with reverence. Pray for her, you who gave your life for God and now spend it in His presence; ask for her help, her healing. We ask this in the name of the Father, and of the Son, and of the Holy Spirit. Amen."

"Amen."

"Nothing changed." Eduard was the first to speak as they watched their sister lying on the bed. "Isn't she supposed to get better?" He looked up at Thomas.

Elizabeth began to cry. "Why isn't God healing her?" Her siblings looked at the youngest princess, wanting to give her comfort, but they were all secretly asking the same question.

Clara sniffled as she shook her head and cried, "He doesn't have to heal her just because we asked." She pulled Elizabeth to her.

"But why wouldn't He?" She spoke into the queen's dress.

The bishop stepped out from the line of observers. "There should be a special Mass of thanksgiving for the return of the relic." He hesitantly retrieved the metacarpal, rewrapping it for safekeeping. He turned back toward the family. "Six o'clock then, tomorrow morning?"

Clara nodded her head in agreement.

Nicholaus waited until most of the royal family had departed from the room. With teary eyes, he went inside.

The queen turned to him and smiled. "Nicholaus." She reached out her hand. "I'm glad you're here." She stood up. "Have a seat." She brushed away her tears. "We must pray that God's will is to let her live." The queen put her hand over her mouth and hugged her husband before leaving the room.

"Princess Annabelle." He grabbed her right hand. "Anna." She moved slightly. "Anna, I'm here, I'm so sorry." His salty tears dropped upon her fingers. "I'm sorry I left you like I did. I'm so sorry, Anna, I love you." Her fingers slightly moved as he kissed her hand.

The king patted him on the shoulder. Nicholaus stood as he wiped away a tear.

"Nicholaus."

"I love her," Nicholaus said before the king could say anything more.

The king swallowed. "I know you do, Nicholaus." He sat down on the chair and looked at Nicholaus.

"I want to marry her."

The king closed his eyes. "Nicholaus, if you would have said those words this very morning, I would have wholeheartedly, and with great joy, consented." He shook his head. "But now, Nicholaus, I only want her to live."

A sad and lonely tear slowly cascaded its way down Nicholaus's cheek. "I'm such a fool!" He looked up at the king. "If I would have not left —"

"Stop, Nicholaus! Don't do that to yourself."

"She came to me and I —"

The king, standing, placed his hand upon the knight's shoulder. "Stop, Nicholaus."

Nicholaus shook his head as he gripped her hand. "I want to marry her — I don't care." He looked up at the king. "I think God wants it, too."

"Even if she does live … she will not … live." The king shook his head. "She'll not be like what she was. She'll never be the same."

"I don't care what she can or can't do."

"Nicholaus, I could not allow that, for your sake."

Nicholaus stared ahead as another tear rolled down his distressed cheek, listening to the king's words: "If it is God's will, then He will heal her. And if she's healed, you may marry her."

Nicholaus's heart fell to the pit of his stomach, but then a slow hope grew inside. The king's words slowly soaked into Nicholaus's thoughts as he kissed her hand one last time and walked toward Isabella's door.

Stumbling into the chapel, Nicholaus fell to his knees. "Father!" He bent over completely. "Help me! I don't know what to do! I see it now: You wanted me to marry her … but I withstood! I defied You … I defied Your will, and now she's hurt. Father, I am nothing! I am Your creature, that is all." He looked up at the crucifix, feeling like a pebble, the size of a thumbnail, inside an immeasurable cavern. "Your will, Father, nothing but Your will." He shook his head as a relief enveloped him with his realization. "I live for You, Father. For Your will, not mine. I will always love her, but if You wish me to watch her in her pain, her struggle, then I welcome the burden. I will do it for You. I will carry my cross."

The king, princes, and bishop sat despairingly around the fireplace listening to the rupturing crackles of the fire as Michael, with a downcast glance, stood by the door of the parlor. All were consumed with their own miserable thoughts.

Bishop Dominicus shook his head. "This is no clearness here." Every eye turned toward him as he asked further, "Why would Prince Phillipus assault her?"

William muttered an impolite answer as he turned away.

The bishop sat up straighter. "You are angry at him for good reason, but what will you do with it?"

William stood. "I'll tell you what I'd like to do with it."

"Will, sit down," Thomas ordered and then looked at his father. "He is locked up, right?"

"Yes," the king stated in defeat.

"I met him," the bishop said. "When he first came to shore in Anchony." He shook his head. "He was very friendly." Thinking about all that had happened since he arrived at the castle, he suddenly realized the injured man in the foyer was the man they were calling Prince Phillipus. He looked over at the king and said in confusion, "That man on the floor when I entered, that wasn't him."

The king nodded his head. "That was him."

"That wasn't a question."

Everyone turned toward the bishop as he stood.

"That was *not* Prince Phillipus of Sethel on the floor out there."

"What do you mean?" Thomas asked.

"I mean that's not him."

"Are you certain?"

"Michael," the king said, motioning with his hand. Michael nodded his head and walked out of the room.

"Positive. My memory is that his hair was blond, and he had a small scar right below his pinky on his left hand." The bishop looked at his own hand as he continued: "I asked him what had caused such a mark; he was amazed that I had even seen it."

"You're saying that man is not Prince Phillipus?" William stated in shock. He looked around from face to face and then bolted for the door.

Thomas stepped in front of him. "Will, stop. Think about what you're doing."

"I am thinking! I think whoever he is, he needs to learn a lesson!"

The king shook his head as a thousand thoughts rolled through his mind. "William."

William looked at his seated father. The king's face spoke the words: Sit down. William took a deep breath and leaned against the wall.

The king stood and waited for Michael's return with the prisoner.

The king, after examining the captive's left hand and finding it scarless, dropped it and looked into his eyes. "Who are you?"

"I'm Prince —" The stranger's nose and cheek were suddenly stinging and bleeding from a well-placed punch; a present from the king's fist for the start of a lie.

"Where is Prince Phillipus?" the king yelled at the prisoner who was trying to recover from the hit.

He slowly stood as he began to chuckle. "I'll never say!"

The king took a step backwards as his nostrils flared. "Who are you?!" The pretend prince smirked and snickered as he shook his head and tasted his blood. All the men looked at each other in disgust.

"A Demolite, no doubt!" William said as he stirred next to Thomas.

"Are all of them?" Thomas pondered out loud.

"Take him away!" the king said as he turned his back to the captive.

Sir Michael and Sir Rogerus pulled him out into the hall as he continued his mantra: "You'll never find him! Never!"

Lord Symon stepped down the stairwell to see the captive being dragged back to the dungeon. He watched the scene as his blood boiled. It took every ounce of strength to watch the man go by. When he had passed, he quickly went to the parlor. He stood in the entranceway and could not wait until he entered to ask, "Sire, what's he doing here?"

All turned toward him. "Lord Symon, now is not the time," the king said as he put up his hand.

Symon looked back down the hall to see the knights and prisoner disappear down a spiral stairwell. He took a breath and looked back into the room. "What has he done?"

They all looked at him strangely. "He is the one that assaulted Annabelle," Thomas said as he glanced at his brother and then the bishop.

Symon walked into the room, shaking his head in confusion. "I thought a prince assaulted her?"

"*That* is our Prince Phillipus." William remarked with disgust.

The king looked at Symon. "You know he's not Prince Phillipus."

The bishop studied Symon's face. "You know him."

Symon looked to the ground and nodded his head, then looked up at the men. "He and his father killed Lord Godewinus, my father. He is my cousin, Arnaldus."

Arnaldus sat in the dungeon, snickering sadistically in spite of his fractured ribs. Reveling in his cunning, he had no fears about the future of his cause. The heart of the Demolites' greatest plan was still at work.

Somewhere, in a secret location, was a man with sandy hair and a scar upon his hand. A man tortured, nearly starved, and chained to a wall — the real Prince Phillipus.

Charity

The queen awoke in her own bed next to her husband, unaware how she had landed in that location. Her thoughts quickly went to her daughter. She quietly tiptoed out of the room, down the hall to Isabella's room — which was now Annabelle's — to check on her daughter. She rubbed her daughter's hand, finding her condition unchanged. She sighed. *Father, I thank You for my daughter.* She looked out the window. Mass would be soon; she must prepare. She kissed her daughter's hand and left as quietly as she had entered.

Alicia awoke with a startle as Ida walked through Isabella's door, announcing, "The bath is ready."

Alicia looked around, disoriented by her change in consciousness. She looked from the princess lying prone, jerking periodically, to the dark window that would soon be turning golden, to Ida. "What?"

"The bath is ready," Ida repeated.

Alicia stood and turned toward Ida, rubbing her aching neck. "What bath?"

Ida stepped in closer, holding a candlestick. "The princess's bath."

Alicia put her hand up in confusion. "What bath?" she asked in distress.

"Well, I wondered the same thing when you knocked on my door, waking me from my sleep, to tell me to draw a bath for Princess Annabelle — but it is drawn now, it is ready."

Alicia shook her head. "I did no such thing. I've been

here since the king took the queen away and ordered me not to leave her side."

"Well, somebody knocked on my door."

Annabelle was on the island, resisting her entry into the water the best she could.

"You need a bath!" Peter insisted.

"No!"

She was perched on the boulder next to the ocean; she jumped off to follow the strange girl.

"Swim! Swim! You must swim!" Celesa urged her forward.

Annabelle awoke and pushed herself off the bed with her right arm. She landed on her back with a thud against the cold stones as her breath was taken away by the new wave of agony pulsating from her left shoulder. Alicia and Ida yelled in shock as they quickly bent down beside her. "Princess!"

Annabelle looked around with her good eye. She soon realized Alicia and Ida were the only ones with her. She felt feverish, her mind muddled. "Mamá?"

Ida answered, "She is going to Mass; your bath is ready." Annabelle looked at her with confusion, but just as quickly as the confusion came, the clarity of the dream took over.

Annabelle held out her hand; they helped her to stand. She staggered as she stood, very lightheaded, drained of blood, and feverish. "I'm hot. So hot." The servants held tight to her to keep her upright.

"I don't think this is such a good thought! You're burning up," Alicia said helplessly.

"Take me. I need water. I need cool water," she stated weakly.

Against their better judgment, Alicia and Ida helped the injured princess down the long hallway toward the bathing room.

"Help me," Annabelle weakly requested as she tried to take off her bloodied dress.

Alicia cautiously resisted. "I don't think we should."

Ida looked at both of them, not knowing what to do.

Annabelle, leaning against the bathtub to keep herself up, gave up on the clothing and started to unwrap her bandage from around her eye.

"Oh, no, don't do that!" Alicia approached her, shaking her head, holding out her hand. "Please, don't do that!"

Ida covered her mouth, afraid of what she would see.

As the layers were unraveled, the disgusting smell of burned flesh permeated the room. Alicia put her hand over her mouth, trying not to be sick. When the grotesque, oozing, infected burned flesh was revealed, Alicia and Ida both ran to the adjacent room and threw up.

Annabelle stared at her reflection in the water; it was so disfigured she barely recognized herself. She was completely aware of every inch of pain as it weakened her legs. *I will bear it all for souls.* The water suddenly crashed into her as every ounce of her was soaked.

A dream, a memory — whatever it was …

She was back on the island in the river swirling around at the bottom of the disorienting waterfall. The mysterious Celesa swam toward her from nowhere and touched her left shoulder and eye as Peter's hand reached for her.

Annabelle sat up in the tub with a gasp. She pushed her hair away from her face — with both hands. She immediately looked at her left arm, as her heart began to pound wildly. Her once broken arm was broken no longer; she moved her arm to its full range, her scapula no longer shattered. She felt her face. Her cheek was no longer stinging from the lacerative remains of the shards of glass; she looked around the room with both eyes, now able to judge depth. She covered up her right eye and was able to see everything. She no longer felt like she was on fire; in fact, she felt no pain at all. Gasping, her tears trickled into the water as the truth hit her: God had reached down and bestowed a miracle upon her.

The embarrassed servants dared to enter back into the room. "We are so sor —"

The servants stared at the princess, unable to utter a sound.

"What's going on in here?" Beatrix opened the door halfway as she looked at the bewildered Alicia and Ida.

Alicia stared at Annabelle, pointing as the servant finally mustered a single word: "Bath."

"A bath?" Beatrix, shaking her head at Alicia, stepped inside the room and closed the door. She followed her finger and jumped when she saw the princess in the tub, rubbing her face. "She can't be in there! She's not well enough!" She looked over at Alicia and Ida, angered.

Annabelle looked up. "Can you help me get the blood out of my hair?"

Beatrix blinked her eyes several times and finally knelt down next to the tub and gently stroked Annabelle's left cheek. "It can't be …"

Annabelle looked up, humbly. "But it is." Joyous tears streamed down her quivering chin as she began to laugh.

Annabelle stared at her reflection in the mirror as she took a deep breath, fully aware that it was only by the grace of God that she stood there, unharmed. *Why would He heal me? I was willing to bear it. Why?*

Beatrix placed a veil over Annabelle's wet, braided hair and crowned it with a tiara. The princess moved closer to her reflection to inspect the beautiful piece upon her head.

She looked back at Beatrix and Alicia, touching the jeweled metal crowning her veil. "I've never seen anything with such beauty."

Alicia and Beatrix stood silently for a moment until there was a knock on the door, and the distant ring of the church bells beckoned parishioners to the mysterious and miraculous Mass.

"Oh, you must hurry if you wish to make it before it starts," Beatrix said as she wiped a tear away with a handkerchief.

Alicia answered the door, finding Sir David. "What is this about the princess wanting to go to Mass?" Alicia opened the door all the way and let him see for himself. He looked to the bed and did not see her; he quickly turned around toward the servants. "Where is —" He stared in disbelief for a moment and then bowed, breathing hard, skeptical of what his own eyes were beholding.

"I do wish to attend Mass." She walked toward the door.

Because the southern wing of the cathedral was barred from the inside by the knights to protect the royal family, Annabelle stepped inside the massive cathedral through the main doors on the western side and was simultaneously elated and petrified as the Introit filled the air. Her eyes looked over the rows and rows of heads facing the tabernacle as the bishop was being vested in front of the altar.

Bishop Dominicus followed the gaze of his helper when his right glove was not offered to him. He turned around, spotting the uninjured princess in the middle of the aisle and waved her forward as every eye turned toward her. The heat in her ears and face elevated; she wanted to flee. She took a step backwards, hitting the knight's foot.

"Princess, what are you doing?" Sir Martinus asked quietly.

"You need to go forward," Sir David said.

Her attention flashed back to the congregation as she realized they all were beginning to bow to her.

Nicholaus glanced over quickly, then completely turned his body to see if his eyes were deceiving him. His mind churned at the figure before him; he walked through the bowing crowd, his heart pounding quicker with every step closer to his Anna.

She looked straight ahead. *Will they not look at me if I don't look at them?* Her eyes fixed themselves on the tabernacle in the far distance; it was the only thing that stopped her from fleeing from the stares, points, and whispers. Her family in the right front of the church — in the southern wing — peeked their heads around the corner in disbelief, pondering if it could really be her, and if it was, why she was not walking toward them.

She stared at the veiled tabernacle. *Christ, give me strength!* Closing her eyes, she breathed deeply as she felt the temperature rising in her cheeks.

His presence stepped beside her left side. She opened her eyes to confirm what she already knew. The strong, loving eyes that had been her companion for weeks gazed upon her with disbelief as his right elbow extended toward her. The terror in her eyes slowly faded as her heart rate decreased. She took his elbow and leaned against his arm, soaking up his strength. She looked up at him and smiled. He smiled back as the backs of his fingers rubbed her pristine cheek in wonder.

Annabelle no longer cared who stared at her; she was safe next to Nicholaus. Together, they walked toward the bishop, they walked toward her family; they walked toward their future.

Author's Note

Dear Reader,

I hope you have enjoyed Annabelle's story thus far. There are a couple details I would like to note concerning her tale. Firstly, all characters are ficitious in this book, including St. Celestria. Though born from my imagination and the needs of the plot, she represents something which is true: the intercessory power of the Body of Christ through prayer, the fervor of the saints for the Eucharist throughout the history of the Church, and the fortitude of all the martyrs since the first century who were willing to give their lives for Christ.

If there was one particular saint who inspired her creation in any way, it would be St. Clare of Assisi. In 1224, she called upon the Eucharistic Lord to dissuade attackers from invading her monastery. Though St. Celestria's tale is not surrounded by the same circumstances, or the same outcome as the actual event, the image of St. Clare holding the monstrance high — as well as her profound faith in Him — fueled my imagination, inspiring a character willing to protect the Eucharist for as long as she could and, ultimately, to die for Him.

Further details of St. Celestria's martyrdom were formed by the necessity of the story. She ended up in the river because water needed to be a refuge.

Secondly, in Annabelle's story, I have tried to present the Church as it conceivably could have been in the 13th century. The truth is that there were no set ways of celebrating the Sacraments universally at that time: Different locations had their own handbooks and customs, which became different rites. After the Council of Trent in the 16th century, the Roman/

Latin Rite replaced all of them except those that had existed for more than 200 years. Today, there are over 20 rites in the Catholic Church — in both Eastern and Western churches who recognize the pope as their leader — with the largest being the Roman/Latin Rite.

If you grew up a cradle Catholic in the United States worshipping according to the Latin Rite, as I did, you most likely experienced the Sacraments of Initiation in a different order. In the early Church and in the Middle Ages, after Baptism (which always must come first), the Sacrament of Confirmation was second, and full initiation into the Catholic Church was achieved and crowned by First Communion (and subsequently reinforced by every Holy Communion thereafter). In Annabelle's story, she cannot receive her First Communion because she has not yet been confirmed, which is why she eagerly awaits meeting Bishop Dominicus. Candidates and catechumens entering the Church through the Rite of Christian Initiation of Adults (RCIA) today experience the same ordering of the Sacraments of Initiation as those who lived in the 13th century.

The history of the reception of the Sacraments of Initiation is an interesting one. Initially, a baby would receive all the Sacraments at once (which is still done in the Orthodox Churches and in the Eastern Rites of the Catholic Church), with a drop of the Precious Blood being placed in the baby's mouth for First Communion. Later, Confirmation was delayed by one or two years. By the 13th century, Confirmation — for children — was celebrated at the age of discretion (around 7 years old) and First Communion was given around age 12. As time passed, the age of administration continued to be delayed up to age 14 (which would further delay reception of First Communion).

In 1910, St. Pope Pius X decreed in *Quam Singulari Christus* (*How Special Christ's Love*) that First Communion should not be delayed past the age of reason. His decree was heeded: First Communion was moved to around age 7. The age of Confirmation, however, did not move along with First Communion, and hence, cradle Catholics now experience the Sacraments of Initiation in a different order.

You might have noticed other differences in Catholic practices throughout the book — such as so few people receiving Communion. In the Middle Ages, reception was so infrequent that the Fourth Lateran Council in 1215 decreed that the Eucharist must be taken a minimum of once a year. I would encourage curious minds to consult NewAdvent.org, which provides the history of all things Catholic and definitions of unfamiliar words that might have been found in the story, especially in the Mass (such as "Introit") or the structure of a church (such as "chancel"). And, if you choose to explore, I pray the Holy Spirit will open your heart and set you on fire for the love of Christ's Bride, the Church, and for Him in the Holy Eucharist — the Source and Summit of our Faith!

Your sister in Christ,
Ruth Apollonia

Ruth Apollonia

A cradle Catholic called to evangelize, Ruth Apollonia envisioned Annabelle's tale and brought it to life when she was a college student. This first book in the series received the Catholic Arts and Letters Award from the Catholic Writers Guild in 2013. Her evangelization efforts, however, are not confined to the pen: She is RCIA director at her local parish in the Springfield-Cape Girardeau Diocese. She lives in southern Missouri where she works as an occupational therapist and continues writing Annabelle's tale as well as other pieces of fiction.